THE TRAIL OF THE
SCOTTISH
BLUEBELL

ANDREW E. CATLIN

The Trail of the Scottish Bluebell

Bedford, VA
Copyright © 2025 by Andrew E. Catlin

ISBN 979-8-9985552-0-6 (paperback)
ISBN 979-8-9985552-1-3 (ePub)

This is a work of fiction. Names, characters, places, and incidents either are the product of the author's imagination or are used fictitiously. Any resemblance to actual persons, living or dead, businesses, companies, or locales is entirely coincidental.

All rights reserved.

Printed in the U.S.A

29 28 27 26 25   1 2 3 4 5 6 7

THE TRAIL OF THE
SCOTTISH
BLUEBELL

ANDREW E. CATLIN

Chapter 1

Friday, April 19, 1861

JED LOOKED UP FROM THE journal on his portable desk to look out the window. The green, Maryland landscape streamed by without him seeing it as the train chugged its way to Baltimore. Every now and then, he caught a whiff of coal smoke coming off the engine. The bitter scent was a reminder of things he thought he had left behind.

Insanity, he thought. *This is pure insanity.*

Looking down at the brand-new journal, he snorted lightly and chuckled to himself. It was a parting gift from his sister, Sarah. She gave it to him at the train station just as he was leaving, extracting a promise to record his daring feats and triumphs in putting down the rebellion.

I don't know whether this insanity is because I'm trying to put thoughts and feelings into this journal, or because of the current situation we find ourselves in, he mused. *I think the whole blasted nation has gone quite mad—me included.*

Jed touched his coat. He heard the paper in his inside pocket crinkle—the paper that ordered First Lieutenant (Brevet) Jedidiah Tremblant, on behalf of Governor Yates of Illinois, to report to the secretary of war concerning the disposition of the Illinois militia. Now, here he was in civilian clothes, riding the rails at the behest of his friend, John Rawlins. The two of them, along with Ulysses Grant, were raising troops in Illinois. Grant was concerned about the lack of information and instruction coming out of Washington since President Lincoln's call for troops on April fourteenth.

Governor Yates liked the lack of direction even less. However, it was a complete surprise to Jed when John handed him his orders to report to Washington for liaison purposes. The brevet promotion by the governor to first lieutenant was obviously meant as a payoff, but Jed let John know he was not happy about going.

"Jed, it has to be you," explained John. "Ulysses went to West Point and so is conducting the troop training. Let me speak plainly. He and I clerked together to become lawyers, and there's no one I trust more. I was your advocate with Governor Yates because I did not want one of the political appointees who play at soldiering to represent us."

"A little warning would've been nice," muttered Jed.

"I beg your pardon?"

Jed jerked himself out of his reminiscing and back to his current surroundings. An elderly gentleman sitting across the aisle was staring at him. Looking again, Jed revised his initial assessment. The man was probably only in his early thirties, but the white hair and mutton chops had thrown Jed off for second. His clothes were as fine quality as Jed's.

"I beg your pardon," apologized Jed. "I was thinking out loud. I did not mean to disturb you."

"The times are disturbing enough," said the man, waving aside Jed's apology. "Forewarned is forearmed, is it not?"

"It would depend upon the warning. A well-intentioned, but poorly delivered warning can wreak more damage than no warning at all."

"Well said," chuckled the man. "Allow me to introduce myself. I am Anthony Duff of Missouri . . . my card."

"Jedidiah Tremblant of Illinois," said Jed, taking Duff's business card. "Are you staying in Baltimore or traveling further on?"

Duff laughed. "Much further on and I will be in the Chesapeake. I don't fancy a swim at this time of the year. The water would not do a thing for my products."

"Oh? What business are you in?"

"I'm a publisher, Mr. Tremblant," answered Duff. "My company produces books. And yourself?"

"I'm a lawyer and traveling on to Washington."

"Ah, answering the call to arms?"

"I am meeting a client there," said Jed blandly, loath to reveal his mission. Fort Sumter had been bombarded a week ago, and everything had gone to hell in a handbasket. Hatred and distrust were the emotions of the day on both sides.

"From Illinois to Washington?" asked Duff with a hint of disbelief in his voice. "A long way to travel for a client."

"This man is like a favorite uncle. Do you mean to tell me there's not one man you know who you would travel that distance for?"

Duff smiled. "Yes, there is a man I would do that for. I have to ask if you will answer the call of your fellow statesman."

"I beg your pardon?" asked Jed, unsure of the person to whom Duff's question regarded.

"His Excellency, President Lincoln," clarified Duff. "He is also from Illinois, I believe. Will you fight for him?"

"Even though Fort Sumter was fired upon, there were no deaths," pointed out Jed. "There's still a chance for peace."

"We can only hope that the right decisions are made." Duff pulled a watch from his waistcoat pocket and glanced at it. "Eleven-fifteen. We will be at the station in fifteen minutes. How are you traveling on?"

"We stop at the Susquehanna Railroad Station. I understand the omnibus can take me to the Camden Street Station."

Duff gave Jed an uneasy look. "I'd advise against it. Spend the extra money and take a carriage for hire from the station. Despite the Baltimore Police efforts to crack down on the Pug-Uglies and the Know-Nothing gangs, they are still a strong presence. You do know that Baltimore is also known as 'Mobtown'?"

"I had heard that," stated Jed. "Is it really as bad as that?"

"Usually not," replied Duff. He glanced at the other people in the railway car. "Look at them. They're distrustful and wary of one another. Changes are coming too fast for the majority of the people to comprehend."

"I beg to differ," said Jed with a smile that was warm and wistful at the same time. "The newlywed couple doesn't seem to be exhibiting the fear you suggest."

Indeed, the couple had eyes only for each other. The second lieutenant, in a starched blue uniform, had his arm linked with that of a young, pretty girl, who was sitting close beside him. They took delight in pointing out items of interest outside the window to one another.

"*Love, the smoke, and is made by the fume of sighs,*" quoted Duff.

"*The sight of lovers feedeth those in love,*" countered Jed. "Do not mock them."

"Never. I just hope their fate is better than Romeo and Juliet. Does he know what he fights for? Will he be liberator or conqueror?"

"A man doing his duty to his country?" suggested Jed.

"That may be how he sees himself now, but how much will he change in the maelstrom of war?" The car jerked as the train slowed down. The landscape outside the window had changed from rural to urban. "Ah, we are arriving. I guess only time will tell about our young lieutenant. Thank you for the conversation."

"You're welcome. I'm sorry if my musing disturbed you."

"Not at all. I was glad for the conversation." Duff's brow furrowed as he stared out the window. "Something is not right."

"What's wrong?" Jed slid over on the bench to look out his window.

The train slowed to a crawl as it approached the station. Jed opened his window and received a stinging face full of smoke and ash. Squinting, he looked out and did not like what he saw.

Groups of men were moving determinedly toward the south. They carried a variety of tools: ax handles, pitchforks, and a couple of pistols. It spelled trouble in Jed's eyes. He pulled his head back in and closed the window.

"I think they are rioting," said Jed. "They're carrying weapons."

"What?!" exclaimed Duff, aghast.

The train slowed to a stop with a squeal of steel brakes and a long, loud gush of released steam. The young couple at the front of the car stood up and made ready to depart. The lieutenant was buckling on his sword and holster, while the woman picked up her reticule.

To Jed, they were focused on one another and oblivious to what was occurring outside the train. Jed picked up his carpet bag and wide-brimmed hat and joined them.

"Excuse me," said Jed.

The lieutenant and the girl faced him with smiles on their faces. The smiles were not for Jed, but for each other. They could not be more than twenty years old. The closeness as they stood together, the look on their faces, and the small, yet betraying, gestures and touches all spoke of the depth of the feelings they had.

Seeing that emotion brought back the despair and sorrow Jed thought he had eliminated from himself. If not eliminated, then banished to the attic of his mind . . . locked away and secured . . . until now. With not just a little bit of effort, Jed shoved the feelings that threaten to overwhelm him back into their niche and slammed the door shut on them.

"Sir? Sir?"

Jed refocused his eyes on the young lieutenant, who was looking at him with some concern.

"My apologies," said Jed gruffly. "I was trying to organize my thoughts. It appears that the city is in the throes of a riot. May I suggest we proceed with caution?"

"What are they rioting about?" asked the lieutenant, looking out the window.

"Maryland has declared itself neutral," said Jed. "However, the eastern portion of the state is for the South. Allow me to introduce myself. I'm Jedidiah Tremblant of Illinois."

"Lieutenant Jonathan Harrison of Connecticut," said Jonathan, shaking Jed's hand. "This is my wife, Maura Harrison. We've been married for three days."

Jed's voice caught in his throat. The girl he originally thought of as merely pretty wasn't that. She was beautiful, incredibly so, with deep green eyes that sparkled like emeralds. Jed saw intelligence, frankness, and concern reflected in them. Maura's complexion was more tanned than what was currently the fashion. It spoke of more outdoor than indoor activities.

"Your servant, madam," greeted Jed, finally finding his voice, which was rewarded by an amused smile.

Maura opened her mouth, but was interrupted by a loud voice proclaiming, "Everyone, please leave the car!"

The conductor had opened a connecting door and was herding people toward the end of the car. Duff, who had been standing in the aisle, was swept along by the wave of people and pushed toward the exit. Jed, Jonathan, and Maura stayed where they were until most of the people passed by.

"I'm sorry, folks," apologized conductor. "Everyone has to get off."

"Why?" asked Jed.

"Orders from the central office," said the conductor. "They want everyone off and for the employees to protect the train. Now, come along."

The three of them were hustled off the train by the conductor, who was then engaged by Duff brandishing a piece of paper. Jed moved aside and was startled to find the platform empty, except for the five of them. Everyone else had either left the vicinity or were taking shelter in the station master's office. It was just then that Jed saw a foot sticking out from between two large wooden boxes situated off to one side of the platform.

Jed walked toward the boxes as the conductor climbed back on the train, saying, "I'll see what I can do," to Duff.

Secreted between the boxes, Jed found a small, scruffy bootblack about eight or nine years old. The boy was clutching a wooden, homemade box, which no doubt contained his supplies. He watched Jed with a wary expression.

Jed knelt down. "Hiding out, boy?"

"Need's a shine, sir?" countered the boy.

"I just disembarked from that train." Jed casually held up a silver half-dollar. "I'll pay you four bits to tell me what is happening."

The boy huddled between the boxes but didn't take his eyes off the coin. It was more than a full day's earnings for him, and Jed knew it. He slowly placed it down on the ground in front of them.

"De folks here is angry 'bouts the soldiers coming through," said the bootblack softly. "De's fixin' to stops dem from gettin' to Camden."

"Federal troops?" asked Jed. The boy gave him a blank stare. "Blue uniforms? Yankees? Where are the police officers?"

"Yessir. All de police is at Camden Yards, not at President Street." The boy snatched up the coin and snuggled back into his hiding place.

Jed stood up and then jumped back as there was a great clang and grinding of gears. The drive wheels of the locomotive spun before catching, and the train began to rapidly back out of the station.

Jonathan had moved Maura away from the train toward the area where Jed was standing. Duff, however, was running alongside the baggage car, banging his fist on the sliding door.

"My crates!" he yelled. "My crates!"

The train outpaced him, and Duff was forced to stop at the end of the platform. That didn't stop the blasphemies and curses he hurled at the train personnel. Jed, Jonathan, and Maura exchanged looks of embarrassed astonishment at the vehemence exhibited by the man. Maura's face flushed a charming shade of red, and Jed averted his eyes to keep from embarrassing her.

"What does he have in those crates?" asked Jonathan. "Pure gold?"

"Books would be my guess," said Jed. "He's a publisher. Although, I don't think it warrants this type of reaction, considering our circumstances."

"Our circumstances, Mr. Tremblant?" asked Maura.

Maura's rich, dulcet voice sent a thrill through Jed. It was a thrill of both pleasure and disquiet. There was no missing her southern accent.

"Yes, madam," said Jed. "The citizens of the city are revolting and trying to stop the passage of federal troops. Troops that are probably heading to Washington to protect that city."

All three of them stopped talking and cocked their heads to the side as sporadic popping noises reached their ears. The popping increased in frequency. Jonathan looked at Jed with a quizzical expression. Jed just looked grim.

"Gunfire," informed Jed to Jonathan's unasked question. "The situation is worse than I thought."

Jonathan pulled his pistol out of the holster and checked the loads. "I must go to the aid of my fellow soldiers. Sir, may I ask you watch over my wife?"

"She will be safe in the station master's office." Jed knelt down to retrieve the Navy Colt revolver from his carpet bag. "I'm coming with you."

"Jonathan?" asked Maura with trepidation in her voice.

Jonathan touched her arm before calling out to Duff. "Come, sir. We go to the aid of our fellow countrymen!"

Jonathan had just started to turn when two loud shots rang out. Jed was knocked aside when Jonathan fell on him. Clutching the young man, Jed eased him to the ground and saw there was nothing he could do. Jonathan's blank gaze stared up at nothing. Looking up, he saw Duff standing there with a surprised look on his face and a pistol in his hand.

"NOOOOO!" Maura wailed.

Somehow, Jed managed to get to his feet and wrapped his arms around Maura before she fell. The whiteness of her shocked face scared him. He had never seen anyone look so pale or who breathed so fast. Her knees suddenly gave way, and he eased her down. Maura sat staring at her late husband.

Standing up quickly, Jed was thinking of going for help but froze when he heard a gun cocked behind him.

"Don't move," ordered Duff, moving around in a wide circle while keeping his pistol trained on Jed.

"Why?"

Duff took in Jed, Maura, and Jonathan before a sorrowful look settled on his face.

"Sic Semper Tyrannis," quoted Duff, angrily. He shook his head ruefully. "This . . ." Duff waved his free hand around him. The pistol never wavered. ". . . should not be happening. I was late and . . . and I lashed out at this poor boy with his misguided intentions in my anger. Don't be a hero, Tremblant. If you try to stop me, I will kill you."

Duff backed up and disappeared behind the station. Jed thought of giving chase, but the distraught nature of Maura Harrison prevented that. She was unmoving on the platform with a vacant expression on her face.

Checking between the boxes, Jed noticed the bootblack had realized the danger and disappeared. More angry people were pouring out onto the street. There seemed to be an ebb and flow to their movements; either toward the sound of the fighting or away from it. Jed hissed between his teeth in exasperation and went to the station office door.

The station master and about a dozen other people were inside the office. Most were standing by the window and now turned to face Jed.

"I need help getting this man inside," said Jed.

No one moved, and many looked away from him.

"I ain't going out there," murmured one man. "Ain't worth my life."

A big man in the back pushed the one who was speaking aside. He and a small woman approached Jed.

"I will help you, mister," he said. "The missus will look after the girl."

"I'll get the flat cart," said the station master. "We can put him in the baggage room. He'll be safe there."

Jonathan's body was wrapped in a spare blanket and placed on the flatbed cart. Once in the baggage room, Jed took off Jonathan's sword belt. He had the station master retrieve Jonathan's kit, and Jed put the pistol and belt inside it.

"Sir, with the city the way it is now, you may not want to leave any valuables on him," suggested the station master.

"Are you going to let people rob the body?" asked Jed harshly.

"I'm not always here, sir," pointed out the station master. "The train you came in on was given orders to pull out of the city for its own protection. The police will not be around for a while since they're dealing with the unrest."

"My apologies," said Jed tersely. He did a quick search of the pockets and discovered a money belt around Jonathan's waist. All the items went into the kitbag.

"The ring, sir," said the station master. "She may be wanting it."

"Just so," agreed Jed, removing the gold band. "I'll send someone for the body. Is there a good hotel nearby?"

"A block north and on your right. Contact Jenkins for the undertaker. He's a good man."

"Thank you." The young woman had gotten Maura off the ground and onto a bench. Jed walked over and squatted down. "Mrs. Harrison . . . Mrs. Harrison, we have to leave."

Maura looked up at Jed and, with a visible tremor, seemed to collect herself. With the assistance of the young woman, she stood.

"I thank you, sir," she said huskily. We should . . . my husband . . . that man . . ."

"Your husband will be safe here," soothed Jed. "We need to get off the street in case the riot progresses this far north."

Maura began to shake. "He's not safe. He's not at peace, being murdered so foully. You are right. We need shelter."

Chapter 2

Saturday, April 20, 1861

JED SAT UNCOMFORTABLY IN THE dining room of the hotel. While the steak and eggs he was having for breakfast were delicious, he wasn't used to being armed when he was eating. His Navy Six sat heavily under his left arm in the special shoulder holster he had made.

Baltimore was still in the throes of the riot. The hotel had hired additional security, even though most of the unlawfulness was down toward the docks. From the hotel, Jed had noticed small groups of men meeting and traveling together. Their actions were not consistent with that of a rabble in his mind but were more organized with a unity of purpose.

Jed glanced down at his journal opened on top of the table. He had written down the events of yesterday and his observations. What surprised him was the feelings he felt, now for all to see in black-and-white. Not only had he written about the dread he felt concerning the upcoming conflict, but also his conviction, determination, sadness, and exasperation about it.

Jed was convinced that the Union of States had to be preserved. If left to themselves, the Southern States would go the way of the Roman Empire . . . into despotism and tyranny, the very things that the Southerners stated they were leaving the Union for.

The sadness from Jonathan Harrison's death came along with a determination to find his killer. It was not an act of war, but outright murder. But Jed was enough of a realist to know that Duff may never be brought to justice.

He had also written about the sadness he felt for Maura Harrison, so newly wed and now so tragically a widow. Looking at his words, Jed almost crossed out his feelings of exasperation. He shouldn't feel put upon, but he did. Jonathan had asked him to take care of his wife before he was killed. It was Jed's Christian and moral duty as a gentleman to help her until she was back with her own family.

A shadow appeared at the dining room door, and Jed looked up to see the person of his thoughts. Maura stood in the doorway looking around. There was a pensive expression about her as she looked over the breakfast crowd. Her eyes alighted on Jed, and relief replaced the tension on her face. Standing up, he moved to the empty chair at his table and held it out for her.

Maura was dressed in a long-sleeved, high-necked, white blouse with a long blue skirt and matching Zouave jacket. Her blonde hair had been put up a little too tightly, but it didn't detract from the beauty of her face. In his school years, Jed scoffed at the idea that a face could launch 1,000 ships, like Helen of Troy. Now, however, he averted his gaze away from her green eyes and countenance before he embarrassed himself.

"My apologies, Mrs. Harrison," he said, after he helped her to sit down. "I had not expected to see you this morning."

"I could not stay cooped up anymore, Mr. Tremblant," replied Maura. "I am usually out and about long before this. I must thank you for the maid you sent to stay with me. It was a comfort and a blessing. I hope it was not too much trouble for you."

"You have had a terrible shock." Jed signaled for the waiter. "I didn't want you to be alone."

"Especially after all those brandies I drank." She looked up at the waiter, and Jed noticed her eyes tightened slightly in pain. "Sliced bread, lightly toasted on both sides, butter, and honey on the side, and may I have a pot of tea?"

"Of course, madam," said the waiter, who broke out in a smile at the sound of her accent.

"Is it possible to get some headache powder?" asked Jed.

"I can send the boy down to the apothecary," replied the waiter. "He should be back before you have finished breakfast."

"Please do so and have the manager place the cost on my tab."

The waiter left, and Maura gestured to Jed's plate. "Please eat before it gets cold. I didn't realize you had a headache."

"I don't. The powder for you."

"Oh." Maura paused. "Is it that obvious?"

"I've . . . seen this situation before." Jed took a deep breath and let it out slowly. "I know we're strangers, but your husband asked me to look after you. If you will let me, I'll see you safely back home to your family."

"Which family is that?" scoffed Maura, more to herself than to Jed. "The Northern one or the Southern one?" She stopped to regain her composure. "I apologize, Mr. Tremblant. I did my grieving last night. No doubt I shall break down and cry on other nights but, right now, all I feel is an anger so vast that it threatens to consume me."

"That is perfectly understandable."

"Is it?" asked Maura. "My father owns a large plantation near Salem, Virginia. Horses, cattle, sawmill, and a couple other things, but no slave labor. He doesn't believe in it. He and Jonathan's father had business dealings, which started about ten years ago. They thought a marriage between Jonathan and myself would be a good thing." She placed the linen cloth on her lap.

"My father and I traveled to Hartford, Connecticut, a month ago for the wedding. During that time, Jonathan not only took me to the usual balls and dinners, but also to his father's factories and other places of industry, because I showed an interest in it. I began to understand the feeling of pride that the Northerners have for the nation." Maura fell silent as a man passed them by to leave the room.

"Jonathan joined the state militia right after South Carolina seceded. His father's influence got him a lieutenancy and a posting in Washington as an attaché. It . . . it was supposed to be a safe position."

Maura began to tremble, and her face flushed red. Her fingernails clawed at the tablecloth in anger. Jed reached over to lay a comforting hand on her arm. Maura looked at his hand in surprise, and he pulled it back. He had momentarily forgotten the social conventions of the East, and Maura visibly regained control of herself.

"I am so sorry," apologized Maura. "I didn't mean to let my feelings—"

"No need to apologize," interrupted Jed. "I must apologize for my forwardness. Ah, your food is coming."

Jed and Maura sat in silence as a waiter placed her order in front of her.

"Mr. Tremblant, I do appreciate and thank you for your help," said Maura, before taking a sip of her tea. "I know Jonathan's family will want his . . . his body sent back home. Would you help me with . . .? I . . . I suppose he is still at the station."

"No, he isn't," said Jed, finishing off his steak. "I had an undertaker named Jenkins retrieved him. Jonathan is at his establishment. We can go there after we have eaten breakfast. Mrs. Harrison, I have a dilemma. There are no trains running in or out of Baltimore at this time, and I've been told that the telegraph wires are down. There is a ship sailing to Washington this afternoon, and I need to report in there."

"Report?" Maura's attention caught the one word Jed now wished he hadn't said.

"Yes, report," he admitted. "I am a . . ." Jed stopped before he said lieutenant. ". . . member of the Illinois State Militia. I am to coordinate between the state and the federal authorities. However, I cannot, in good consciousness, leave you alone here with such unrest in the city." He dabbed at his mouth, then placed the cloth back on his lap.

"I want to catch your husband's killer, Anthony Duff, but that will not happen here. The police are too busy dealing with the violence from yesterday. I'm going to report him to the authorities in Washington."

"Were many people hurt?" asked Maura.

Jed sighed. "The newspapers are reporting the deaths of four soldiers and twelve citizens. They're calling it the Pratt Street Massacre."

"Is that true?" asked Maura, aghast. "They couldn't have possibly meant for Jonathan's death to be anything else but murder!"

Jed coughed uneasily. "Jonathan's death was not counted as one of the soldiers' deaths. His killing was completely overlooked by the newspapers."

Maura sat even more upright than she had been as her face went completely white. The skin across her jaw went taut as she clenched her teeth. Jed knew this was another blow, and he didn't know how many more she could take.

The waiter reappeared with a headache powder and placed it on the table beside Jed. Maura picked it up and poured the contents of the packet into her tea. After a quick stir, she drank the concoction. Pouring herself another cup, she and Jed finished off their meal in silence. Jed could tell she was thinking about something by the movement of her eyes and the mechanical way she was eating. To what end, he did not know.

"Mr. Tremblant, I have come to a decision," said Maura with a calm Jed did not like at all. Her hands were wrapped around her tea cup as she stared straight ahead. "I am already in your debt for what you have done. If you will permit, I would like to come with you to Washington after we've seen Mr. Jenkins."

"I purchased a second ticket in the hopes that you would leave Baltimore," said Jed. "Will you be continuing on to Salem from there or north to Hartford?"

"Neither. I have other plans."

Jed wanted to ask what her other plans were, but instead he said, "I'll arrange to have our trunks taken down to the ship."

Maura turned her head and gave him a genuine smile. "I meant to ask you how you managed to find my luggage. It was a surprise to see my trunks in the room this morning."

"I thought you would need them, and I had need of my own," said Jed.

He found the baggage car at a departure yard just north of the station where it had been placed for safety. What Jed didn't add was that, after retrieving their trunks, he had opened Duff's crates. Those boxes didn't contain books, but over one hundred pistols and ammunition for those weapons. Jed had the crates sent to Fort McHenry, the only bastion of federal power in Baltimore that Jed knew of.

After breakfast, Jed hired a carriage, and a short time later, he and Maura were walking into the undertaker's funeral home. Mr. Jenkins was a short, jovial man who exuded comfort and solicitation. Jed introduced Maura to him.

"Mrs. Harrison, may I offer my deepest regrets on the passing of your loved one," greeted Jenkins in complete sincerity. "I am here to ease your burden, if I can."

"Thank you, Mr. Jenkins. I know my husband's family will want to bury him in Hartford, Connecticut." She handed Jenkins an envelope. "This is their address and funds to cover the cost."

Jenkins looked inside and gasped.

"Madam, you have overpaid by a goodly amount," said Jenkins. "Even for my best coffin and a swift passage."

"It is for your best coffin, a swift passage, and someone to accompany my husband back there," said Maura. "I will not be able to go with him."

"Ah, I understand." Jenkins put the division of the nation into just those three words.

"May I see him?"

"He is laid out in the back parlor, but I've just gotten his uniform cleaned," said Jenkins. "If there are other clothes you wish him to wear . . .?"

"He wore that uniform proudly to preserve the Union," said Maura. "I know he would like to be buried in it. If he is covered, that would be acceptable."

Jenkins, who had seen all sorts of erratic and unusual bereavement behavior, nodded and led the way. Jonathan was laid out on a cooling table and covered with a blanket. His pale, serene face had lost all the animation and passion Jed saw in it yesterday.

Maura stepped beside the body as Jed and Jenkins stayed back. Her fingers brushed his face as a single tear rolled down her cheek.

"My darling Jonathan," said Maura softly. "I will avenge your death. I ask now for your forgiveness for the things I will have to do or say. May God grant you eternal rest."

Maura turned away, and Jed let out the breath he'd been holding. All the tension and anger inside her had fallen away to be replaced by a quiet stillness.

Maura grasped Jenkins's hand warmly and smiled graciously at him. "Mr. Jenkins, I cannot begin to express my thanks to you. I know my husband is in good hands. I, however, find myself in need of a good dyer. Would you be able to recommend someone?"

"Yes, I can. She does quality work using only the best dyes."

"Very good. I hate to ask, but would you take care of that for me if I send you my trunks?"

Jed started to speak, then closed his mouth on his thoughts when Maura slowly turned to look at him. He took half a step back and shook his head.

"Uh, yes, I can," said Jenkins slowly, unsure of what was happening.

"Perfect," said Maura, smiling at him. "I will send instructions with the trunks. Mr. Tremblant, shall we go?"

Jed offered his arm and led Maura toward the front door. As he put on his top hat, he attempted to understand what this woman was trying to do. To leave her trunks here meant risking the loss of them, apart from the fact that she would be severely restricting her selection of wardrobe. Jed knew she had three trunks, two were hers and one belonged to Jonathan, according to the labels on them.

Outside, Jed hailed the carriage he had hired and helped Maura into it.

Inside, she beat him to the punch. "When does our ship leave, Mr. Tremblant?"

"It leaves in about three hours. We should get there early in case there's trouble along the way. A dyer, Mrs. Harrison?"

"Mr. Jenkins is too much of a gentleman to mention my attire . . . or the color of it. I should be wearing black. This is the darkest color of my current dresses."

"Wouldn't it be better to have that done once you've returned to your home? No matter which home that is."

"I'm not going home," said Maura. "I will accompany you to Washington to give an accounting of what transpired with Jonathan's death. Then I will be returning. Anthony Duff is here."

"Maura!" exclaimed Jed. "I mean, Mrs. Harrison. It's too dangerous."

"I'm not a hothouse flower or simpering debutante without a brain in her head," said Maura, matter-of-factly. "I grew up on the plantation, working in the field more than in the house, much to my mother's dismay. If you say one word about a woman's place, I'll start reciting names and deeds of adventurous women."

That very thought of a woman's place had been on the tip of Jed's tongue. He drew in a deep breath as he stroked his handlebar mustache to marshal his arguments.

"Let us hope you do not end up like Lady Macbeth or Gertrude, Queen of Denmark."

"They are but fictional creations of Shakespeare," countered Maura.

"Maybe so, but *Hamlet* and *Macbeth* are still stark reminders of the consequences of revenge and retribution. Do you mind if I continue to try to talk you out of this course you have set?"

"You may do so but only once a day."

"Twice a day."

"Once a day."

"Once a day but two times on Sunday," offered Jed.

Maura took a deep breath and gave a great sigh. For a second, Jed saw the sad girl just before Maura snorted in disgust and the calm, beautiful façade was firmly back in place. Jed knew she would not appreciate his noticing her emotion and, thus, her vulnerability.

What was it about this girl that made him want to help her? She had to be six to seven years younger than he was, but her deportment was of one with more maturity. Jed guessed it was a culmination of many factors . . . his upbringing, the violence that threw them together, that she was alone in a strange, unrestful city, and other things. Not the least of which was her beauty and grace.

Her high cheekbones, fine nose, and full lips gave her face a classical beauty that any artist would long to paint. Maura was tall. Jed knew himself to be six feet high, and he only had to lower his brown eyes about an inch or two to look into her green ones. Her carriage and ease of movement spoke volumes about her grace and elegance.

I'm a fool, thought Jed. *All too soon, she'll be off for home, despite her vow of revenge.*

At the hotel, Maura arranged to have her three trunks sent to Jenkins. Two were to go to the dyer to have the contents dyed black, while the third would be shipped back to Connecticut with Jonathan's body. She packed one valise for herself to go with her to Washington and told the manager to hold her room.

Jed settled his bill and also had the manager hold a room for him that was next door to Maura's. He packed the essentials in his carpet bag and arranged to have his trunk moved into the new room. He then met Maura at the front desk.

"I'm not sure what accommodations they have on the ship," he said. "I think we should have some food and then go there to board."

"We just finished breakfast not more than two hours ago," said Maura, a little flabbergasted.

"Yes, and I don't know when we will eat again." Jed led her into the dining room. "I've been on campaigns before. It's best to prepare for any eventuality."

After they sat down and placed their orders, Maura asked, "Where did you campaign and how did you learn all about soldiering?"

"I was stationed out west to fight against the Indians when I was younger. I was taught Clausewitz's principles of war."

"We have a few Indians near the plantation. They are peaceful."

"I'm sure they are . . . now," said Jed. "I admire the Plains Indians, but their way of life is not our own. I think this upcoming conflict will prevent a clash of cultures but only for a few years."

"I know the gentlemen of the South. Taught from birth that they are the masters of their own fate, and there's nothing better than their way of life. They will not bow to orders coming from the Northern States." She sighed heavily. "Blood has been shed."

"Yes, all we can do is prepare for the worst."

"Like your Claus-a-hoozit?"

Jed chuckled. "Clausewitz. He was a Prussian general in the colonial army during the French revolution. He wrote a paper about the principles of war. They're not bad principles to follow in life either."

"What are they?" asked Maura as their food arrived.

"The first principle is mass," said Jed. "That means concentrating your strength or force at a decisive place and time. The second is maneuver, which is placing your enemy in a position of disadvantage."

"Like being on top of the hill and having your enemy at the bottom," pointed out Maura. She nodded to the waiter as he filled their tea cups.

"Not necessarily. What if you have taken the hill and your enemy is in the valley, but he is encamped on the only source of water for twenty miles in any direction?"

"Oh, yes. I understand."

"The next one is objective or the goal, which should be clearly defined and attainable. After that is offense. You must take the initiative and not let your actions be forced upon you."

"So, mission, maneuver, objective, and offense . . . that's four."

"Three S's: surprise, security, and simplicity." Jed reached over to pick up a cube of cornbread.

"Surprise I understand," mused Maura as she watched Jed break up the cornbread into his stew. "Security is to keep yourself from being surprised. What is simplicity?"

"When you were a child, did you ever make convoluted plans that never worked out?"

Maura nodded.

"It means to keep your plan simple and ensure that they are clearly understood."

"Any others?"

"Economy of force, which means don't use a cannon to kill a mouse or commit too many of your forces to secondary efforts."

Maura shuddered as she finished off the last of her cucumber sandwich. "I hate mice!"

Jed smiled. For all of her seeming maturity, Maura was still only eighteen.

"The last one is probably the most important, in my mind. It is unity of command. It means to ensure there is a command structure under one responsible commander. I'll write the principles down for you if you like." Jed looked down at their empty plates. "I think our objective now should be to get to the ship."

"Yes, sir, Commander. Shall we go?"

Jed had the hired carriage take them to the docks. He loaded their two bags before helping Maura step inside. The trip was a grim reminder of the recent spurt of violence in the city. Store windows had been smashed, and goods were strewn across the street. Cobblestones had been pried out to be used as weapons. That and the debris made the carriage sway dangerously this way and that, either hitting or avoiding the obstacles.

They passed one scene of six police officers confronting three shabbily dressed men on a side street. Bile rose in Jed's throat when they passed by one black man. The man was off to one side, bloody and beaten. In his hand was a torn and dirty American flag.

Still, Jed could sense the city was calming down. People were out greeting neighbors and gossiping about the riot. He was a little surprised when the driver stopped the carriage a block away from the docks. Jed leaned out to inquire as to why they had halted.

"Sorry, sir," said the driver. "I dare not get closer. There're gangs at the docks."

Taking off his hat and holding onto the doorframe, Jed stood to look. Indeed, as the driver had said, there were several rough-looking men lounging around the pier entrance. They didn't stop everyone, only those trying to get out to the ships. They let a couple of people through but turned away others.

"We have to get out here," he said to Maura. "It looks like there's going to be trouble."

Maura stepped down and stood off to one side as Jed paid off the carriage and retrieved their luggage. She watched the men at the pier gateway.

"Can you carry my carpet bag, while I carry your valise?" asked Jed. "That will leave me a free hand for my pistol if I need it."

"I have a better idea," said Maura. "If we force our way onto the ship, we'll be stuck there until she sails. That will leave them plenty of time to go get help."

"What do you suggest?"

Maura linked her arm in his in a manner unbecoming a widow or new acquaintance. It was more of an infatuated girl or a . . . Jed swallowed hard to get his heart out of his throat. He couldn't even think of the word for a fallen lady because that term would never apply to Maura. Still, with parts of her anatomy pressed against him, Jed began having thoughts he shouldn't have.

"Pick up the bags and don't say a word," whispered Maura before she laughed gaily. "Your accent will give you away."

"I like my plan better," he murmured as he lifted their luggage.

"That way would've conceded the initiative to the enemy." Maura smiled as she pulled him toward the pier. "Besides, no gentleman would ever let a lady carried her own baggage."

Chapter 3

"Why, I do declare, I never understood why my great-aunt Winnifred carried on like that. I mean, honestly, I didn't mean to step on her dress on purpose, and I'm quite sure it hadn't been the first time it happened to her!"

Jed tried to keep the amazement off his face as Maura kept up a prattle about everything and anything. In the twinkling of an eye, she changed into one of those empty-headed debutantes who grace the social scenes in search of husbands. Two men stood in front of them as they approached the ticket office and the gate to the pier.

Out of the corner of one eye, Jed spied a police officer standing across the quay by the Custom House. The officer watched what was going on but made no move to interfere with the men. Jed had just enough time to wonder if the officer was acting on his own initiative or had orders from superiors before he and Maura had to stop because of the two men in their path.

"I don't know how poor Daddy is faring down at the plantation and with us just stuck up here. It's a miracle, an absolute miracle, that you got us these tickets to Washington. I am positive we shall continue on to Salem unhindered from there." Maura stopped talking and widened her eyes in surprise at the man in front of her. She broke out in a wide smile. "Why, land o' goshen! Isn't it so nice that the boat sent these men out to help us?"

"Look, lady—oof!" The man almost doubled over when Maura plucked her valise out of Jed's hand and shoved it into his stomach. He barely managed to hold onto it and his breakfast. The second man was startled but managed to catch Jed's carpet bag that Maura tossed before it could do any serious harm.

"If you gentlemen will just follow us," ordered Maura as she sailed effortlessly around the two with Jed in tow. "As I was saying, I'm sure Daddy has just made a muddle of things. The season is almost upon us, and I'm sure he hasn't done a thing about it."

"Uh, ma'am?" interrupted the second man, as his buddy wheezed and tried to catch his breath. "We ain't with the ship."

"You're not?" Maura produced a baffled look. She seemed to shrug it off and beamed a smile at them. "Well, it's perfectly natural mistake." She faced Jed. "Be a darling and retrieve our bags. Oh! Oh! Don't forget to tip these men for their trouble. I don't know what kind of state I'll find the house in. Not a word have I heard. I guess it's to be expected with the wires being down."

Jed overtipped the man and picked up their bags. Maura latched lovingly onto his arm as they turned toward the pier.

The second man looked at the coins in his hand. "Ma'am, the telegraph lines ain't down."

"Really?" That one word hit a note that should've made Jed's ears bleed. "That's just wonderful! Oh! Oh! We have oodles of time! One quick telegraph! Where is the closest? Go on to the ship, dear, and get us situated. Left side of the boat so we're not in the sun. Now, where is that telegraph office?"

"In the Custom House, ma'am."

"Thank you so very much." Maura took about ten steps and then hurried back. She looked at Jed with pleading eyes. "I forgot. I need some money."

Jed smiled and handed her a twenty-dollar coin.

"Ooo, I love you!" exclaimed Maura as she took the coin and pressed herself against Jed to kiss him on the cheek before hurrying off in a flurry of flounces.

Jed stood as if frozen, but he felt anything but. The warmth of her breath and the softness of her lips on his cheek was an unexpected, but pleasant, surprise. Despite the petticoats, corset, and outer garments she wore, the curvature of her body pressed against him made Jed feel warm all over. The old feelings he had long denied were being awakened.

"That's money long gone," joked the first man, now that he had regained his composure.

"Humph!" grunted Jed in agreement. He coughed delicately to establish a sense of decorum and turned around. No one tried to stop him as he boarded the ship.

The steamer was a side-paddle wheeler. Numerous ships of its kind lined the piers and dotted the waterways, along with sailing barks, sloops, and other merchant vessels. Jed was escorted to his cabin; Maura's was next door. He placed their luggage in his room and went up to the top deck. From there, he could see the Customs House and the quay beyond the steamship line buildings.

An hour passed by, and Jed was getting anxious. There was no sign of Maura, and he made ready to leave the ship to search for her. He had just placed a foot on the gangplank when a loud hail made him look up.

Maura hurried toward him, carrying three or four boxes, a tied-up paper package, and a large wicker basket. Jed walked down to the pier and relieved her of her bundles.

"Where have you been?" he asked quietly as they boarded the ship.

"I had to send a few telegrams and ensure they were received." Her tone was at odds with the smile on her face. "Also, because of your largesse, I had to go shopping to keep up the pretense to those men on the docks."

"I'm sure your father's all right," said Jed. "It'll be nice for him to hear from you."

"What?" Maura looked at him in confusion. Her face then cleared up in understanding. They were still beside the gangplank with people and crew milling about. "Is there a place where we can talk privately?"

"The upper deck is relatively empty."

The upper deck was indeed deserted, but Jed knew it wouldn't stay that way for long. Passengers would be coming up to take in the sights and watch the ship leave the dock. Now that he was no longer worrying about Maura safety, Jed took in the views of the bustling city and the scents on the wind.

There was, of course, the malodorous smells but also the tang of spices on the quay, the smoke from coal, and hidden underneath it all, the clean scent of water.

"I did send a telegram to my father," said Maura. "I also sent one to the Harrisons and one to the Federal War Department."

"What?" exclaimed Jed. "Why?"

"This is a copy of what I sent." Maura handed him a piece of paper. "I had to use your name."

Jed looked at the paper and read:

Plot to destroy ship Allegheny within week stop recommend moving it immediately stop will be in Washington in the morning stop J. Tremblant Illinois Militia

When Jed looked up, Maura continued, "The maid you provided for me is courting a man who sympathizes with the South. He told her they plan to use a device to blow up the ship and all the soldiers on it. I used your name because I don't think the people in Washington would've believed a woman."

"Unfortunately, they would not." He chuckled. "No more than I would have before I met you. Feel free to use my name anytime."

"Will they heed the warning? I would hate to think of all those men killed because the War Department did nothing."

"If they respond, it would be miraculous." He looked out over the harbor. "If they do, they will send soldiers from Fort McHenry."

"Why send soldiers from Fort McHenry? Why not just send a message to the ship?"

"The principle of security," advised Jed. "I'm guessing Fort McHenry has its own telegraph. A message to the ship could be intercepted and destroyed. The men on the dock can't stop a company of soldiers. However, given the tension in the city, marching troops through the streets would be ill-advised."

"How will we know?"

"We may never know. Information, especially military information, is fleeting . . . here and gone. The only thing we can do is wait and see if anything happens."

The two of them watched and waited in silence. More passengers ascended to the upper deck, and it soon became a noisy place. Not that Baltimore Harbor was quiet. The myriad of ships sailing in and out ranged from steamers to rowboats to everything else in-between.

Maura and Jed were startled by a blast from their ship's whistle. With clanking and a loud crash, the gangplank to their ship was pulled back onto the pier and the lines loosed. A low thrum vibrated through the deck as the paddlewheels began to rotate. Slowly at first, they pulled away from the pier and began to head down the Chesapeake Bay.

"When will we be in Washington?" asked Maura.

"Tomorrow morning, probably around seven or eight o'clock. Are you really coming back to Baltimore?"

"Yes, Mr. Tremblant, I am," answered Maura in a tone that brooked no discussion. The skin of her face tightened with a painful memory. She shivered slightly as if to throw off the stronger emotion before looking back at Jed. "Jonathan deserves it. I am curious, though. You're in the Illinois Militia. What rank do you hold?"

"First lieutenant."

"But you said you've been in the Army before?" quizzed Maura.

"Out west," replied Jed tersely, looking out over the water.

"I'm sorry. I didn't mean to bring up bad memories."

Jed's mouth quirked at the irony. The two of them had bad, if not horrible, memories. This war almost guaranteed everyone would have their own share, and here he was, calmly cruising down the Chesapeake Bay with a lovely woman for company.

"I was young and stupid. My father wanted me to join his law practice, but I was filled with vim and vigor to go trounce the Indians. After all, they were just savages standing in the way of progress. I quickly learned it was not so. After five years, I returned and join my father's practice." Jed chuckled. "Three years later and I find myself on a steamer to Washington."

"You have experience," said Maura. "They should have made you a colonel."

"You are correct. I could have easily purchased a colonel's rank and raised my own regiment or had my father lobby the governor. I, however, had no pretensions toward that. I signed in as a second lieutenant. My friend, John Rawlins, had the governor brevet me to first lieutenant since I was to be sent to Washington."

"I'm glad they sent you," said Maura.

They stayed on the upper deck, watching the shoreline pass by. Out on the water, the fishing boats were returning with their catch. Wooden docks weathered gray jutted out into the Patapsco River. Their pilings were green with algae. Plantation houses and farms dotted the edge of the river. Jed saw several barges being loaded with produce. The waters of the Bay turn golden as the rays of the setting sun reflected off it.

"This is my first time on a large boat." Maura smiled as she watched a flock of ducks in the water.

"Ship," corrected Jed. "A boat only carries three to four people. Ships are larger." He looked at the sun which was now kissing the treetops on the western shoreline. "Shall we go down to see what our ship has to offer in the way of refreshments?"

Maura smiled weakly. "I have a surprise for you. Would you get the wicker basket out of my cabin? No peeking, please. I will meet you in the salon."

Jed went to Maura's cabin and picked up the wicker basket. He didn't look; however, he did bring it up to his nose and inhaled. The delicious smell of fried chicken and bread set his mouth watering.

Back at the salon, Maura had secured them a table. Other people were there, some of whom were dining from their own dinner baskets.

"You peeked!" accused Maura, correctly guessing from the smile on Jed's face.

"No, I did not. The aroma gave it away. Where did you find a dinner basket?"

"At a store that had been vandalized," said Maura, opening said basket. "Two of the six plates were broken, and the cutlery was missing. I replaced the knives, forks, and spoons with a mishmash of odds and ends. I bought it for practically nothing." She pulled a bottle of wine out of the basket. "If you could get this open, I'll . . . Jiminy! I forgot the glasses!"

"Allow me." Jed walked over to the salon's bar and came back with the opened bottle and two tumblers. "They're not wine glasses, but they should do."

"Thank you. As you may have guessed, we have fried chicken, rolls, pickled beets, pickled dill green beans, a crock of butter, and a small jar of honey." She gave a little wince. "I'm sorry, but there wasn't a big selection to choose from."

"It smells divine." Jed poured wine into the tumblers. "Your thinking so far has been better than mine. You led us past the ruffians and onto the ship without a fight. You sent off a telegram about the Allegheny and still managed to astonish me with this repast. Your family must value you greatly"

Maura looked at Jed for a couple of seconds and, cocking an eyebrow at him, gave him a nod of acknowledgement.

"Mr. Tremblant, I greatly appreciate the compliment." Her normal demeanor left her to be replaced by a bland, uncompromising expression. The change startled Jed. "I will not, however, be swayed or turned from my task."

"Mrs. Harrison, I meant it just as a compliment, nothing more," said Jed flatly.

Maura sighed and said, a little abashed, "I do crave your pardon. I . . . I . . ."

Jed's irritation that had started to build inside of him dissolved. He had meant it as a compliment, and she took it as an attempt to get her home to safety. The trouble was they had been thrown together by circumstance and knew nothing of one another.

"I must offer my apologies, too," he said. "May I try to explain?"

Maura nodded, not trusting her voice.

"My father has a very successful law practice in Chicago. We are very rich, and I grew up very spoiled. I cared more about myself than any other person. Responsibility and accountability were not a part of my repertoire. My father had my whole life planned out for me, but I wanted to go out West to fight Indians and be a hero. I basically ran away from home to join the Army."

"I was given the rank of second lieutenant. I was so full of myself; I didn't even realize that my father had probably secured the commission for me. Fortunately, I had a commanding officer who realized how green I was and taught me how to be a soldier, an officer, and a gentleman. It was a humbling and embarrassing experience, but I learned. Native guides taught me how to speak Comanche and Arapahoe and the way an Indian lives. My commander had his family with him. I fell in love with his daughter and she with me. I had been out west for two years before we were married.

"After five years, there was a . . . a tragic incident. My wife died. Nothing violent . . . just one of those things. I couldn't bear to stay there. Everything reminded me of her. So, I resigned my commission and went home to Chicago. That was three years ago."

Jed refilled his glass when he paused for a moment.

"The differences between the North and the South were muted in the Territories. Social conventions are not highly observed as they are in the East. Back home, I became fully aware of how big the division was becoming. Honestly, I really didn't care about that or anything else. I have two sisters: Chastity is seventeen and Sarah is fourteen.

"The two of them, more than anyone else, kept me going for the past three years. Sarah gave me a journal to write in when I was posted to Washington. She handed it to me with explicit instructions to write about my adventures and my feelings. I think she wants me to go back to being the brother I was . . . or rather, the brother she remembers. The one who did nice things for her and cared about her, when he wasn't being completely self-centered." Jed grinned a little and ran his hand through his hair.

"I do care for her, but it's not that easy to show since . . . well, the reason I'm telling you this is because I do care, Mrs. Harrison. I want you to understand the dangers. Your actions alone concerning the Allegheny would have you either shot or hung as a spy. Duff appears to be a southern spy sent to Baltimore to foment trouble. Hunting him will be extremely dangerous. The South will try to protect him. The North will not assist you because you are a woman, but I will help you if you let me."

Maura seemed to sense Jed's unwillingness to talk about the event that brought him back east. She nibbled on a wing as she sat in contemplation. Setting her piece of chicken down, she looked at Jed.

"Mr. Tremblant, I, too, am the oldest sibling in my family. I have two brothers and two sisters, and I dread what this war will lead them to. Despite the competence and bravery of the southern gentlemen, I believe the North will prevail. The manpower and industrial disparity between the two is too great.

"I loved Jonathan. To have him shot down like . . . like . . . like a dog is . . ." Maura shook in anger. After several deep breaths, she regained control of herself. "I will never forget that, and I will avenge him. I will heed your warnings and, as to your offer, let us see how things stand in Washington. If you'll excuse me, I would like to turn in."

Jed stood up to pull out her chair. "I'm sorry if I upset you."

"You've been honest with me, Mr. Tremblant, and have done more than what was expected. I do appreciate it. My anger is the only thing right now keeping me on my feet. I should retire."

Jed watched her leave before packing up the basket. A saloon waitress came over to collect trash to be thrown overboard. Looking at her mahogany skin, Jed wondered if the waitress was free or not and if she knew of the events to come. Shaking his head because he could no more see the future than she could, Jed headed to the cabin to go to sleep.

"Good morning, Mr. Tremblant."

Jed pushed himself off the top deck railing and turned around.

"Good morning, Mrs. Harrison. You're up early. I trust you slept well."

"Tolerably," said Maura, although there were dark circles under her eyes. She was dressed in her blue skirt and matching jacket, but a black shawl draped across her shoulders had been added to her outfit. "I see you brought the basket."

"I must confess that I peeked. Scones, butter, honey, and apple cider. I thought it would be better to bring it than have to go back down for it."

"Sound thinking," said Maura. "Is that Washington?"

"Yes. The steward told me we should be docking in less than an hour. That's the town of Alexandria to our left."

Maura pointed off to her right. "That huge building with the round center and what looks to be scaffolding around it . . . that's the Capitol Building, is it not?"

"I believe so," said Jed. "At least that's what I gather from the newspaper illustrations I've seen. Shall we have some breakfast at our table?"

Breakfast was unhurried, and the conversation was congenial. After Jed had repacked the basket and disposed of the rubbish, he sighed and then chuckled at himself. Maura gave him a questioning look.

"Mrs. Harrison, you will not hear any more arguments from me. I didn't sleep well because, well, just because. I will not try to turn you from your task. Will you allow me to assist you in Baltimore to find Duff?"

Maura stared at him for a second. "What of your orders? Your commission?"

"I hope I can persuade Secretary Cameron of the importance of finding Duff—a southern agent who transported arms into Baltimore for the rebellion. He needs to be apprehended."

Maura reflected on Jed's words for several moments.

Jed was a little impressed; most women of his acquaintance would have readily accepted his offer without thinking about it.

"Thank you, Mr. Tremblant," she said at last. "I accept your offer. Oh, it looks like we're going to dock."

Their steamship was indeed approaching the piers adjacent to the Washington Navy Yard. Jed hurriedly picked up the wicker basket.

"Please, go and pack your things, if you haven't done so already," said Jed.

"I've done so," replied Maura with a quiet smile.

"Good. I will meet you at your room in a few minutes."

Maura and Jed went their separate ways, only to meet up a little while later at the door to her cabin. The steamer was slowly pulling into a dock. Jed picked up Maura's valise and stood by the railing to watch the ship tie off.

The pier was wide with a number of wagons, teamsters, and stevedores moving goods and chattel. Jed spied blue-uniformed soldiers at the end of the pier. The soldiers appeared to be inspecting passengers and cargo.

"Mr. Tremblant? Is that man over there holding a piece of paper with your name on it?"

Jed saw a neatly dressed man in a brown suit standing on the pier. The sign he was holding had 'J. Tremblant' written out in large, black lettering. Standing next to the man was a Marine officer.

"Uh, maybe this time, you had better be the one to be silent," said Jed with a smile. "At least, until we get off that dock."

Maura looked around, her head twisting to look between the Marine officer and all the other soldiers.

"Why, Mr. Tremblant!" she exclaimed with in a much-exaggerated southern drawl. "I do believe you may be right."

After they disembarked, Jed and Maura walked to where the two men were standing.

"I'm Lieutenant Jedidiah Tremblant of the Illinois Militia."

The man with the sign let out a big sigh of relief. "Thank goodness. I'm Martin Dowling. I'm here to escort you to the Honorable Mr. Cameron. I have a carriage waiting. Captain Murphy?"

"This way, gentlemen," said the Marine officer.

Maura raised an eyebrow but didn't say anything. She simply followed behind Jed, who was carrying both bags. Captain Murphy led them past the soldiers to a carriage that had been waiting just past the end of the pier. He turned and was a little startled to see Maura there with them.

"Uh, Miss . . . ?" he started to say.

"She's coming with us," said Jed.

Captain Murphy and Mr. Dowling looked at one another.

"Gentlemen, her husband, who was a lieutenant in the Connecticut militia, was killed on Friday during the riots in Baltimore," said Jed. "As a gentleman, I could not leave her alone in that city. She is also a witness to what transpired there."

Captain Murphy offered his condolences to Maura as a carriage driver took the luggage and stored it away. Murphy nodded to Dowling and then turned away to resume his duties. Mr. Dowling also expressed his sympathy and stepped away to allow Jed to assist Maura into the carriage.

"Poor, weak, defenseless thing, am I?" Maura whispered as she laid a hand on Jed's arm.

"I don't believe that for second but don't let them know," he whispered back.

The tenseness in Maura's face was replaced by a genuine smile. She gave his arm a squeeze as she stepped into the carriage. Jed followed, allowing Maura time to arrange her long skirts and sit down. Dowling sat in the rear facing seat.

The carriage ride took them past the unfinished Capitol Building and up Pennsylvania Avenue. Martin, insisting that they call him such, learned this was their first time to Washington and pointed out interesting buildings and locations as they rode by them. They were soon passing the President's House and stopped just west at a large brownstone building.

"The War Department," said Martin as he stepped down to the cobblestones. He looked at Maura and seemed indecisive about what to do with her.

"Lead the way," said Jed. "We shouldn't keep Mr. Cameron waiting."

Martin opened his mouth and then closed it. With a nod, he graciously led the way into the brownstone. As they walked into the building, Jed looked back and saw the coachman unloading their luggage. They followed Martin to the second floor where he entered an outer office before stopping in front of an inside door to knock. A voice on the other side bid them enter.

Inside the room was Simon Cameron, the Secretary of War. Jed had seen engravings of the man in the newspapers. Cameron appeared to be in his sixties with a high forehead and white hair combed over the top.

"Lieutenant Jedidiah Tremblant of Illinois," announced Martin. He turned to introduce Maura but realized he didn't know her name. He coughed to cover up his faux pas and turned toward Cameron.

"Thank you, Martin," said Cameron. "That will be all. Tremblant, what's happening in Baltimore and what has the Allegheny to do with it?"

Before Jed could answer, footsteps sounded outside the room. Martin, who was walking out, backed up to make room for the tall man dressed in a black suit to stand in the doorway.

"Simon, I have a little time before I have to go to church," said President Lincoln. "What is new in the reports?"

Chapter 4

Sunday, April 21, 1861

"I BEG YOUR PARDON," APOLOGIZED President Lincoln. "I did not realize you had guests, Simon."

The president stepped the rest of the way into the room, dipping his head slightly through the doorway. Jed was sure it was an automatic reaction for the tall man. The dark suit, the tall, lean frame, and the chin-curtain beard had all been illustrated in the newspapers. However, not one drawing caught the intelligence or intensity of Lincoln's deep-set eyes.

"Mr. President," greeted Cameron. "May I introduce Lieutenant Jedidiah Tremblant of the Illinois Militia and . . . I am terribly sorry, Miss. I did not get your name."

"Mrs. Maura Harrison," said Maura before Jed could say her name, "of Virginia."

Cameron and Dowling looked aghast that there was a real, live southern-born lady in the office of the secretary of war. Jed held his breath, waiting to see what the others were going to do.

Lincoln raised himself to his full height and smiled. "I am honored to make your acquaintance, Mrs. Harrison. I do wish it was under better circumstances. I hope you'll excuse us, but we have matters to discuss before I have to leave for the church."

"Mrs. Harrison's husband was murdered on the nineteenth in Baltimore," said Jed quickly. "He was a lieutenant in the Connecticut Militia. The murderer, one Anthony Duff, is, I believe, an agent for the South."

President Lincoln slowly closed his eyes as if in pain. Cameron rummaged through the papers on his desk looking for a report. Martin turned this way and that, unsure of what to do or say.

Lincoln opened his eyes and gently took one of Maura's hands. "Mrs. Harrison, I cannot begin to express the sorrow I feel at the loss of your husband."

Her eyes glistened with unshed tears.

"If there is anything I can do for you, you only have to ask," he said.

"Bring my husband's killer to justice," said Maura, shaking with emotion.

"Your pardon, but I do not have a Lieutenant Harrison listed as one of the soldiers killed by the mob in Baltimore," stated Cameron, holding up a paper.

"Nor was he listed in any of the Baltimore newspapers," commented Jed. "Lieutenant Harrison and his wife were riding the same train I was on, along with Duff. We all disembarked at the Susquehanna Railroad Station. Duff was transporting arms and ammunition to Baltimore, and I think the riot occurred earlier than he expected. He lost possession of his crates of weapons. When Lieutenant Harrison proposed to go fight the rioters, Duff shot him in the back in a fit of anger."

President Lincoln stood still for several moments, analyzing and assessing what he just heard. He looked at the clock on the mantle of the room's fireplace and blew out a breath of air.

"Simon, would you send your young man here over to the residence and convey my regrets to Mrs. Lincoln that I will not be able to attend church today?"

"Of course, Mr. President." Simon turned to Martin. "Convey just his regrets. Nothing else."

"Yes, sir. May I suggest that I sent for an illustrator?"

Cameron bristled and snapped, "This is not the time for that! Just do as you're told!"

Martin turned away crestfallen, but Jed stopped him.

"Did you mean to get an illustrator, so we capture a likeness of Duff?" asked Jed, to which Martin nodded.

Cameron snorted to disguise his discomfort.

"Regrets to Mrs. Lincoln first, illustrator second," he said Martin. He then added gently, "As quick as you can."

Martin gave Jed a smile of thanks and left quickly.

The president gave Cameron a look of admonishment before turning to face Jed. "May I suggest we have a seat? People complain of cricks in their neck when they have to look up at me for too long."

He assisted Maura into a padded chair beside Cameron's desk before sitting down himself. "Now, Lieutenant Tremblant, if you'd be so kind as to start at the beginning of your tale and tell us what is supposed to occur to the *Allegheny*."

"Mr. President, I'm afraid Mrs. Harrison is going to have to tell you. She sent the telegram under my name, with which I have no issue," Jed said.

Jed went on to tell of his encounter with Duff on the train and the subsequent chain of events that led up to Lieutenant Harrison's death. He related his observations of Baltimore the day after the riot and of men and the police officer at the pier.

"I cannot state if the police officer acted with authority or on his own volition," said Jed. "Either way, it presents a disturbing trend. Mrs. Harrison?"

Maura filled in her parts of the tale. She told how her maid at the hotel heard about the plot to destroy the *Allegheny* by some infernal device, and the sending of the telegram.

Lincoln and Cameron exchanged a look before the president stood up and the others followed. Lincoln spotted Martin, who had returned during Maura's telling. "Is the illustrator here?"

Martin nodded.

"Lieutenant Tremblant and Mrs. Harrison should meet with him. We will convene afterward. Mr. Dowling, if you could show them the way?"

Martin led the way out of the room. Jed started to follow but turned around at the doorway.

"Is the *Allegheny* still residing in Baltimore Harbor?" he asked quietly.

Lincoln and Cameron exchanged glances before Cameron said, "Yes, it is still there. We're using it as a receiving ship. It is thought that we will capture the men when they make the attempt."

"Mr. President, Mr. Cameron, I don't mean any disrespect, but what if they float a mine or use a torpedo against the ship?"

The three of them stood silent for a moment. Then Lincoln sighed. "Thank you, Lieutenant. We were a little suspect of receiving such a telegram from a dubious source. Go see the illustrator."

Jed and Maura spent an hour with the illustrator in another part of the building until Duff's face was there for all to see on paper. Martin paid the man and sent him on his way before leading Jed and Maura back to Cameron's office. A new man in a brown tweed suit, holding a bowler hat, stood in the inner office. There was no missing the silver badge pinned to the outside of his jacket. Everyone stood when Maura entered.

"Lieutenant Tremblant and Mrs. Harrison, may I introduce US Marshal John Stockdale," said Cameron. "I've given him the details, and he will be issuing a warrant for the arrest of Anthony Duff. Do we need anything else, Marshal?"

"No, sir." Stockdale bowed to the president. "I'll have wanted posters printed and mailed to other jurisdictions, except Baltimore City. I think I should hand-deliver those myself and take a look around."

"Thank you, Marshal," said President Lincoln. "If you have any trouble or need any help, please let us know."

"Yes, Mr. President."

Jed stood aside as Stockdale left. President Lincoln escorted Maura back to her chair.

"Thank you, sir," said Maura, as she sat. "If you'll excuse what I'm saying, you're not the person I was expecting to meet. I mean, you're different than . . ."

Lincoln chuckled. "No, you were expecting to see Mr. Cameron. I'm not always the ogre the newspapers portray me as. Hopefully, I can be the president you want me to be." He sat down next to her. "I've sent a telegram to Governor Letcher in regard to the murder of your husband and the warrant for the arrest of Anthony Duff."

"Oh!" Maura looked a little startled. "Thank you, but, um . . . er . . ."

"Why didn't I send one to Jeff Davis? Mrs. Harrison, I have states in rebellion, trying to tear apart this nation, and we are a nation. We are not just a grouping of independent states. We must stand together, or we *will* fall apart, and I do mean every single state standing together. I cannot afford to give any sort of recognition or legitimization to the Confederate government."

"Governor Letcher is part of that government," argued Maura.

"Ah, but he was elected by the people before Virginia seceded. A fine point, I grant you, but it is one I can use."

"Has he replied?" asked Maura.

"No, and he may not reply," stated Lincoln. "What will you do now? Will you return home?"

"No, Mr. President. I will be returning to Baltimore."

The President could not have looked more shocked than if Maura had gotten up on the desk and danced a jig. Even Cameron was a little taken aback.

"Why on God's green earth would you return to that forsaken city?" asked Cameron.

"Anthony Duff is there. Mr. President, Mr. Secretary, with your permission, I would like to accompany Mrs. Harrison," said Jed.

"You have to ask permission?" asked Maura.

"Mrs. Harrison, Lieutenant Tremblant is a soldier," said Cameron. "He has orders to work for me in the War Department. He can't ignore them."

"If I may point out, Mrs. Harrison—" Lincoln was interrupted by knocking at the door.

"Enter!" bellowed Cameron.

A young man in shirt sleeves came timidly. With an unintelligible mutter, he handed a piece of paper to President Lincoln. The man then beat a very hasty retreat.

President Lincoln read the telegram and then read it again. Standing up abruptly, he paced to the window. A red flush crept up Lincoln's neck, and thunderclouds formed on his brow. Whatever was on that paper did not bode well for someone.

It took a few minutes for the president to regain his composure. When he turned away from the window, the anger was gone, replaced by determination and a bit of sorrow.

"There is no easy way to say this, Mrs. Harrison, so I'll just read it.

To: President Lincoln
From: President Davis
I am sorry to hear about the soldier's death, but you foisted this war upon us. Your unrelenting determination to interfere and subjugate the Confederate States will only result in more deaths. These deaths will be on your conscience. Your soldier's death was regrettably an act of war.

Lincoln looked at Maura with real sympathy in his eyes. Jed understood what President Davis was saying. War, with all its horror, had started, and Davis considered Duff to be a soldier and a patriot.

"Mrs. Harrison, we would do everything in our power to bring this man to justice," said Lincoln.

"Mr. President, may I keep that?" asked Maura, indicating the paper he was holding.

Lincoln hesitated and then said, "Of course."

"The man is obviously a spy. We need to start taking measures to protect ourselves from spies and provocateurs," said Cameron.

"Mr. President." Maura stood quickly, as the men fumbled to their feet in courtesy. "May I speak with you privately?"

"I don't think that would be appropriate," said Cameron uneasily.

"Oh, la," poo-pooed Maura. "I am not an assassin, Mr. Cameron, and I've no desire to compromise the President. Please, sir, it is important."

Lincoln chuckled. "I'll listen to what you have to say. Gentlemen, if you please."

Jed was the first one out the door, followed by Martin and then Cameron. They looked decidedly unhappy about the situation as the President slid the pocket doors together, shutting them out of the inner office.

There was nothing to do but wait. Time seemed to crawl. Jed tried to relax, but his mind kept wondering what Maura was talking to President Lincoln about. He nibbled on a leftover drumstick from the basket he had retrieved from their pile of luggage. After an hour, Jed was ready to jump out of his own skin and break into the office. He looked over Cameron, who was sitting in a chair, going over reports and apparently unconcerned.

"Sir?"

Cameron forestalled Jed's question with a deep sigh and a raised hand.

"Lieutenant Tremblant, in the short time I've known President Lincoln, I found him to be of immeasurable intellect and indomitable will. He's not the baboon or ape who has been illustrated so many times in the newspapers. He will not be swayed by pretty face or sweet words."

Jed started to bristle, but Cameron held up his hand again.

"I mean no insult to the lady or to you, sir. I merely say that the President is a man unto himself and entirely capable. Patience is a virtue, Lieutenant Tremblant."

"Yes, sir," said Jed with a sigh. "Sorry, sir."

Cameron waved aside Jed's apology. "I, too, must confess a great curiosity about exactly what Mrs. Harrison had to say. These are not matters that the President should be concerned with today. I have Baltimore in turmoil, and General Butler has landed in Annapolis. The South is seizing ships and forts, and we have only one regiment to defend Washington. We are routing troops around Baltimore, and we hope that one blow to the South in the summer should end this rebellion."

There was nothing to say, although Jed did not believe that one swift blow would end the conflict. It was a little more than five minutes later when Maura opened the doors just enough to let herself out. To Jed's eyes, she looked like she had achieved what she wanted but was now a little scared of the consequences.

"President Lincoln has requested your presence, Mr. Cameron."

"Thank you, Mrs. Harrison." Cameron headed to his office. "Martin, please see if our guests need anything. We will be finished momentarily." He closed the doors behind him.

"What can I do to make you more comfortable?" asked Martin.

"There's nothing I need, thank you," said Maura graciously.

Jed shook his head and asked Maura, "Is everything well?"

"The president expressed concerns and facts that . . . well, that were not to my liking. However, my responses showed him my resolve. We . . . We reached an accord."

"You are going back to Baltimore then, I take it?" asked Jed.

"Yes, Mr. Tremblant."

Jed had learned patience on the plains out west, which was a far cry from his impetuous youth, and where it also meant survival. Even so, he wanted to ask Maura the nature of her conversation with the president, but she seemed to be inwardly reflecting on it, and he didn't wish to disturb her. The doors to Cameron's office slid open, causing Jed and Maura to jump.

"Mrs. Harrison, Lieutenant Tremblant, if you would please come in," said Cameron. "Martin, I'm afraid I must ask you to wait downstairs."

"Of course, sir," said Martin. He nodded to Maura and took his leave of them.

President Lincoln was waiting for them in the office. With a bow, he led Maura to her chair before sitting down himself. Jed and Cameron found their own chairs.

"Lieutenant Tremblant, I believe you are the only one here unaware of our discussions," said Lincoln. "Please, allow me to enlighten you, but I fear it will not be to your liking."

"I know Mrs. Harrison will be returning to Baltimore to search for Mr. Duff," said Jed.

"Yes, despite my warnings and dire predictions. The Secretary and I agree that southern spies in Baltimore cannot be allowed to remain there. Therefore, we are sending you with Mrs. Harrison. Mrs. Harrison has proposed, and I have accepted, that she will be my agent to uncover plots and plans against the federal government. I've discussed it was Secretary Cameron, and you will be assigned to the War Department with the rank of captain. We will notify Governor Yates of the change of your status. Simon?"

"Captain Tremblant, any information Mrs. Harrison obtains will be given to you. You'll send such information on to us—in code, please. I cannot stress how sensitive the codebook is. Please, don't lose it."

Cameron shifted his body to face Maura more directly. "Mrs. Harrison, I'm sure the president and Captain Tremblant have expressed the extreme danger you're placing yourself in. If the situation wasn't so dire, I would call a halt to all of this. However, you are now the President's spy. It is imperative that Maryland does not join the rebellious states. Governor Hicks has declared that his state will remain neutral. He is facing the same problem as Virginia."

"Virginia seceded, Mr. Secretary," said Maura.

"Yes, and the western counties of that state are not in accord with the Ordinance of Succession. Maryland is the same way. Governor Hicks does not want his state split apart. Your objective is twofold. One is to find and stop any southern spies, including Anthony Duff. The other is to gather information on the officials of Baltimore City. We know the mayor and the police commissioner want Maryland to join the Confederate States. We need to know who else is in their camp."

President Lincoln stood and handed Maura a sheet of paper.

"I hope this meets with your approval, Mrs. Harrison. It was witnessed by Mr. Cameron," said Lincoln.

"Thank you, Mr. President."

"Do you really think it is necessary?" he asked.

"Mr. President, the feeling up north is that once you have gathered your troops, one push toward Richmond and beyond will end the rebellion. Mr. Cameron and Mr. Dowling believe it too. I pray that it is so, but I do not believe the South will give up so easily. I do believe the North will triumph. You have superior manpower and industry." She handed the paper back to Lincoln. "Will you keep this safe for me for when I shall need it?"

"Of course, Mrs. Harrison," said Lincoln. "Tonight, you and Captain Tremblant will be my guests at the residence. We shall have a special train take you back to Baltimore in the morning."

"Sir, that would not be advisable," said Jed. "We need to keep Mrs. Harrison's contact with you and the War Department to a minimum. A special train would also attract attention. I already purchased two tickets on the packet to go back to Baltimore this afternoon. We should be there tomorrow morning. Mrs. Harrison will also need funds."

"Funds?" asked Cameron in surprise. "Whatever for?"

"The furnished house that she will have to rent," explained Jed. "Servants, food, and most importantly, paying for the information you need. I am a lawyer, and I know the cost of such information. She will need to start with fifty thousand dollars."

"Start with fifty . . .," sputtered Cameron in astonishment.

He looked at President Lincoln to see if he was as upset as he was about the amount. Lincoln, however, was deep in thought. He stroked his beard before pulling himself out of his reverie. "She cannot just go up and demand that these people tell her of their plots and plans, Simon. It will require social gatherings, balls, dinners, building confidences, and, yes, paying informants. Today is Sunday. Let us know which bank you wish to use, and we will have the money sent there."

"The money cannot come from the government, Mr. President. We will need a third intermediary," said Jed.

"Why?" asked Maura.

"It's an axiom of police officers when investigating crimes to follow the money. To find out where it comes from and where it goes. If a southern sympathizer at the bank or someone inquiring into your accounts sees that you're receiving large funds from the United States government, it would raise suspicion and could be detrimental."

"Mrs. Harrison, there is still time for you to change her mind," said Lincoln gently. "I will still honor our agreement if you do."

Maura straightened up with a sharp inhale of breath. Jed saw the bitterness and anger on her face just before it resolved into a fierce determination. Lincoln sighed because he saw the same thing, too.

"Goodbye and good luck, Mrs. Harrison," said Lincoln, standing up. "Please, do not take any unnecessary risks.

Simon, would you please have Martin call a hansom to take them back to the pier?"

"Thank you, Mr. President," said Maura as she turned to leave.

Jed made to follow her, but a hand on his arm restrained him. Looking over his shoulder, he saw that the hand belonged to the president.

"I've just seen a casualty of this war I had not expected to see," said Lincoln unhappily. "I do not like this endeavor, probably no more than you do. I am hoping this gives her a purpose beyond revenge and retribution. Please understand that you will not be able to keep her completely safe. I told her that you two are partners and need to work together."

"I find her to be intelligent and adaptable. However, I do feel her revenge will place her in harm's way," said Jed.

"Keep her safe, Captain Tremblant."

"I will do my best, Mr. President."

Jed headed downstairs to where Maura and Martin were waiting. As Jed left, he heard Secretary Cameron complaining to President Lincoln about the money. With Cameron upstairs with the president, Jed told him that they needed a hansom cab to take them back to the docks. Martin left to get one and Jed turned to face Maura.

"Are you mad at me?" asked Maura.

"No, Mrs. Harrison. President Lincoln told me we are partners in this endeavor, but I thought we were that when I . . . we agreed to travel back to Baltimore to hunt for Duff. We will not find him by roaming the streets. We need to find his supporters and associates."

"The mayor, the city council, the police board to include the commissioner . . .," said Maura.

"You have a better chance to affiliate yourself with them. I have no chance at all. I can start tracing the weapons Duff brought into Baltimore. I need to find out where they came from and who purchased them."

"Mr. Dowling is returning," whispered Maura. She turned to face the door. "Mr. Dowling, I see our cab is ready. Will you direct us to where we may obtain substance for our little boat trip?"

"I can do better than that. Is this your basket?" Martin picked up the wicker case. "Tell the driver to wait. I'll be right back."

Martin hurried off, and Jed went out to tell the driver about the delay. He stored their luggage in the cab while he and Maura waited for Martin to return.

Several minutes later, Martin came back with an obviously heavily laden basket. He placed it in the cab and then assisted Maura to step up.

"Will we see you again, Mrs. Harrison?" he asked. Jed was sure there was nothing more that Martin wanted than to see the beautiful girl again.

"It is doubtful, Mr. Dowling. My business here is concluded, but in these times, who can tell? Thank you so much for everything. Where did the food come from?"

Martin blushed. "I raided the president's kitchen. I didn't think he would mind."

"Oh, dear," moaned Maura theatrically. "The poor man is as thin as a rail already, and I'm stealing his lunch."

The three of them broke out laughing; even the driver chuckled. Jed expressed his thanks to Martin, had a word with driver, and climbed into the cab.

"Back to Baltimore, Mrs. Harrison?"

"Back to Baltimore," she agreed. "I think, since we are partners, you might as well address me as Maura."

Chapter 5

Monday, April 22, 1861

"Good morning, Jed. I see the Union flag still flying above Fort McHenry."

Jed had risen early and was already on the upper deck of their steamer to watch the approach to Baltimore. At the sound of Maura's voice, he turned around. She was wearing her blue dress with a black shawl. Her hair, instead of being in ringlets as was the style, was done up in a bun on top of her head. The change in hairstyle made her look older than her eighteen years.

"Good morning. I trust you slept well."

"I think I was too exhausted from the night before to notice how much noise the ship makes," said Maura with a weak smile. "That and the motion."

"I'm sorry to hear that," said Jed. "I must say you do look exceptional this morning."

"Why, I thank you, kind sir, even though I know you're talking out of both sides of your mouth," said Maura with a slight smile. Jed smiled along with her. "I was lucky enough to find a cleaning lady who could help me with my hair and dress. You were correct. I need to hire help, at least a maid. I don't know how to find a house to rent."

"I've been giving that some thought. I suggest you talk to Mr. Jenkins. As an undertaker, he knows everyone and will be an important contact. He will also try to remain neutral." Jed looked back at the port. "As for your help, you're going to have to be very careful. There is a saying that a master has no secrets from his valet. I'm sure the same is true for lady's maid."

"Very true, probably even more so. The lady's maid is very often a confidante. I'll go to see Mr. Jenkins this afternoon. I hope he can help."

"If he can't, he will know someone who can."

"Jed, the president explained several things to me. He did try his best to try to dissuade me. I'm going to have to socialize and associate myself with the southern sympathizers here to obtain information." Maura hesitated before continuing. "That means you cannot be with me. No one will speak to me about anything but pleasantries if you're nearby. Do you . . . do you understand what I'm saying?"

"I do understand, because I've been wrestling with that problem all night. No solution came to my mind, I might add. Once we get back to the hotel, I will not be able to chaperone you anymore. However, I feel that once your clothes are dyed black, they will give you protection against all but the most hardhearted and callous."

"Mr. Tremblant!" Maura put her hand to her chest as if to protect the clothing she wore against any advances he should make.

Jed chuckled without meaning it to divert the two or three curious stares that her cry attracted. He then bowed to her an apology, not so much for what he said, but for the couple of seconds he needed to compose a response.

"Maura, this game is in earnest," he said softly. "You must keep your wits about you. I know you to be intelligent and resourceful. Society gives a widow a lot of protection."

"And some vulnerabilities," added Maura, giving Jed a fake smile that would've fooled anyone but him. "There will be some men who will see it as an opportunity to replace the husband—matrimonially, intimately, or both."

Jed's face turned sour. The very thought of another man having designs on Maura turned his stomach and set his blood simmering. He knew men who had no morals and no qualms about taking advantage of a woman. To those opportunists, the only things that mattered were her means or her attractiveness, usually in that order. To divert his mind, Jed looked out over the water.

"Maura, look," he said, nodding his head in the direction of Fort McHenry.

"Oh, that is something new."

As usual, at the star-shaped fort, soldiers patrolled the battlements, but the orderly rows of canvas tents outside the fort were new. Groups of soldiers in blue uniforms were conducting drills.

"There must be a company of infantry or more," mused Jed.

"They must've brought them in by ship. I'm sure the railroads are not running, and marching through the city would only inflame the citizens," said Maura.

"I agree, which means Secretary Cameron and President Lincoln regard Maryland seriously. The orders to move those troops took place days ago, and they are crack unit."

"What do you mean?"

"Look closely. At the balls and parties you attend, do you not observe what the men and women are wearing? Do you not see who is talking to whom, and who's being snubbed? The same goes for military units." Jed nodded toward the drilling soldiers. "Their uniforms are consistent and clean. Their marching is well ordered without fumbling or missteps. They have had training."

Maura studied the camp for several minutes. "There is a line of widely spaced soldiers standing away from everyone else. And look at those cannons."

"The line of soldiers are pickets—sentries to prevent a surprise attack," explained Jed. "Those cannons on the northwest side of the fort are pointing at the city instead of at the harbor. I wonder if the commander of the fort threatened to shell the city if the fort was attacked."

"Would he shell the city?" asked Maura with a little trepidation in her voice.

"I would think only if he is attacked by a citizen mob from Baltimore," stated Jed. "The big question is about the Maryland Militia. Which units are for the South, and which are for the North? I don't know if the Baltimore City Police were overwhelmed or not on the nineteenth, but I would guess that policemen are for the South or at least their leadership is."

"Those cannons look massive, but will they really shoot as far as the city?"

"Yes, they will." Jed pointed at a large hill. "However, if I were in command, I would occupy that hill to the west. Fort McHenry was designed to stop a ship invasion of Baltimore. That hill is closer, which means they would have better accuracy and could march quickly into the city."

"Look." Maura pointed at the docks. "The *Allegheny* is still there. There's smoke coming from her smokestacks."

"I hope they are moving her." Jed grimaced as he tried to make up his mind. "Would you mind if I went over there to quickly check?"

"Of course not. I can wait on the ship until you return. You can leave your carpet bag with me. Will they talk to you?"

"I hope so," chuckled Jed. "I have a letter stating I am the special envoy for Secretary Cameron. Although that may hold no weight since the *Allegheny* belongs to Secretary of the Navy Gideon Welles."

"Go and see what they have to say. I will wait here until you get back."

Their ship soon docked two piers away from where the *Allegheny* was berthed. Before leaving the ship, Jed checked the loads on his pistol. Along his way, Jed noted police officers and men watching the comings and goings of the passengers and cargo. He was glad Maura had remained behind. The two of them together would surely have been noticed.

At the *Allegheny's* gangplank, Jed was stopped by a sentry. After requesting to see the captain, Jed was allowed on the deck to wait under the eyes of another soldier. He was soon joined by an officer in a blue uniform.

"I am Commander William Hunter," said the officer. "I understand you wish to see me."

"Captain Jedidiah Tremblant." Jed handed over his letter. "I came aboard to find out what your intentions are, sir."

"Secretary Cameron?" asked Hunter, handing back the letter. "I'm under orders sent personally from Secretary Wells to sail the *Allegheny* to a berth at Locust Point next to Fort McHenry. We will be moving in ten to fifteen minutes."

"Thank you, sir. Secretary Cameron was worried about the safety of the *Allegheny* in the wake of the riots."

"Things have been a bit nervous," admitted Hunter. "Be careful. There are men watching the docks."

"I've noticed." Jed shook Hunter's hand. "Smooth sailing."

Hunter quirked a smile. "Not much chance of it being otherwise for the short distance we have to go. Good day."

As Jed headed back to Maura, he noticed two men standing around who were decidedly unhappy about the *Allegheny* firing up its boilers. At the gangplank to his ship, Jed stopped and watched the *Allegheny* slip its lines and head out into the harbor. The two men left thereafter in a hurry.

Jed quickly decided. He walked to the end of the pier and hired a porter. He escorted the porter to Maura's cabin. Maura was a little surprised to see the other man.

"Mrs. Harrison, I've hired a porter to get you to your hotel. There appears to be ruffians hanging around," said Jed.

"Oh!" exclaimed Maura. She wrung her hands nervously.

"Now, missy," said the porter with a smile. "Dey's always dose dat hang around. Dey don't means no harm. We'll gets you to your hotel with no trubble."

"Thank you. That is my valise." Maura handed the porter a coin. She turned to face Jed and held out her hand. "Mr. Tremblant, it was a pleasure to make your acquaintance."

Jed took her hand and bowed over it before taking his leave of her. As he left the pier, one man and a police officer were taking notes of all passengers getting off the ship. There were also two groups of men in civilian clothes marching around carrying pikes. Jed was glad he took the precaution of separating himself from Maura, no matter how much he disliked doing it so. Confederate and Maryland flags were prominently displayed.

After walking several blocks to the hotel, Jed checked in at the front desk to see if he had received any messages. Learning there were none, he had a seat in the lobby. Only a short while later, Maura breezed in, much to Jed's relief, followed by the porter carrying her luggage.

While Maura was still in the lobby, Jed headed to his room. He was pleased to see that his trunk had been moved to the new room. As he finished unpacking his carpet bag, there was a light rapping at his door. Maura stood alone in the hallway when he opened it. Her valise was on the floor beside her.

"I saw the men watching the docks, too," she said quietly. "We will have to be careful about being seen together."

Jed felt a twinge of sadness about her statement, but realistically, he knew this was coming. The truth be told, Maura did not look thrilled at the prospect either. Jed knew this setback would not stop her from searching for Duff.

"We'll have to come up with some way to communicate," said Jed. "Don't write your name or mine on any correspondence you send to me."

"We need to meet secretly, like . . ." Maura abruptly clamped her mouth closed. Her face turned a brilliant shade of red as she diverted her gaze away from Jed. Her guilty look was more than enough to show her betrayal of Jonathan's memory, even for such a minor slip of a well-used phrase.

"No, not like lovers," said Jed, completing her sentence. "We need to be even more secretive than that. If we are discovered, it will not be a censor from society we will have to endure. Now, go get some rest. You need to see Mr. Jenkins later today."

Jed watched Maura walk to the next door down the hall. If Maura didn't find a house to rent, he was going to have to change rooms. It was a mistake to take the room next to hers. Jed grimaced as he thought that he should probably change hotels. Jed looked up quickly as Maura gasped when her door swung open.

"Step back!" Jed pushed her aside and pulled his pistol out of its holster.

A black silhouette confronted Jed as he moved in front of Maura. Only two things kept him from shooting: the first was the woman's dress; second was that the figure had no head. Jed carefully lowered the hammer on his pistol and stared at the mannequin in the black dress.

Looking in the room, he saw two trunks against the far wall. There was an envelope on the bed with 'Mrs. Harrison' written on it. Picking it up, he handed the envelope to Maura.

She read the letter quickly. "This is from Mr. Jenkins. He took the liberty of returning my trunks, but the dress was still damp from the setting of the dye. They placed it on a mannequin to finish drying. When it is done, he will send a man to pick it up. I can call on him at any time."

"Maura . . ." Jed started to say, but she walked past him to look at her dress.

"Mr. Jenkins was right. The woman does excellent work. She managed to get different shades of black in the fabric to emphasize the design." Maura took in a ragged breath. "Mr. Tremblant, I think I would like to rest now. I will go see Mr. Jenkins in an hour or so."

"Of course, Mrs. Harrison," said Jed with a bow. He didn't like that they were back to using their formal names and a little miffed because he didn't know what to do to change it back. "I'll go see the commander at Fort McHenry."

"Thank you." She shut the door, but it couldn't silence her muffled sobs coming from behind it.

JED TOOK A CARRIAGE SOUTH through the city, passing by Camden Railroad Yards. As they rounded the huge hill he and Maura had spotted from the ship, Jed had the driver stop so he could get a better look.

"What is this location called?" he asked the driver.

"It's Federal Hill. Some still call it Signal Hill because it was used to send signals about incoming ships."

"Federal Hill?" asked Jed.

"City officials renamed it after the Constitution was written some time ago," said the driver.

"Thank you," said Jed as a carriage started toward Fort McHenry.

Just shy of the fort, a sentry halted the carriage. Jed climbed down and showed his papers to the soldier. After paying off the driver, with a little extra for the information and additional stop, Jed was escorted into the fort and the commanding officer's quarters.

"Captain Jedidiah Tremblant, sir," said Jed, introducing himself.

"Captain John Robinson," said the officer with a smile. "Commanding officer for the next couple of days. Please, call me John."

"Jed. You won't be staying here?"

"The Army has reassigned me to recruiting duty in Detroit, Michigan. A great number of troops are coming to this fort, more than a mere captain is allowed to command. The Army just sent troops over to Fort Carroll commanded by a major."

"The secretary is worried about Maryland."

"Along with a great number of other people," said John. "One of which is Governor Hicks. Right now, he's touting the neutrality of Maryland, but that's for the sake of those who put him in the governor's chair. He is of the American party, also known as the 'Know-Nothing' party. The gangs in Baltimore were literally fighting one another on election day to affect the outcome. I even heard that they tried to use a cannon one time. The 'Know-Nothing' gang came out ahead, and Governor Hicks got elected."

"I think Governor Hicks is afraid that if he goes to one side or the other without being forced into it, there will be open warfare in his state, which will divide it just like the nation. General Butler recently landed in Annapolis with a large number of troops. That will go a long way to deciding which way the governor will jump."

"However, Baltimore is the key. It's a hotbed of southern sympathizers." John pulled a sheet of paper out of his desk and handed it to Jed. "Read this."

Jed had an idea what the notice referred to when he saw 'People of Baltimore!' blazoned across the top. He read it quickly. It was a call to arms for the citizens of Baltimore to confer off the baseness and oppression of the North for the sake of their State of Maryland. Reading it again, he saw no reference to the Confederacy, only encouragement to give organized aid to the 'Powers That Be' and that the bloody deeds of the nineteenth were written across the southern sky. It was dated Sunday, April 21, the previous day.

"It's a nice touch that the printer used Justice as the emblem at the top," commented Jed sarcastically. "The writer implies the mayor and police are in support of this... revolution without really saying so. Although, I do find the reference to President Washington in this notice trite."

"I agree," said John, taking the paper back. "Don't be fooled. Mayor Brown and the police are solid southern sympathizers. The mayor sent militia to destroy railroad bridges north of the city. Marshal George Kane—the marshal of police—stated that the one thousand or so Baltimore men who voted for President Lincoln were the worst sort of people. After Friday's riots, the city has had an influx of southern gentlemen."

"I rode with one on the train on that day," said Jed. "He said his name was Anthony Duff. He was transporting firearms and ammunition into the city. The events of the riot separated him from those crates, and I had them sent here."

"So that's where they came from!" exclaimed John. "Things have been a little hectic. I didn't get a chance to look at them because of the riot, and then I had a visit from Police Commissioner Davis on Saturday."

"What did he want?"

"He was concerned for the safety of the fort. He stated that a mob would be descending, and he wanted to move the Maryland Guards inside the fort to bolster its defenses. That militia unit is two hundred strong, and I have only sixty men."

"What did you do?"

John chuckled. "I politely declined the offer, mainly because I knew they were trying to take over McHenry. We walked around the fort where he could see that I had several crews aiming cannons at the city, using the Washington Monument on the top of Mount Vernon as an aiming point. Its height makes it readily visible from anywhere in the city. I then told Commissioner Davis that if a mob attacks the fort, there will not be another mob in Baltimore for ten years to come."

The Trail of the Scottish Bluebell

Jed broke out laughing. "I can see that no attack came forth. They must not be ready to die for the cause."

"I'm just glad I didn't have to fire upon a monument to our first president," said John.

Jed turned serious. "Anthony Duff murdered a lieutenant of the Connecticut militia. I sent the weapons here because I wanted them to be safe."

John looked a little perplexed. "I don't recall anyone from Connecticut being killed in the riot. Are you sure?"

"I was there when Duff shot him in the back. I filed a complaint with a US Marshal. The wanted posters will be in Baltimore in a day or two." Jed described Duff. "The Confederacy is treating it as an act of war between two soldiers."

"The man deserves to be hung," growled John. "I'm guessing Duff was not in uniform."

"No, he was in civilian attire. I'm looking for him, as well as doing what I can to keep Maryland in the Union."

"You're incognito yourself," said John. "Watch your back. Apart from the southern sympathizers, Baltimore is not a safe place. Who do you have helping you?"

"No one," said Jed, not wanting to mention Maura.

"No one?" repeated John. "Valet? Servant?"

Jed shook his head. He had left his valet back in Illinois. Officers were expected to have a servant as a privilege of their rank. Jed originally planned to send for his valet after he had settled in Washington. It didn't look like that was going to happen anytime soon.

"I haven't had the time," Jed answered.

"Ah, it's about who you know and who knows you," chuckled John. "Be my guest for lunch. There are merchants coming here after noon. You should meet them. Merchants like stability and order. I'll give you all the information I have about Baltimore and its personalities." John stopped for a second and rubbed his hand up and down his large mutton chops. "Duff has white hair, you say? I have a problem that I think you can solve, and it may help you in your endeavors."

"What may that be?"

"Come with me," said John with a smile.

61

John notified his servant that Jed would be staying for lunch, then they left the two-story brick building.

Two more brick buildings, identical to the one they just left, angled halfway around the circular parade ground in the center of the fort. Hearing a flapping sound above him, Jed looked up and felt a sense of pride to see the United States flag blowing in the breeze on the tall flagpole.

"It's not the same flag that flew over the fort during the British bombardment," stated John as he led Jed past the fort's arched entrance to the next door. Following John through the door, Jed found himself in the guardroom with three cells. A guard scrambled to his feet at the site of Captain Robinson.

"At ease and please go stand by the flagpole." After the guard left, John called out, "Private Tanner?"

"Sir!" came a voice from the middle cell.

Inside the cell was a short man—only a boy in Jed's eyes—dressed only in shirt sleeves and blue uniform pants held up by white suspenders. He stood at attention facing the iron bars of his cell door.

"Captain Tremblant, this is my problem," said John. "Private Tanner here had a girlfriend, who decided the color of his uniform was not to her liking. He proceeded to get very intoxicated and, in his inebriation, decided he could change her mind by talking to her. He left the fort without a pass and traveled to her parents' residence on my horse. Luckily, my color sergeant noticed Private Tanner was missing and correctly guessed where he had gone. Due to Private Tanner's alcohol consumption, he became disoriented enroute, allowing the color sergeant and two other soldiers to reach the residence ahead of him and bring him back without incident."

Jed watched Tanner as John described his infractions. Tanner was in serious trouble, but he stood ramrod straight, despite the shame and embarrassment showing clearly on his face.

"Private Tanner, do you have anything to say in your defense?" asked John.

"I have no excuse, sir," replied Tanner clearly but with a slight crack in his voice.

"As you said so before," said John. He turned to face Jed. "It appears that a couple of citizens were buying Private Tanner drink after drink and goading him to go see the girl. I believe they were hoping for an incident to occur."

"Sir, I'd never!" exclaimed Tanner in outrage.

"You almost did, Private," said John coolly. "As you see, Captain Tremblant, I do not believe this was entirely Private Tanner's fault, but I simply cannot release him either. Discipline must be maintained."

"An interesting problem," commented Jed. "Shall we discuss it over lunch?"

"Of course. At ease, Private Tanner. We will inform you of our decision shortly."

"Yes, sir."

"Hold on," said Jed, just before they walked out. "Private Tanner, how old are you?"

Tanner hesitated before answering, "I believe sixteen, sir."

"Can you read and write?'

Yes, sir. A priest at the orphanage in New York taught me my letters."

"Very good."

Jed and John walked out of the guardroom and sent the guard back in.

"You want me to take Tanner as a servant?" asked Jed.

"Tanner's conscientious and capable. Hopefully, he will outgrow his amorous tendencies. He has spent more time in Baltimore than any other soldier here. He would be of great assistance to you."

"I agree, but will he agree to it?" Jed then shook his head. "Forget that I asked a question. Tanner doesn't have much of a choice in the matter. Dereliction of duty, public drunkenness, horse theft . . . just to name a few of his infractions in a time of war."

"You talk like a lawyer," commented John as he held open the door to his office.

"I am in Illinois. Still, my job here is to gather information and find southern spies. I would like him to understand what that entails."

"Go into the city and throw a rock," suggested John. "You'll undoubtedly hit a southern spy. I don't like all the skullduggery, but I do understand the need. As I said, Tanner is smart and can read and write. He'll understand what you're doing. You should know, I was told one of the civilians plying him with liquor had whitish hair."

Jed raised an eyebrow but said nothing.

"My officers will be here shortly for lunch. Do you want them to see you or would you rather not?"

"We should not tell them I'm working for the secretary of war or that I'm trying to uncover southern plots and conspirators. Let's say I'm investigating Anthony Duff in regard to the homicide. I can give them his description."

"A cautionary tale for my officers will be a good thing," said John. He smiled in approval when he saw his table and been set for five people, then sniffed delicately. "Ah, ham. Michael does wonders with the food. Fortunately for me, you cannot have him."

LATER THAT EVENING, JED SAT alone in the hotel dining room, well pleased with the information he had received today. He had a better understanding of the city government and who played what part in its functioning.

The merchants he had met supplied him with owners and business names for most of the industries in and around Baltimore. The most prominent name was Ross Winans, the inventor. Winans had actively urged the people to throw off the tyranny of the federal government on the eighteenth, the day before the riot. Jed made a mental note to check on Winans's foundry and see what he was doing.

Tanner had readily agreed to work for Jed. Not liking the constant drudgery and work that was required from him at the orphanage, Tanner enlisted in the Army. Jed told Tanner about the seriousness of his work, and Tanner understood the need for secrecy as only a used-to-be street urchin would. He was currently bedded down in the servants' quarters at the hotel. Jed had not told him anything about Maura.

Of course, Jed had been worrying about Maura all day and wondered how she had fared with Mr. Jenkins. A discreet cough behind him brought his attention to the manager of the hotel.

"Sir, there's a person wishing to see you," said the manager with great reluctance.

"Oh, well, show him in," said Jed.

The manager harrumphed. "It is not a man, sir, and we do not allow this type of person in here."

Jed's thoughts went to Maura. "You won't allow her in here because she dyed her clothes?"

The manager looked confused, then understanding came to his face. "Mrs. Harrison will always be welcome here should she wish to return. You are obviously not expecting this young woman, and I will send her on her way."

"Mrs. Harrison has departed?" asked Jed with a sinking feeling in the pit of his stomach. Maura had left no word as to her whereabouts.

"She departed early this afternoon," said the manager.

"This young woman asked for me specifically?"

The manager nodded.

"I'm a lawyer, and she may be seeking me out for legal counsel, but I have no desire to meet this woman in my room. Is there some place private where we can talk?"

The manager hesitated before saying, "We have a private dining room in the back with an entrance in the rear. If you wish, I will send her around to it."

"Thank you. Would you please send up my servant Tanner, so he can take notes of this meeting?"

"Of course, sir."

Jed followed the manager to the private room. It was small with only enough space for a round table, two chairs, a buffet, and a settee. Taking in the plush settee, he guessed this room was probably used for more than an intimate dinner. A couple of minutes after the manager left, a quick knock sounded at the door, and Jed let Tanner in. Moments later, the young woman was ushered in.

The woman was short and thin. Her long, mouse-brown hair was pulled back away from her face and hung down to the small of her back. She was pretty; her face had been scrubbed clean, but Jed saw the dirt underneath her fingernails. Her long-sleeve muslin shirt was open down to her corset which she wore on the outside. Her skirt had been hiked up to show her scuffed boots and an inch or so of skin above them.

"Two o' you will cost ya double," she said in a weary voice.

"I'm Jedidiah Tremblant. I understand you wish to see me."

"Yeah. Miss Maura sends her regards."

Chapter 6

"SHE WHAT?" EXCLAIMED JED, AT the same time Tanner asked, "Who's Miss Maura?"

"You two sounds like the opening act at the penny theater" The woman laughed. "Anyways, Miss Maura sends me to fetch ya."

"Where is she?" asked Jed.

The woman gave him a disgruntled look. "Ya wants me to describe it or do ya wants to see it yourself?"

Jed took a deep breath, held it, and then let it out slowly. He nodded to the woman and held out his hand. The woman looked askance at him.

"My sincerest apologies," said Jed. "I was a little . . . befuddled. I hope you will forgive me, Miss . . . ?"

The woman took his hand hesitantly. "Chrissy . . . Christine Schaefer."

"It's a pleasure to meet you, Miss Schaefer." Jed bent over her hand. "It will take me a couple minutes to get ready. Would you care for anything to eat or drink while you wait?"

"And in return?"

"Nothing. It's just courtesy. So, please, can we get you anything?"

"Gin and . . . and . . ."

"Tanner, would you please obtain Miss Schaefer's drink and whatever food is readily available. I will return shortly."

When Jed returned, Chrissy was eating sausage with mashed potatoes and corn bread. A tumbler half full of clear liquid rested on the table by her elbow. Tanner stood on the opposite side of the room, blushing furiously. Standing in the doorway and unobserved by the either of them, Jed didn't understand why Tanner was blushing until he caught Chrissy winking and smiling at Tanner.

Jed bit the inside of his cheek to keep from laughing out loud. After arranging his face into a normal expression, he coughed. Chrissy straightened in her chair and looked guilty for moment before she assumed a bland expression.

"Please, finish your dinner," said Jed to Chrissy. He turned slightly to look across the room. "Tanner, I don't believe I will need you anymore tonight. Meet me tomorrow morning at eight in the dining room."

"Yes, sir." Tanner left the room quickly.

"You really should not tease him, Miss Schaefer." Jed sat down on a chair opposite her.

"He's young and needs a thrill," said Chrissy with a laugh. "Not that he would knows what to do with a girl if he gets one."

"He had a girl here in Baltimore," said Jed flatly. "She threw them over because he's for the Union."

Chrissy pursed her lips in distaste. "I'm sorrys to hear that. He shoulds have come to see me. I work with all sides."

"How very pragmatic of you, Miss Schaefer. Tell me, how did you meet Mrs. Harrison?"

"Who?"

"Miss Maura."

Chrissy's face cleared in recognition. "Oh, she's a good one. Our idiot of a mayor closes the saloons today." She threw up her hands in exasperation. "I think he wants to keep the soldiers sober for when the blue boys come here, but it means a lot of men had no place to go.

"We has a young girl named Alexa at the brothel. She's half my age, and wes take turns hiding her when the men are around. Madame Suzette, however, wants her brandy and sent Alexa out to get it.

"I don't knows what happened, but Miss Maura, all in black and breathing fire, comes into the brothel followed by Alexa. She marches right up to Madame Suzette and demands to know what this child is doing out on the streets. She said she saw the child accosted by two ruffians. Ruffians! Did ya ever hear such palaver? Anyways, the men make off with the drink, and Miss Maura brought Alexa back." Chrissy took a swig of her drink and plopped a big forkful of potato into her mouth. It took a second or two before she could continue.

"Madame Suzette only heard that she lost her brandy. She loses her temper and didn't sees Miss Maura as the lady she is. Madame starts yelling at her, blaming her for losing her drink, and calling her names that aren't used outside our establishment. When she ran out of breath, Madame hauled off and slapped her."

"She what!?" gasped Jed in horror.

"Slapped her," repeated Chrissy as she took a drink. "Right across the face. Well, Miss Maura took it, and despite the red mark on her cheek, it didn't faze her. Madame Suzette realizes that Miss Maur's not the tramp she thought she was. She orders Miss Maura out. Miss Maura stood there for a second and then left without a word."

"It couldn't have beens more than half an hour later when Miss Maura walked back in with Officer Fletcher. Madame pays Fletcher so she can stays open. Officer Fletcher is not looking happy. Miss Maura, she pointed ats Madame and say she was a woman that hit her."

"Fletcher asked Madame if that is true. Madame told him this tramp made her lose her money, and she had to teach her a lesson. Well, Fletcher's looking gloomier and gloomier and keeps glancing over his shoulder at the door. Guess who walks in at that moment? No one else than the marshal of police, George Kane, himself."

Chrissy took another slug of gin and smacked her lips in satisfaction. A surge of fear coursed through Jed's body. He knew Maura would have to get close to certain people, but he never imagined it would be the head of the police department.

Chrissy continued. "Well, Marshal Kane starts asking Madame questions, like, did you not see her mourning attire? Did you not see that she is a lady? Did ya ever thank her for helping the girl? I tell you, Madame was turning white in anger.

"She then hisses she's been paying off the police for years, and if he expects her to continue, they need to leave. Madame then makes a mistake by saying they better get ready for when the boys in blue come back, because her girls will be willing and ready. She then adds that, when that happens, those of southern persuasion can find their entertainment elsewhere.

"I coulds tell that Marshal Kane didn't like that at all. The next thing I know, he's ordering Fletcher to arrest her and close the brothel down. Me and the others start complaining that we gots no place to go if they throw us out. The Marshal said he didn't care.

"Miss Maura piped up and asked the Marshal if she can talk to him. They steps outside, and when they come back, Marshal Kane has Fletcher arrest Madame Suzette and takes her away. Miss Maura is all embarrassed but says we have two days before the brothel is closed and that she is taken responsibility for us with the marshal." Chrissy's face beamed in adoration.

"Miss Maura spent the rest of the afternoon with us. We tells her how things work." Chrissy broke out laughing at Jed's horrified expression. "Not that. Money to be paid to the police and city officials. What we charge and the part the girls gets to keep. We gots to talking about the things we know and the secrets we've been told. Ya ready?"

"I beg your pardon?" stammered Jed.

"Are ya ready to go?" asked Chrissy slowly, putting her utensils on her plate.

"Of course, Miss Schaefer." Jed stood, moving around to assist her with her chair. Chrissy looked startled and a little flustered by his courtesy.

Jed picked up his hat and held the door open for her. In the hallway, he turned to walk toward the front desk, but stopped when Chrissy coughed loudly behind them.

"Rear entrance for the likes of me," said Chrissy without rancor.

"I don't seem to be working at peak efficiency," said Jed ruefully.

"Men usually calls on me, not the other way around."

They exited the hotel and walked up the alleyway to the main street.

"It's been a strange day for us all. Miss Maura put me in charge of the girls, while she makes arrangements. Makes ones proud to be given such."

"Arrangements? What sort of arrangements?"

"I don't know," said Chrissy as Jed waved down a cab. "Miss Maura said that."

"Said what?"

"Said she would make arrangements," answered Chrissy in exasperation. She climbed into the cab on her own. "Look, are ya coming or not?"

"I'm coming. As you said, it's been a strange day for us all. I'm sorry if I upset you."

Chrissy gave him a strange look and then smiled. "Most gents don't apologize to the likes of me . . . or, ifs they do, they don't means it. When ya sees Miss Maura, don't be jumping all over her. She's trying to do right by us."

"I will not 'jump' all over her." Jed smiled.

"Maybe ya should. She's a beauty and could make a mint," mused Chrissy.

Jed choked on her words.

Their destination was a short distance away in the Mount Vernon area. The carriage pulled up in front of a stately mansion not more than a block away from the Washington Monument. Jed knew his family could afford a house like this in such an affluent neighborhood, but he was not sure Maura could, even with the funds promised to her. He descended and held out a hand for Chrissy.

"Thanks ya, but no," said Chrissy. "I've gots to get back and check on the others. Pay the driver, will ya?"

He chuckled as he paid and tipped the driver to have him take Chrissy wherever she wanted to go. Chrissy waved as the cab drove off.

Jed walked up the white marble steps and knocked on the front door. After a few moments, he knocked again.

The door swung open to reveal a woman in her late forties. Her white blouse and gray striped skirt were covered by a large tan apron. The feather duster in her hand and the exasperated look on her face told Jed he had interrupted her work.

"Good—," he started to say.

"She was right about the mustache," interrupted the woman. "Come in. She's waiting for you."

"Uh?"

The woman gave a loud huff. "If you're not coming in, I'm closing the door."

Jed quickly entered the foyer. "I'm sorry. This evening has been very strange. An unknown woman brings me here, and you are not Mrs. Harrison."

"Chrissy was not my choice to approach you," said the woman. "I'm Mrs. Petford, Mrs. Harrison's companion. My husband passed away ten years ago. I'm Mr. Jenkins's second cousin, and he recommended me to Mrs. Harrison. My cousin said Mrs. Harrison needed me for her work."

"You have my condolences about your husband. Do you know what work Mrs. Harrison is doing in Baltimore?"

"To find a murderer named Anthony Duff," she replied. "To scotch any attempt by the South to add Maryland to the Confederacy. To uncover any plots and spies that are here in Maryland. Does that cover it, Mr. Tremblant?"

"Everything but your views on secession, Mrs. Petford."

"Slavery is an evil that needs to be abolished," she declared. "The gentlemen of the South believe their superiority entitles them to keep the Negro in chains. They fail to see the reverse side of the coin where, if one man, no matter what color his skin is, can be enslaved, anyone is vulnerable to the shackles and whips."

"I had not really thought of it that way. I believe slavery is wrong, but my main concern is for keeping this great nation together."

"If the questioning is over, I have work to do." Mrs. Petford brandished her feather duster. "We won't be interviewing for servant positions until tomorrow, but we do need at least two clean bedrooms tonight. Go on; you'll find her in the kitchen."

Mrs. Petford headed toward the back of the foyer where a grand mahogany staircase rose majestically upward. As she began to ascend, she pointed to a door off the hallway to her right. Jed went through the door and found Maura cooking over an iron stove. The savory smell of stew filled the air.

"Good evening, Maura."

Maura looked over her shoulder. "Oh, Mr. Tremblant . . . Jed, you're here. I do hope you were not put too much out of countenance by my invitation." Maura was in a black everyday dress with a white bib apron over top of it. To Jed, it almost looked like a habit.

"It was unique. I think my reputation may have suffered with the hotel manager." He smiled. "Although, the ease with which he handled the situation indicates he has done this before."

"You mean with Chrissy?" Maura's eyes looked down at the pot, refusing to look up as she continued to stir. "She was the only one I could send. Neither Eunice nor I could be seen there."

"Eunice?"

"Eunice Petford," clarified Maura. "She's my companion."

"I just met her. She seems perfect. Isn't this taking a risk to meet like this?"

"A small one," conceded Maura. "We haven't hired any servants yet, and I wanted you to meet Eunice in case she has to contact you."

"And Chrissy . . . ?"

"That was a situation not of my choosing. I was slapped by Chrissy's employer, but it presented the perfect opportunity to meet Marshal Kane. He is for the Confederacy and would like nothing more than to cleanse Baltimore of its freed Negroes. He told me Virginians are flooding into Baltimore and his police force is preparing to repel the northern aggressors." Maura took a taste of the stew and reached for the pepper grinder.

"When the owner spouted off about how the North was going to take over Baltimore, he had her arrested and was going to throw the women out on the street. I didn't want the women to suffer, and the marshal didn't want the, uh, establishment supporting the North. We reached a compromise."

"A compromise?" Jed wondered what Maura had to give for the marshal's help.

"The women get to stay, but not work, for two days. I'm responsible for making sure they don't work. They didn't like it but saw the necessity. Jed, I was shocked! Most of the women there wanted to continue that . . . that way of working. It gives them finances and freedoms they otherwise wouldn't have." She shook her head.

"There are two or three who wanted to quit, and I've written to Mr. Jenkins to see if we can find them positions. As for the rest . . ." Maura moved the pot off the stove and faced Jed. "These women have a wealth of information. Men talk to them all the time. I'm going to purchase a building for them in a more affluent neighborhood. I want the upper crust of Baltimore's male society coming to it."

"You're going to run a . . ." Jed was aghast. He couldn't bring himself to say whorehouse.

"No, I'll just own it," said Maura flatly. "Chrissy will be running it. The women will make a better commission than they did under the previous owner, and I will be paying them extra for information they hear. Jed, Duff is a Confederate spy. I will use any means available to find him."

Maura stood there, her eyes as hard as flint, daring Jed to say anything. He knew that any confrontation would be a losing proposition for both of them. He had hoped deep down that she would find this dangerous action an impossibility and quit. Jed snorted when he realized she had found informants he would've never thought of using.

"It's been a long day." Jed decided to diffuse the situation by using her culture against her. "By any chance, do you have anything to drink?"

"Oh! Oh!" gasped Maura in embarrassment. "Where are my manners? Please, have a seat. Which do you prefer? I have a red wine and water on the stove for tea."

"Wine would be fine."

"Let me find the glasses." Maura opened and closed cabinet doors, searching for the wineglasses.

"Is it safe to enter?"

Eunice Petford stood in the doorway. She still had her apron on but had left the feather duster behind.

"It's safe." Jed moved around to pull out a chair for her.

Eunice nodded her thanks and sat down. "She hasn't told you of her big plan?"

"You mean about the, uh, working ladies' establishment? Yes, she has."

"You're not going to try to stop it?" asked Eunice haughtily.

"No, it's a reasonable plan. When I had to litigate a case, the pertinent information came not from those directly involved but from those on the periphery. It was the clerks, secretaries, waiters, footmen, grooms, maids, and even those in the criminal element—pickpockets, yeggmen, and the like. Maura's going to have to cultivate friendships with the movers and shakers in Baltimore's government and society, and also with those who work underneath them."

"Or against them," suggested Eunice with a smile.

"I've represented a few of that type," said Jed.

Maura set a glass of wine down in front of Jed on the big country table. "We're having beef stew. Would you like a bowl?"

"No, thank you. The wine is all I need."

"Jed, I talked this over with Chrissy. A number of tenement houses and brothels are owned by the well-to-do and managed by others. To attract the class of men who may have the information I need, we will be making it more into a gentlemen's club. I've never been in one, so I need some idea of what to do."

As the three of them ate, Jed talked about the club he belonged to in Chicago to Maura and Eunice. To Jed, it was a place to relax and meet friends. He stated his likes—the big comfortable chairs, the well-stocked bar, and the library. He also described the gaming room and the overindulgence by some members. He had one suggestion for Maura that had her bristling.

"What do you mean the women shouldn't be allowed on the first floor?" she asked him. "How will the men know they're there?"

"They'll know. It's convention that women aren't allowed into a club. The women will make the men feel ill at ease, and you'll lose clients. The male staff on the first floor can direct and guide patrons who wish to indulge upstairs. There should be a separate entrance apart from the club. I'm sure the women have, uh, favorite customers who will come to the new location. The women will also have to be trained."

"Mr. Tremblant!" exclaimed Maura. Eunice sputtered and spat the food in her mouth halfway across the room. Jed looked at them, bewildered.

"I would've thought they wouldn't need any training for their line of work," said Eunice sourly as she wiped her chin.

"Oh! No... No, I... uh...," stammered Jed. He blushed. "I meant, since it will be a better class of clientele, they should be taught poise, grace, and diction."

"Diction?" scoffed Eunice.

"Why would I wants to be taught diction?" asked Jed, mimicking Chrissy's voice. He shook his head. "I can't believe I'm saying this, but better clientele means they can charge a higher commission. Men who visit such establishments are looking for a change from their normal routine. Lady-like behavior and interest in the client himself will get the men to talk more, which is what we want them to do."

"I will talk to Chrissy about it," said Maura. "On another topic, Marshal Kane definitely wants Maryland to secede from the Union. There's a dinner party tomorrow night at his house, and he has invited me to attend. Mayor Brown and several members of the city council will be there, along with their wives."

Jed didn't feel good about Maura going to such an affair. These men were firmly for the Confederacy and, if they learned Maura was a spy, would feel twice as betrayed because she was presenting herself as a Southerner. She was so new to Baltimore that she could easily be made to disappear without any fuss at all.

"I'm sure the two of you will be fine. Just don't take any unnecessary risks," Jed said.

Maura and Eunice exchanged a glance before Eunice said, "I was not invited. We had not met yet."

"Jed, I will be fine." Maura laid a hand on his arm. "I won't take any unnecessary risks, but this is an opportunity to meet these men. One of them could lead me to Duff." She fished a piece of paper out of the pocket of her apron. "This is my account with the Bank of Maryland. You can send it on to the . . . the investor."

Jed could see that Maura had not told Eunice the entire truth. That gave him more confidence in her ability to make it through the dinner. Although, truth be told, he was not concentrating so much on their mission as much as he was on Maura's hand resting lightly on his arm and burning through his defenses to his heart.

He took in her bright green eyes and flawless complexion, her classical features, and the way her full lips twisted into a smile. Jed wanted nothing more than to place his hand on top of hers and protect this young woman of eighteen.

However, he knew if he did so, he would be rebuked and rebuffed with a strong chance of alienating her. The anger at losing her husband had not left her. It had only been tamped down but was still visible to those who knew how to read expressions. Jed had seen it a dozen times in the eyes of the victims he had represented in Chicago. It was there in Maura, all the anger and hurt of being a victim.

The victim's feelings came with the conviction to make sure the wrong that happened to them never happened again and to hurt those who caused their pain just as badly as they were hurt. Unfortunately, Maura knew who caused her pain and focused on it, like a hound chasing a fox. Jed's major concern was what would happen if she and Duff ran into one another.

"What's our first mission?" asked Eunice.

"To keep Maryland in the Union," answered Jed.

"That is our objective," countered Eunice. "We should plan for something other than listening in on conversations and hoping we hear something."

"We know Mayor Brown and Marshal Kane are pushing for secession. They've tried to take over Fort McHenry." He related his conversation with Captain Robinson. "We can add Commissioner Davis to the list of secessionists. Everyone we add is another source of information."

"Duff was bringing in pistols," stated Maura.

"And ammunition," added Jed.

"There should be records of what arms come into Baltimore and where it's stored," said Maura.

"No doubt that will be locked up at their offices or homes." Eunice's eyes widened. "Are you saying we should become yeggmen?"

"Of course, not. We won't be stealing anything. We'll just be copying any information we find there," Maura said.

Jed did not correct Maura, although her distinction would be moot if they were caught breaking into offices and homes they had no right to be in. He decided to change the subject.

He spread his arms wide, palms up, to indicate the entire room. "How did you manage to find this house?"

"Mr. Jenkins found it," said Maura. "An elderly gentleman died without heirs, and his estate has been in the probate court for some time. Mr. Jenkins convinced the judge, in these troubling times, it might be better that the house was occupied than not. I am currently renting it for a minimal expense until we can finalize the sale."

"Minimal expense?" asked Jed.

"I believe the term 'Southern Army widow' was used," said Maura with some asperity. "Mr. Jenkins didn't tell the judge which army Jonathan was fighting for."

"It helps establish your bona fides," said Jed.

"My what?"

"Credentials. That you are a southern widow who has moved into this house has been established in the court... or, at least, by a judge," elaborated Jed. "You'll not only have the dinner to attend, but you must call upon your new neighbors."

"And interview and hire the staff, purchase food and necessities..."

"Don't forget," interrupted Eunice with a smile. "We need to burgle the mayor's office to see what he may be hiding."

"All in good time," laughed Jed. "Let's not become yeggmen yet. First, we need to find out where his office is and how it's guarded. *That* should be our first mission."

"Oh, I thought you would be after the steam gun," said Eunice.

"Steam gun?" asked Maura.

"It's at Winans's foundry. It doesn't use gunpowder and is supposed slice down a battalion of men in less than a minute."

Chapter 7

Tuesday, April 23, 1861

IT REALLY WASN'T ALL THAT hard for Jed to learn about the steam gun. It had been published in papers all over the nation and heralded as Ross Winans's technological marvel. As a matter of fact, *The American* had, this morning, mentioned it in another article along with the fact that Winans was forging pikes and casting balls of every caliber. Jed read the article over his breakfast.

Why bother at all with spies? he thought sourly. *We can just wait for the news to be published to tell us what we need to know.*

Jed was irritated and knew exactly what the cause was. It wasn't the article, but the fact that Maura would be wining and dining with the bigwig, southern sympathizers of Baltimore City tonight. His main fear was she would be anxious and in too much of a rush to catch and punish Duff that she would take risks and get caught.

Of course, he had cautioned her the night before and had been mocked by her acting like an empty-headed society damsel. Every single one of his warnings was met with an astonished, "Well, I do declare!" which just grated on his nerves. Mrs. Petford had opted for discretion, easing out of the room when Jed and Maura reduced the conversation to a juvenile version of "Yes, you will . . . No, I won't . . ."

Their argument ended with them glaring at each other. He realized they were in danger of ending their mission before it began. It was not his most auspicious moment.

Jed swallowed his pride and made amends immediately. Maura, of course, had her color up and was not about to forgive and forget . . . not without having her say. The strange thing was the more she ranted, the calmer Jed became.

After a couple of minutes, Maura stopped and glared at Jed. "Well, have you nothing to say?"

"Duff," replied Jed.

The color fled from Maura's face. Her hands gripped the table edge so tightly that her knuckles turned white, and her arms shook. Her facial features pinched together in shock, and for the first time, Jed saw her beauty disappear.

After several deep breaths, Maura closed her eyes against the pain she felt, then slumped down a little. "Mr. Tremblant . . ."

"Jed," he interrupted softly with a smile.

Maura opened her eyes and smiled back.

"Thank you, Jed. I had not realized how nervous . . . yes, and scared I was. I was just arguing with you to hide it. Strange that that name is enough to bring me to my senses. I'm so dreadfully embarrassed. Can you ever forgive me?"

"There's nothing to forgive," Jed told her. "I was not at my best myself. This is also so new to me that I'm having a little trouble adapting to the changes."

Maura was silent for a second before she asked, "We aren't going to get Duff, are we?"

"Do you believe that? You have the backing of the president of the United States. There's a federal warrant out for his arrest. US Marshal Stockdale is coming to Baltimore to look for Duff. One of us on our own has only a small chance of finding him, but we are not alone. We need to work together."

Jed and Maura had continued to talk for an hour afterwards. They managed to coordinate how they would communicate and prioritized the list of people and places they needed to investigate before Jed headed back to his hotel for the night.

Jed placed his chine cup back in its saucer as he thought about what needed to be done today. Since Maura had a multitude of things to do along with the dinner tonight, he would take on the task of investigating Winans's foundry.

He had not expected the local newspaper to give him the information he needed.

Well, not all the information, thought Jed, remembering there had been no mention of what the steam gun was going to be used for or who was going to use it.

Just then, Tanner entered the dining room. Jed gave an analytical look at the sixteen-year-old. The civilian clothes he wore on his gangly frame had to be over a year old, based on his shirt sleeves and pants legs being an inch or more too short. The blue Army suspenders holding up his pants contrasted with his faded red shirt. Tanner needed a new wardrobe.

The maître d' stopped Tanner at the door to the dining room. The two of them had a short, whispered discussion before Tanner pointed at Jed. The maître d' looked at Jed and raised an eyebrow. Nodding, Jed waved to have Tanner come forward.

"Did you sleep well?" asked Jed as Tanner walked up to stand beside the table.

"Well enough, sir."

"Breakfast?"

Tanner looked down as he shuffled his feet. "I ate with the servants, sir."

"What's wrong, Tanner?"

"Nuttin', sir," came the sullen response.

Jed sighed. "Tanner, please sit down." Tanner did so with some reluctance. "What's the problem? Come on . . . out with it."

"Sir . . . sir, I don't know what I'm doing!" stated Tanner. "I've never been a servant. The breakfast I had was plain, but better than I got with the Army. When I made to pay for the meal, the other servants laughed. They told me you will pay for everything."

"It's my responsibility," said Jed. "I'd forgotten how new all of this would be to you. I'm sending for my valet. He should be here in a couple of days. He'll be able to teach you what you need to know. I didn't hire you for your skills as a servant. I did so because you know this city better than I do. I need you to keep me from making mistakes. In the meantime, we need to keep up appearances."

"In my room is a canvas bag with my soiled clothing in it. I want you to talk to the concierge and the desk clerk about finding a good laundress. Talk to all three of them about the riot and their feelings about secession and anything else they may have heard. Be circumspect and careful."

"What will you be doing, sir?"

Jed turned the newspaper toward Tanner and pointed to the article. "Read this and tell me what you think."

Tanner read the article. "He needs to be arrested."

"What for?"

Tanner looked perplexed. "He's helping the enemy. He's making weapons and ammunition for them."

"Is he? Or is he stockpiling these items in anticipation that the federal government will need them in this conflict?" argued Jed.

"Oh! Uh . . ."

Jed held up his hand. "I don't believe it, but the foundation of our legal system is that a person is innocent until proven guilty. Winans is too vocal about the rights of states and the need to defy federal authority, but that is just his opinion. What we need is proof. That is why I'm going to his foundry this morning."

"Will you find what you need?" asked Tanner.

"I hope so, but Winans is extremely intelligent. I'm anticipating it will be hard to find the proof I need." Jed sighed. "The desk clerk will give you the key to my room. Talk to those people and also get their opinions on the Baltimore City Police Department."

"Yes, sir." Tanner stood.

"Oh, and Tanner?"

"Sir?"

"Light starch on the shirts, please."

Having sent Tanner on his task, Jed left the hotel and hailed a carriage to take him to Winans's foundry. As the conveyance took him deeper into the industrial area of Baltimore, Jed saw the immense potential that Baltimore could have on the war.

Coal smoke hung over the area, and the gritty taste cleaved to the back of his throat. Tall brick smokestacks belched out the black smoke from the furnaces that spoke of the industrial might of the city. The foundry was surrounded by a high wall with broken glass embedded in mortar on top. A massive, wrought-iron gate blocked the entrance; two men stood inside. Jed paid the driver to wait and walked up to the entrance.

"Watcha want?" growled a heavy, bearded man, just as Jed opened his mouth.

A little civility, thought Jed, but he held his tongue. Instead, he said, "I'm here to see Mr. Winans about a commission."

"He ain't here."

"Can you tell me when he will return?" asked Jed, trying to keep from being irritated.

"No."

"Can I, at least, talk to the foreman?"

"Mister, nobody is getting in here, except them that work here," said the other man. "You want to see Mr. Winans, you have to go to his office downtown. We got orders. Nobody's allowed in."

Jed returned to his cab. It was obvious he wasn't going to get into the foundry unless he snuck in. The glass on top of the wall would make that difficult but not impossible. He was glad to hear that Winans had another office. Hopefully, he could gather information at the other office as to what the Southerners had planned.

"Do you know where Mr. Winans's office is located in the city?" he asked the driver.

"Yes, sir," replied the man. "That's where the paperwork is done. All the rest of Mr. Winans's work is right here around Mount Winans."

"Mount Winans?" asked Jed.

"Old Man Winans bought the whole area around here and renamed it. It was named Mount Claire before he bought it. What did you want to see him about?"

"I have a commission to see if he can make a certain piece of machinery."

The driver looked around uncomfortably. "You got the rights to it? The reason I say that is, I had a couple of gentlemen riding in my cab. They was talking on how Old Man Winans came by some of his contraptions through other people's work."

"Have you heard anything about his steam gun?" Jed held up a one-dollar coin.

"The papers have been touting that he made it, but I've heard that some guy named Beckingdale, or some name like that, actually made it."

Jed tossed the coin, which the driver expertly caught.

"What's your name?"

"Robbie," answered the driver.

"I am Jedidiah Tremblant of Illinois. Are you for the Union or for the Confederacy?"

Robbie snorted. "I'm for keeping my family under a roof and fed. And keeping my horse and cab in good order. You're a Union man and a military one, to boot."

"It shows that much?" asked Jed, half in humor and half in trepidation.

"It's the bearing," said Robbie. "That and you stated you're from Illinois."

"I'm going to have to watch what I say. Unfortunately, I'm afraid a lot of people around here are going to become more closed-mouthed."

"They still talk in my cab," said Robbie as Jed climbed in and sat down. "Where can I take you?"

"Back to the hotel, please," said Jed. "Thank you for your help."

Robbie clucked his horse into movement. After traveling north for several blocks, the cab turned left onto another street. At the end of the block, Robbie turned right to go north again. Jed glanced up but could not see Robbie because he was above and behind him.

"Mr. Tremblant?"

"Yes, Robbie?"

"There's someone following us. A horseman came out of the foundry as we pulled away. He's been behind us ever since."

"I guess I obtained someone's attention. How far back is he?"

"Four . . . five hundred feet," guessed Robbie.

"Turn right at the next street. I'll jump out and hide in a store. That way I can get a look at who's following me."

"Three streets up is better . . . more crowded."

"Robbie, how would you like to work for me? One dollar a day for any information you hear about the insurrection."

"Fares will cost you extra."

"Agreed." Jed shifted in his seat and prepared to jump off the carriage. He would have to jump far enough out to avoid being run over by the wheels.

"Sit still," ordered Robbie. "Wait until we're around the corner."

"Meet me outside the hotel tomorrow morning at eight o'clock."

"I'll be there." Robbie pulled the reins to make his horse turned to the right. "Wait for it. Now!"

Jed was up and hanging off the side in a second. With a push to avoid the rear wheel, he dropped lightly onto the cobblestone street. A heavily laden, delivery wagon was beside him, and Jed quickly ducked behind it.

Looking under the wagon, he saw the four hooves of the horse come around the corner and head down the street. Jed peeked around the wagon and saw a young man in soot-covered work clothes watching Robbie's cab with some intensity. Jed stood straight up to watch the man trail after it.

The street was as busy as Robbie said it would be. Big freight wagons vied for the road with cabs and carriages. Those who were walking on this fine April day crowded the sidewalks to avoid risking life and limb by being out in the roadway.

Jed was watching an omnibus roll up the street, so he could cross over to the other side behind it. He was just about to make his dash when he froze. Sitting in the omnibus, chatting amicably with another gentleman, was Anthony Duff.

There was no mistaking the blondish-white hair, but Jed still took a step forward to get a better glimpse. A horse nearly careened into him, and Jed had to jump back to the safety of the stopped delivery wagon.

"You!" a voice called from horseback.

Jed looked up at the rider to find himself staring at the bearded face of the gatekeeper from Winans's foundry. Two more soot-covered men were on horses behind him. The gatekeeper looked ahead at the boy following the cab before glaring back at Jed.

"Get 'em!" he bellowed, pointing at Jed.

It amazed Jed how quickly the crowded sidewalk emptied of people. He ducked back behind the wagon, and one of the men cursed because he couldn't get at Jed from horseback. Jed made to start up the street toward the corner, and all three horsemen moved to block his path. Turning quickly, Jed dashed down the alley that was blocked by another parked wagon.

Jed didn't stop, but vaulted up on top of the wagon, ran over the crates, and dropped down on the far side. There are niches, cubbyholes, open crates, and narrow stairways cluttering the entire length of the alley. There was nothing at the far end.

"Go around to the other side and cut 'em off!" the gatekeeper yelled.

Hearing the other two men break into a gallop, Jed took in a deep breath and let it out slowly. He figured he had about seven to ten seconds before they came into the alley. His Navy-six pistol was still in its holster, but reluctance stayed his hand. Gunshots would bring unwanted attention, especially from the police. It wasn't clear to him which side they were on. Jed looked around the alley with a critical eye he had developed while fighting Indians. He broke into a smile.

He heard the gatekeeper at the entrance to the alley begin to climb over the wagon. A glint in the gatekeeper's hand was from the wicked looking knife he was holding.

"Where are ya, you . . .?" said the gatekeeper as he jumped down and searched under the wagon.

"Right here," Jed said from behind him.

Quickly incapacitating the gatekeeper, Jed stepped into the shadows when hoofbeats sounded from the other side of the alley. He waited as the two men swung down and tied their horses to a nearby hitching post. Jed forced himself to relax as he carefully watched his opponents. One of the men stopped to pick up a piece of pipe as the other one moved forward, pulling a knife out of a scabbard. They cautiously made their way down the alley, but when they spotted the gatekeeper, they rushed forward. As they passed him, Jed stepped out from behind a crate and swung his pistol at the nearest man's head. The solid thunk knocked the man unconscious and caused the second man to spin toward Jed. The sound of a cocking gun made him freeze in his tracks.

"Drop the pipe and get down on your stomach," ordered Jed. The man did so. "Good. Hands behind your back, please."

Jed tied his wrists together and then his ankles with rope he had taken from the wagon. Jed did the same to the gatekeeper and the other man. Picking up both knives, he tested the edges.

"What . . . what are you going to do?" asked the conscious man.

"I could scalp all of you," said Jed, matter-of-factly. "I've seen it done and know how to do it, but it's messy. I don't relish getting blood on my clothes. However, I do need to do something to serve as a reminder and warn others not to interfere with me. Ah, I think I know what to do." Jed moved toward him with the knife in his hand.

COMMISSIONER DAVIS LOOKED ILL AT ease as he waited in an ornate room. Disturbing the marshal of police was not something that one did lightly. There was a rattle at the door just before it opened, and George Kane walked into the room.

The man radiated energy. Davis knew he had been active in Maryland politics since 1849 when Kane was the collector for the Port of Baltimore at age thirty-two.

The trimmed, full beard gave Marshal Kane's face a distinguished look. However, it was his eyes that caught a person's attention. They stared out with an intensity that made Davis nervous. It also might be that his eyebrows, which looked like an inverted Vs, added to the focus of his stare.

"Are there problems with the shipments, Davis?" Marshal Kane asked. "I cannot think of any other reason for you to come to Mrs. Harrison's house while she is showing it off."

"We're packing up the weapons and ammunition at police headquarters, and they will be ready to move shortly," answered Davis. "The militias had a couple of setbacks. A Union officer took command of one unit and took back all the arms that had been moved out of his armory. The additional arms and canons that another unit had obtained were declared surplus to that unit's needs and moved to another location along with most of their regular firearms."

"Dammit!" cursed Marshal Kane. "We would be in the Confederacy already if we had taken over Fort McHenry."

Davis looked down at the floor. "That was my fault, sir. Had I realized how weak the garrison was then . . ."

Marshal Kane placed a comforting hand on the commissioner's shoulder. "We all get a share of that blame. By the time we realized the situation, those blue boys had reinforced the fort. Of course, there's no doubt in my mind that Robinson would've fought and shelled the city if he had been forced to. If I could have been certain that bombarding the city would have brought us into the Confederacy . . . well, we are beyond that point now. What have you come to see me about?"

"There has been an incident," said Davis. "Three men were found tied facedown over their horses. All three were naked and had their faces and heads shaved. It must've been a dry shave because their skin was nicked in several places. Two of the men were unconscious from head blows. The third man stated they work for Ross Winans.

"The man said a Northerner came by the foundry looking for Mr. Winans. They turned them away at the gate and then followed him as was their instructions. The Yankee ambushed them and cut off their hair and clothes with a warning not to try to follow him again."

"One man against three?" asked Marshal Kane with incredulity. "Do we know who he is?"

"No. He appears well-to-do, well-dressed, and educated. He's tall with brown hair and an elaborate mustache." Davis held up a hand. "Before you ask, yes, the man can identify him but wants nothing to do with him . . . said he moved like a cat. Scared him almost to death."

"Get the officers to go around to the hotels and boarding houses," said Marshal Kane. "I want to know who he is. Mr. Winans and his inventions are too important to the Confederacy to risk."

"I've already sent out the order to find him, and I'll obtain a blank warrant."

"No, no warrant," mused Marshal Kane. "Just find him. I can't leave this dinner party. I have the young widow who I need to influence."

"Sir?" Davis raised an eyebrow in consternation.

"Nothing like that!" harrumphed Marshal Kane. "Yes, she's beautiful, but her father owns one of the richest plantations in Virginia. She has taken this house and plans to reside here. Her wealth and beauty could be of great benefit to the cause. The vote for succession is coming, and she may be of use to influence that vote."

Eunice moved away from the door where she had been listening and smiled at getting her first intelligence coup. She had to tell Maura, who would then send a message to Mr. Tremblant.

Chapter 8

Wednesday, April 24, 1861

"Mr. Jedidiah Tremblant?"

Jed looked up from his morning coffee to see a tall, bearded man in a dark blue uniform-type coat looking at him. Standing, he extended his hand.

"Marshal George Kane, I presume, based on the illustrations I've seen of you. How may I help you?"

"My officers happened upon three men who were tied to their horses," said Marshal Kane. "I was wondering if you knew anything about what happened to them."

"Of course," said Jed, sitting back down. "Please, join me. The coffee here is excellent."

"Thank you." Marshal Kane took a seat.

Jed waited until they had both been served fresh cups of coffee. He reached to the floor and pulled two knives out of his attaché case, placing them on the table.

"I went to Mr. Winans's foundry to purchase a commission," said Jed. "I was told that Mr. Winans was not available, and I left. Those men from the foundry followed me, and when they caught up with me on the street, they pulled out these knives. Marshal, I don't know why they picked me, but they clearly demonstrated their intentions by drawing weapons."

"So you took the law into your own hands," commented Marshal Kane.

"I am sorry for that. I spent too many years on the frontier where you're responsible for yourself, and law, order, and justice can only be enforced by you alone."

"Unique form of punishment."

"They scared me," said Jed. "I wasn't thinking clearly. Is there going to be trouble?"

"I don't believe you were scared, but, no, there won't be any trouble." Marshal Kane took a sip of his coffee. "They received what they deserved. When my officers explained to them they were lucky to be alive and it might be better for them to let the entire situation drop, they didn't wish to pursue it any further. Unless, of course, you wish to bring them up on charges."

"I'm rather embarrassed by my actions, especially here in a civilized state. I have no wish to bring more scrutiny upon myself."

"I will consider the matter closed then." The marshal stood. "You're correct. The coffee is excellent."

"Your men did excellent work tracking me down," commented Jed.

"Tall, excellent clothes, blond hair, and a large mustache." Marshal Kane chuckled. "It wasn't that hard."

"Ah," said Jed in understanding. "I look forward to their efforts in finding other culprits with such ease."

"Meaning?" There was no mistaking the coolness in Marshal Kane's voice.

"No meaning beyond that they are police officers, and it is their duty to apprehend criminals and protect society," replied Jed urbanely.

"Of course." Marshal Kane's face showed he clearly knew what the man in front of him was implying. "Good day, Mr. Tremblant."

"Good day, Marshal Kane."

Jed watched the head of the Baltimore City Police Department leave. He expected the police to come but not the top man of the organization. Finishing his coffee, Jed picked up the newspaper and went to the front desk to ask the clerk to find Tanner for him. He then headed outside.

Dark clouds hung in the sky, and every now and then, big drops of rain dropped down as a portent of the incoming storm. Jed stopped at the top of the hotel's front steps and looked around. He then walked up the street to the corner.

"You're late," said Robbie, who was standing beside his horse. "You're lucky Ole Dick here is a patient sort of animal."

"I apologize. I had an unexpected meeting with Marshal Kane over breakfast just now."

Robbie raised his eyebrows but didn't say anything.

"Can you deliver a letter for me to Mrs. Maura Harrison?" asked Jed as he handed Robbie an envelope. "The address is written down. Your payment for the remainder of this month and next month is on the seat of your cab."

"I didn't see you put it there," said Robbie, a little startled. "Delivery fee?"

Jed chuckled and shook his head, fishing a coin out of his pocket. "Of course."

Robbie looked up at the ominous gray clouds billowing overhead. "I'd better deliver it then. Bad weather means more fares. You need a ride somewhere?"

"No, thank you." Jed winced as a raindrop hit him in the left eye. "I'm heading back inside. You try to stay dry."

Robbie laughed. "No money in that!" He turned serious. "Be careful yourself. You've attracted the attention of a powerful person. He'll have people watching you."

"What about you?" Jed steeled himself not to look around.

"I can take care of myself," said Robbie. "No one really notices a cabbie."

"Be careful, Robbie." A couple more drops of rain hit Jed in the face. In a louder voice, he said, "I'll be staying in today. I won't be needing you. Can you be here tomorrow morning?"

"Yes, sir." Robbie tipped his hat before he climbed back up on his cab and drove off.

Jed walked into the hotel just as the rain started to really come down.

"Mr. Tremblant?" The desk clerk caught Jed's attention. "I am sorry, but your man is not in the hotel. Do you want us to try and find him?"

Jed wondered where Tanner could be. "No, I sent him on an errand. I'm sure he's probably being delayed by the weather."

A brilliant flash of light quickly followed by a loud clap of thunder emphasized Jed's remark on the weather. The desk clerk jumped at the sound, laughed nervously, and let out a sigh of relief. "Of course, sir. Is there anything else we can do for you?"

"Not at this time."

Jed sat down in the lobby, flipped open his newspaper, and set his top hat on a nearby table. He selected a chair mostly hidden behind a large potted palm that gave him a view of the front entrance. He sat and he waited.

Minutes passed by, and the rain became heavier. Jed had learned patience from the Indians on the frontier, where the first one to move was probably the first one to die.

A man in his early thirties with a thick brown beard hurried into the hotel. He stopped just inside the entrance to shake the water off his hat and coat. His eyes, however, searched the lobby. His gaze took in each person there, categorized them, and dismissed each one. All except Jed, who remained hidden.

The man strode purposefully toward the front desk. He put his hand into his coat pocket and pulled out something that flashed silver. He had almost reached the desk when he looked to his right and spotted Jed.

Jed pretended to read his newspaper, but he caught a look of chagrin pass over the man's face. Changing direction quickly, the man sat down in a chair where he could watch the area of the potted palm with feigned nonchalance.

"Mr. Tremblant?" Jed looked up to see the manager approaching him. The manager leaned down and said softly, "The young woman is back in the private dining room."

"Thank you," said Jed, unobtrusively slipping the manager some money.

Standing slowly, Jed casually made his way to the front desk.

"I will be in my room if anyone asks for me," he told the desk clerk.

Jed walked up the front steps, taking his time. Once he was out of sight of the lobby, he hurried to his room. Once there, he threw his top hat on the bed and grabbed his overcoat and wide-brimmed hat. Jed relocked the door, headed down the back steps, and knocked on the private dining room door.

"Come in."

Jed entered the room and found Chrissy lounging on the settee. Catching sight of him, she stretched out seductively, rubbing her hands up and down her body.

"Only ones of ya?" she pouted. "Aw, I was hoping fors a double."

"Marshal Kane came to see me this morning here at the hotel," said Jed briskly. "I'm being followed, so we can't stay here."

Chrissy's sexiness disappeared in an instant. She quickly got up and went to the door, moving Jed aside with some amusement on his part. Looking to the left and right, Chrissy grabbed him by the sleeve and pulled him toward the rear door.

"Wait here." She pulled a scarf over her head just before she went out into the rain.

Chrissy came back a minute later and motioned for Jed to follow her. The two of them headed down the alleyway. Just before they walked out of the alley, Jed pulled his hat lower over his face and took Chrissy's arm. She hissed and tried to pull away, but he kept ahold of her elbow.

"Quit that," he whispered in a low growl. "Left or right?"

"Left," said Chrissy. "We's going to the building that may be Miss Maura's new club. She wants ya to sees it." She then reached over to grip his arm tightly. "What's ya go and gets yourself seen by the police, and no less than the Marshal!"

"Unavoidable, but would you rather I had been cut and stabbed?"

"O' course not," countered Chrissy. "I's rather there were none of it. You're justs bringing attention to Miss Maura."

"I definitely do not want to do that." A cab rode toward them, and Jed waved it down. "Is it far to the building?"

"Too far to walks in the rain," said Chrissy, climbing up into the cab.

After he sat down beside her, Chrissy gave the driver the address. Several blocks later, they stopped in front of a large, three-story, stone building. As Jed paid the driver, he noticed they were in the middle of a prominent business area.

He and Chrissy headed up the broad marble stairs, and the front door opened. A middle-aged, potbellied man beckoned them in. Jed stepped inside and stopped.

"It's a bank," he said.

"One of the finest ever built." The man extended his hand. "I am Nicholas Winser, the broker."

Jed looked at the marble columns that rose sixteen feet from the marble floor to the decorated ceiling. Wrought iron teller cages lined both sides of the front half of the main floor. The back half was an open area with enclosed offices along the back wall. White marble stairs located just before the offices led upstairs to the second floor. Even in the dim light from the storm-clouded sky, the entire building exuded wealth and power.

"It's a bank," repeated Jed.

"Yes," replied Nicholas with patience. "The bank had the misfortune to invest heavily in railroad stock of a company that went bankrupt. That caused all the customers to pull their money out of the bank, which went under. I'm afraid this is the only building available that complied with the qualities you were looking for."

"I . . . ?" choked Jed, surprised by Nicholas' implication that he was looking to purchase this building.

The front door opened, and everyone looked that way. Maura, wearing a black mourning dress, came in, folding her umbrella. She was followed by Eunice and a young Negro woman, who looked to be about Maura's age.

Maura was stunning in Jed's estimation. Despite the rain and humidity, her golden hair hung down in perfect ringlets with a black hat fastened on top. He saw the energy and determination in her eyes as she took in the interior of the building.

"Ah, we are all here," said Maura. "Mr. Winser, I see you have met Mr. Tremblant. He is a lawyer and will be my factor for the purchase and renovation of this building if I decide to buy. Would it be all right if Mr. Tremblant and I look around?"

"Of course, please, be my guest," said Nicholas. They split into two groups with Jed and Maura in one and everyone else in the other.

"Shall we start on the third floor?" asked Maura, to which Jed cocked an eyebrow quizzically. Jed guessed the top floor would be for Chrissy and the other women from the brothel. Using the basement would create an air of secretiveness and skullduggery that they didn't want. The second floor was unusable because it opened out to the first floor. "I don't see Mr. Winser climbing the stairs that fast or that far."

"Ah!" said Jed.

They made their way to the top floor. Jed guessed that this was where the executives of the bank had their offices, based on the large room size and luxuries, like a fireplace or iron stove in each room. This would be a vast improvement from Chrissy's last location. Several of the offices were devoid of any furnishings, and Jed assumed whoever had occupied them took what they could when they left.

"Do you think it will work?" asked Maura hesitantly.

"Absolutely," assured Jed. "As long as we let Chrissy manage this portion of the business. We should not concern ourselves with anything that goes on upstairs or down, only the information we can obtain from either. Still, I'll have to wire my family for funds to pay for the building and the renovations."

"That will not be necessary." Maura stopped when they heard footsteps on the stairs coming up toward them.

The young Negro woman ascended the stairs. She quickly spotted Jed and Maura and made her way to them.

"Mrs. Petford asked me to come up and check on you," she said, giving a wary glance at Jed.

"Tabitha, Mr. Jedidiah Tremblant," said Maura. "Jed, this is Tabitha Freed. My father sent her and nine other people from the plantation up here to help me. They've taken over the servant duties at my house."

"Sent?" asked Jed, not liking the connotation of that word.

"He asked us, Mr. Tremblant," said Tabitha. "We're all freed with papers to prove it. Mrs. Harrison has explained everything to us."

"Not quite everything," corrected Maura. "I told them about Anthony Duff and how we are looking to stop this insurrection. My father transferred a large portion of his cash-in-hand to my bank account. I could buy three or four of these buildings without blinking an eye."

Jed was a little shocked by her revelation. "That . . . uh . . ."

"That is beside the point," interrupted Maura, waving a hand dismissively in the air. "What is important is the information I heard last night. Governor Hicks is having the Maryland Legislature consider the question of secession."

"What? When?"

"This weekend starting on Friday, the twenty-sixth. The governor has called for a special session. The mayor and chief of police are saying that since Annapolis is overrun with Union troops, Governor Hicks will be holding the session in the town of Frederick, Maryland."

"Do you know where that is?" asked Jed.

"No," admitted Maura. "They're supposed to be meeting there to lessen the northern influence. I was thinking that Duff may be there to try to influence the vote."

"He may be," admitted Jed. "Even if he is not, we should go. I'll buy us to railroad tickets for this afternoon, if it's possible . . . tomorrow morning, at the latest. We need to arrive before the twenty-sixth."

"Jed, I cannot go," said Maura plainly. "First, it's incongruent for me to be touting the Union cause when I have tried to establish myself as a southern sympathizer. Second, by asking for Mayor Brown's and Marshal Kane's help in establishing this club, I may be able to keep them out of Frederick, and thus, they will be unable to influence anyone there." She paused for second. "Third, Anthony Duff may not be going to Frederick. It would be better if we covered both cities."

Jed thought about it. "I agree. I'll send a report to the War Department. Was anything else discussed at the dinner?"

"Just the usual gossip of who's engaged to whom and the latest scandal," replied Maura. "The men were worried that Governor Hicks will be urging for neutrality rather than secession. Eunice heard Marshal Kane say they are stockpiling and taking weapons from the police headquarters."

"It sounds like a good idea to keep them here and away from Frederick." Tabitha cocked her head to one side. "I think I hear the others a'coming."

The clatter of feet reached their ears. Nicholas was huffing and puffing all the way up, and he stopped at the top to wipe the sweat off his face with his handkerchief. Chrissy looked around in wonder; Eunice was her normal imperturbable self.

"Oh, my!" gasped Chrissy. "Oh, my! This is . . . this is our . . . our floor?"

Maura nodded, and Chrissy gave a little shriek of joy before dashing from room to room to look at each one. Jed chuckled at her antics but turned his attention to Eunice when she cleared her throat loudly.

"Mr. Winser, are these the only steps?" she asked.

"No, ma'am." Nicholas went to a corner at the rear of the building and opened a door.

Jed looked in and was surprised to see a stone, circular stairwell going down.

"This stairwell goes down to the basement," said Nicholas. "There's an exit there, another on the outside of the first floor, and another hidden one on the second floor. I believe it was used by the cleaning people."

"Outside on the first floor?" asked Maura.

"There is a bronze door in the rear of the building that opens to the staircase," explained Nicholas. "If you wish, you can get a stone cutter in to open the staircase to the interior of the first floor."

"That . . . thank you," said Maura. "I will keep your advice in mind. I, for one, would like to see the rest of the building. Will you accompany me, Mr. Winser?"

"Delighted," said Nicholas, with a smile on his face for the beautiful girl.

Eunice and Tabitha went downstairs with them. Jed was happy to see them go down the stairs before Nicholas began asking questions about Chrissy or their use of the third floor.

"This is amazing!" exclaimed Chrissy in delight. Then the joy flow out of her face. "Will we be able to moves here? I knows we need's a second set of stairs."

"Come with me, Chrissy." Jed led her to the hidden staircase door. Opening it, he stepped back so she could see. Chrissy, with bewilderment on her face, leaned forward, looked, and with a squeal of delight, threw her arms around Jed's neck.

Jed was beyond shocked. Being much taller than the diminutive Chrissy, she jumped upward to get her arms around his neck. Jed had no option but to wrap his arms around her to keep them both from falling over. Chrissy was laughing and pressed right up against him. For such a small girl, her body radiated a lot of heat, or at least, that's what Jed thought.

"Uh, Chrissy," choked out Jed, the tightness in his throat having nothing to do with her arms around his neck. He reached up to loosen her arms.

"Yes?" she asked coquettishly as she slowly slid down his body. She remained pressed up against him, turning his face bright red.

Jed, still holding onto her arms, moved Chrissy carefully, but firmly, away. Chrissy pouted at him and then broke out laughing.

"Ya knows that with these stairs, ya can slides right in any times ya wants and slides right out again." Chrissy's hips move forward and backward slightly.

Jed held onto her arms because he was afraid if he let her go, Chrissy would sidle right up against him again. His cravat seemed to be choking him, but he dared not reach up to loosen it.

"I am well aware of the innuendo," he said.

"Don't knows what that is," replied Chrissy. "I'm justs talking about a little bit of fun. It's to shows my appreciation for ya buying this building."

"I'm not buying the building. Miss Maura is."

"Oh." Chrissy's face went bland as she thought through the ramifications of Jed's statement. She took a step back, and Jed dropped his hands from her arms. "I thought's ya're buying it. Guess I'll has to show my appreciation to her."

At Jed shocked expression, Chrissy cackled. "Won't bees the first woman I've been with." She grinned and took a step closer. "You ands I cans still has a little fun, huh?"

Jed held up a hand. "I appreciate the offer, but I have a train to catch. Please, Chrissy, Miss Maura lost her husband during the riot." Jed blinked as he calculated the days. "Hmm, only five days ago . . . seems like longer. Her emotions are . . . " Jed paused for words.

"Yeah, I's know what ya mean. She aren't fragile and delicate, although she's really is. Everything's up justs under her skin."

"You are correct in that assessment," said Jed. "Will you do me a favor and help her while I'm away?"

"You really's do have to ride on a train?"

"I'll be gone for several days. Will you and the other ladies be able to move in here if Maura purchases this building? There may not be any furniture."

"Not likes we have much of a choice," laughed Chrissy. "Besides, we's slept in worse. Though, I wills have to reminds Miss Maura to brings the beds in at night."

Jed choked and coughed.

Chrissy smiled. "I need's to check out the stairwell." Just before she disappeared down the stairs, she shocked Jed by lifting her skirt to her knees and placed her hands on her derrière.

"Any times ya want to slip in, Mr. Tremblant, come on by."

Chapter 9

Wednesday, April 24, 1861

JED STOPPED BY THE TELEGRAPH station to code and send out a message to Secretary Cameron. He reported the Southerners' attempt to move the militia into Fort McHenry, what the newspaper article said about Winans's foundry, and the special session of the Maryland Legislature. Jed wrote that he would send another message once he arrived in Frederick. Frederick lay fifty miles west of Baltimore, and the train was scheduled to leave the station in an hour. He needed to get moving. After getting confirmation that the War Department had received his message, Jed rushed to his hotel.

He had just finished packing his carpet bag when there was a knocking on his door. Jed pulled his pistol out of its holster, cocked it, and hid it behind his back before he opened the door. He was a little astonished when he saw his valet standing there.

"Sir, you cannot possibly be going out like that?" chided his valet. "That coat . . . that cravat . . ." The man shuddered.

"Good morning, Bryce," said Jed to the man who is impeccably dressed, despite his travels. He was a little over a decade older than Jed and had been his valet ever since Jed had returned from the frontier three years ago. "Although, it is almost afternoon."

"Master Jedidiah, that holster is ruining the cut of your coat and is completely unnecessary here in civilization," said Bryce with a sniff and a disdained look at Jed's pistol.

"I wouldn't be too sure of that." Jed uncocked his firearm and put it back in his holster. "When did you arrive?"

"A short while ago." He pulled an envelope out of his inside pocket and handed it to Jed. "The manager sends his abject apologies. He said your servant left this message at the desk yesterday morning, but it was misfiled. Your servant . . . ?"

"A sixteen-year-old soldier who got into trouble. He has never been in service."

"Obviously."

Jed opened the letter and read it.

When Jed looked up, Bryce asked, "Are you traveling somewhere?"

"I'm taking the train to Frederick in an hour." Jed caught Bryce up on just about everything that had occurred since he left Chicago. When Jed finished, Bryce stood there with a stunned look on his face.

"I . . . I don't know what to say," gasped Bryce. "Murder, spies, President Lincoln . . ."

"And a young soldier turned servant who decided to investigate on his own," said a miffed Jed, waving the letter in the air. "Of course, his way did work better than mine. I went to the foundry and was set upon by three men. Young Mr. Tanner simply went and asked for job. He just waltzed right on in."

"Sounds like an enterprising young man." Bryce pulled a pocket watch out of his waistcoat and looked at it. "Ahem, your train, Master Jed . . ."

"Why do I always feel like I am eight years old whenever you are around?" asked Jed as he picked up his carpet bag. He smiled. "It's good to have you here."

"When you were eight, I tanned your hide for stealing Cook's cherry pie."

"Yes, but not for stealing the pie. It was because I lied about taking it. You made quite an impression on me."

"I was striving to do so at the time," said Bryce, straight-faced.

"As I said, it's good to have you here, Bryce. I hope to return in three to four days, but I might be longer. Do you have enough cash to—"

Jed stopped talking when Bryce held up his hand.

"Your father made sure I was supplied with everything I need. I will take Mr. Tanner in hand, if he ever shows up, and check on Mrs. Harrison. Now, go save the Union."

JED MADE IT TO THE train with ten minutes to spare. He barely had time to stow his carpet bag and find a seat before the train whistle blew. With a lurch, the train slowly began to roll out of the station.

Looking around, Jed checked out the other passengers. Twice. It wouldn't do to get Frederick to find out he'd been riding in the same railroad car as Duff. The car was filled with people. There were three families, along with five men and one woman traveling separately.

The lone woman, who appeared to be in her mid-twenties, had curly chestnut brown hair done up in a blue bonnet that matched her traveling dress. She was sitting alone in the front of the car closest to the engine. Jed was five rows back and noticed a paunchy man in his mid-fifties paying a lavish amount of attention to her. Jed was sure she was aware of the attention and tried to avoid him by gazing out the rain-streaked window.

The older man kept trying to catch her eye but was unsuccessful. He finally straightened up to smooth out his coat and lapels. Just before he stood, Jed got out of his seat and move forward with the man just a few steps behind him. The woman was sitting on the rear facing bench and looked up in surprise as Jed slid into the forward facing seat closest to the aisle.

"Ma'am," said Jed as a way of apology, just before he hiked his long legs up onto the seat beside her.

He caught her look of utter surprise and open mouth just before he hunched down and pulled his wide-brimmed hat over his eyes.

The man sputtered in indignation behind him, but the only way to get to the remaining empty seat would be to climb over Jed's legs. With a loud huff, the man returned to his original seat.

"Sorry, ma'am," murmured Jed softly. "I did not think that you would have wanted or appreciated that man's attentions."

"I did not," she replied in quiet tones. "Your gallantry saves me the trouble of fighting off the senator's advances."

"Senator?"

"State senator from Maryland's eastern shore," clarified the woman. "Thank you, Mister . . . ?"

"Tremblant, Jedidiah Tremblant."

"Of the Tremblants of Illinois?"

Jed nodded.

"My name is Ruth Goldberg. Your family is famous from the supreme court cases your father has had there."

"Has the senator settled back down?"

Ruth glanced up and replied with a smile. "He is grumpily ensconced behind his newspaper."

"Thanks be to God." Jed put his feet down and straightened both his hat and his posture. "I was developing a crick in my back."

Now that he was sitting up, Jed found himself looking down at Ruth. He guessed she was barely over five feet tall. Her blue traveling dress emphasized her narrow waist and hourglass shape. She was not the stunning beauty that Maura was but had an ethereal look that drew a person's attention to her. The light coming through the window reflected the red highlights in the hair that had escaped from her bonnet.

"How long would you have stayed that way if the senator continued to show interest in me?" asked Ruth.

"Until he lost interest or until we arrived in Frederick, which is my destination."

"I'm glad he lost interest," stated Ruth, with humor written all over her face. "We can't be arriving there with you all hunched over and disabled."

"You are stopping in Frederick, also?" asked Jed. "If you'll pardon my saying so, it's unusual for a woman to travel alone." At Ruth's look of embarrassment, Jed quickly added, "I'm sorry. I did not mean to pry."

"No, Mr. Tremblant, it is unusual," said Ruth. "You deflected unwanted advances toward me, so I believe I can trust you at least this much. My family is Jewish, and I had a . . . transgression when I was sixteen. Because of it, I am unwelcome in our society. My father, however, recognized my spirit and intelligence. He's the one who supports and employs me. I am supposed to keep an account of what occurs within the legislature."

"He sent you here alone to report on the legislative session?"

"As a businessman and the leader of our community, he needs to keep abreast of what the elected officials are doing. I have not failed him in any of the assignments he's given me."

"There is atonement, and then there is . . ." Jed clamped his mouth shut. He was about to imply that Ruth's father was prostituting her for information, but even if Jed thought it was so, the man was still Ruth's father. Ruth glanced out the window, but her resigned look told him she knew what he was going to say.

"Miss Goldberg, may I act as your escort while you are in Frederick?"

Ruth's eyes widened in surprise. "Mr. Tremblant, I appreciate the offer, but we are of the same age. Will not people assume the worse, which would damage both of our reputations?"

"I'm prepared to dissuade anyone who mistakes our relationship for something tawdry."

Ruth's eyes rested for a moment on the bulge of Jed's coat underneath his left arm. She quickly appraised the rest of his physique. "Yes," she murmured. "I believe you could. Tell me, Mr. Tremblant, are you making this trip on your own or are you under orders?"

"If I was under orders, I would be wearing a uniform," replied Jed. "What are your feelings on the insurrection?"

"My viewpoint is colored by my people's history," said Ruth with a slight smile. "I do not approve of slavery since the time the Egyptians enslaved us. Unfortunately, our community is as divided as the country. Rabbi Einhorn, who is an abolitionist, had to flee Baltimore after the riots for fear of his life. Rabbi Raphall of New York and Rabbi Illowy have spoken in favor of slavery."

"Ah, but what about the slaves kept by the Hebrews who are mentioned in the Bible?"

"The Christian Bible? I have to admit slaves are mentioned in the Torah. Do you know what the Torah is?"

"It's your religious scrolls kept at a synagogue. I beg your pardon. I should not have used the Bible as a reference."

Ruth smiled. "Both works were written by men, translated by men, and subject to the whims of those who decided what should and should not be placed in those works."

"So, you think a woman should have been involved in the publishing of these works?" asked Jed.

"How do we know women weren't involved, as unlikely as it seems? All I'm saying is that interpretations and translations are subject to the bias and prejudice of those doing the copying . . . and who is to say that the original was written down in its entirety? If a part of a letter from a saint did not fit with your philosophy, would you leave it out to promote your cause? It could be that both religious works should be double or triple the size they are now."

Jed thought for a moment. "I would like to say no, but in these times, I can see it being done all too easily. I also cannot say if I would fall into temptation or not."

"It seems that we are both on the same side," said Ruth. "If you are going to escort me, then perhaps we should work together. Each of us will hear and see things that the other will not. My father is afraid of the Confederacy. Apart from the slavery issue, he's worried about the viability of the nation where individual states have more power than the central government. The Confederacy is united now against President Lincoln and the Union. If the North ceases to be their enemy, will the Confederacy split apart so that each state is a separate country?"

"They may or they may find another enemy. Or they may become as tyrannical as ancient Rome," suggested Jed. "I agree to a partnership. Do you like opera?"

The rest of the trip passed by quickly in pleasant conversation. They agreed to go to the theaters in Frederick because the legislators would most likely attend. Before he left Baltimore, Jed had learned that there would be a traveling opera company performing in Frederick.

Ruth agreed to attend Mozart's *Die Zauberflöte* but reserved judgment on all Shakespearean plays until they discovered which one, if any, was being performed. Jed agreed with her, being familiar with *The Merchant of Venice*. He knew that play would be particularly offensive to her because of her religion.

Jed put his foot down on going to any Shakespearean sonnets as he only attended those because his mother made him. The rainy countryside flowed by as they discussed their individual likes and dislikes of theatrical productions.

It was a little past two o'clock in the afternoon when the train pulled into the Frederick station. It seemed like everyone disembarked, and the platform soon became crowded. Jed managed to get a porter to help Ruth with her luggage while he exited the station to find a transport.

Unfortunately, everyone else had the same idea. Jed snorted in frustration at the complete absence of cabs and wagons outside the station. Ruth came out, followed by the porter who had a handcart with her trunk and two medium-sized cases on it. There were still a couple of dark clouds in the sky, but it appeared the storm was breaking up.

"I take it there's no transportation available," commented Ruth.

"No, but graciously, it has ceased raining."

"We have a saying in Maryland concerning the weather: wait five minutes. The weather can change that fast."

"Where's you headin', sir?" asked the porter.

Jed told him of his hotel and Ruth's boarding house.

The porter replied, "De hotel is down Patrick Street on the right. Go up Carroll Street and turn left. De hotel is just past Market Street. De boardin' house is up Public Street. I can see that these get to where they belong."

"I will trust you to deliver the lady's luggage safely to the boarding house," said Jed, handing a couple of coins to the porter. "I'll retrieve my bag at the hotel. I understand the legislature is supposed to meet at the courthouse."

"Yes, sir. Thank'ee, sir," said the porter, pleased with Jed's tip. "I don't think they is all goin' to fit in the courthouse, though . . . too small. De courthouse is a block north from the hotel on Church Street."

"Shall we?" Jed offered his arm to Ruth.

The day was turning out to be a fine spring day as the sun broke through the clouds. The smell of daffodils was caught on the breeze. People stared out their doors and windows at the arrivals.

"Did you notice?" asked Ruth quietly.

"Do you mean the Union flags and banners? How could I miss them?"

"Is it a good thing or bad thing?"

"A good thing, I think," said Jed. "It shows the people's feelings and choice without the intimidation aspect that federal troops in the town would produce."

"My father told me the citizens in Frederick were for the Union," stated Ruth. "Here's your hotel." They walked north on Public Street to the corner of Church Street "Oh, look at the people!"

Ten to twelve people stood outside the courthouse. They had broken up into several groups of well-dressed men greeting one another; some warmly and others with cool reserve. Observable through the windows of the courthouse, a couple of men inside were gesticulating and pointing.

"The porter was right," said Jed. "The courthouse is too small. They'll be forced to move to a larger meeting hall. We should go and get you to the boarding house. We don't want them to give your room away to someone else."

Ruth took a look at the men gathered around the courthouse. "They will not get anything done today?"

"No. The members will be arriving all day. I venture that today the leaders and Governor Hicks will be establishing protocols and seating arrangements . . . and soothing ruffled feathers."

Ruth laughed lightly. "I think there will be a great deal of those. The legislature was not supposed to convene this year, and some will not be happy about it because either they are inconvenienced by having to be here, or they were hoping to remain neutral and not vote this year."

"Or both," added Jed. "I believe this is your destination."

Jed and Ruth headed inside to meet the landlady. They learned that two legislators' wives had arrived with their husbands. With the break in the weather, the wives were out on the lawn enjoying tea. Ruth quickly ushered Jed out the front door with an agreement to meet him for dinner before heading onto the lawn to meet the wives.

Walking into the crowded lobby of his hotel, Jed was glad he'd telegraphed the hotel, reserving a room and getting a confirmation reply. He walked up to the front desk where a harried clerk was sorting keys and trying to match them to the names in the register.

The clerk glanced up quickly and looked back down before saying, "I'm sorry, sir, but all of our rooms are taken."

"It is a good thing to know that you have a room for me, then," said Jed gently. He pulled his wallet out of his inside coat pocket and extracted a piece of paper from it. "You may want to read this."

The clerk looked at the paper and picked it up gingerly, as if it was a snake. The clerk's muscle on his jawline clenched and his face blanched.

"Excuse me, sir," stammered the clerk. "I will return shortly."

The clerk went through the door behind him into a back room. True to his word, he soon returned following behind a portly man who Jed guessed to be the owner or manager. "Mr. Tremblant?"

Jed nodded.

"I do not know what to say. We had not expected for our rooms to be requisitioned for the elected members of the State."

"Oh, I understand," said Jed. "Whatever will you tell the person who was supposed to stay in my room?"

The owner gaped, his eyes widened, and he began to sputter as Jed's words sank in.

"I would let him have the room if I were you," came a voice from behind Jed.

Jed turned around and found himself face-to-face with the industrialist Ross Winans. Jed recognized him immediately from his picture in the newspapers.

"Mr. Winans," greeted Jed.

"Mr. Tremblant," said Winans. "of the Tremblants of Illinois. Let's get you registered, and then we can have that discussion you wanted to have with me in Baltimore."

"But, sir!" exclaimed the owner.

"Eject the junior senator from the Eastern Shore," said Winans. "Just tell him when he comes in that someone miscounted, and there is no room for him. It will be unlikely he'll get this far west again. Mr. Tremblant, shall we have a seat over there by the window?"

Jed walked to where two, large, upholstered chairs had been placed. He sat down in the far one, facing the door.

"What do you want, Mr. Tremblant?" asked Winans. "Please don't insult me by saying this is a coincidence. Being from Illinois, I assume you are a Union man."

"True," admitted Jed. "Maryland is strategically located and what happens within its borders is of importance to a great number of people. I'm here to observe this impromptu session of the legislature."

"You're a spy," said Winans, with obvious disgust. "I thought you were a man of breeding. Do you plan to assassinate those of us who wish for secession?"

"I thought you were a man with intelligence," retorted Jed calmly. "If I was a spy, I would hardly travel or give out my name, which is obviously well known. I am here only as an observer. Do you believe in your cause so much that you side with the South?"

"Are you saying that you will not try to influence us?"

"I will talk to people and try to make them understand my point of view," answered Jed. "If that is influencing them, then yes, but that is as far as I will go."

Winans eyed him warily. "I believe you," he said finally. "I apologize for my earlier assumption. I am for each state to be allowed to decide its own laws and direction. More and more, I see the federal government stripping these rights from each state. The federal government is growing too powerful and is taking liberties it should not."

"So you'll vote for secession?"

Winans sighed deeply. "No, I cannot. As much as I would like to, the Committee on Federal Relations has told me we do not have the authority under current Maryland law. My comrades who, as you would put it, are for the South and I have had several discussions on the matter. The question will be put to a vote, but I do not see it passing. However, I will let you know that we will be asking to have the question of secession put on the ballot for the next state convention."

"I thank you for the information," said Jed. "I've seen the courthouse and believe it will be too small for your use. It might be prudent to scout for a larger meeting hall."

Winans looked over, caught the clerk's eye, and signaled him to come over.

"Young man, where's the largest meeting hall in town?" asked Winans.

"That'd be Kemp Hall," said the clerk in an awed voice. "It's three stories high, has glass windows, and iron stoves on each floor! It's at the corner of Market Street and Church Street."

"Thank you," said Winans. "Mr. Tremblant, care to take a brief sojourn with me?"

"I'd be honored, but wouldn't that be colluding with the enemy?"

Winans chuckled. "Undoubtedly, but Governor Hicks has declared Maryland to be neutral, and for the time being, I must abide by that decision. Shall we?"

The two of them headed to Kemp Hall where Winans spoke with the proprietor. He tentatively reserved the hall for the next four months, promising to come back the next day to finalize the agreement. Jed raised his eyebrows in astonishment at Winans's timeframe.

"Mr. Tremblant, Maryland is being occupied by federal troops. The mayor of Baltimore has destroyed train bridges north of the city to stop troops from traveling through it. We, the elected officials, have much to discuss, even if the vote on secession will not take place during this session. I'm walking back to the hotel to see if Governor Hicks has arrived to apprise him of Kemp Hall. Will you join me?"

"I think I will take a walk around town," said Jed. "I usually try to get in a constitutional before dinner. Thank you, Mr. Winans."

"You're welcome, Mr. Tremblant. I ask you to keep your eyes open for when the government you serve begins to suppress and take away the rights and liberties of the citizens. Maybe we can have another discussion on that day. Good day, Mr. Tremblant."

As he watched Winans start back toward the hotel, Jed figured he should be able to time his walk around town so that he arrived at the hotel to meet Miss Goldberg for dinner.

The quaint town situated on the Monocacy River was enjoyable to walk through on the spring day. In addition to the blooming flowers in the air, there was the smell of food being cooked for dinner. Rolling hills to the west led to the South Mountains. The mountain range hazed in a bluish color dominated the western horizon. They were the northern extension of the Blue Ridge Mountain range.

Jed's walk took him up to the train station, then he turned to head back down Carroll Street when he froze.

Ahead of him, with two other men, was Anthony Duff.

Chapter 10

Wednesday, April 24, 1861

THE ORANGE SUN WAS JUST above the crest of the South Mountain, and dusk was beginning to settle in on Frederick. Even so, there were a fair number of people strolling or standing around that made Jed hesitate from confronting Duff. There was a good chance Duff could escape, and Jed didn't want to risk a gun battle with all the people in the area.

Duff stopped two blocks away from the hotel and had a brief, but intense, discussion with the two men who accompanied him. One was a big bull of a man with ham-sized hands. The other was thin and weasel-like with a scraggly goatee. Duff and the thin man disappeared down a side street.

The big man reached into his pocket and, to Jed's amazement, pinned a red, white, and blue Union cockade to the front of his shirt. The man lounged against the fence at the street entrance, trying to appear nonchalant, but he scrutinized everyone who walked past him.

Guessing that Duff had some plan that he was working on, Jed backed up. Heedless of who may see him, Jed ran down the cross street, cut the corner, and ran up the street parallel to Church Street until he reached the side street where he thought Duff may be hiding. Jed pulled out his pistol and cocked it. Moving silently from one area of concealment to another, he made his way up the street.

Creeping along stealthily, Jed quickly spotted the thin man hiding behind a bush. The man was twitchy and clearly nervous. Snorting mentally, Jed thought the man wouldn't have lasted three days out on the frontier.

Duff, it appeared, had more woodcraft. He was expertly hidden in the shadow of the stone chimney. Only the sparkle of the setting sun off his gold watch chain betrayed his location. Using all the skills he learned while fighting Indians, Jed managed to get within three feet of Duff.

"Do not move, Mr. Duff. My pistol is pointed at your back."

Duff froze. With exaggerated slowness, he dropped the club he'd been holding down by his side. Stepping slowly out of the shadows, he turned to face Jed.

"Ah, Mr. Tremblant, I believe," said Duff. "I am led to believe you're after my head, based on the warrant you swore out. You ruined one of my plans in Baltimore simply by moving that ship."

"*You* were going to blow up the Allegheny?" asked Jed in shock.

"Boss?" asked the thin man in consternation as he looked back and forth between the two men.

"Have them come out," ordered Jed.

"Come here, Rufus, and you, too, Jack," said Duff.

Rufus hesitantly sided up next to Duff, facing Jed. They were both wearing a Union cockade on their clothing. Behind them, Jed saw Jack, the big man, take notice and move a couple steps toward them.

"Wearing the ribbons to put the pro-North delegates at ease, so you can attack them without any fuss?" asked Jed.

"Not exactly," replied Duff. "Camouflage for an assault, yes, but it would be for a couple of the southern-sympathizing delegates. Not enough to incapacitate them; just enough to leave them battered and bruised. It would've been seen as typical northern aggression. I tried the same thing with the young soldier from Fort McHenry, but his commander incarcerated him before anything happened. I'm not happy with Captain Robinson. After his statement to Commissioner Davis, it was impossible to get the mob to attack the fort, but, please, do not infer that there's not fighting spirit there."

"I would never suggest that the Confederacy does not have fighting spirit," said Jed. "It may be that just their morals need a little work."

"Boss?" whined Rufus, clearly agitated.

"Be still, Rufus," warned Duff. "We don't want to get Mr. Tremblant nervous, especially when he has his revolver pointed at us. Some things, Mr. Tremblant, need to be done, no matter how unpleasant it may be to do them."

"Oh, Mr. Tremblant!"

Jed's muscles went tight, and he stepped back to put a little distance between Duff and himself. Ruth Goldberg hurried toward them from the end of the side street. The dimming light made it hard to see, and she closed half the distance between them before she saw the gun in his hand and before Jed could call out a warning to her.

"What are you— Oh! Mumph!"

A tree-trunk of an arm wrapped around her waist as a meaty hand clamped over her mouth. Ruth was lifted off the ground as she futilely pulled and pushed against Jack's superior strength.

"It appears we are at a stalemate," said Duff with a smile. "I have no doubt that you can shoot both myself and Rufus, but are you willing to risk the girl's safety? It's already clear that she knows you."

Jed looked at Ruth, who was struggling to free herself. What made matter worse was the more she fought, the more Jack smiled. It was a lecherous smile, and the man's face took on a feral look.

"Miss Goldberg . . . Ruth, stop struggling," commanded Jed. He looked back at Duff. "You three go your way, and we will go ours. Agreed?"

"Agreed," said Duff. "Come along, Rufus."

Jed uncocked his pistol.

"Boss, he still has a gun," said Rufus warily, as he backed away from Jed.

"Mr. Tremblant is a man of his word." Duff moved next to Jack. "He will keep it as long as we do not break the truce. Let the girl go."

Ruth continued to attempt to break free. Her feet were off the ground, and her legs swung from side to side.

"She's got a nice caboose," growled Jack, licking his lips and grinding his pelvis against her derrière.

Ruth gave a muffled squawk of protest. Duff held up his hand as Jed started to reach for his pistol.

"Put her down and let her go," said Duff.

His tone was mild, but Jed saw the tightening around his eyes. With great effort, Jed moved his hand away from the butt of his pistol.

"Put her down," said Duff again.

"No," said the big man slowly. His hand came up to grip one of her breasts. Ruth froze in shock as did Jed. "She's got big ones. She and I are gonna have a good time."

Jed shook off his stupefaction and started to reach for his pistol. Duff, however, was quicker. His hand came up and swept in front of Rufus. Rufus stood still for a split second before his hands came up to his throat.

As Rufus started to choke, Duff stepped behind Jack and punched him rapidly in the back. Jed pulled out his pistol and cocked it as he saw the flash of the knife in Duff's hand disappear and reappear again and again.

The big man roared in pain and anger, and he tossed Ruth aside. He turned toward Duff, who got in a couple more stabs before dancing back out of reach. Rufus collapsed onto the ground, twitching before falling still. Jack took several shuffling steps toward Duff before he toppled heavily, like a tall tree that had been chopped down.

Jed kept his handgun pointed at Duff as he quickly moved to where Ruth was on the ground and knelt beside her. She gasped for breath and was shaken but seemed unhurt.

Duff, in apparent unconcern for the weapon pointed at him, walked to Rufus. After checking him, Duff cleaned his blade on Rufus's shirt and hid the knife away inside his coat. He slowly moved closer to Jed and Ruth, squatting down six feet away from them.

"Miss, I want to offer you my humblest apologies for your treatment," said Duff softly. "I hired them for a specific purpose, and it is my fault they could not adapt to changing circumstances. I am heartily sorry for the indignities perpetrated upon your body, but the man who did so will never do it again." He looked at Jed. "Do we still have a truce?"

Jed sighed and put his pistol away. "I will have to notify the sheriff or marshal . . . two dead bodies, you understand."

"Of course," said Duff, "but I doubt he will be anxious to arrest the man who stopped a would-be rapist. However, I will be gone before you managed to convince him to arrest me." He stood up, looked down, and sighed. "Again, miss, I am very sorry."

Duff nodded to Jed and headed down the side street to be lost in the gloom of the evening. Jed had a momentary flare of frustration that he was letting Duff get away. That feeling was quickly replaced by anxiety as to how Maura would react when he told her that he had let Duff escape.

All those feelings he damped down as Ruth began to shake. Sitting down on the ground, Jed gathered her up in his arms to hold her tight.

"He killed them! He killed them both!" gasped Ruth.

Jed opened his mouth, but snapped it shut as two men he had never seen before came hurrying around the corner. He relaxed a little when he saw they were not armed and had concern on their faces.

"A man told us you needed help," said one of them. "We sent for the sheriff. Are either of you hurt?"

"No," replied Jed. "She's just in shock."

"Bob, go get a blanket."

The other man ran down the street, and Jed heard him pounding on a door. He soon returned with a short, stout woman carrying a large quilt. Several men followed behind them. One of them had a silver star pinned to his vest.

The woman took in the two dead bodies. With a sharp hiss, she walked over and gently tucked the quilt around Ruth.

"Pick her up, and we'll put her on the sofa in my house," the woman told Jed.

"Hold on, Mabel," said the sheriff. "I need to find out what happened here."

"Come along, then," ordered Mabel. "You can talk to them there. There's no sense in having her see this . . . this sight anymore. Pick her up, sir, and follow me."

Jed struggled but got his feet under him and stood up with Ruth in his arms. Ruth, for her part, wrapped her arms around his neck and snuggled closer. Jed felt deeply embarrassed by the intimacy, but also knew she needed a sense of security.

Jed was a little uneasy. Women in Chicago started pursuing him as soon as he returned from the territories because he was a Tremblant, rich, and single . . . usually in that order. Of course, at the time, he didn't want to feel anything at all. Now, he was starting to feel emotions he hadn't felt in a long time—first for Maura and now Ruth. Jed felt it may have been because both women had been placed in danger, but he was not sure. Feeling a little confused, he cradled Ruth in his arms as he carried her toward the house.

He followed Mabel into her cozy, clapboard house. The parlor had a couple of plush easy chairs and a large sofa and was lit by two oil lamps on wooden end tables. Jed carefully maneuvered around a low table in front of the sofa and set Ruth down. Before he could pull way, her arms tightened around his neck, and she lifted herself up to press her lips against his.

Jed froze. Ruth's lips were full, soft, and packed a punch that left Jed befuddled. She pressed against him, setting his blood a-boiling until a loud harrumph behind them startled the two of them enough that they broke apart.

Jed disentangled himself from Ruth's arms and straightened to find the sheriff scowling at him. Mabel was blushing furiously and trying to hide her smile behind her hands. Ruth settled back down on the sofa with a little self-satisfied smile playing on her lips as she pulled the quilt up to her shoulders.

"I . . . uh . . . I . . . uh-hum . . . ," stammered Jed as he felt heat rise up from his collar to his face. He took in a deep breath. "Sheriff, I am Captain Jedidiah Tremblant. The two men in the street were killed by Anthony Duff, a southern spy and murderer."

Jed went on to describe his encounter with Duff in Frederick, giving a full description of the man. The sheriff left them briefly to talk to his deputies and have them start searching for Duff.

"I'll be right back," Jed said to Ruth. "I'll be on the porch."

Ruth closed her eyes and nodded. Jed stepped through the front door and stepped to the side as he searched the street. The sheriff finished talking to his deputies and came back to stand beside Jed.

"As if I didn't have enough problems with the governor and state legislature being here . . . ," the sheriff started to gripe. "Western man, aren't you? I saw you step aside at the door so you wouldn't be silhouetted by the light."

"I've been west but not that far. I've lived for a while in the Indian Territories. Most easterners seem to lose their survival instinct. I don't intend to lose mine." Jed took a measure of the man in front of him.

"Do you think this man Duff will still be around here?"

"No, or he'll be hiding where we can't find him," replied Jed. "Do you think his plan would've worked?"

"Attacking his own people to get sympathy and support and blaming it on the North?" asked the sheriff. "It may have. Emotions are running high and outside interference through bullying, blackmail, threat, or any other tactic like that could tip this from the frying pan into the fire."

"I agree," said Jed. "That's why I'm just an observer here."

"More than just an observer, I'd say. Well, your missus has had quite a shock. It'd be best if you're by her side."

"Uh, we're not married, sheriff," stated Jed uncomfortably.

The sheriff gave him a look and raised an eyebrow. "Engaged?"

"I just met her today on the train," admitted Jed.

The sheriff let out a whoosh of air. "Son, I don't know whether to tell you to run for the hills or to poke you in front of a Justice of the Peace with my shotgun."

"I think I was the most surprised one in the room," said Jed. "It might have been the shock of seeing those men killed in front of her."

"Unfortunately, I believe we're going to see a whole lot more of that before this conflict is over."

"You don't believe one decisive march on the Confederacy will end this?"

"No, I don't. I had some schooling in Virginia. Those southern boys are taught to fight, and they'll fight well. Their main problems are that they are short on industry and people. The North should win, but it won't be an easy fight." The sheriff's face took on a look of disgust as he thought of something. "Of course, there's still a chance we could lose."

"What do you mean?"

"You've been observing too much of one side of this thing," said the sheriff dryly. "You need to watch not only the enemy, but those who are on your side as well." He sighed as if he was very tired. "It's started already. Men who don't know one end of a rifle from another are raising and commanding troops. Deals are being made on all sorts of supplies. Hoarding to drive prices upward has begun."

"You're joking," gasped Jed aghast.

"Nope," said the sheriff, "and, if that is happening here in the small town, think of what's happening in the big cities like Washington, Baltimore, New York, and the like. C'mon, enough of these gloomy thoughts. Let's head in and see if Mabel's straightened out your gal."

"Straightened out . . . ?" choked Jed.

The sheriff smiled. "Mabel is tough and strict. All the boys behaved around her daughters, and all her boys were raised to be gentlemen around the ladies. Now, she and her husband hug and kiss all the time, but as she would remind them, they were married. Mabel doesn't take kindly to hanky-panky between unmarried folk."

Jed briefly wondered what Mabel would think of his helping to set up a gentlemen's club with a brothel on the third floor of the building. He decided he really did not want to find out and followed the sheriff back inside the house.

Ruth was sitting up on the sofa holding a mug of hot tea in her hands. Mabel was sitting beside her. She placed the teakettle on a trivet on the low table in front of the couch.

"May I offer you gentlemen some tea?" asked Mabel, straightening up.

"Thank you, but no," said the sheriff. "I have to get going to see if my deputies have found that man. Then I must see the mayor to let him know what has happened."

"I must also decline," said Jed. "I have letters I must send out and must get back to the hotel. I wanted to see if Miss Goldberg is feeling well enough to let me escort her back to the boarding house."

"I told her she can stay here, but she says she doesn't want to impose," griped Mabel.

"I am feeling much better," said Ruth. "I promise I will take it easy."

"Very well, then." Mabel walked to the front door, pulled a shawl off one of the hooks situated there, and draped it around her shoulders. "Whenever you're ready to go."

Ruth brought her mug up to her lips with both hands as Jed sort of floundered with his mouth wide open. Based on her twinkling eyes, Jed was sure Ruth was using the mug to hide her smile. Snapping his mouth shut, Jed recovered himself and put on his best behavior.

"Are you ready, Miss Goldberg?" he asked.

Ruth put down her mug, twisting her head from side to side to hide her smile. Pursing her lips together, Ruth stood up and held out her hand. Jed gave her a smile, which was returned, as he led her to the front door. As they left and walked up the street, Jed heard a swish of cloth every now and then to remind him that Mabel was behind them.

"Mr. Tremblant, I would like to apologize for my action earlier," said Ruth, in a voice a little louder than usual. "I was in shock."

"It was understandable, Miss Goldberg. Please, let the matter be forgotten." He murmured, "Was that good enough for her?"

"Hmm-hum," hummed Ruth in agreement. She then continued softly, "I am sorry."

"For kissing me?" whispered Jed.

Ruth smiled and whispered, "No, not that. I'm sorry you had to choose between that man and me. If I hadn't come blundering in . . . Why were you holding a gun on him?"

"He murdered an Army officer." Jed hesitated for second and then told Ruth about Duff but not his orders from President Lincoln or about Maura. He finished by saying, "I've been looking for him. You've seen what he's capable of, and I know he's working for the Confederacy."

"Now I am doubly sorry," replied Ruth.

"Don't be. I spoke with Mr. Winans this afternoon. He and the other secessionists are not going to vote for secession. He stated they don't have the authority, but they are going to try to get the question on the ballot for the next state convention."

"Truly?" asked Ruth. "If that is so, I must get a message off to my father."

"It might be best to wait until after the vote," suggested Jed. "Duff was going to assault a couple of the pro-South delegates to elicit sympathy for their cause. What Mr. Winans has said and how he votes may be two different things. If Duff had succeeded, it may have swayed their vote."

"He was going to attack his own people?" gasped Ruth in shock. She drew back a little and looked at Jed shrewdly. "You are a government man, however much you protest the fact."

"I believe I was supposed to be taking you to dinner," said Jed, changing the subject as they approached the hotel. He looked over his shoulder. "Would you care to join us for dinner?"

"Lord, no," said Mabel. "You two go on. I've got to get back to set my own supper out for my brood. Take care, Mr. Tremblant. If you try anything, I'll hear about it."

"I'll be on my best behavior," promised Jed. "I'll take her right back to the boarding house afterwards."

"*Oy vey*," muttered Ruth under her breath.

Chapter 11

Monday, April 29, 1861

"How did you like the first act?" Jed asked Ruth as the theater curtain closed. Jed had surprised her with two box seat tickets for tonight's performance of Mozart's opera.

There'd been no time earlier to attend the theater with the vote for secession still up in the air, but that morning, the vote had been called. Now, the heat of the day was dissipating, as was a lot of the fervor of the Maryland delegates.

The delegates' first meeting in the Frederick courthouse on the twenty-sixth proved the building was too small for their needs. Governor Hicks had given a speech before the assembly on Friday that promoted neither the North nor the South, but neutrality, with the possibility of Maryland being a mediator for both sides. The legislature adjourned and met the next day at Kemp Hall.

Jed had barely made it into the packed hall on Saturday to hear the delegate from Prince George's County put forth the question of Maryland secession from the Union. The Committee on Federal Relations then reported that, under the Maryland Constitution, they didn't have the authority to vote on secession. The vote was unanimous against the proposal, much to Jed's surprise. Even though Winans had told him about it, Jed fully expected the southern sympathizing delegates to vote for the measure, instead of going by the law.

Each night of the legislature, Jed had spent his evenings talking to the delegates, while Ruth had met with their wives. Jed and Ruth met for dinner each night to discuss what they had learned. He was a little amazed at the amount and type of information Ruth obtained from the spouses. After dinner, they wrote their reports and took them to the telegrapher. Because the state legislature was meeting in Frederick, the telegraph station stayed open much later than usual.

The vote this morning was the one Jed worried about. It proposed that the question of secession be placed on the ballot of the next state convention. Governor Hicks's speech must have swayed some of the delegates because the vote was fifty-three to thirteen against the proposal. However, the issue of neutrality remained. The legislators didn't want to open the railroad lines to the North and were working on a resolution to be sent to President Lincoln to remove federal troops from Maryland soil.

Maryland had not seceded from the Union, but neither was it actively supporting the North. Jed felt all the compromises made over the past two decades were being played out here as elected officials strove to maintain a middle ground. Jed had received word from his father of the mustering of troops in Illinois and elsewhere. There was no middle ground to be had.

The opera tonight was the first chance they had to relax, and Ruth insisted Jed call her by her first name. She was dressed in a burgundy off-the-shoulder gown, the color of which complemented her complexion. Looking down at the crowded theater from their box, she asked, "How did you manage to get these seats? They are excellent! I've seen this opera before, but the players are doing an admirable job. However, I do take issue with the high priest, Sarastro, stating that Pamina needed a male to instruct her, rather than her headstrong mother, the Queen of the Night. I see nothing wrong with a headstrong female. Do you?"

"I like strong women," said Jed. "Not stubborn or pigheaded, which is sometimes taken for strength. I like to do my arguing in a courtroom."

"You and your wife don't fight?" asked Ruth, with a smile.

Jed stood up abruptly, feeling as if she had slapped him. Turning stiffly away from her, he stared out over the orchestra section without seeing anything.

"We used to." His voice was as soft and as cold as a snowflake.

"I am sorry." Ruth lightly touched Jed's arm. "I had not meant to cause you any hurt, but you're very closed mouth about your family. I only know you are working for your father, and your sister gave you that journal you write in. I just assumed you were married, even though you don't wear a ring."

Jed took a seat, shaking slightly. He tried to swallow. Ruth hurried to the doorway to hail an usher, then rushed back to sit beside Jed, grasping his hand as he gasped for air.

There was a discreet knock at the doorway, and Ruth hurried to answer. After the gurgle of pouring liquid, she came back, handing Jed a tumbler half full of amber fluid.

"Drink this," she ordered.

Jed took a big gulp. The whiskey hit the back of his throat, burning all the way to his stomach. Jed choked, gasped, and went into a coughing fit before he managed to regain control of his breathing.

"Are you okay?" asked Ruth anxiously.

Jed blinked his eyes to clear away the tears. "Her name was Beatrice. She was the daughter of my commanding officer at the post when I was stationed out west. After I had been at the post for two years, we became engaged and then married. It couldn't have been more perfect. A little over three years ago, I was out on patrol. When I returned, I was told she'd come down with influenza and had died." He shook his head as if to clear away those memories. "I don't know why I'm telling you this."

"Was it because I mentioned your wife?" suggested Ruth. "Did she like the theater?"

"Yes and no," replied Jed with a smile of remembrance.

All of a sudden, he went stiff, and the smile on his face disappeared. Then, with a sharp inhalation, Jed shuddered. He took a sip of his whiskey and slowly smiled.

"She didn't care for the high drama. She liked the plays that stretched your imagination." Jed sighed. "She would've loved this, and she would be in agreement with you about the high priest's attitude in regard to a woman's place."

"I'm glad. What else did she like?"

Jed gave her a rueful smile. "Do you know that two weeks ago I wouldn't have discussed Beatrice at all? My little sister Sarah was, I think, despairing for me. She didn't like the quiet, moody person I had become. I could not stay out west. Everything there reminded me of her and the things she loved." He sipped his drink while he gathered his thoughts.

"There was the wide expanse of the plains, the seemingly endless stretch of blue sky above, and the countless stars shining in the night sky. She loved all these things and more." Jed chuckled in memory. "Even the burning heat, the freezing cold, the flash floods, and the tornadoes." Jed began to fidget.

"Are you all right?" Ruth asked.

"I'm sorry. This is not the way I planned for the evening to go. We should be celebrating, but . . ."

"But . . . ?"

Jed's mustache twitched from side to side. "I'm starting to feel a little confined in here. I must apologize for not being better company."

"You are excellent company." Ruth stood. "We just chose the wrong entertainment. What do you say to a stroll under the stars?"

Standing, he held Ruth's small jacket for her. She put it on with a murmur of thanks. Jed escorted her out of the box and down the stairs to the theater's exit.

Outside, it was a cool spring night. Jed took in a deep lungful of air and felt his muscles relax. He had not realized how tense he had been. Ruth twined her arm in his and brought her other hand over to gently squeeze his upper arm.

"I think you are made for the outdoors," she commented as they walked down Church Street. The roadway was lit by oil streetlamps along with the glow coming from the residences on either side of the thoroughfare. "Is this better?"

"Yes, and thank you," said Jed, feeling a little embarrassed.

"For what?"

"Understanding." He placed his free hand over hers. "I've always felt better outdoors. I think that's why I ran away from home in the first place." He turned a little melancholy. "I came back after Beatrice died and locked myself away in an office for the past three years. Sarah kept trying to get me to do things and talk to her."

"She sounds like a perceptive and intelligent young woman," said Ruth.

"Try persistent and determined," said Jed dryly. "She dragged me to balls, cotillions, theaters—anywhere there were people. I have always had trouble telling her no."

Ruth laughed. "There is always one beloved member in any family who can make us do anything they want."

"What about your family?"

Ruth let out a big sigh. "I come from a large family. I have five brothers and three sisters, but because of my indiscretion, they will have nothing to do with me. I am shunned by everyone." She snorted with derision. "I fell in love."

"Ruth, you don't have to tell me this."

"I would like to, if you care to hear it."

Jed stayed silent and nodded.

"I've . . . I've never told anyone. My family knows, but it's never mentioned. Only the work I do for my father allows me to be near and talk to them.

"When I was seventeen, I met Jonathan Brattox. He was tall and handsome, and his father ran a successful shipping company. He is also a Christian. I was smitten; so much so that I agreed to run away with him. We were going to be married in New York City. Unfortunately—or fortunately, depending upon your point of view—his father's telegram caught up to us in Philadelphia."

"I saw it but never read it. Jonathan told me it was nothing, but the next morning, his side of the bed was empty. He left me there alone. Later that same year, he married a proper girl for one of his position and standing." She pulled an aristocratic face to look down her nose at Jed before starting to chuckle.

"I had to sell some of my jewelry to pay the hotel bill and buy a ticket back to Baltimore. When I arrived at my father's house, I was made to stand in the foyer. When my father finally agreed to see me, he asked if there was anything he could do for me . . . like I was total stranger to him."

Ruth's lips curled in distaste. "That was when I realized how far I had strayed. During my affair, I gained quite a bit of knowledge about the Brattox Shipping Company. I also knew the parable of the prodigal son. With nothing left to lose, I asked my father for employment and hinted at the key facts that I knew. The hints were enough for my father to put aside his ire. I am now nothing more than a servant in my father's house."

"Ruth, I am sorry for your troubles."

"It was of my own making," said Ruth. "At least, I was not thrown out onto the streets."

"Will your father ever forgive you?"

"It would have to be both my father and my mother to forgive me," said Ruth solemnly. "I think, in a way, they have, but the traditions of our people prevent them from fully accepting me back into the family. My father, as an elder, must respect those traditions. With my mother, it's more personal. It had not helped that my mother and Mrs. Samuelson had planned on me marrying Mrs. Samuelson's son Jacob. Mrs. Samuelson tells my mother how lucky her son was not to have married me at least once or twice every week."

"I'm afraid I'm not very familiar with Jewish traditions," said Jed.

"What of your father? Did he accept you back after you ran away from home? You did, of course, marry the girl."

Jed's mouth twisted into a slight smile. "Yes, I did, but I was gone for five years. This is probably an example of a double standard. I was the prodigal son who was welcomed home. We had the fatted calf in the way of a huge celebration dinner, several balls to introduce me back into Chicago society, and before I knew it, I was ensconced in an office in my father's law firm. I barely remember any of it."

"You were still hurting from the loss. I was too, for the longest time."

"I would still be in that office if my friend John Rawlins hadn't pulled me out of my chair and put me in front of the governor to swear an oath."

"Before Governor Hicks?" asked Ruth.

Jed made a face. "I have *got* to stop talking to pretty girls."

His quip made Ruth break out in laughter.

"No, I'm not in the Maryland militia. It was Governor Yates of Illinois, but please, keep that to yourself."

"I will," promised Ruth. She took on a wistful look. "Do you know this is the first time I've been able to discuss this?"

"Include myself with that," said Jed, choking up a little. "I've never been able to talk about Beatrice to anyone, since . . . Well, it's been a very long time."

"How long did you wait before going out with another woman?"

Jed pulled out his pocket watch and looked at it. "Oh, I'd say, tonight."

"What? Oh! Oh, you . . . Oy! When was the last time you kissed a woman?"

Jed broke out laughing. "Last Friday. There was this woman in Mabel's house . . ."

"Oy vey," muttered Ruth, shaking her head.

"When was the last time you kissed a man before that?"

Ruth let out a sigh and said gloomily, "Nine years ago."

Ruth looks so downcast that Jed stopped walking, cupped her chin with his hand, and raised her face to gently kissed her on the lips.

The kiss lasted for only a second, but in that time, all sound and movement stopped.

THE DOOR TO JED'S HOTEL room flew open as Jed and Ruth entwined around one another. They took a stumbling step into the room, and Jed tried to jiggle the key out of the lock while keeping his lips pressed to Ruth's.

Jed's fingers snagged the key out of the lock, and he tossed it aside as he swung his foot around to close the door. They gasped for breath as Ruth pulled Jed's frock coat off his shoulders and down his arms. They kissed again and again as her hands untied his cravat and tossed it aside.

Her short jacket easily came off, and Jed dropped it to the floor. He reached behind her, but he had the devil of a time trying to undo the small buttons on the back of her dress. His frustration level was rising as was the tightness in his pants.

The shoulder holster and pistol were the next thing to thump onto the floor, followed closely by Jed's vest. Ruth was reaching her own frustration point as she tore his shirt open, buttons flying everywhere. She looked at his naked upper body and gasped.

Jed's physique was hard and muscular, marred only by a nine-inch scar traveling from his left shoulder downward across his pec and a round puckered scar on his right abdomen. Pulling her close to kiss her again, the heat of his skin radiated through her dress.

Jed broke the kiss and turned Ruth around. He gave a discontented grunt as his fingers worked the tiny buttons at the back of her dress. Ruth picked feverishly to untie her skirt and all the petticoats underneath it. He felt her shivered with desire and anticipation.

Jed knew he had to take his time. Ruth would have to wear this dress when she left, and he didn't want her to look like a painted lady when she did so. He also knew there would be repercussions, even if they were only between the two of them.

Jed's trembling fingers undid the last button as Ruth's last petticoat fell to the floor. She felt him pull at the tie to the lacing of her corset and sighed in relief as the restricting garment loosened. It followed the petticoats to the floor and Ruth turned around, dressed only in her pantaloons.

She started to move forward to kiss Jed again, but he held onto her bare shoulders.

"Ruth, are you sure?"

The trembling of his hands spoke of his need. The huskiness of his voice exposed his desire. However, it was the concern for her in his eyes that made Ruth smile up at him warmly.

"Yes." Ruth untied the ribbon at the top of her pantaloons and let the garment drop.

His eyes followed her pantaloons downward, and Jed inhaled sharply. Ruth was more than very nicely put together. She was voluptuous.

More so than Maura, observed Jed, who was immediately shocked and embarrassed for having so callous a thought. He then wondered again what it was about these two women that attracted him so, but only for second.

Parting her soft lips, Ruth grazed her tongue lightly across his lips. Jed pulled her to him, feeling her soft breasts press enticingly against his bare skin. His tongue darted out to return her favor, and Ruth moaned in desire as she kissed him back passionately.

When he brought his hands up to Ruth's breasts, she shivered in pleasure. His fingers caressed the soft mounds, feeling their weight and strumming across her nipples. It was then his turn to gasp and shiver as he stiffened in more ways than one. Ruth used one hand to trace and feel the bulge between his legs. She left off teasing him long enough to push his buttonless shirt and suspenders off his shoulders.

Placing a hand on her shoulder for balance, Jed pressed one foot against the other to pry off his shoes and try to get his feet free from his entangling pants. Ruth simply tucked her feet up behind her, one at a time, to take off her footwear. Jed had to finally resort to stepping on the toe of each sock to pull his feet free from both the sock and his pants.

"That was graceful," chuckled Ruth, now dressed in only her stockings and a look of mirth in her eyes.

"Better than being tactless by wearing them in bed." Jed moved closer to Ruth, looking down upon her face.

Her eyes opened wide, and she gasped out loud as Jed's fingers touched her between her legs. She shook as his fingers brought back her desire and longing. She pulled his head down to kiss his lips as they shuffled toward the bed.

Jed tried to lay her down gently, but Ruth refused to let go of him. She half fell onto the bed with Jed on top of her. He managed to get his hands on the mattress to break his fall, so he wouldn't crush her. Panting with long-suppressed passion, Ruth pulled at his hips until he was between her legs. Jed couldn't hold back, and with a thrust, they were joined together with cries of joy.

Chapter 12

Tuesday, April 30, 1861

THE SUN HAD NOT CRESTED the horizon, but the light from the false dawn filtered through the window revealing the nude form of Ruth laying half on top of Jed. Both were shiny with sweat, and their muscles quivered from exertion and passionate gratification.

"Ay-yay-yay," cooed Ruth dreamily. "That felt so good!"

"I'm so glad you got pleasure out of it," teased Jed as he rubbed up and down her back. "I enjoyed myself, also."

"Don't be a schmuck." Ruth slapped her hand lightly on his chest. "Honestly, you made me feel . . . things I haven't felt before. Where did you learn those things?"

"Spent time with the Indians." He kissed the top of her head. "I stayed in Indian villages, sometimes up to a month at a time. I slept in teepees—like a large tent—with entire families. You pretend to ignore what goes on between a man and a woman next to you, but you do learn some things. The squaws were especially forthcoming and descriptive to Beatrice when she stayed with them."

"She stayed with the savages?" exclaimed an astonished Ruth, sitting up. Her long, dark hair cascaded down, framing her face and covering her breasts just barely enough to be enticing.

"They're no more savage than we are. They have different customs and laws that are strange to us. We are as equally incomprehensible to them." Jed pulled her down for a kiss.

"Let me tell you one of their legends. The Coyote Spirit or Old Man Coyote, as he is known in some parts, is a trickster.

He also represents playfulness and wisdom hidden in humor. There are several personifications of him.

"One day, Old Man Coyote was walking with his younger brother, who was very sad. When asked about it, the younger brother lamented that his wife had been stolen from him by a young, strong warrior.

"Old Man Coyote chided his younger brother, stating that when a warrior took a woman to be his wife, things would be wonderful for several years. Then, the warrior would lose interest after being with the same woman for so long, and he would go out to steal another warrior's wife.

"Old Man Coyote asked his brother if he was going to take his wife back. His brother told him he would never do that because he had too much honor, and he respected himself too much. Old Man Coyote laughed at him and told him that his own wife had been stolen three times."

Ruth's eyes widened in astonishment, but she didn't say anything.

"The younger brother berated him, saying that all the other warriors were laughing and making fun of him behind his back. Old Man Coyote chuckled, saying it did not matter what they thought. He was laughing for his own reasons under the buffalo blankets.

"He told his younger brother that she had become more obedient because she remembered that she had been abducted. She was now eager to please and fulfill his every desire. In bed, she was a hot one, because she learned things while she was with another. Old Man Coyote would rather have a stolen wife than not."

"That's . . . That's . . ."

"Immoral? Barbaric?" suggested Jed. "Old Man Coyote happily took back his young, pretty wife each time. Indian women have more freedom and rights than women do in our society. I always thought the moral of the story was that people should not be stuck in a rut but should expand their horizons."

After thinking about it for a minute, she leaned in to kiss him again. Ruth sat up on the edge of the bed and looked out the window. Stretching her hands above her head, which gave

Jed an excellent view of her physique, she said, "It's morning, bubelah. Will you help me with my buttons?"

"Bubelah?" questioned Jed as he hopped out of the bed to gather their scattered clothes.

"It's a term of endearment." She tied her garters around the tops of her stockings. Pantaloons, corset, blouse, petticoats, skirt, and jacket went on, one after another. The sun was just peeking over the horizon when Ruth was finally dressed.

"Give me a minute," said Jed as he grabbed his pants. "I'll escort you back to the boarding house."

Laying a hand on his arm to stop him, she said, "No. Even this early in the morning, I will be seen, and it will cause gossip. If you're with me, the gossip will double and become a certainty." Ruth chuckled. "We have been awake most of the night, and I need some rest."

"Ruth, I . . ."

Putting her fingers on Jed's lips to stop him, Ruth added, "This was something we both needed, my bubelah. I have no expectations beyond last night. Can you live with that?"

"Well, at least, you didn't say we come from two different cultures," huffed Jed, getting one leg in his pants. "I can live with that as long as you understand that I will still be your friend, and I will be walking you back."

"I would like to remain friends," said Ruth. "As for walking me back, you're going to be too slow."

With that said, she opened the door and took a quick peek around. Seeing no one in the hallway, she sailed through the doorway, blowing Jed a kiss before she shut it. Jed almost fell over trying to get his other leg into his pants. With a sigh, he plopped down on the bed, sure in the knowledge that he couldn't get dressed and catch up with her before she got back to the boarding house.

The sun was just passing noon before Jed walked out of the hotel. He was rested and found he was oddly at peace with himself. A small part in the back of his mind seemed to scoff at him for taking so long and sent sharp little reminders that Beatrice would not have liked what he had done to himself over the past three years. His late-wife loved life, and he hadn't really been living since she went to heaven.

His first order of business was to check on Ruth and see how she was. He also wanted to see what she would like to do this evening. The town orchestra was performing a concert at the town square pavilion. He headed toward the boarding house.

"Mr. Tremblant! Mr. Tremblant!"

Jed looked further up the street to see who was calling him. A man waved, and Jed had to look twice before he recognized Tanner coming toward him. Wearing a brown striped suit, white shirt with a necktie, and a bowler hat, Tanner looked completely different from when all he had to wear was his clothes that were too small.

"Tanner, it is good to see you," greeted Jed. "I see you have a new wardrobe. Why are you here?"

Puffing up a little in his new finery, Tanner pulled an envelope out of his coat pocket. "I was sent to bring you this message."

Opening the envelope, Jed saw that the letter was written in Bryce's hand. It read:

Master Jed,

I felt this was too sensitive for the telegraph and sent young Tanner to you. Mr. Duff is in Baltimore, and someone is searching diligently and rather incautiously for him. That person has been taking serious risks and may be in danger. There have been two close calls that I know of.

If your duties allow, you may wish to return.

Bryce

P.S. Please send Tanner back so I can continue with his instruction. He is bright and industrious, but he asks too many questions instead of accepting things as they are.

"Mr. Bryce said you might be coming back with me. The next train leaves in two hours. He said it was urgent." Tanner waited expectedly.

Hissing between his teeth in frustration, Jed considered this new development. He was quite certain that Maura would go to any lengths to capture or kill Duff. If she were captured by Mayor Brown and Marshal Kane, she could be taken to Richmond for trial or simply made to disappear. Either prospect had a terrible and terrifying conclusion.

"Have you purchased the tickets?" asked Jed.

Tanner shook his head no.

Jed headed back to the hotel. "We will pack my things, then you will go buy the tickets and wait for me at the station. I have someone I have to see."

"I can pack your things," said Tanner.

"Even if you could get the key from the clerk, there are a couple of hidden items I would rather not leave behind."

"Oh."

Returning to his room, Jed recovered his codebook that was hidden under the top dresser drawer. The knob of one of the brass bedposts came off, and pulling on a string, Jed fished his sensitive messages out of the hollow tube. Tanner looked on in amazement.

"Can you pack everything else?"

Tanner nodded.

"Good man. I'll see you at the station."

Leaving Tanner to his task, Jed hurried to the boarding house. Unfortunately, he learned Ruth and several other ladies had gone out for tea. Inquiring politely, Jed was told there were four possible locations where they may have gone.

Ruth was not present at the first or the second tearoom. Checking his watch as he hurried to the third one on his list, Jed knew he was running out of time. Yes, Ruth had said she had no expectations, but Jed didn't consider himself the type of cad who would make advances toward a woman and then leave without a word.

The third tea house was adjacent to a small park, and the proprietor had set up tables outside for his customers. Two of the tables with fine linen tablecloths spread over them were occupied. Large, rectangular fans hung from tree branches above the tables, but on this fine spring day, none were in use.

Ruth was sitting at one of the tables with three other ladies. After wiping his face with his handkerchief from his back pocket and dusting himself off, Jed walked over to the group.

"Good afternoon, ladies." Jed held out a hand to Ruth. "I'm sorry to interrupt your tea, but I wondered if I might request the presence of one of your members for a few minutes?"

"Excuse me," said Ruth as the three other ladies twittered between themselves. Jed led Ruth about thirty feet away but still in plain sight of everyone. "I thought you would be at the afternoon session."

"I was planning to, but one of my servants showed up here in Frederick with a message. Anthony Duff has gone back to Baltimore since we thwarted his plans here."

"Don't you mean since you thwarted his plans?" asked Ruth with a smile. She then turned serious. "So, are you going back to chase after him?"

Jed checked his watch. "I am leaving within the hour."

"Oh, I . . ." stammered Ruth. "Why are you here? I told you I had no expectations."

"So you told me. I, however, have a code of conduct that does not include sneaking off without a word or leaving behind a carefully crafted letter." Jed became flustered. "I . . . uh . . . I mean . . . Last night meant a great deal to me. I . . ."

"Shh," hushed Ruth, holding up a hand. "Last night helped me as much as it did you, and I'm grateful for it. We both have jobs to do in this conflict, and hopefully, we'll see one another again. I will always consider you a true friend."

Jed scuffed his feet. "Nothing more than a friend?"

Smiling, Ruth said, "Maybe a little more than that but not much beyond. We cannot marry, not without losing our families and friends. You need to hurry, Jed, or you're going to miss your train."

"My train can go to blazes," stated Jed flatly.

"I don't like it any more than you do. I was hoping to spend more time with you. However, you won't be able to live with yourself if Mr. Duff does something atrocious, and you aren't there to stop him."

"You're right," sighed Jed. "I'm sure before this conflict is resolved, we will all be doing things we wish we didn't have to do." He grimaced. "I never thought I would be chasing a spy or gathering information."

"From what I've seen, you're very good at it," said Ruth.

"Mostly luck on my part." Jed laughed.

"Really? Could it be that you understand and comprehend Duff's behavior better than you think?"

"Luck," reiterated Jed. He then relented. "It might also have been the training I received from our Indian scouts."

"Either way, I was happy to have met you." Ruth laid a hand on Jed's arm. "Be careful. Mr. Duff is playing for keeps. If the roles were reversed on the street the other day, I'm not sure he would've honored the truce."

"I don't trust him, either. He's bent on bringing Maryland into the Confederacy and will use any method to do so. If you had not been a woman . . ."

" . . . things may have gone differently," finished Ruth. She broke out in a smile and blushed. "Very differently, after the opera."

Coughing discreetly to regain his composure from her audacious statement, Jed chuckled. "Very differently, indeed. You must be careful. Duff knows you, and he knows you're acquainted with me. Hopefully, he'll think you're just that, an acquaintance."

A lone train whistle, faint in the distance, echoed between the hills. Both Jed and Ruth sighed, because they knew their parting was at hand.

Holding out her hand, Ruth said, "Take care, Mr. Tremblant."

"You, too, Miss Goldberg." Jed surprised her by kissing the back of her fingers. Letting go, he turned to leave.

"Mr. Tremblant," said Ruth quickly, laying her hand back on his arm to stop him. "If you ever need help, my father's place of business is on Lloyd Street, three buildings up from the synagogue."

With that said, she let go of his arm and turned back to her group of ladies. They were all looking at her and Jed with speculation dancing in their eyes. Jed gave them an exaggerated bow and left.

He walked quickly toward the train station. He didn't want to leave Ruth behind, but she was probably safer here than in Baltimore.

Looking up Carroll Street, he spotted Tanner standing outside the train station. The young man sagged in relief when he caught sight of Jed. The train whistle blew again, this time much closer. Turning his head, Jed saw the plume of smoke from the engine's smokestack rising above the trees about a half a mile away.

"I was starting to worry if you were going to make it." Tanner handed Jed two tickets and picked up his and Jed's carpet bags.

"I see your clothes are not the only thing that's new," stated Jed, looking at Tanner's piece of luggage. Making sure they couldn't be overheard, he asked, "What specifically has occurred? Bryce's letter was a little vague, except to say that Duff was back in Baltimore."

"Miss Maura is convinced he is there but has not seen him yet. She's been reading Mayor Brown's and Marshal Kane's correspondence whenever she goes to their homes for dinner. She's even tried following them a time or two. One letter she read stated the agent in Frederick couldn't complete his mission because of you. That's why she thinks Duff has returned to the city."

"Anything else?"

"Yeah, after we heard the legislature voted not to split from the union, the police started arresting the people who are speaking out against the Confederacy. Several newspaper offices were broken into and destroyed. It was said that the vandalism was caused by the rioters."

The train was pulling into the station with a loud hissing release of steam and the screech of steel brakes. After checking with the conductor, Jed and Tanner stepped up onto the passenger car and stowed their bags in the overhead rack.

"I must admit I was a little perturbed when you went to work at the foundry," said Jed as he sat. No one else was near them, and Tanner sat facing him.

"I'm sorry, sir. It won't happen again."

"Don't be ridiculous, . . . uh . . . I have to apologize. In all this time, I never learned your first name."

"Ezekiel, sir. Most people call me Zeke."

"A good biblical name," said Jed with a smile. "Anyway, your plan worked much better than mine, and I'm upset with myself for trying to bull my way into the foundry. I want you to continue gathering information. I wonder if we can get you hired in Winans's office?"

"Sir, it might be better if I was in the mayor's office or the marshal's office," said Tanner. "I learned at the foundry that the city was paying for the repairs on the steam gun, and they plan to ship it to the Confederacy in about two weeks."

"We cannot let that weapon fall into the hands of the Confederacy. Even if it is only half as devastating as the newspapers make it out to be, it will seriously impact the war if the South can reproduce it. I think you should stay at the foundry until we can determine when it will be shipped."

"Why don't we just destroy it?" asked Tanner.

"It may come to that, but I would like to have it captured. It could be of great importance to the Union. General Butler is in Annapolis, reestablishing the railway north from Washington. He's in the perfect position to intercept it. We need to get the diagrams of the steam gun."

"They're kept right next to the gun, sir," said Tanner. "The people from the city want the plans where they can get to them. I'm pretty sure they will go with steam gun wherever it's shipped to."

"We just need to find out when and how it will be shipped," said Jed. "Can you get back into the foundry?"

"Yes, I told them I had to move my widowed mother in with my older sister, so I had yesterday and today off from work. I can be back there tomorrow morning." Tanner turned a little pensive. "Sir, Mayor Brown and Marshal Kane were very upset about the secession vote. They're not at all happy with Mr. Winans or the rest of the state delegates. According to Chrissy, they're planning on staging their own revolt with as many counties as they can get to go with them."

"So Maryland will be split just like the Union?"

"Yes, sir. East and West, by the look of things. The Fifty-third Maryland and the city police are training more. They're also stockpiling weapons, ammunition, and gunpowder in warehouses, private homes, even cemeteries. Mr. Bryce's writing down lists of where everything is and who's responsible."

"I often made fun of his lists when I was growing up. I think, however, it might be a good idea for us to start keeping track of all the things we have learned. Your job, right now, is to keep an eye on the steam gun. Since you're going back to the foundry, you need to keep your distance from me. I'm too well known to Marshal Kane and Duff. Can you get a message to Chrissy if you need to contact me?"

"Yes, sir." Tanner blushed brightly. "I can do that."

"Don't take the plans for the steam gun, even if you have a chance," warned Jed. "I'd like to get them both at same time, if I can get General Butler to listen to me."

"You work for the Secretary of War, don't you? What makes you think he won't listen?"

"He's a general, and I'm a captain," explained Jed. "He outranks me, and his way of thinking might be that if Secretary Cameron wanted me to tell generals what to do, he should've made me a general. It might be a good idea for me to go to Annapolis and introduce myself."

"And our friend?"

"I'm going to her house to talk to her tonight. I need to find out what she knows about Duff being in Baltimore."

"He has been sending information to Mr. Bryce, but nothing about Duff," said Tanner.

"That's why I want to talk to her. She may be trying to get information all by herself. Wait a minute, what you mean by 'he'?"

"Mr. Bryce told me to refer to our acquaintance as he, and from what Mr. Bryce told me, our friend is looking for Duff himself."

Jed thought about it for a moment or two. "I'll talk to him. Using this terminology makes sense. We should also have code names so that our identities are not revealed."

"How about Z for me?" supplied Tanner enthusiastically.

"You don't think anyone will connect Z with Zeke?" asked Jed kindly.

"Oh," said a crestfallen Tanner. "I guess our code name should be something that isn't part of us."

"We can call you Fort, because you came from Fort McHenry and very few people can associate you with it," suggested Jed.

"That's great! We can call you Chief, like an Indian chief."

The Trail of the Scottish Bluebell

"Let me talk to Bryce about it. Now, you'd better find another seat. Let Chrissy know when they're going to move the steam gun, how they're going to move it, and its route, if you get that information safely. Stay at the foundry until it ships just in case there are any last-minute changes."

"Yes, sir." Tanner stood, retrieved his carpet bag, and moved away from Jed.

Jed spent the rest of the trip writing in his journal. He actually felt flushed and nervous as he related his liaison with Ruth in broad euphemisms. What was strange to him was that, as he traveled further away, Ruth's image became less defined in his mind as Maura's image grew. Was it because Maura was in more danger now than Ruth?

Not liking the way his thoughts were going, Jed emulated Bryce's canon of order and preparedness by making lists. First, there were the codenames to be made. Second, if he stayed in Baltimore any length of time, he would need a more permanent and private residence than a hotel room. Third, he would have to meet General Butler within the next couple of days to establish a rapport with the man. The steam gun was not as important as keeping Maryland from seceding, but in Jed's mind, it was a close second.

Finally, Jed knew he had to find out what Mayor Brown and Marshal Kane were planning. Nothing in their actions to get Maryland to join the Confederacy was overt, apart from Marshal Kane's telegraph to the men of Virginia after the Baltimore riot, calling on them to come and defend the city. It was the covert stockpiling of weapons and ammunition that worried Jed. If Baltimore revolted and was savagely suppressed by Northern troops, the fighting would spread across the entire eastern portion of the state.

Later that evening, the train pulled into the B&O station in Baltimore. Jed was pleased when Tanner left the platform without so much as a glance at him. At his hotel, Jed sent for Bryce and went up to his room to unpack. A few minutes later, Bryce showed up with a covered tray.

"I don't know if you have had the chance to eat, Master Jed, so I took the liberty of preparing you a tray."

"Thank you, Bryce. I haven't eaten." Jed sat at the desk as Bryce put the tray in front of him. The smell of fried catfish, roasted potatoes, fresh bread, and squash made his mouth water. A fine, white wine accompanied the meal. "I will be leaving soon to see Mrs. Harrison."

"I expected as much. That is why I sent young Tanner to you. The tales I've heard about her activities have been . . . disturbing. Did Tanner not return with you?"

"I sent him back to the foundry. It's important we find out when they plan to ship the steam gun." Jed went on to explain his plan to capture the steam gun while it was enroute to the Confederacy. "We also need codenames for one another to hide our identities."

"Yes, sir, and you need more suitable quarters than just this room. I located a proper house to lease. It is set away from other houses in the neighborhood and is private. We can see it tomorrow, if you like."

"Bryce, you are wonder." Jed bit into his chicken, which had been marinated before it had been fried, making it delicious. He took a second bite just to savor it. "I was thinking the same thing about a house on the train ride here. Tomorrow is fine and tell them to have the lease papers ready. Right now, I must see Mrs. Harrison."

Bryce went over to the wardrobe and pulled out Jed's dark-gray cloak.

"You said yourself that it hides you better in the dark than your black one," said Bryce, in reply to Jed's raised eyebrows. "Go to the rear entrance and knock. Ask if they can spare any rockfish. When they reply they have no fish on the premises, you will say you will go out on the boat tomorrow and catch some."

"Challenge and password?" asked Jed in amazement.

"It started as an excuse to be at the door," explained Bryce. "The servants won't know you."

"Except Miss Freed," said Jed. "I'm off."

"Sir, before you go, a Mr. Dowling from Washington hand-delivered these two packages for you the day before yesterday."

Jed opened the large envelope first. In it was his orders assigning them as a special investigator to the War Department under the command of the Secretary of War. Jed let out his breath slowly. These orders placed him outside of everyone's command. In essence, he was his own man and only accountable to Secretary Cameron. The second piece of paper in the envelope was a short note:

I hope you will not have need of these, but I felt you should have them just in case. L.

Jed looked over at the crate, which was a little more than a boot box in size. Bryce produced a screwdriver from somewhere, and Jed used it to pry the lid off.

"Oh, my!" gasped Jed when he saw the markings.

"What is it, sir?"

"A present from the president," replied Jed.

"I beg your pardon?"

Jed reached in and pulled out six rectangular cardboard boxes and eighteen square boxes from the sawdust packing. The boxes had "C. Sharps & Company" written on it along with ".30 caliber Pistol." Opening one of the rectangular boxes, he gingerly lifted the small gun out of the oilskin it was wrapped in.

"I have heard of these, but this is the first time I've seen one," said Jed. "It's a Sharp's derringer." He looked at the writing on one of the square boxes. "Thirty caliber with a rimfire cartridge." He pulled a bullet out of the box. "See . . . the powder is in the casing behind the bullet. No percussion caps. No chance of the cap falling off and having a misfire."

"But will it work?" asked Bryce skeptically.

"We'll find out." Jed loaded two pistols and put one in each of his coat pockets. Nodding to Bryce, Jed headed out the door.

The moon was only two-thirds full, but it still gave plenty of light to see by. Jed headed to Maura's house, keeping away from police officers and any large groups of men roaming about. The back door to Maura's house was opened by a middle-aged Negro woman. Jed went through the challenge and password before he was escorted into the kitchen area.

"Mr. Tremblant!" The young, black woman rushed toward him.

"Hello, Miss Freed." Jed felt the tension lessen from the servants in the room. "I'm here to see Mrs. Harrison."

"Thank the Lord you're here," exclaimed Tabitha in both relief and anxiety. "Miss Maura put on britches and a coat and went to the place where they're keeping the weapons. Miss Petford didn't know she left and is beside herself with worry and anger. It's not safe for black folk be on the street after dark, but I was just getting ready to go after her."

Chapter 13

Tuesday, April 30, 1861

"What does that cockamamie woman think she's doing?" fumed Jed as he hurried down the street. "In britches, no less!"

Tabitha had given him the address of the warehouse to which Maura was going and had given him two more locations where Maura might be if she was not at the first one. Even though Bryce had told him they had a list of where arms and ammunition were being stockpiled, Jed was a little shocked by the quantity of weapons being stored according to Tabitha's list.

It was edging on to midnight as Jed moved from the residential district to the business one. Almost all traffic along the street had diminished to nothing. Even though the cobblestones were hard on his soft-soled shoes, the hard surface allowed Jed to hear patrolling police officers before they saw him. Skillfully eluding them, he was soon at the warehouse.

The large, brick building took up half a city block right on the edge of the docks and loomed a good thirty feet above the street. The roof had a window-lined, cupola-like structure on top for ventilation. Three massive, double doors faced the street, each large enough to allow the biggest wagon to pass through it with ease. Two entry doors for regular foot traffic were situated in between each of the huge doors.

There was no missing the three men standing guard out front of the warehouse. Jed was sure that, if there was a back door, it would also be guarded. Looking this way and that as he moved from shadow to shadow, he didn't see Maura anywhere. Then a slight movement drew his gaze upward.

A figure dressed all in black was scaling up one of the downspouts. There was a flash of a pale face in the moonlight as the person looked around before climbing higher. Jed was positive this was Maura and quietly moved down the street.

She had gone up and over the edge of the roof by the time Jed had reached the downspout. The large downspout was firmly attached to the wall, and thankfully, it was not raining. Gripping the downspout with both hands, Jed started climbing.

Two-thirds of the way up, Jed froze. The clack of hobnailed shoes on stone grew louder as someone approached. A man carrying a shotgun came around the corner from the back of the warehouse. Jed put his chin to his chest to hide his face and stayed perfectly still. The man passed by and went around the corner at the front to greet to guards there. Letting out a slow sigh of relief, Jed continued his climb.

Up on the tarred, wood roof, Jed saw that one of the square window frames was open. The frame was four feet square with four panes of glass mounted in it. Crossing silently over to it, he eased his way inside and stood on one of the large support beams. The person he had spotted before was making their way across the beams toward the rear of the warehouse.

The first floor was lined in brick and illuminated by oil lamps. There were crates and barrels clustered in groups all over the floor, except for three lanes leading to the large front doors. A thirty-foot-wide balcony circled the interior walls, leaving an open space in the middle to the floor below. The balcony was also cluttered with items and crates. A dozen men or so gathered around a table on the first floor. One of them had whitish-blond hair—Duff!

The light from the oil lamps barely lit the upper area where Jed crouched. The other intruder was making slow progress toward the group of men, holding something in their hand. Moving as fast as he dared, Jed closed the distance between them.

"Gentlemen, the state legislature has shown their true colors," Duff said. "It's up to us to free ourselves from that great evil in Washington and become masters of our own destiny. The time is close to when we throw off those who would enslave us and dictate how we should live. Each of you knows what to do."

The person on the beam had stopped and was looking at the group. In the dim light, Jed saw Maura's face, ugly in the fury that possessed her. Her hair was bound up in a black scarf tied tightly around her head. Shaking with hate, she lifted the pistol and pointed it at Duff.

"Maura, no!" hissed Jed softly. She was trembling so much, he knew her chances of hitting Duff at this range were almost nonexistent.

Maura gasped sharply and pivoted on the beam to face Jed. Her hand swung around to point the pistol at him. That was a mistake, because it hit a vertical support beam, and the gun went flying.

Jed watched in alarm as the firearm seemed to slowly fall, end-over-end, to the brick floor. When it hit, the pistol went off with a loud bang, and the bullet ricocheted once with a high ping before splintering a wood crate.

"Come on!" hissed Jed amidst the yells of alarm and consternation.

"I had him!" said Maura vehemently.

"No, you didn't!" said Jed angrily as he led the way back to the open window. "If we get out of this alive, I'll show you why!"

The guards outside barged in with weapons drawn. The group had scattered to find cover. In the confusion, Jed and Maura made their way to the window without being noticed.

Just as Maura went through the window, however, someone yelled, "Up there!"

Half a dozen shots rang out. Most of the bullets hit the beam as Jed dove out the window. One shattered a pane of glass beside him, and he heard one whiz over his head.

Now that they were focused on him, Jed knew pursuit would be swift and sure. He saw Maura start to go down the downspout just before he spun back around. One man was at the back door, and Jed fired off shot at him. The man cried out and fell. Jed quickly triggered two shots at the front doors as more bullets crashed through the windows around him.

After sliding back several feet on his belly, Jed jumped to his feet and raced to the downspout. Heedless of his safety in his rush for speed, he mostly slid down the pipe, skinning his arms and legs. Maura, having just climbed down, gasped at him in surprise when he landed right beside her. Grabbing her hand, he pulled her into a run toward the docks.

Shouts and yells accompanied the banging open of the doors of the warehouse. There were too many pursuers to try and escape on the streets. Any police officer they ran into might just as easily turn them over to their accusers as protect them. Their only escape was in the water.

"There they are!" came a shout, followed by several shots.

Jed pushed Maura away and began weaving back and forth. He would've been pleased that Maura followed his example if the situation wasn't so dire. From the sound of the voices, the range was too far to be accurate with the pistol, but they could possibly get in a lucky shot.

With the loud boom of a rifle, a whistling projectile zinged past his head—exactly what Jed had been dreading. He and Maura were close to the edge of the dock. Ten more feet and they would be in the water. Just at the edge, there was another boom, and Maura catapulted over to splash, unmoving, into the water.

Jed grimaced as he dropped off the dock but held on to the edge long enough to take off his cloak and throw it out on top of the water. He then jumped in next to Maura.

Her face was ashen and blood seeped from the back of her head. With trembling fingers, Jed felt the wound and, feeling no bullet hole, breathed a sigh of relief, hoping it was only a graze. Footsteps came closer, and placing his hand over her nose and mouth, Jed dove under the water.

Muffled shots and booms echoed from above, and the water was riddled by bullets and buckshot around the area of his cloak. Swimming alongside the stone blocks that made up the pier, Jed got around the edge and under the wooden portion of it.

Surfacing, he jerked as another fusillade let loose. He knew they would soon spread out and start looking for swimmers or bodies. Gripping Maura with one arm, he swam as fast as he could away from Duff and his compatriots.

The water was very cold, still chilled from the melting of the winter snows. With Maura injured, they couldn't swim to safety, not without risking the chills, and carrying her through the streets to her house without being stopped had little chance of success. Duff and his men had, no doubt, raised an alarm to be on the lookout for anyone in wet clothes.

As they swam from pier to pier, Jed's feeling of desperation rose. There were ships docked here, but no small boats he could steal. He knew they needed to get out of the water very soon. His extremities were starting to lose their feeling, and the weight of his clothes, along with hauling Maura, was sapping his strength.

Even with the grease he put in each chamber, Jed knew the immersion of his Colt had rendered it useless, except as a club. He was unarmed and had a wounded woman to care for, with a lot of unfriendly people around. Jed snorted as a thought came to him. This was just like being out West, but in a more supposedly civilized environment.

Jed stopped a couple of times to check on Maura. It appeared the bullet had grazed the top back portion of her head, probably when she was bent over. If she'd been standing upright, it would've killed her outright. Jed shuddered at the thought.

When he thought he was far enough away, Jed climbed out and pulled Maura onto a low wooden pier. Her wound was still bleeding, so he took the wet handkerchief from his coat pocket and the one from his back trouser pocket to use as a bandage. He retied her black scarf around her head to hold them in place.

Something hard hit against his leg as Jed sat back to regain his breath. Reaching down, he felt a hard, squarish object in his coat pocket. Anticipation shot through him as he pulled one of the derringers out of that pocket.

I wonder if the casing kept the powder dry, thought Jed in fervent hope. He pulled the other derringer out, removed the bullets, and dried everything off as well as he could before reloading the pistols.

Men with torches were searching around the pier where the Jed and Maura had gone into the water. Jed had gone about two hundred yards, but it was only a matter of time before they started looking up and down the bank. While wringing as much water out of his clothes as possible, a stench arose that had Jed wrinkling his nose.

With numerous steamers and packets sailing in and out of Baltimore, the harbor had become a depository for all sorts of trash and filth. Jed hoped they wouldn't catch anything and Maura's wound wouldn't become infected. Looking around, he spotted large bales of cotton lined up on the pier, waiting to be loaded on board a ship.

Pulling Maura up, he slung her over his shoulders. He put an arm between her legs and grasped her wrist with his hand. He used his other hand for balance.

"I'm glad you're wearing britches and not a dozen or so petticoats," murmured Jed.

At the first bale, he lifted Maura up and placed her on top of it. He then started walking toward the end of the pier, stopped, and turned around. Walking past the bale, Jed went to the side of the pier, wrung out his clothes to create a large puddle there, and backtracked to the bale.

Pulling himself up gingerly to avoid leaving telltale watermarks, Jed climbed up and lifted Maura onto his shoulders again. Even though the cotton was tightly packed inside the bale, it still made for a spongy and uneven surface to walk upon. Jed slowly made his way to the end of the long line of bales.

Placing Maura down again, Jed jumped off the bale and then pulled her down. Crossing over to a side street, he laid her down. Picking up a couple handfuls of dirt from a nearby garden, he went back to cover their water trail as best as he could. Hurrying back, he hefted her over his shoulders and moved quickly away from the pier.

Jed was getting worried. His original plan was to find someplace to hide until they could get word to Bryce, but Maura had not made a sound since she'd been shot. Her breathing was shallow, and she needed medical attention immediately.

Having no choice, Jed headed toward Mount Vernon with Maura slung over shoulders. It was the closest place he knew of where they could get help. He was not familiar with the area, but he knew Maura's house lay to the northwest of his location. About a block away from the pier, Jed caught sight of flickering torchlight playing on the walls of the buildings at the next corner. Ducking into a doorway, he pulled out one of his derringers. Two men, carrying torches and pistols, came up to the corner of the intersection and stopped.

"What in the hell happened?" asked one man.

"Two men sneaked into the warehouse," answered the other. "They shot John as he tried to get out, but we got one of them, judgin' by the blood on the dock. The other is tryin' to swim the harbor."

"He won't get away," guffawed the first man.

"Nah, the water's freezin' and they have boats out lookin' for him. Duff's got men all over the docks in case he tries to sneak back into town."

"What are we here for then?" asked the first one.

"Checkin' to make sure there ain't a company of blue bellies hiding around. I'm thinkin' that if there were soldier boys, they would've surrounded the building. Those two were probably just a pair of thieves who stumbled on our meetin'. C'mon. I don't want to get on Duff's bad side if we're surprised again."

Relaxing as the two men moved off, Jed pocketed his derringer. At the corner, he looked down the street, and seeing the men's backs were to him, he quickly crossed over and continued down the side street.

Guessing that Duff had about twenty men with him, Jed figured most of them would be either in the boats or on the shoreline. His main concern now was evading any policemen along his path. Therefore, it was a shock when Jed turned a corner and nearly ran into a middle-aged couple. Jed swayed back to avoid bowling the two people over.

"Steady, man," advised the gentleman, reaching out to hold onto Jed's arm. The two people were dressed for a night out and must be just returning home. The man's look of alarm changed to one of disgust as he let go and shook out his hand. He took a delicate sniff. "You're soaking wet!"

Jed caught on to what the man was thinking and unfocused his eyes before slurring his words. "Sees! Youse gets so drunk and goes for a swim thats I have to pulls youse out." Jed swayed a little back and forth. "Oh, goods evening." He looked around aimlessly. "Uh, we wanted to sees the Wash . . . Washington Monument."

The corners of the man's mouth took a decidedly downward turn.

"You're quite aways from there, sir. Go up Lloyd Street there. At the end of it, you'll find a number of policemen who can assist you. Good night."

"Good night, sir . . . Mad . . . Madame," hiccupped Jed, bowing and pretending to almost fall over from Maura's weight. "Whoa there! We'll be there soon."

The husband and wife walked quickly away from Jed. He heard the man's snort of disapproval at his supposedly inebriated state. Jed weaved and stumbled his way onto Lloyd Street, which ran diagonally to the road he had been on. Jed's feelings were mixed. He had both hope that there was now help at hand and dread about the comment concerning the number of policemen out and about.

Not far up the street, Jed came to a building with strange writing on it. Just past that were the offices of Mr. Samuel Goldberg. Jed tried the door, but it was locked. Looking up at the two stories above the storefront, he saw curtains in the windows and hoped that the Goldbergs lived above the office.

Not wanting to bang on the front door on a deserted street, Jed backtracked to a narrow pathway running alongside the synagogue to the back alley. The back door was also locked, and Jed had no option but to rap on it loudly with his fist.

Getting no response, Jed gritted his teeth and banged on the door again. He swallowed an oath as a light flickered in two of the windows behind him.

One window banged open, and a woman in a voluminous robe with a scarf tied around her head leaned out. "What is going on out here?"

Jed winced at the noise she was making.

"Who are you? What are you doing there?"

The window above the door Jed had been knocking on slid open, and a man with a salt-and-pepper beard looked out. Another window opened behind Jed, and he was starting to feel a bit crowded in the alley.

"Yes?" asked the man above Jed.

"Mr. Goldberg?"

The man nodded.

"May I talk with you? I am a friend of Ruth's."

"Is that—?" Goldberg's eyes grew wide as they adjusted to the dark enough to see the body slung over Jed shoulders.

"No, no," assured Jed. "Please, I need your help."

Goldberg ducked back inside, and the back door opened. He motioned Jed to come inside. Jed no sooner stepped through the doorway when he saw two young men, one about twenty and the other around eighteen, pointing pistols at him.

"Who are you?" asked Goldberg sternly.

"Jedidiah Tremblant. I met Ruth in Frederick. She's still there."

"Hiram? Hiram?" yelled the woman from across the alley. "What is going on?"

Goldberg relaxed, but the aim of the two men did not waver. In the candlelight, Jed saw the resemblance between the three of them. Goldberg went into the alley, making a shushing motion with his hands.

"It is all right, Mrs. Samuelson," he said, turning to look at everyone who had opened their window. "Someone needs our help. Go back to sleep. I will talk to the other elders in the morning."

"Fine thing," snorted Mrs. Samuelson. "Waking us out of a sound sleep. No telling—" The shutting of her window cut off her voice.

Goldberg came back inside, shutting and bolting the door. He stayed out of the line of fire of the two pistols pointed at Jed.

"Ruth wrote to me about you," stated Goldberg. "What is she supposed to be doing in Frederick?"

"The same as I was," said Jed. "Reporting on what the state legislature was voting on, especially in regard to secession. Please, can you help? She has a scalp wound and is unconscious."

"She?" asked Goldberg in surprise, looking in shock at the black trousers and shirt. He shook off his amazement. "Saul, go get Doctor Bassky. Aaron, tell your mother we have an injured woman." Goldberg then pointed at Jed. "You . . . follow me."

Chapter 14

Thursday, May 2, 1861

"Mr. Tremblant."

Jed jerked awake and jumped to his feet. His hand went to his left side where his Colt normally hung, but it wasn't there. It hadn't helped that he had been dreaming of chasing and being chased by Anthony Duff through the streets of Baltimore. It took him a moment or two to orient himself to the unfamiliar surroundings and person standing in front of him.

"Easy, Mr. Tremblant, easy," soothed the bearded man.

Jed's brain switched on to recognize Doctor Bassky.

The good doctor visibly relaxed as Jed's senses kicked in. "Okay, now?"

"Yes, I'm sorry if I startled you," said Jed. "How is Mrs. Harrison?"

"She has regained consciousness but is still a little weak. I think jogging through the streets with her over your shoulder emptied most of the water from her lungs, which prevented problems from surfacing or being worse than they are. Still, I wouldn't recommend it for most of my patients. Don't go tiring her out."

"I won't. I promise," said Jed. "Thank you, Doctor Bassky. When do you think we can move her?"

"How far?"

Jim was about to mention her house in Mount Vernon but instead said, "To a home here in Baltimore . . . by carriage, of course."

"Of course," repeated Doctor Bassky with a slight smile. "Tonight, if she's not jarred and if she's up to it. Good day, Mr. Tremblant. If you need me, call me. I am discreet."

"Which is very much appreciated. If you will excuse me." Jed left the room and went down the hall. When he knocked on the door, it was opened by Mrs. Goldberg. One of her daughters stood beside the bed Maura was laying on, with the sheet and bedspread pulled up to her neck.

Maura smiled faintly when she saw Jed standing in the doorway. "You need to shave."

"You're looking much better than you did when I brought you here." He stepped up next to the bed. A disapproving sniff from the older Goldberg and a giggle from the younger made Jed take a step back. "May I introduce Mrs. Esther Goldberg and her daughter Hannah?"

"We have met." Maura tried to clear her throat twice. "Mrs. Goldberg, will you please pour me a glass of water?"

Mrs. Goldberg went over to the low dresser by the window and picked up the pitcher on top of it. Her face screwed up into a grimace as she gently shook the pitcher. It was easy to see that it was empty.

"Hannah, we need some fresh, clean water."

"Yes, mamma." Hannah took the pitcher and left the room.

"Are you going to ask me to leave?" asked Mrs. Goldberg after the door closed.

"That wouldn't be prudent," said Maura. "Jed, what happened?"

"What do you remember?" asked Jack cautiously. "About the warehouse?"

"I remember the warehouse and getting out," replied Maura. She didn't look Jed in the eye, and he couldn't tell if her contrite tone was one of apology or hidden anger. "We were on the roof, but I can't remember anything beyond that."

Jed gave a glance at Mrs. Goldberg. "We climbed down the downspout. The men inside the warehouse chased after us as we ran toward the harbor. You were shot a grazing blow just as we reached the water's edge. I brought you here because they were looking for us. I'm very grateful the Goldbergs took us in and helped us in our time of need."

"I, too, am grateful." Maura held out a hand to Mrs. Goldberg. She tutted and covered Maura back up, while giving a glare at Jed to avert his eyes. "However, I need to get home before I'm missed."

Jed and Mrs. Goldberg exchanged a glance over the recumbent Maura.

"Maura, you've been unconscious for almost two days," said Jed softly. "You've already been missed, but I sent word to your house. You had an accident and injured your head. The doctor won't allow any visitors to see you until you're better."

"Oh," gasped Maura as she seemed to shrink a little. "I missed a dinner at Marshal Kane's house."

"There will be others," interjected Mrs. Goldberg, patting Maura's hand.

"Of course, you are right," said Maura with a smile, but Jed knew Maura wasn't referring so much to the dinner as to the missed opportunity to gather information. "I must still get home and receive visitors."

"Doctor Bassky said you can leave tonight if you feel up to it," said Jed. All three of them looked up when there was a knock at the door. The sudden paleness of Maura's face and the tightening of her throat muscles to keep her stomach down was not lost on Jed. Before Mrs. Goldberg could get to the door, it opened, and Hannah came in carrying the pitcher.

"Father would like to have a word with you downstairs," said Hannah to Jed.

"If you will excuse me," said Jed as he headed out of the room.

"Will you help me get up?" he heard Maura ask.

"You're not well enough yet," said Mrs. Goldberg sternly.

" . . . and I won't get better lying in bed," countered Maura.

"You've said that to us lots of times," added Hannah, which produced a loud harrumph from Mrs. Goldberg.

"If you insist," grumped Mrs. Goldberg, but with a hint of respect in that phrase. "Hannah, get the bucket and be ready."

Jed beat a hasty retreat downstairs. Listening to Maura be ill was not something he wanted to do. He knew her indomitable will would get her on her feet, despite any dizziness or nausea. On the ground floor, he found Hiram Goldberg in his office.

"Tea?" offered Mr. Goldberg as he indicated for Jed to sit down. There was a steaming pot and two cups on a silver tray in front of him.

"Yes, thank you," said Jed. "Mrs. Harrison is awake and trying to get to her feet."

"She is a lot like my Esther. When she wants to do something, it's best just to stay out of her way."

"You have no idea," muttered Jed. "We will probably be leaving this evening, unless she has a relapse. I cannot thank you enough for your help. Oh, and I also must settle up with Doctor Bassky."

"I will send one of my sons over to find out what you owe. Now that your one lady is out of immediate danger, shall we talk about the other?"

"Ruth?" asked Jed in shock and disquietude.

"You know, my daughter, the one you met in Frederick?" asked Mr. Goldberg deadpanned. He then chuckled. "Her correspondence since meeting you has been, let's say, brighter."

"Mr. Goldberg . . ." Jed started to say but stopped when the older man held up his hand.

"I'm afraid of losing her again. Did she tell you what happened to her?"

"Yes, she told me. We discussed a bit about our respective families."

"Is that a judgment of us?"

"No," replied Jed. "I'm not familiar enough with your culture to make judgments. As for Ruth, she blames herself. She made no condemnation of her family. As I think on it, she is grateful for being allowed to stay." Jed chuckled. "Although I don't think she takes too kindly to Mrs. Samuelson."

"That harpy!" exclaimed Mr. Goldberg angrily. "A woman with nothing better to do than to snoop and spy on her neighbors."

"Words can harden one's heart," commented Jed.

"Yes, and love can soften one. It is far past the time to welcome her home."

"May I suggest that you ask her what she wants? She values the work she's doing for you."

Mr. Goldberg sighed. "Ruth does exceptional work, but I cannot ask her to continue. It would put her outside our cultural rules again." He shook his head. "Then, again, she may not belong here anymore."

"She wants to," said Jed. "She wants to be part of the family."

"And so she will be, but on her terms; not ones her mother and I set. I will take the train to Frederick tomorrow to talk to her."

"I know she would be delighted to see you," said Jed.

"May I ask, as Ruth's father, what are your intentions toward her?"

Jed thought about it and, after a few moments, said, "I want to help her. She told me there could be nothing between us but friendship. Our two cultures would never accept the two of us together."

"Unfortunately, that's true," said Mr. Goldberg ruefully. "You're Gentiles to us . . . Those that have strayed from God. We . . . We are the Christ killers to your religion's dogma. I don't know if either of you can give up your religious beliefs. Could you?"

"I think out West that wouldn't be a concern," stated Jed. "There, it is only what a man or woman does that matters."

"As of now," amended Mr. Goldberg. "Time will change attitudes as civilization moves into that expanse. Still, it is a land of opportunity . . ." Mr. Goldberg's face grew thoughtful. "May I talk more with you on the West?"

"Of course. If you're thinking of going west, it might be best to wait. Texas has joined the Confederacy and who knows which way Kansas will go. However, I will be more than happy to talk to you about it. What would you do there . . . farm . . . ranch?"

"Stores and banks, but it will have to wait until I return. You'd better head upstairs to check on the lady."

"I will, but I need to arrange a carriage for this evening. I wish I could get a hold of a cabbie named Robbie. He has one for hire, and he can be trusted."

"I know of him," said Mr. Goldberg. "I'll have one of my sons stop by his house to leave a message. When do you want him here? Around eight?"

"Yes, that would be fine. I need to get Mrs. Harrison home. Every hour we stay here, we put you in more danger."

"Ehh!" discounted Mr. Goldberg with an exaggerated shrug of his shoulders. "My people are always in danger."

"Why invite trouble?" countered Jed.

The rest of the day passed by quietly, except for Maura getting ill once from trying to stand up too quickly. Watching out the window, Jed observed a lone policeman making inquiries up and down the street. There were also two men, dressed in militia uniforms, who had patrolled around the neighborhood twice that Jed saw. They hadn't questioned anyone, but they were looking at everyone.

Robbie drove his carriage up to the front door of the Goldberg's establishment later that evening. Maura had squawked a little at the notion of Jed carrying her down the stairs. Mrs. Goldberg put an end to her argument by saying that if Maura fell down the steps, she would just drag her out to the carriage no matter what shape she was in.

"Good evening, sir," greeted Robbie as he set the break and climbed down to help Jed, who had carried Maura out of the house. "Here you go, miss."

"Watch her head," warned Jed.

"I can . . . talk for myself," panted Maura, who was very pale and unable to focus her eyes.

"You might need this." Mrs. Goldberg handed Jed a large bowl and a clean towel.

"Thank you. I owe you more than I can repay."

"Shalom," said Mr. Goldberg. "That means peace. We use it as a greeting for hello and goodbye."

"Peace," mused Jed. "I wish we had more of it. Shalom, Mr. Goldberg."

"I'll be gone for two days to go to Frederick."

"Frederick?" questioned Mrs. Goldberg. "Why are you going to Frederick?"

"I have business there," stated Mr. Goldberg. "I'll discuss it with you later tonight."

"Indeed, we shall!" Mrs. Goldberg stormed back into the house.

Mr. Goldberg shrugged his shoulders and turned to follow his wife, waving his arms to make Hannah and his two sons precede him. Even though the Goldbergs were not looking, Jed gave them a nod of thanks before climbing into the carriage.

"Go easy, Robbie, and watch the potholes," Jed said. "How are you feeling, Maura?"

Maura gasped as a carriage jerked into motion. Her hand covered her mouth as she fought down the nausea. With a determined swallow, she collected herself and leaned back into the cushions, closing her eyes.

"Jed?"

"Yes, Maura?"

"Would I really have missed him?"

"Yes, I believe so. Firing up or down at someone is tricky enough. I could see your hand shaking, either from emotion or because you had not rested after climbing the downspout. The fact that I hit anyone at all was pure luck. I was trying just to keep their heads down."

"Hannah has made you her idol. She told me everything you did after I was shot—swimming underwater; carrying me from the docks; evading the patrols looking for us; staying by my bedside the entire time . . ."

"I was not at your bedside the entire time!" huffed an embarrassed Jed.

Maura gave him a weak smile. "I cannot see Mrs. Goldberg allowing it. You have become a larger-than-life hero in Hannah's eyes."

"I hope she's not going to spread the tale around," worried Jed. "We would both be in danger if she does."

"She—" The carriage hit a bump, and Maura had pressed her lips tightly together. "She seems to understand the need for secrecy. Her mother said she will remind the girl that this is real life, not some penny novel."

"I hope so."

"I also want to thank you for saving me," said Maura as the carriage took a turn.

"You're welcome, but please let me know next time."

"Jed?"

163

"Yes?"

"Hand . . . hand me that bowl."

APART FROM THAT ONE LITTLE incident, the trip proceeded without any problems. Robbie stopped a block away from Maura's house, and Jed got out to scout around. A quick look revealed a dark street only lit at intervals by the oil streetlamps. On silent feet, he sneaked up the street to see if anyone was around who would be on the lookout for them.

Sans hat, cloak, and cane, Jed knew he cut a conspicuous figure. Lack of proper attire was not quite as bad as wearing shiny buttons or jewelry out in the Indian Territory, but in this setting, it could be just as deadly. Sticking to the shadows, Jed saw just one or two casual passersby at a distance from the house but no one in the immediate vicinity. He hurried back to the corner to wave Robbie forward.

Robbie pulled up and stopped the carriage in front of Maura's house. Jed quickly opened the carriage door and helped Maura out until he could lift her into his arms. He took a step toward the house before stopping and turning around.

"Don't expect you can pay me with your hands full," joked Robbie. "Tomorrow morning?"

"Yes and thank you."

Robbie nodded and drove off. Jed turned back to the house and went around to the kitchen door. Maura didn't say anything but quirked an eyebrow when Jed bypassed the front door. Maura knocked on it lightly, and the side door sprung open.

"Praise the Lord!" gasped Tabitha. "I've had heart palpitations for the past two days. The mayor and his wife, the marshal and his wife, and a host of others have all been here to give their get-well wishes. It's been all I could do to fend them off. The marshal is due to stop by here tonight. Miss Eunice is upstairs at the front door trying to keep him away. Just don't stand there, get inside."

"I will," said Jed dryly. "As soon as you move out of the doorway."

Tabitha stiffened at the perceived rebuke but stood aside to allow Jed to enter. The butler in his shirt sleeves and a housekeeper in her robe hurried down the service steps.

"You can put me down now," said Maura to Jed.

"And risk having you faint or get ill?" asked Jed with a shake of his head. "You need to be in bed and rest for at least a couple more days."

"You heard Tabitha. Marshal Kane is coming here . . . tonight. I need to have him see me. You know it's too late for this to be a social call. You actually want him storming in here to find me?"

"No." Jed turned to Tabitha. "Have you told anyone where the accident occurred?"

"Yes, I told them it was in the morning room," she replied.

"Show me. You two, follow us."

"What are you doing?" asked Maura as Jed headed toward the stairs.

"Making sure everyone's story matches." He stopped at the top of the stairs and looked at the housekeeper. "Will you please bring up cleaning solution for getting blood out of a carpet?"

"Yes, sir." She quickly departed.

The morning room was to the left of the main door as one entered and was laid out to greet visitors. Plush comfortable chairs were placed for conversation with a low, rectangular, marble-topped table in the center. A lady's desk was against the back wall. A curio cabinet sat next to the desk. Its shelves held porcelain figurines, small miniatures, and Oriental knickknacks. Eunice was in the room, and the relief she felt at seeing Maura was evident on her face.

"I told them she hit her head on this low table," said Tabitha as Jed set Maura down gently into a chair.

"The wound is to the back of her head, so she would have to be falling backward," said Jed. There was an area carpet underneath the table. "Could you have slipped on the floor and hit your head?"

"It would be too far away from the table," said Maura as the housekeeper entered the room. "I would need to take several steps backward before falling over. How about tripping on the carpet?"

"You would trip forward, not backward," said Jed.

Everyone stayed silent, thinking about the problem.

The butler coughed. "A mouse, Miss Maura?"

"I hate mice!" exclaimed Maura. "But I grew up on a plantation and killed more than my fair share of them. I'd shy away from them, but that would be it."

"Not if you were surprised and had a broken heel," thought Jed out loud. "I need a pair of her shoes quickly."

Tabitha took off at a run. Jed kneeled by a corner of the table and pulled a folding knife from his pocket.

"What are you doing?" asked Eunice.

"Head wounds bleed," hissed Jed as he pricked his thumb. He put a very thin smear of blood on the underside edge of the table and blew on it to dry it as his thumb dripped onto the carpet. Placing his thumb on the carpet, Jed moved it around until there was a bloody oval. He looked up at the housekeeper and asked, "Can you take out just enough that there will be a pink stain left?"

"It'll set," said the housekeeper. "We could've saved your thumb and just used some of the blood from the meat in the kitchen."

"I should have thought of that." Jed wrapped his thumb in his handkerchief.

"It's all right, Justine," said Maura to the housekeeper. "We can get a new carpet."

Tabitha came back holding a pair of shoes. They were black and ankle-high with a three-inch heel on them. Justine started working on the carpet stain as Tabitha handed the shoes to Jed.

"One heel is loose already," she said.

Jed took the shoe with the good heel. Digging the heel into the carpet about five feet away from the table, he leaned on the shoe with all his weight and twisted it. There was a small ripping sound just before the heel snapped completely off.

"Where would you put these?"

"Down in the boot room to be repaired," answered Justine before Tabitha could. "In the repair box. Here, take this, too."

Justine handed Tabitha the pail she had brought up. Tabitha took it and the shoes and hurried out of the room.

"It's time to get you upstairs," said Jed to Maura.

"I can get upstairs on my own," snapped Maura.

Everyone froze and looked toward the front door when someone banged on it loudly.

The butler went to the window to look out. "It's the marshal, and he has a number of police officers. It looks like they're surrounding the house."

"That settles that question." Jed scooped Maura up in his arms. "He can't see you down here in that black outfit, and he surely can't see me here."

"Go," said Eunice. "I'll try to stall him."

Chapter 15

Thursday, May 2, 1861

"Good evening, sir. I'm afraid—OOF!"

Marshal Kane stepped into the foyer and stiff-armed Maura's butler against the wall. Three police officers with revolvers in their hands brushed past him and fanned out throughout the ground floor.

"Sir—"

"Quiet," ordered Marshal Kane, chilling in the calmness of his voice. "Where is your mistress?"

"She's upstairs in bed, but—"

The butler's words were cut off as Marshal Kane pulled him by the shirt front away from the wall, and then slammed him into it again. Sighing in exasperation, he grabbed the gasping butler by the arm and propelled the man into the first room off to the right.

The morning room door opened, and Eunice stepped into the foyer. Her eyes opened in alarm, and her hand flew to her throat. "What are you doing, Marshal Kane?"

Kane stepped to one side, blocking her retreat further into the house. He held up one hand, indicating the door that he just pushed the butler through.

"This way, if you please."

The parlor was lit by a single oil lamp. Kane shoved the butler onto the sofa. When the door at the far end clicked open, the marshal spun around and dropped into a crouch. He didn't take his hand off the butt of his pistol until Tabitha and Justine were prodded in by one of his officers.

"Found these two hiding in the kitchen," said the officer.

"What were you two doing?" asked Marshal Kane.

Justine placed her hand on Tabitha's arm. "Just resting before bedtime, sir," Justine said.

"Really?" scoffed Marshal Kane. He looked at his officer. "What were they doing?"

"Sitting at the table drinking tea, I think."

Kane closed his eyes. "Then say that instead of they were hiding. You two, sit down. Officer, watch them."

Turning, Kane saw Eunice standing beside the curio cabinet. He pointed at a chair, and she sat on it.

He strode out into the foyer. The two other officers were coming back from checking the ground floor. Kane met them at the foot of the main stairs.

"Anything?" he asked them.

"No, sir," answered one. "There was just the butler on this floor, and the two servants we found in the kitchen. The other five must be upstairs. We have not found Mrs. Harrison's companion yet."

"She's in the parlor. Gather the others up and bring them to the parlor," ordered Marshal Kane. "After that, search this place from top to bottom, but do it carefully. I don't want anything broken or torn apart. Do you understand?"

Both men nodded.

"Good. Get going. I'll be calling on the mistress."

The two officers raced up the steps to the second floor and then climbed up to the servants' level. Marshal Kane took a second to straighten his frock coat before marching up the steps. He paid no attention to the muffled cries of surprise, bewilderment, and outrage coming down the stairs from the floor above. Walking to the double doors leading to the master bedroom, he flung them open with the crash.

"Oh!" gasped Maura. She was sitting up in a large bed with a lamp lit on the bedside stand next to her. She clutched her pale green embroidered dressing robe around her neck before putting her hands back underneath the covers. A white wimple covered her head. "Marshal Kane! What are you doing in my bedroom? You must leave at once!"

The master bedroom was opulent and elegant. A large triple dresser stood against the wall opposite the bed with a matching cedar chest near the footboard. Left of the door, the attached bookcase faced two windows that overlooked the street. Paintings of mountains and countryside adorned the walls.

"I think not, Mrs. Harrison," replied Marshal Kane. The sound of people being forcibly hustled down the stairs was clearly audible. "No one has heard from you in two days. With all the unrest and the number of darkies you keep for servants, I and a certain number of gentlemen became concerned for your safety."

"You may tell them I'm recovering from my fall and should be up and about soon," stated Maura tartly. An officer hurried past the bedroom's open doors, then backed up to look at Maura. "You brought your men into my house?"

"Get on with your search," growled Marshal Kane to the officer before closing the bedroom doors.

"Search?" asked Maura angrily.

"My apologies," said Marshal Kane, not sounding sincere at all. "I should have closed the doors when I came in."

"I want you and your men to leave!"

"It has come to my attention, and I just received confirmation tonight, that a Lieutenant Jonathan Harrison was killed during the Pratt Street Massacre," said Marshal Kane, moving so that he stood right next to Maura. "He was an officer of the . . ." His face took on a look of disgust. "Connecticut Militia. He was also married to one Maura McKenzie Harrison. The woman who I thought had breeding and taste."

Marshal Kane froze at the ratcheting sound of a hammer being cocked from underneath the bed covers, and his eyes grew very wide.

"I'm still a little dizzy," said Maura sweetly. "However, at this range, I'm sure I can shoot off some piece of your anatomy or, at least, hit you in the belly. Why don't you sit down, George, before something unfortunate happens."

Marshal Kane backed up to a chair that had been placed close to the bed. Sitting slowly, he kept his hands in plain sight on the arms of the chair.

"You heard I was married to a northern officer, and you automatically assumed the worst, didn't you?" Maura eased her right hand from under the covers. Her aim of the four-barrel derringer did not waver.

"These are not trusting times," said Marshal Kane. "One of our warehouses was broken into two nights ago by a spy. We have not seen or heard about a northern spy since that time. You have also been incommunicado. There are those who think you may be working for the North. Why would you marry a Yankee?"

"Could it be that I married for love?" asked Maura rhetorically, waving the pistol around and causing Marshal Kane to stiffen in alarm. "Of course, there's the possibility that my father had entered into a financial agreement with Mr. Harrison, the senior; that it was not an equitable arrangement, and I married the son to prevent shame and dishonor to my father. Does it matter that the son desired me and wanted me, no matter what the cost?"

"Why did you ship his body home without accompanying it?"

"The Harrisons are extremely rich, and my being there would inflame a complicated situation. Do you believe they would welcome me with open arms or that I wished to be associated with them?"

"You don't have to show off your vocabulary to me," said Marshal Kane, relaxing back into the chair.

"Inflame . . . aggravate, it doesn't matter. Have you ever been on the receiving end of northern vindictiveness?"

"Yes, I have," replied Marshal Kane. "Why stay here? Why not go home?"

"If I go home, my father would feel the contract was not fulfilled. He'd feel honor bound to compensate the Harrisons. I wed their son, went to bed with him, and played the dutiful wife. My family doesn't owe the Harrisons anything else!"

"The contract is void. That is, if it was drawn up before the Confederacy declared its independence," said Marshal Kane. "How did you injure yourself?"

"What?" Maura seemed to shake herself out of her reverie, and her face lost the bitterness. Inhaling deeply, she blew out a cleansing breath before smiling sheepishly and uncocking the pistol. With deft movements, she put it away in the pocket of her robe. "As you said, Marshal Kane, there's been some unrest lately. The North shall surely overcome us if we fight among ourselves."

"So, you're for the South?" Kane steepled his fingers together.

"My home is there," said Maura.

"You still have not told me how you injured yourself."

"I was in the morning room when a mouse scurried right under my feet. I took a step back and then I was falling. I woke up several hours later with my head bandaged. My heel had caught on the rug and broken. I was told I hit my head on the marble table."

Kane winced in sympathy. "You're lucky to be alive."

"Now, if you'd be so kind as to open the door. My reputation has suffered enough by having it closed."

"My men know this is business, not pleasure," replied Marshal Kane, although he did open the doors. "How true of a daughter are you to the Confederacy?"

"You ask me that like you need me to do something," said Maura suspiciously. There was a crash from a nearby room. "You can ask your men to stop searching, can't you?"

"Unfortunately, no." He opened her closet and began searching. "I must report back that a thorough search was made."

"Well, look all you want, and you might as well tell me what you want from me while you do so."

"We would like you to get to know someone. He is a Northerner and has caused a couple of problems."

"Why haven't you just . . . well, you know?" Maura felt a little sick to her stomach. She was sure she knew who Marshal Kane was referring to.

"That was proposed, but then those Black Republicans in Washington would send others. We know who this one is, and we can keep track of him to find his accomplices."

"Who is he and where is he now?" asked Maura.

"He is Lieutenant Jedidiah Tremblant of the Illinois Militia." Kane moved away from the closet to open the drawers of the dresser. "He was sent here to spy on us. We know he was in Frederick when the legislature voted on secession. The Tremblants of that cesspool of the state have dabbled in land and law. It is therefore inadvisable to bribe him."

"I have not said I would meet him." She shook her head, grimacing at the real pain it caused. "It will not do. I cannot disguise my voice, and the moment I say anything to him, he will know I am from the South."

"Yes, but there is one point in your favor." Kane shut the last drawer. "Your late husband was a Connecticut officer and, if you let him know that you have northern sentiments, . . ."

"Sir!" exclaimed Maura. "I would lose all the friends I've made here and my standing!"

Marshal Kane smiled. "Those of us who know will stand by you. You would be a heroine if—let's say *when*—Maryland becomes part of the Confederacy. Events are happening or will happen very soon."

"Very well," said Maura.

Kane swelled with pride. However, he deflated when she added, "Although, I will need certain assurances if I am to play the role of the spy."

"What kind of assurances?"

"A letter from President Davis saying I'm spying . . . no, *working* on behalf of the Confederate States of America." Marshal Kane's mouth gaped open. "Also, a letter from him or whoever is in charge of finances stating that Rosedale, our plantation, is free from any past financial obligations."

"You can't be serious!" gasped Marshal Kane.

"Of course, I am." Maura daintily arranged and smoothed out the covers over her. "I will not be an object to be used and cast aside at the whims of fate, like those working women who were going to be cast out onto the street by you. Nor do I relish being tried for treason when I return home."

"I do not have that type of authority," growled Marshal Kane.

"Someone does, especially if Maryland is to become a Confederate state soon. In the meantime, I will ask Mr.

Tremblant to dinner this Saturday. You, the mayor, and your wives will be invited."

"I've met the man," said Marshal Kane. "Coming to dinner with him would not be a good idea."

"According to the newspapers, the state legislature did not vote for secession," said Maura primly. "Nor would they allow for the question to be placed on the next ballot. You said Tremblant was in Frederick, which means you suspect he influenced the senators. He will be basking in his glory, and his guard will be down. The dinner will give you a chance to reassure him of your continued support for the state of Maryland."

Marshal Kane looked at her in amazement. "I'm shocked and awed by the deviousness of your plan. You're exactly the right person to worm her way into Tremblant's confidence."

"You know, if you're keeping an eye on him, then I suppose, he's keeping an eye on you. If he finds out about this totally unwarranted search, it would make him more predisposed in my favor but," Maura gave Marshal Kane a stern look, "nothing will get done without those letters."

"It will take time," equivocated Marshal Kane.

"Are you sure you have that time to waste?" asked Maura. "It would be a shame if we could have prevented this man from interfering with Maryland joining the Confederacy but didn't because of the lack of a piece of paper."

"Set up your dinner, Mrs. Harrison." Marshal Kane headed for the door. "If I can, I'll have your assurances then."

"Marshal Kane?"

Kane stopped and looked back at her.

"You have not looked under the bed."

Marshal Kane sighed and went down on one knee. Maura pulled up the bedspread enough so that he could see that there was nothing underneath the bed. Giving her a disgruntled look, Marshal Kane got back to his feet.

"Where is Mr. Tremblant now?" asked Maura.

Marshal Kane's mouth twitched in embarrassment. "We don't know. He was in Frederick but returned here to Baltimore."

"Then it's probably a good thing I will be helping you. Do you know where he's staying?"

"At the Kent Hotel." Marshal Kane tipped his hat at her. "Until Saturday, Mrs. Harrison."

"Good evening, Marshal Kane."

Kane headed back downstairs, calling for his men on that floor to join him. He went into the parlor where all the servants were gathered under guard.

"You." He pointed at Tabitha. "Show me the morning room."

Looking around hesitantly, Tabitha stood. Justine also did so.

"Where do you think you're going?" asked the police guard.

"Miss Maura don't let none of her women servants go off alone," answered Justine.

"Let her come." Kane stood aside to let Tabitha precede him.

In the morning room, Marshal Kane took in the layout before moving to the marble table. After looking at the stain on the carpet, he felt around the edge of the table. He didn't say anything as he examined the small red flakes that had adhered to his fingers. He rubbed his fingers over the stain in the carpet. "It's still wet."

"We've been trying to get the bloodstain out," stated Justine.

"It looks like it's set into the pile. Your cleaning skills need improvement. You left blood on the underside of the table." Justine looked at the floor in shame. "Where are the bandages and her shoes?"

"Downstairs," said Tabitha.

"Show me."

Tabitha and Justine took Marshal Kane to the basement. Lingering food odors vied with the earthy smell of the root bins and the sharp tang of polishing solution. Tabitha opened a door to the laundry room, letting warm, moist air to escape.

"The bandages have been boiled," she said. "They're soaking in that vat. Don't put your hand in. It's borax and potash in there."

Marshal Kane grabbed a large laundry paddle leaning against the wall. Gently stirring the contents of the vat, he lifted several strips of white cloth out of the water.

"At least, your laundry skills exceed your cleaning skills," commented Marshal Kane. "Shoes?"

"In the boot room." Justine indicated a door just down the hallway.

Marshal Kane walked into the room and examined the shoe with a broken heel. Tossing the shoes nonchalantly back into the bin, he didn't say a word as he headed back upstairs. With a flick of his head, his men headed outside. He took one more look around and walked out.

ALL THE SERVANTS BREATHED A sigh of relief as the butler hurried to lock the front door. Excited conversation burst forth from everyone until Justine clapped to silence them.

"I know everyone's excited," she said to them. "Miss Maura's still upstairs resting from her accident. Wondering will get us nothing but trouble. Tomorrow will be here before we know it. Miss Maura will let us know why the police were here. Now, go back to bed, and remember, we don't talk about Miss Maura outside this house."

All the servants, except for Tabitha and Eunice, headed back to their beds. The two women hurried to the master bedroom.

Maura was still sitting up in her bed. "Are they gone?"

"Yes," replied Tabitha.

Maura slumped wearily back into the pillows. "Jed?"

There was a click as the bookshelf swung away from the wall. Behind it was a triangular, open space underneath the stairs going up to the floor above. Jed, slightly hunched over, came out and pushed the bookcase back into the position.

"A priest hole?" Eunice asked.

"Let's call it a hideaway hole," said Maura, throwing off the covers and standing up. "It came . . . with the . . . house."

Jed dashed forward and caught the swaying girl before she fell. He quickly lifted her back onto the bed. As he covered her up, he got a tantalizing view of her shapely legs all the way up to her knees. "Ahem." Jed turned away. "You need to rest."

"You heard him." Maura kept her eyes closed to keep her head from spinning. "They have something planned, and it's going to happen soon. You've seen the list of stockpiled weapons and equipment they have. I can't be an invalid! There's too much to do!"

Jed remained silent, remembering the helplessness he felt the times he was wounded. Of course, then he had Beatrice to nurse him through it. Maura's Jonathan was gone. He was also afraid that any affection and consolation he gave her now would be misconstrued as pity and condescension.

"Maura, listen to me," he said.

She just lay there with her eyes closed. "I'm listening," she replied after a moment's silence. "I'd rather not look at anything right now."

"Whatever they have planned will not happen until after Saturday," said Jed. "Plan the dinner and regain your strength. They are still trying to repair the steam gun. Remember that Duff is going to be in the middle of it all."

Maura's eyes snapped open, and Jed could see her mind working.

"I promise I will rest in bed all day tomorrow. I will send an invitation for dinner to your hotel." Maura moved a little to one side. "Oh, your pistol."

Fishing the small derringer out of the pocket of her robe, she held it up for Jed.

"Please, keep it. The bullets in there went for a swim in the harbor, so I can't be one hundred percent certain they will fire. President Lincoln sent me six guns with ammunition. I can't even imagine the cost. I will send over two dry boxes of ammunition later."

"Might not fire? That would've been nice to know when I was threatening Marshal Kane with it."

"My apologies. You didn't need it, so the point is moot. Tomorrow I will see the commanding officer at Fort McHenry and warn him. He's not going to like that I don't have any specifics as to what is going to occur."

"Tabitha, Eunice, would you mind if I had a word or two alone with Jed?"

"I most certainly do mind," snorted Tabitha. "You being alone up here in your bedroom with a man?"

"I was up here alone with Marshal Kane," retorted Maura.

"No you weren't, and you know it," argued Eunice. "You had Captain Tremblant hiding in the closet."

Maura giggled at the absurdity of the situation. Jed couldn't help but smile and coughed a couple times to stifle his own laughter. Tabitha tried to be serious about it but couldn't contain her own laughter. Eunice smirked and shook her head.

"Given the nature of her injury, I believe your mistress is safe from any advances I would make," said Jed.

Maura cocked an eyebrow at the word *would*. "You can wait just outside the door if you like."

Tabitha blew out a sharp breath of air through her nose, but she gave Maura a smile and a nod as she went out into the hallway.

"Don't be too long. She needs to sleep." Eunice left the room.

"... advances you would make?" asked Maura after they were gone.

"You wanted to speak with me alone," reminded Jed, deflecting the question.

"In your travels tomorrow, can you go to the gentlemen's club? The renovations are being done, and I've not been able to check up on them. I need to make sure they will finish on time. Could you also check on Chrissy and see how she's doing?"

Maura's face took on an embarrassed look, and she stared down at the bedspread.

"I wanted to say I'm sorry about the trouble I caused at the warehouse. I ... I ... Every time I think of Jonathan, I'm filled with such rage. It ..." She had to stop speaking because of the emotion choking her.

"We will get him, Maura," said Jed softly. "It may be tomorrow, or the next day, or a year from now. I will not let it be forgotten or go unpunished. Jonathan's spirit may rest easy. As for the warehouse, you forgot your Clausewitz."

"I beg your pardon?"

"Simplicity, which also means planning. I don't believe I told you the catchphrase for planning."

"And that is . . . ?"

"Prior proper planning prevents . . . uh . . . poor performance," quoted Jed, omitting one vulgar term.

Chapter 16

Friday, May 3, 1861

THIS IS NOT HOW *I thought I would be spending my morning,* thought Jed.

Yet, here he was, standing in the middle of the main floor of a half-torn-apart bank, soon to be a gentlemen's club if the foreman would stop quibbling about every little detail.

No, Jed decided. He wasn't arguing about every detail. He was trying to change the floor plan so he could use less material and finish ahead of the completion date. The contract had an early completion bonus on a graded scale. The earlier the foreman completed the work, the more he would be paid.

"Unless there is a specific, valid reason to change the plans, they will remain as they are," said Jed to the foreman, "and at the quality that was quoted when the contract was signed."

The foreman opened his mouth to argue but saw the resolve in Jed's eyes. He blew out a long breath of defeat.

"As you say, sir. We'll go to and get her done."

Jed clapped the man on the shoulder. "The day you complete this project, I'll stand two rounds for you and your men at the neighborhood bar. You can tell them that."

"Thank you, sir," said the foreman with a smile.

Jed headed toward the back of the building where a large walk-in safe was located. The new club manager was inside taking inventory.

"How are you doing, Mr. Lachlin?" asked Jed.

Timothy Lachlin was stocky, in his mid-forties, with a trimmed, dark brown beard. He had been in service as a youth, but seeing no real chance of advancement made him seek his future elsewhere. He had schooling and clerked for a shipping company and an accounting firm. After that, he had operated a successful bar until the election riots had completely vandalized and destroyed that establishment.

Mr. Jenkins had recommended him. Jed and Maura found Lahlin to be well spoken, knowledgeable about society's rules, and a union man.

During their interview a week ago, he told them, "As our good police marshal has said, I am one of those worst kind of people. I voted for Lincoln."

After Maura and Jed had outlined the parameters of how the club was to be run, Timothy sat back and stared at them for a moment or two.

"Let me see if I have this correct," he finally said. "You want me to run a gentlemen's club for the upper-class of Baltimore, particularly those of southern persuasion. If the staff hears anything of importance, they are to let you know. By things of importance, you mean like armed revolt?"

"Caches of weapons and supplies," said Jed. "Shipping of these items; talk of sabotages or inciting riots; and things like that. Oh, and of anyone being in Maryland who shouldn't be here."

Timothy broke out laughing, "That's half the population!" He brought this humor down to a chuckle. "Sorry, but you just described the two of you. Mr. Tremblant, I can guess why you're doing this. Mrs. Harrison, by your accent, you're from the South. I don't understand your motives."

"I am from Virginia, and my reasons are personal," said Maura. "Let it be sufficient to say that I was shown the potential of what this nation could be, provided that it is not torn apart."

"Fair enough, but you do understand that the two of you will not be allowed into the club after it opens."

"I am responsible for the women on the third floor," said Maura in a tone that brooked no dissension.

"Tell me about the women," said Timothy.

"They were thrown out of the house they had been in because the madame made derogatory comments about the

South to the Marshal," said Maura. "That remark got the madame arrested and the house closed down. Now they are working for us and will be collecting information. They all want to keep working, as they put it."

"I have to tell you that I was going to turn you down because of the, uh, let's say, third-floor establishment. However, you're telling me that these women have chosen to be, uh, working girls?"

"Ask them," suggested Jed. "I had the same doubts and reservations that you have now, but these women like the freedom, both personal and financial, that this life gives them. They also understand the serious risks they could run into."

Holding up his hand, Timothy had told them, "Don't say anymore. I think you're playing a very dangerous game, but given the times, I can see the necessity for it. I've already had one business burned out from under me. I don't want to have a repeat of that. I'll take care of hiring staff who will keep your names away from the club."

"I'm afraid Mayor Brown and Marshal Kane know I purchased the building and that it's just intended to be a club," said Maura. "I asked them to be on the board."

"Keeping your enemies close?" asked Timothy. "The board is usually the people who hire the manager."

"Unless you're a genteel Southern lady who's used to getting her own way to protect her investment," said Maura with a smile.

They had hired Timothy, and he was the one who suggested using the vault to store the club's valuable assets, like their liquor, supplies, and cash. Jed would've left the construction in Timothy's hands, but Maura insisted that he had enough to do, and it should be either Jed or herself.

Now that she was injured, that left Jed to check on the progress. And here he was.

"I'm doing well, sir," answered Timothy in response to Jed's question. "We're almost fully stocked, and I found a grocery for the fresh foodstuff we will need daily—mint, lemons, and the like."

"How are you and the women upstairs getting along?"

"A couple of them thought they had the run of the entire building, but Miss Schaefer set them straight. I'm amazed at the amount of information they have obtained. I could, if I was so inclined, set up a very good business doing blackmail. Miss Schaefer and I thought it would be better to coordinate our information rather than send up duplicate reports. Mrs. Harrison stops by every other day to check on them. I have to say, the women upstairs are ecstatic about their percentage of the profits. Do you think the construction of the club will finish on time?"

"The majority of the renovation is completed," replied Jed. "The remainder is the finishing touches that take time, according to the foreman. He's trying to cut the time down, but the club will open on Thursday. Mrs. Harrison has already sent out the invitations. Woe be to the foreman if he's not done by then."

"The staff and I will be ready. We only—" Timothy looked at Jed with disdain. In a very neutral tone, he said, "I'm sorry, sir, but the club is not open yet, and only certain members are allowed access at this time. Are you a member-to-be?"

Jed felt a prickling sensation between the shoulder blades as he heard footsteps behind him.

"No," replied Jed with an ingratiating smile. "I understand Mrs. Maura Harrison is the owner of this establishment. I have just received an invitation to dinner from her and hoped to make her acquaintance a little sooner. I'm also in town on business, and I'm looking for a club to join."

"A woman?" derided Timothy. "No woman will be allowed past the front doors, owner or not."

"Well said," came a voice from behind Jed. "Causing trouble, Mr. Tremblant?"

Jed turned. "Not in the least, Marshal Kane." He looked past Kane at the man with him. "You must be Mayor Brown. Allow me to introduce myself. I'm Jedidiah Tremblant of Illinois."

"A pleasure to meet you, Mr. Tremblant," said Mayor Brown, shaking his hand. His face and tone were pleasant, but Jed got the impression that this meeting was anything besides that. "What brings you to our fair city?"

"Business," replied Jed cryptically. "However, I have received a dinner invitation from Mrs. Maura Harrison. I understand she is a widow and one of the great beauties of your city."

"That she is," replied Mayor Brown. "Her father owns a plantation in Salem, Virginia. We're hoping to make her stay pleasant and one of a more permanent nature."

"Property."

"I beg your pardon?" queried Mayor Brown, perplexed.

"Property," repeated Jed. "Nothing binds a person more to a place than owning property there. If she does indeed own this building, which I'm seriously beginning to doubt by that man's account," he gestured at Timothy, "then she has a stake here. Of course, businesses can be run by a manager or by a board. It takes a residence to firmly establish one to a community or city."

"You should bring that up to her when you're at dinner," said Marshal Kane.

"Not if she is as beautiful as is rumored." He gave a shudder. "Discussing money with a beautiful woman, or any woman, would be the last thing on my list of things to talk about with them. I assume, since she's here, that she and her parents have no affection for those deluded, idiotic, dimwitted morons who actually believe in the Confederacy."

Marshal Kane took a step forward, and Jed could tell he had gotten under his skin. However, Mayor Brown put a restraining hand on the bigger man's arm and stopped him with just a touch. Kane settled down, and Jed reappraised the dynamics between the two men.

He had thought the marshal was a mover and shaker of the pro-South faction in Baltimore. With that one gesture, Jed saw the mayor in a new light.

Jed heard that Mayor Brown had walked alongside the federal troops during the Pratt Street riots. One soldier claimed the mayor had snatched his rifle out of his hands and fired it into the crowds. Jed had assumed that, if it were true, it was a heat of the moment action. Now, he was wondering if it wasn't a deliberate act. The mayor could have been trying to incite the crowd to further violence, or he could have wanted the bullet to miss whoever the soldier was going to shoot.

Jed took a step back as a new, more chilling, thought came to him. It could've been that the mayor was actually shooting at a target of his own choosing. Duff had said the riots had started too soon. It could be that the mayor eliminated an adversary or rival during the riots.

"I believe you just maligned quite a few people who are neither idiots nor dimwitted," stated Mayor Brown pleasantly. "Will you think of yourself as such when the federal government takes away your rights and dictates how you should live?"

"Life, liberty, and the pursuit of happiness?" asked Jed. "Or are we discussing freedom of religion, freedom of speech, and the right against unreasonable searches, like last night?"

"If you are referring to the police being at Mrs. Harrison's residence, there was a reason for that," said Mayor Brown. "We had been told she'd been injured, but no one had heard from her for two days. We became concerned and desired to check on her well-being. I, myself, was turned away from her door the day before, which worried me. It's strange that you know of it."

"She sent me an invitation to dinner on Saturday. Being new to the city, I checked out the location of her house and heard some gossip. She must be feeling better to host a dinner party."

"I've been assured she's getting better," said Mayor Brown. "I will also be at the dinner on Saturday. May we continue our discussion on constitutional rights then, especially in regard to the Tenth Amendment?"

"The rights of states versus that of federal authority?"

The mayor's question had clearly been couched as a dismissal. Jed took one last look around. "You have an excellent club here. Maybe one day you will invite me to join it."

As Jed walked out the door, Marshal Kane said, "An invitation to this club? Not hardly."

"Don't be too hasty, George," advised Mayor Brown. "Do you have your men following him?"

Kane nodded.

"An invitation here would put him at a disadvantage. He would have no one else to call upon if we wanted to isolate him. It's also a place where we may be able to compromise him."

"With the whores upstairs?" scoffed Marshal Kane. "A censure from society here in Baltimore would mean nothing to him. I told you what he did to those three workers from Winans's foundry. He is used to fighting and blood, and he's very good at it. I'm sure he was one of the two men who were at the warehouse the other night."

"We need to find out who he's working for and who's assisting him," said Brown.

"I believe Mrs. Harrison is the key to obtaining that information," said Kane with a smile.

"Will she, though? Even with the urgency with which I requested their response, President Davis could take days to send us what we need . . . if indeed, he responds to us at all."

"Gentlemen!"

The men turned around to see Timothy coming out of the vault holding two crystal tumblers with an inch of amber liquid in each glass.

"I must thank you for evicting that man from the premises. I would also like to ask your opinion on this twelve-year Scotch whiskey I've just obtained."

Chapter 17

Saturday, May 4, 1861

"Good evening, sir."

"Good evening," said Jed to the butler. "I am Jedidiah Tremblant of Illinois."

"Yes, sir. You are expected. Mrs. Harrison is receiving her guests in the drawing room."

Jed allowed the butler to show him to the room. Paul had schooled his features so there wasn't even a hint of his recognizing Jed. Lilting notes from a piano stopped as soon as Paul opened the door.

Maura, in a low-cut, black gown, was the first person Jed saw, despite the fact that she was seated at the piano across the room. Her beautiful face drew his gaze. To Jed, her sparkling eyes and smile told him in more than words how happy she was to see him.

There was a very slight movement of her shoulders, and her entire countenance changed. She lifted her hand and was assisted to her feet by the Maryland Militia captain standing next to her. Jed's perception expanded, and he finally began to notice the other people in the room. Besides the captain, there was a lieutenant from the Maryland Militia standing beside the piano. Closer to the sofa was Mayor Brown, Marshal Kane, and two women in their mid-to-late forties. Opposite them, by the window, was a police captain in his blue uniform, a woman about his age, and two younger ladies. Jed had to try very hard to keep from laughing as one of those ladies was Chrissy Schaefer.

"Mr. Tremblant, I am so glad you could attend our dinner," said Maura, coming over to greet him. "May I introduce Mayor George Brown and his wife, Anna, and Marshal George Kane and his wife, Anne."

"Gentlemen," said Jed, nodding acknowledgment to their names. "Ladies."

"This is Captain Daniel Wilcott and Lieutenant Herbert Frijack of the Maryland Militia," said Maura, leading Jed over to the piano. "By the window are Police Captain Ezekiel Boxer, his wife Suzanne, Miss Dorothy Caston, and Miss Chrissy Schaefer.

Captain Boxer was a thin man in his late twenties with large mutton chops running along the edge of his jawline. His gaze coolly appraised Jed as only a police officer could. Chrissy looked very pretty. Her hair was washed and styled in ringlets. The high-necked, billowed-sleeved, pink dress she wore gave her an air of elegance that Jed had not seen before. Miss Caston was a dark-haired, dark-eyed beauty, who was also appraising Jed but in a very different manner than Captain Boxer was.

"I am pleased to make all of your acquaintances," said Jed. "Marshal Kane and I have met before. Mayor Brown and I were introduced yesterday."

"Oh! I was not aware of that," said Maura graciously. "I'm glad we can all be friends here, despite the recent unpleasantness."

Captain Wilcott and Lieutenant Frijack both stiffened at Maura's statement but forced themselves to appear at ease. Jed was sure their sympathies lay with the Confederacy. It was obvious they had been warned and coached about the nature of this dinner.

"I understand your husband recently passed away. I am very sorry for your loss," Jed said.

"Thank you for your condolences," said Maura. "He was an officer in the Connecticut Militia."

"A terrible loss for the Union cause," commiserated Jed. "You're from Virginia, though."

"My father owns a . . . homestead near Salem, Virginia."

"You can say plantation without my turning into a fire-breathing dragon," laughed Jed.

"Even if they own slaves?" sneered Lieutenant Frijack.

And so it starts, thought Jed.

He knew the dinner was a test to see if Maura could get into his confidence. If that was impossible, then the three younger men in the room would come into play. From his study of the Maryland Militia, Jed knew Captain Wilcott was regarded as the best pistol shot in the militia, if not the entire state. Lieutenant Frijack was an expert swordsman and had fought at least two duels. This dinner, if it did not go as the mayor and marshal had planned, would definitely end in a duel or an arrest . . . or both, if Jed survived the first two men.

Luckily, both Jed and Maura were on the same side and that was something no one else in the room knew, apart from Chrissy. That gave them the advantage in this increasingly perilous game of spy craft. Scouts were venerated for the important, but dangerous, missions they had to perform. Spies, on the other hand, were considered worse than pond scum, even by those on their side.

"Even if," replied Jed. "The issue does not diminish the amount of sympathy I feel."

"What if he was a—" Lieutenant Frijack started to say.

"Gentlemen," interrupted Marshal Kane. "I believe we are distressing Mrs. Harrison."

"My humblest apologies," said Lieutenant Frijack with a low bow to Maura.

"I must also apologize for my imprudent comments," said Jed.

"Please, think nothing of it," said Maura, laying a hand gently on Jed's arm.

"It appears that my appearance has interrupted your piano playing. I heard you when I came in, and I greatly desire to hear more. May I request a lively piece to lighten the mood?"

Maura smiled, crossed back over to the piano, and accepted Captain Wilcott's hand to sit down. Jed smiled as both militia officers stood beside her, facing him, as if to protect Maura. He was sure they weren't even aware they had done so. Maura rested her fingers lightly on the keys and began playing an upbeat version of *Dixie*.

Mayor Brown turned white. Marshal Kane looked like he was going to blow a blood vessel. Both of their wives were dangerously close to swooning. Chrissy was choking from having to swallow her laughter. Boxer, Wilcott, and Frijack were just stoic, making Jed even more certain of the nature of their orders. Maura's fingers flew over the keys until she finished with a flourish.

Chrissy and Jed applauded, quickly followed by the others. Maura stood up to bow low in acknowledgment. While still bent over, she raised her head to smile at Jed.

A fire must have been lit under Jed, based on the sudden heat he felt and the tightness of his collar. Her unsurpassed facial beauty was enhanced by her smooth shoulders and deep cleavage. Jed knew she was putting on a show for the others, and he would have to play along. Maura gave him the briefest of winks before she stood up.

"A very nice tune, but I can't say I've ever heard it before," said Jed. "I would venture to guess that it won't become popular in Baltimore."

"How about this one?" asked Maura, playing the first several stanzas of *My Country 'Tis Of Thee*.

"A much better selection," stated Jed with a smile.

"We have some time before dinner. May I suggest a walk around the monument? The flowers are blooming and are lovely. Mr. Tremblant, would you escort me?"

"I'd be honored."

Jed extended his arm to Maura. They walked out the front door and down Monument Street toward the immense 178-foot-high column with the statue of George Washington standing on top of it. The four blocks leading to the monument had wide streets. There was a central courtyard on each block with a street on either side of each courtyard. Cool shade trees and well-maintained flowering foliage graced each of the four rectangular parks. Gazing up at the statue, Jed wondered what Washington and the founding fathers would've thought about these times.

"Of course, they had their own problems with keeping the States together," said Jed. "Compromises had been made to remain unified against England. It's hard to believe that war was less than a hundred years ago."

"What are you thinking?" asked Maura softly.

"I was wondering what old George up there would've thought about all this," answered Jed. He looked back over his shoulder. "Everyone is following behind us. Is Miss Caston one of Chrissy's girls?"

"No," said Maura. "She was accompanying Captain Wilcott when he arrived at the house. I'm not aware of who she is or what part she plays in this. You know you have to appear besotted with me as far is the mayor and the marshal are concerned."

"I already care for you, Maura," whispered Jed without thinking.

"Don't say that!" hissed Maura, jerking her arm away.

Jed looked back and saw Mayor Brown frowning and Marshal Kane stifling a smile. Captain Boxer removed his wife's arm from his and took a step away from her.

"I apologize if my words have offended you," said Jed, just loud enough that the others could hear. "I understand that not all Southerners are traitors; nor are all Northerners saints. If you wish, I will say my goodbye here and call upon you another time."

"No, please stay. It is I who must apologize. I only wish to maintain my late husband's ideals."

Maura took Jed's arm again. "Have you been to the top of the monument? We have enough time for short stay up there before dinner."

Jed and Maura headed to the monument's entrance. The other couples behind them stood around looking at one another until Mayor Brown directed Captain Wilcott and Lieutenant Frijack to follow them.

Inside, Maura put a foot on the first step. "One!"

Laughing, they counted the steps as they raced up the circular stairway. It took a minute or two to reach the top and exit the circular, domed room at the top, which put them out on the balcony. Baltimore and its harbor opened up before them in a grand vista. Warm air wafted about them, and the scent of spring flowers was intoxicating.

"Two hundred and twenty-seven," said Maura.

"I counted the same," said Jed. "We have about a minute before they get up here."

"You do realize this is the trap?"

"As soon as I walked into your drawing room. Captain Wilcott is a superb shot, while Lieutenant Frijack is an excellent swordsman. I believe the good Captain Boxer is here to arrest me, in case they fail."

"My commitment is unchanged," said Maura. "Remember—"

Maura stopped talking as footsteps coming up the stairs reverberated from the domed room behind them. Jed looked down at Maura as she looked up at him, both realizing that their time alone was ending for today.

Much to Jed's surprise, Maura slid one arm around his waist as she stepped close to him. Her other hand came up around his neck and pulled his head down. Their lips met as she pressed her body against his.

Jed inhaled and almost moaned as a tremor seemed to vibrate through him. He put an arm around Maura's narrow waist as the kiss went on. Her lips seemed alive, even though the kiss was soft. A loud cough behind them broke the two of them apart.

"I beg your pardon," said Captain Wilcott. "I didn't mean to intrude."

"It is a good thing you did, sir," said Maura with great aplomb. "Otherwise, we might have been late for dinner. Shall we head down, gentlemen?"

As Maura headed down the stairs, she said, "Turn around, Lieutenant Frijack. We mustn't be late for dinner."

Jed and Captain Wilcott exchanged a glance of complete understanding, despite their being tentatively on opposite sides. They shrugged their shoulders as they made to follow Maura back to her house. Jed knew the kiss was a ploy to deceive the men coming up the stairs. However, he was having a hard time putting his emotions back in check. Maura had told him she would do anything to get to Duff.

Conversation about the war was generally avoided through dinner. Maura had ceded her position at the head of the table to Mayor Brown, and she sat at the opposite end. Jed found himself seated in the middle between Mrs. Kane and Miss Caston.

During the first course, Jed discovered Maura's cook was exceptional. The canapes a la bordelaise was served with fresh ham instead of salted, like so many preserved foods. The paprika in the butter sauce was perfect.

The shrimp bisque, served as the second course, was also very good. Jed tasted the brandy and sherry in it, but his mind wasn't so much on the food, but on a seasoning—salt. He knew salt was very important for preserving food and wondered who the major salt producers were and where they were located in the Confederacy.

Mrs. Kane was reluctant to talk to Jed and turned away from him to talk to Captain Boxer on the other side of her. Fortunately, Miss Caston was more than amicable to discuss any topic with Jed. She warned him to watch out for bones as a servant placed a poached striped bass in front of him. The delicious aroma of butter, garlic, lemon, dill, and chives tickled Jed's nose and made his mouth water.

Jed learned that Dorothy, as she wished him to call her, lived with her parents and was often in the company of Captain Wilcott. The fourth course, an asparagus salad, was presented. Dorothy went on to say how splendid Jed looked and wondered about his part in the upcoming conflict. Jed thought she might be a little too giddy about the prospect of the war. She apologized to him for thinking all Northerners were cold and unfeeling.

"I've never been north of the Mason Dixon line," chatted Dorothy over the lemon ice course. "I've never met a man from Illinois. I understand it's very cold and snows all the time."

"It does get cold in the wintertime, but we have the seasons too. If you want to see constant snow, you must travel much further north. However, I have to say how very pleasant it is here in Maryland."

193

"Is it?" asked Dorothy, leaning a little toward him.

Jed stiffened as he felt her hand touch his leg. He actually stopped breathing as her fingers slid to the inside of his thigh and gently squeezed. Just as quickly, her hand withdrew. A quick glance around the table showed Jed that no one had noticed their interlude.

Jed cleared his throat. "It does seem to be getting more interesting."

"I'd be honored if you would stop by my parents' house tomorrow at six," cooed Dorothy. She leaned closer to whisper, "It could get much . . . much more interesting."

Jed didn't think of how interesting it could be but of how much trouble he would be getting into. Thankfully, that was the only overture she made.

The main course appeared. A sizzling rib roast was placed in front of Mayor Brown to the delighted exclamations from Maura's guests. The platter was whisked away to a sideboard to be carved by the butler. A savory aroma filled the air as a perfectly cooked piece was placed in front of everyone. Talk turned to the theater and the new plays being introduced.

As the gingerbread cake was being served for the last course, Lieutenant Frijack, seated opposite Jed, asked, "Mr. Tremblant, I've been meaning to ask, exactly what business are you in?"

"I'm a lawyer, sir," replied Jed. "My business is dealing in the law."

"But you must have clients here?" pressed Lieutenant Frijack, who had taken up playing with his knife like it was a sword. "I think reading law books would be dusty and tiresome."

"One must have clients to receive payment," replied Jed. "However, it would be unethical of me to name my clients or what work I do for them. It is imperative that I retain their trust. There was one lawyer I know of in Chicago who used his client's information for his own gain. That was to the detriment of said client. The client shot and killed him and was later exonerated for justifiable homicide." Jed chuckled. "I have no desire to meet such an end."

"Nor should any of us," agreed Mayor Brown. "Unfortunately, I fear there will be more bloodshed."

"And what will Maryland do?" asked Jed.

"Gentlemen," announced Maura, standing up, which forced all the men to their feet. "Since the conversation has turned to work and politics, I believe the ladies and I shall retire to the drawing room. Cigars and brandy will be brought in shortly. If you desire anything else, please let one of the servants know."

With that, Maura and the other women left the dining room. The butler served brandy in round snifters to each man. Three humidors had been placed on a side table from which the men could select a cigar. Each man selected his cigar and sat back down.

"To answer your question, Mr. Tremblant, Maryland has already signified its position when the state legislature did not vote for secession," stated Mayor Brown, before taking a pull of his cigar. "I, personally, have too much to worry about with the city of Baltimore. I'll leave those decisions to . . . the men elected to deliberate and set the course for the state."

Despite the mayor's calm demeanor, Jed still heard the anger in his voice when he had said *men*. Jed knew some units of the Maryland Militia were stockpiling arms above and beyond the allocated number and type. The police department had moved numerous arms and ammunition out of their headquarters to the warehouse, and the city itself was paying for repairs to the steam gun.

The steam gun was becoming a major concern for Jed. The repairs were still ongoing, and the gun was starting to become a focal point for the citizens of Baltimore. It had taken on an almost magical property in their minds as a way to keep federal troops out of Baltimore. Jed hoped to hear from Tanner soon.

"My understanding, Mr. Mayor, is that the legislature did not vote so much against secession, but clarified their position that they did not have the authority to vote on the question," said Jed. "For them to do so would've been a violation of their oath of office."

"Do you believe they would've been consigned to Antenora?" asked Mayor Brown. "Will that be the final fate of the West Point officers who resigned instead of blindly following the dictates of an oppressive government?"

"Consigned to where?" asked Lieutenant Frijack.

"Antenora," answered Jed. "It's the second ring to the ninth level of hell in Dante Alighieri's *Divine Comedy*. You might know of it as *Dante's Inferno*. The ninth level is a gigantic frozen lake with Lucifer frozen in it. Antenora is the ring for oath breakers who have betrayed their country. I believe those people are frozen in solid ice. Perpetually cold, as is fitting."

A flash of anger passed across Lieutenant Frijack's face, which Jed contributed to his showing the lieutenant's ignorance at not being well-read. There might have been a twinge of dread at being told the final vision for committing certain actions.

"I am not God, Mr. Mayor," said Jed, turning back to face Mayor Brown. "Do I wish for a peaceful resolution? Yes, because I think the alternative will be more terrible than anyone realizes."

"Why not just leave us—," Lieutenant Frijack caught himself, "the Confederacy alone?"

"Like God's judgment, I do not have any voice in national policy," said Jed with a smile. "Maybe that's the one thing the people who are saying that the rights of the states supersede that of the federal government do not understand. Leaving aside the issue of slavery, we are in the United States, not an association of individual states. We can be great as a nation but only if we are united in fulfilling our destiny."

"The North's destiny or the South's destiny?" asked Marshal Kane.

"The nation's." Looking at the stub of his cigar, Jed snuffed it out in the ashtray beside him. "I must say how enchanted I am to make Mrs. Harrison's acquaintance. I believe it is time to rejoin the ladies."

"But our discussion—" Lieutenant Frijack started to say.

"Will not be solved by any of us here," interrupted Mayor Brown before anything was said that could not be withdrawn.

"It's still incumbent upon us to do what we can to prevent the impending calamity." Jed changed the subject. "I must say the rumors are true."

"Which rumors?" asked Marshal Kane suspiciously.

"The ones that say Mrs. Harrison possesses extraordinary beauty."

The ladies were in the drawing room. Miss Caston was plinking out a tune on the piano with help from Maura. Jed recognized it as Stephen Foster's composition, *Virginia Belle*. Chrissy waited by one of the windows.

"Good evening," greeted Jed, to which Chrissy gave a curtsy. A particularly bad piano note made him wince. "Miss Caston seems in fine form."

"Be careful," said Chrissy softly from behind her fan. "She isn'ts . . . isn't a working girl. She and the captain has . . . have something going on. The last several duels he has been in were because of her."

Jed's lip curled in disgust. "She made overtures to me and wants me to meet her tomorrow. No doubt the good captain will be there. It appears that both get a thrill from death."

Dorothy finished playing the piece to the polite applause from everyone. She moved away from the piano to stand beside Captain Wilcott, and Chrissy went over to take Lieutenant Frijack's arm.

"How about a parlor game to end the evening?" asked Maura. "Does anyone have an objection to Cross Purposes? No? Does everyone know how to play?"

"I'm afraid I don't," replied Chrissy.

"It's very simple. Everyone must have a seat, and I will whisper a phrase to each person. I will then go around the room asking each person a question. You can only answer the question with the phrase I have given you. Any hesitation or incorrect response will mean you must stand up. The last person sitting is the winner and will win a prize."

Everyone sat down and Maura went from person to person whispering in their ear. When she came to Jed, she bent over and said very softly, "Your phrase is 'Yes, indeed'."

The game proceeded through the first round with good humor invoked all around. Marshal Kane's phrase was the opposite of Jed's because when he was asked if he liked fried grasshoppers, he replied, "No, indeed!"

Jed's question almost made him blush when he was asked if he liked the women of Baltimore.

Lieutenant Frijack lost in the second round when he was asked how he liked Miss Schaffer. He managed to get out the word 'with' but choked on 'honey all over.' Mayor Brown gracefully stood up rather than say living in this wife was 'a fate worse than death.' Mrs. Boxer could not answer 'the more, the merrier,' when asked about the beaus she knew before her marriage.

Glasses were refilled before the start of the third round. Maura then walked over to stand in front of Jed.

"Are you a spy?" she asked.

Mayor Brown's eyes grew wide and both Marshal Kane and Captain Wilcott sputtered into their drinks. Everyone had gone silent, including the servants.

Jed smiled up at her. "Yes, indeed!" Then he burst out laughing.

Fortunately for Jed, the question and the answer so discombobulated almost all the other people so much, that by the end of the third round, only he and Chrissy were still sitting.

"Mr. Tremblant, you're not really a spy, are you?" asked Maura.

"Yes, indeed," replied Jed seriously.

"Aw, shucks. I was hoping you'd say no."

"Yes, indeed," said Jed with a chuckle.

"Miss Schaffer, how do you like men?"

Jed knew her phrase to be 'hot, sweet, and strong' but was a little surprised when she stood up.

"I yields the floor to Mr. Tremblant," said Chrissy. "Congratulations."

"That was fun. I hope I did not embarrass anyone too much," said Maura. "To the victor, goes the spoils. A bottle of my best port . . . produced, fermented, and bottled at my father's plantation."

"I will treasure it and think of you," said Jed. "If you all will excuse me for a minute."

Jed went to use the necessary. As he was returning, Tabitha signaled him to follow, and she took him into a small study adjoining the parlor. Holding her finger to her lips, she nodded toward the keyhole.

"He's smitten with her," he heard Captain Wilcott say. "There's no doubt of that given the way he kissed her on top of the monument. I will know for sure if he shows up tomorrow at Miss Caston's house."

"But is she taken with him?" asked Marshal Kane. "Women are too flighty; to prone to go wherever their fancy takes them."

"I believe Mrs. Harrison is not like most women," said Mayor Brown. "She cares for her home and family. She remained here to protect your father's honor and wealth from northern rapacity. It's even more evident by the papers you gave her, George."

"I know," said Marshal Kane. "And the devil of the time I had getting them too. More troops are coming in from the North. We must do something soon."

"We're almost ready," said Captain Wilcott. "Can we keep Tremblant distracted for the next three weeks?"

"Mrs. Harrison will," said Marshal Kane with derision. "Those papers give her some protection, but they also bind her to our cause tighter than any chain could. If she incites problems, copies of those papers will find their way into northern hands."

"Where is Mr. Tremblant?" queried Mayor Brown.

Jed quietly backed away from the door and hurried back to the drawing room. Using his fingers to groom his mustache, he approached Maura.

"The last to arrive must also be the first to leave," he told her. "I must take my leave of you. May I ask if you will go riding with me tomorrow?"

"You may ask," answered Maura with a twinkle in her eyes. "I'm not sure what my answer will be."

She glanced over at Mayor Brown and Marshal Kane. Both gave small nods, while the militia officers stood around looking decidedly unhappy. Captain Boxer waited patiently with a bored look.

Dorothy looked vexed, but Mrs. Kane's hand on her arm kept her from saying anything. Chrissy, of course, appeared ready to break out in giggles at any second.

"Would you go riding with me tomorrow at one?"

"Half past one, if you please," amended Maura. "I will need time to change after church. Where do you attend church, Mr. Tremblant?"

"Old St. Paul's Episcopal Church on North Charles Street," replied Jed. "I will call on you at half past one. Ladies, gentlemen, I bid you good night."

"I will see you out," said Maura as she followed Jed to the front door.

"Well?" asked Maura softly.

"I think it went well," whispered Jed. "We're not under arrest or in a duel. I will see you tomorrow. By the way, where is Mrs. Petford? I expected to see her here tonight."

"Haven't you guessed? She should be just through searching Mayor Brown's office by now," said Maura.

Paul closed the front door between them.

Chapter 18

Sunday, May 5, 1861

"Good morning, Robbie."

"Good morning, Mr. Tremblant," said Robbie from the front of his carriage. "Going to Old St. Paul's church?"

"Yes, I am." Jed climbed in, and Robbie clucked at the horses to get them moving. "How's the family?"

"They're doing well, sir," replied Robbie. "I've heard something that's not general knowledge yet. General Butler is moving several regiments north from Annapolis to Relay House. He'll be just eight miles south of Baltimore."

"Relay House?" mused Jed. "That's where the railroad tracks run to Harpers Ferry and branch off to Washington."

"Yes, sir. It's where the railroad crosses over the Patapsco River. A bit of rolling stock has gone south from Baltimore. All of it went past the Relay House. I imagine a few people are going to be a bit upset about Butler's march."

"If I remember my maps correctly, this will cut off all rail movement from Baltimore to the south. Fort McHenry controls water movement in and out of the city. With troops at Relay House, that will prevent any large shipments to the Confederacy coming from Baltimore."

What Jed didn't tell Robbie was that he had already contacted the commanding officer at Fort McHenry about inspecting sailing vessels leaving the docks. Jed gave a brief thought to trying to see General Butler after church, but he was taking Maura riding and the opposition knew that.

There was no doubt they would be keeping an eye on him, especially when Maura was with him. Maura would go to Relay House if he asked her, but a sixteen-mile round-trip on horseback would be arduous. Although, this would just be the thing which he could do with Maura for show. It would make Marshal Kane and the others think that he trusted her, and she could report the trip back to them.

"Robbie, can you drive us down to Relay House?"

"Yes, sir. It'll be a couple of hours both ways."

"Good," replied Jed. "Please go to Mrs. Harrison's residence and inform her I need to change our plans. Tell her of General Butler's movements and ask her to prepare to leave immediately."

"I'll also convey your apologies for the short notice." Robbie chuckled.

Jed laughed. "Yes, please. Drop me off at the church. I'll take a cab back to my hotel. That way it will look like I receive the information from someone in the congregation. I'll be waiting at my hotel."

"That's a convoluted way of thinking about things." Robbie pulled up in front of Old St. Paul's. "Necessary, though, since you're being followed . . . again. It's a gent on horseback wearing a tan coat."

Jed got out of the carriage and, as he was paying Robbie, spotted the man on the horse. As Jed entered the narthex of the church, he spotted Tanner standing off to one side. Tanner walked past him, and Jed felt something slip into his coat pocket. After ensuring no one was watching, Jed took a piece of paper out of his pocket and unfolded it.

The steam gun is repaired. They are planning on testing it on Tuesday at an abandoned farm just south of Towsontown off The York Turnpike. I drew a map on the back showing where the farm is located.

Jed blew out his breath. He knew he would have to see the test to assess the potential of the steam gun. The pro-South faction in Baltimore put a lot of time, effort, money, and publicity into promoting this new invention. It could change the course of the war. Folding up the note, Jed placed it in his inside coat pocket. He entered the church and sat in a pew.

When he couldn't sit still, he stood and left. Returning to the hotel, he was surprised to find Bryce packing his belongings.

"I thought you would be at church," said Jed.

"We're moving to the new house today, Master Jed," said Bryce, folding Jed's new suit into a trunk. "It will make it harder for the scoundrels to search our rooms."

Jed opened his mouth and then closed it. "Ah, I should've guessed that they had done that."

"They were very good about it, but they did happen to leave a few things askew."

"Disgraceful," Jed deadpanned. "General Butler has moved troops to Relay House, which is eight miles south of here. I'm going to be driven down to try and see him, and I'm taking Mrs. Harrison, if she's available. Mr. Tanner passed me this note before church."

Bryce read the note and studied the map to memorize the location. He handed the paper back to Jed. "Boots for the journey, Master Jed?"

A little while later, Robbie stopped his conveyance in front of the hotel. Maura and Eunice were waiting in the carriage.

"I declare!" Maura exclaimed as Jed opened the carriage door. "You simply cannot change our plans without giving me several hours' notice."

"Good morning, Mrs. Harrison." Jed sat down facing the two women. "Good morning, Mrs. Petford. Robbie, to the Relay House, please."

As the carriage started down the street, Maura asked, "Are we being followed?"

"Yes, a man wearing a tan coat and riding a sorrel horse. I imagine he'll be a little saddle sore by the end of this evening. Tanner gave me a message that the steam gun is repaired and they are going to test it this Tuesday."

"May I come with you?" asked Maura.

Jed almost said no but thought back to Maura's determination.

"It will be dangerous, and if you're seen with me, they will never trust you again. You'll have to wear men's clothes that will hide you in the woods, similar to the ones you wore at the warehouse."

"Sir, you cannot propose to have this lady dressed up as a man again!" snapped Eunice.

"I suppose breaking into the mayor's office was very ladylike," said Jed rhetorically. He suspected Eunice craved the freedom and excitement of these new endeavors but without forethought and planning, which in his opinion, was foolhardy and dangerous.

"Maybe not, but it would have been worth it had I found anything of value. His private ledger showed all the same locations we already know about."

Jed opened his mouth for a retort but then snapped it shut. For all the good things Mr. Jenkins had done for Maura, recommending his cousin as her companion was not one of them. She had taken her duties, both as a companion and a spy, too seriously. Eunice would do anything, even to the point of recklessness.

To Jed's way of thinking, Chrissy would've made a better companion than Eunice. The problem with that was Chrissy's profession. Enough men knew of Chrissy's line of work for it to be detrimental all the way around.

Of course, he couldn't just dismiss Eunice. She wasn't his companion. Jed was also afraid of what Mrs. Petford would do if Maura sent her back to Mr. Jenkins. She knew too many secrets. He had to neutralize her somehow before she returned to rely on the benevolence of her cousin.

They traveled for an hour or so without anyone speaking. Jed's mind kept coming back to the phrase 'rely on the benevolence of.' Slowly, he sat up straight as a thought came to him. Maura cocked an eyebrow at him as if to ask what took him so long.

Eunice wasn't trying to keep Maura within society's norms and values for society's sake. She was doing it for herself. Chrissy and the ladies at the club had opened Jed's eyes. The girls and women who chased after him in Chicago only seemed to have matrimony on their minds. That single-minded pursuit made them appear empty headed and insipid. Now, Jed understood they were doing what they could within the boundaries set for them to secure their future.

Beatrice, like most western women, was more independent and self-sufficient than her eastern counterparts. She was the one who had started the change in Jed's way of thinking. Maura, Ruth, and even Chrissy—all strong women—had brought him to this point of understanding how women may feel trapped by their place in society. In some ways, it was worse than slavery.

Women could not vote, although Jed felt a portion of the male population should not be allowed to vote either. For the most part, a woman's wealth and power was given to and used by her husband, father, or male guardian. It took a strong woman to retain her wealth and power.

Turning his mind back to Eunice, Jed now saw where all her motivation and apprehension was coming from. If something were to happen to Maura, Eunice would lose her position and have to go back to her cousin. The near fatal incident at the warehouse must've scared her out of her wits. She was trying to do the most dangerous jobs to keep Maura away from them. Fortunately, she hadn't run into any unexpected encounters. Maura was the one who planned out Eunice's missions, and Jed postulated that Eunice didn't have the experience to adapt to changing situations.

Understanding the problem and dealing with it were two separate things. Eunice could go with Maura to all the social functions. The secret, clandestine missions that put Maura in danger was where Eunice raised her objections. Objections that, if raised in public, could be noticed by the wrong people. Jed was concerned that Eunice's recklessness could have her saying the wrong thing at the wrong time.

"Mrs. Petford—" Jed started to say.

"You're putting me out to pasture, aren't you?" interrupted Eunice dejectedly.

"Not in the least," replied Jed. "Maura needs a companion at her public outings and at her house. You have been instrumental in accomplishing our goals, and I don't want to replace you. We all do dangerous jobs. There's no getting around it in these times. What would Maura do if I was not here?"

"Continue as she has been and send her reports to the War Department."

"And if those reports are intercepted and lead the Confederates back to her? That is why I am sending the reports and leaving any mention of the two of you out of them. Everyone here knows I'm from Illinois and a Northerner. Mrs. Petford, if something should happen to Maura, what would you like to do?"

"To continue the fight and be useful," she replied.

"Don't answer me now, but I want you to think on how you can continue to do that," said Jed. Eunice opened her mouth to protest but stopped when Jed held up his hand. "I'm not getting rid of you. It's an alternative plan if we need it. I will support you in anything you want to do."

"Eunice, I make plans all the time," said Maura. "That way if one plan fails, I'm not at a loss for things to do. My late husband taught me that. I want you to remain my companion."

"But I'm going to have to let you do things your way, aren't I?" groused Eunice.

"I prefer to make society conform to me than the other way around," declared Maura loftily. "However, please feel free to poke, prod, thump, or abuse anyone who gives me offense."

Eunice laughed, a real honest-to-goodness laugh. Jed had expected it to be a braying sound, but it pealed out like a silver bell.

"Oh, I needed that," said Eunice with a smile. "Thank you, Mr. Tremblant. I was afraid of losing this position. I still am. You don't know the dread I feel about going back to my cousin's house to sit day after day. Don't get me wrong, he's a good man, but you two have given me so much more."

"Folks, I hate to break up this conversation, but there's a unit of Union soldiers blocking the road," said Robbie.

Jed was in the rear facing seat. He stood up and hunched over to look out the door window. There was indeed a squad of soldiers blocking the road. Further beyond them, Jed saw the makings of a much larger camp.

Robbie pulled his horses to a stop in front of two soldiers, one of whom took hold of a horse's bridle. Three other soldiers kept their rifles pointed at the carriage.

"Step out of the carriage and no sudden moves," ordered one of them. "You, up there! Tie off the reins and stepped down."

Jed was about to open the door when Eunice stopped him. She leaned out the window. "I have no intention of stepping onto this muddy roadway," she informed the soldier imperially. "Nor do I intend my mistress to do so. We are of no danger to you. Summon your commanding officer, and we will speak to him."

"Ma'am, we're ordered to search everything that moves on this road," said the soldier. "No exceptions."

"Young man, I am not wearing suitable footwear for this mud, and I do not wish to argue the point with you. We will wait right here for your officer."

"See here . . ." snarled the soldier.

"I'm just hired to drive the horses," interrupted Robbie before things got out of hand. "Wouldn't it be better to just get your officer here?"

He didn't like it, but the soldier sent someone for his commanding officer. The remaining four soldiers kept guard on the carriage. Robbie walked off the road to sit down with his back against a tree. After a while, an officer strode toward them from the direction of the camp. Jed got out to greet him.

"Sir, I am ordered to search all conveyances," the lieutenant of the Eighth New York said without preamble.

"I'm Captain Jedidiah Tremblant of Illinois," said Jed, handing over his orders. "I came down from Baltimore to see General Butler . . . quietly."

The lieutenant read the orders, and his eyes widened as he got to the part about Jed working for the Secretary of War. A couple of minutes later, Robbie was up on the driver's seat with a soldier sitting beside him to escort them to Relay House.

After presenting his orders to Edward Parker, General Butler's aide-de-camp, Jed waited outside with Maura and Eunice for over an hour before General Butler came out. The only thing Jed knew about the man was that General Butler had a law practice in Boston and was considered to be very shrewd in the labor disputes area. It was rumored he had even represented both sides in the same case. What Jed saw was a man of average height with a paunch around his middle. His hair was long on the sides and back of his head, but the top was completely bald. The baggy eyes and droopy mustache gave his face an air of displeasure at having to meet Jed under the circumstances.

"Captain Tremblant?" greeted General Butler.

"Good afternoon, sir." Jed saluted.

General Butler grimaced and waved off the salute. "I was told this was a matter of discretion." He looked pointedly at Maura and Eunice. "I am not accustomed to such dealings."

Obviously, General Butler seemed to regard Jed being here as a lark, since he had brought women along. Still, he could not ignore one who had orders directly from the Secretary of War. General Butler's eyes seemed to be looking everywhere and appraising everything. The general took special note of Maura's beauty. A couple of officers holding papers stood beside her as they awaited their turn to talk to the General.

"Sir, Mrs. Harrison's husband was a lieutenant in the Connecticut Militia. He was killed during the riots on April nineteenth in Baltimore. I've been ordered by the Secretary of War to investigate southern activities in Baltimore and the surrounding area. I am also ordered to put a stop to them."

"Spies and informants," sneered General Butler.

Jed saw his worth decreasing rapidly in the General's eyes. "Be that as it may, sir, we have located several warehouses and private establishments where arms, ammunition, and equipment are being stored for either shipment to the Confederacy or for armed revolt in the state of Maryland. There's also the steam gun invention being held at the Winans's foundry."

"I've heard of the steam gun," said General Butler, suddenly interested. "Is it truly as fearsome a weapon as the newspapers make it out to be?"

"Baltimore city officials have paid to have it repaired," said Jed. "They're planning on testing it Tuesday and then shipping it to the Confederacy. I hope to watch the testing if I can. Since you are now situated in Relay, it will probably go through Ellicott Mills toward Harpers Ferry."

"And the stores of equipment?" asked General Butler eagerly. "When do you plan to seize them?"

"I have no orders regarding them, apart from keeping an eye on where and what is being stored. I do know that something is being planned in Baltimore by southern sympathizers. I don't know what it is yet."

"I must get back to my duties, Captain. Keep me abreast of developments in Baltimore. I will do what I can to assist you."

Without another word, General Butler turned and left. Jed looked at the bewildered faces of Maura and Eunice. Jed extended an arm to each of them and led the two ladies back to the carriage.

As he helped them up, Jed glanced around. Two cannons were being set up on a hill overlooking the railroad bridge. Breastworks were being dug and positions were being fortified. Jed also saw a large number of green troops lounging around.

"Back to Baltimore, Robbie," said Jed as he climbed inside. He asked the ladies, "What do you think of General Butler?"

"It appears he doesn't have much use for spies," said Maura hesitantly. "His men were bringing him lists of . . . contraband that they had captured."

"Humph!" harrumphed Eunice. "Didn't you see the way his eyes lit up when Mr. Tremblant mentioned the warehouses? I'd only trust him to do what would benefit him the most!"

"Troop training does seem to be lacking," admitted Jed. "It might be that his troops had just marched to this location and were establishing their camp. He did manage to occupy Annapolis without incident, and his orders are to stop troops and equipment from being shipped to the Confederacy."

"I still don't trust him," stated Eunice.

"Neither do I, but if he is driven by avarice, we now know how to manipulate him into working for us. I'm glad he's here. Duff cannot flee south through this location. I will send several wanted fliers to General Butler and his aide-de-camp. The reward on Duff should spark General Butler's interest."

Eunice snorted with amusement, but Maura looked distressed and troubled.

"Maura, I know you want to . . . capture Duff yourself, but this conflict is spreading," said Jed. "There's talk of pulling troops from the Indian Territories. I've gotten a couple of letters from friends who are still there. They've told me the Texans are boasting about taking over New Mexico."

"Why would they want to do that?" asked Maura. "Texas is the largest state, but isn't New Mexico it mostly deserts and Indians?"

"They are descendants of the Spaniards and people from the East looking for new life, towns, cities, and farms living there. It's not all bleak deserts." Jed had to chuckle. "I wouldn't even call the desert bleak. It has a beauty all its own, but that's beside the point. If the Confederacy expands westward to the Pacific, it opens new trade routes and strengthens their position."

"I don't understand," said Eunice.

"The Confederacy is lacking in major industry," explained Maura. "We're an agrarian culture. Jonathan," Maura's breath caught in her throat, "Jonathan used to say no one was more willing to fight for secession and less prepared to do so than the South."

"Too true," agreed Jed. "That's why we need to watch the stockpiles of weapons in Maryland and make sure they don't leave the state. The Confederacy will have to purchase and import large quantities of supplies and equipment. That takes gold and silver."

"The gold fields of California," said Eunice in understanding.

"Yes, and other mineral wealth from the West and beyond that, to China," said Jed. "Maura, if you still wish to see the testing, I will meet you just before daybreak on Tuesday at the stable north of the Washington Monument. Are you prepared for this endeavor?"

"I know you don't wish me to do this, Eunice," said Maura. "However, I must see the men who come there for the testing. I've met a number of families in Baltimore society. They may be unknown to Jed, but I may be able to identify them." She turned to look at Jed. "I will be at the stable."

Chapter 19

Tuesday, May 7, 1861

THE GRAY DAWN BARELY GAVE off enough light for Jed and Maura to ride out. Jed had made the arrangements at the stables for the horses on Monday. He spent the rest of the day helping Bryce set up the new house.

The house, a large Gothic revival mansion, was indeed secluded at the end of a cul-de-sac. Light gray stone gave it an impressive and imposing look. A stable, built to match the house, rested a short distance away.

Bryce hired a complete complement of servants, all carefully vetted and interviewed. Two extra groundskeepers patrolled the estate to keep unwanted guests away. The grounds were mainly wood and field, so there wasn't a lot of upkeep to do, but the area was extensive enough so the hiring of two groundskeepers wouldn't attract extra attention.

Jed considered hiring Robbie as his coachman but was hesitant to do so. He knew he could trust Robbie but was afraid of hindering the information coming in from the other hacks. Finally, he offered Robbie a choice, and Robbie chose to remain as a cabbie.

Jed must've looked an unusual sight to anyone looking out of their home in the predawn light. He wore his usual wide-brimmed hat but had replaced his fine clothes for the fringed buckskin of his scouting days in the West. He belted his Colt in a holster around his waist with a Bowie knife on his left side. The dark leather saddle bags he carried showed the wear and tear of several years use. A lanky stable boy surprised Jed when Jed walked into the stable to get the horses.

"I thought this would be less conspicuous than the dresses I usually wear," said Maura as Jed stared at her openmouthed.

Maura had been sitting on a bale of hay. Her long, strawberry-blonde hair was piled up under a brown felt hat with a floppy brim that half hid her face. A billowy checkered shirt and baggy pants hid her figure. Scuffed boots added to the stable boy image.

Jed shook his head. "This is going to take some getting used to. Good morning, Maura. You're right. Those clothes are better suited for this than your other outfits. Shall we get started?"

The two horses Jed had rented had their tack laid out by their stalls. It only took a couple of minutes to get them saddled. Leading the horses outside, they mounted up. It was a little disconcerting for Jed to see Maura sit astride her horse. He was used to women sitting that way on a horse out West, but since his return to Chicago, he had become accustomed to women riding sidesaddle. Of course, it would be silly for Maura to ride sidesaddle in the disguise she was wearing.

Riding up the York Turnpike, they were soon out of the city. The sun was just over the horizon, and the day promised to be clear and warm. Maura was an excellent rider. No one else was on the road as yet, but farmers were up and about doing their chores.

"Are you usually this quiet in the morning?" asked Maura jokingly.

"Usually," responded Jed with a smile. "That was one of the things Beatrice complained about."

"Beatrice?" asked Maura. "Was she your . . . I'm sorry. I didn't mean to intrude."

"It's quite all right," said Jed. "Yes, she was my wife. She died three years ago from influenza. Strange, isn't it? For the past three years, I could barely talk about her and now, . . . well, it doesn't hurt as much to talk about her as it used to. Until several days ago, I wouldn't have talked about her at all."

"May I ask what she was like?"

"Of course," replied Jed. "She was seventeen when we met, and the daughter of my commanding officer, Captain Johnson. She was a firebrand and fearless . . . a lot like you. Having grown up in the West had given her more independence and freedom than is the norm for most women."

"And she fell in love with you right away," added Maura.

Jed broke out laughing. "Not hardly. When we first met, she thought I was the most insufferable, arrogant, wet-behind-the-ears tenderfoot who had ever lived. I was, but her father saw I had two attributes he greatly prized: determination and persistence. I also had an aptitude toward learning Indian languages. I spent a lot of time among the Indians. Beatrice accompanied me to the relatively safe Indian villages, mostly to keep me out of trouble, but I learned a great deal about their culture from her."

"Is that where you got those buckskins? They suit you, even though you look like a mountain man in them. I'm surprised you wore boots instead of moccasins."

"They're in my saddle bags along with extra ammunition, jerky, pemmican, and dried fruit. Oh, and a canteen. This outfit was given to me by the Cheyenne. I wore it through most of my time in the Army. Bryce brought it with him when he came here from Chicago. It seemed fitting to wear them for a scouting mission."

"Aren't they unbearably hot during the summer?" asked Maura.

"Exceedingly so. Still, they don't catch or tear like cloth—saved me from losing large patches of my skin numerous times."

"You're always thinking ahead," said Maura. "You forgot your rifle though."

"I almost brought it but decided against it. We're supposed to observe and report without being seen. If I need my rifle, we've done something wrong."

"Aren't you supposed to be prepared for any eventuality?" She slumped a little in her saddle and looked sad. "Jonathan taught me that. He just wasn't prepared for the encounter that killed him."

"No one could have been prepared for that encounter," stated Jed bitterly. "Least of all, me. I hadn't expected a deadly Confederate spy; one willing to do anything to further his cause."

"Why do you think he didn't kill you that day?"

"I think it was because I didn't tell him what my actual position was," replied Jed. "I'd led Duff to believe I was going to Washington to see a client. In his mind, I was a civilian. Make no mistake, though. If I had tried anything, I would've ended up like your husband. I'm truly sorry for your loss."

"I know," said Maura bitterly. "I'm filled with rage and anger that Jonathan was killed in so despicable a fashion. Shot in the back without warning or remorse. President Davis's message showed me the true colors of the Confederacy by condoning Jonathan's murder and turning it into what he believed was a patriotic act. I will do anything to avenge this affront and let Jonathan's spirit rest in peace."

Jed turned off the road and stopped his horse under the foliage of a grove of oak trees. Maura halted her horse beside his.

"That abandoned house and falling down barn should be the farm." Jed pointed to the buildings about three hundred to four hundred yards away. "We need a place where we can watch."

"Why not right here?"

"There's no underbrush, and we're visible from the road. The ridgeline behind the barn is too far away. I think that small hill to our right with the woods on top is the best place to observe. There's sufficient vegetation to hide us and the horses."

"That makes sense." Maura gave Jed a sideways look as they started their horses toward the hill. "You have nothing to say about my plans to avenge Jonathan's murder?"

"What is there to say?" Jed chuckled. "You have berated me each time I brought up an objection. I figured it was easier on my ears not to object. We have the same goal with regard to Anthony Duff. So far, no one has seen him or admitted to seeing him."

Jed rode easily and appeared to be relaxed, but his head turned this way and that, taking in everything. The path he led them on kept them under the cover of the trees lining the stream that wound its way toward the base of the hill.

"Could he have left Baltimore after we saw him at the warehouse?"

"That's a possibility," admitted Jed. "However, we know the secessionists in Baltimore are planning something big within the next three weeks. My best guess is that Duff is playing a major part in whatever they have planned. I think it's going to be an armed revolt in the eastern part of this state."

Maura gasped in horror as a thought came to her. "Would troops at Fort McHenry open fire on the city if that happens?"

"I don't know, but I could see that happening if the entire population of the city decides to join the Confederate cause."

They reached the top of the hill, and Jed secured the horses in a spot on the back side of the trees where they wouldn't be seen. He carried the saddle bags as he and Maura walked to the side of the hill facing the abandoned farm. Their vantage point was behind bushes, but they could see the entire farm and the road. Jed spread a rough wool blanket out for them to sit upon and pulled binoculars out of the bag.

"We might have a while to wait," he warned Maura.

"It's not raining, and the sun is out," said Maura cheerfully. "Thank you for letting me come."

Jed glanced at her. Even in the old, baggy clothing and floppy felt hat, Maura's classical profile was still entrancing.

"You're welcome." He returned to his binoculars. More horses and wagons appeared on the road. "I have not forgotten your oath, but I must say you are a remarkable woman."

"Thank you," demurred Maura. "Will the war be as terrible as I think it will be?"

"Probably worse," admitted Jed. "I've heard of post commanders turning over their forts, with all assets, to southern—Confederate—state militia before resigning their commissions to join the Confederate Army. When Jefferson Davis and John Floyd held the position of secretary of war, they both moved secessionist officers into key positions and transferred large amounts of ordinance and ammunition to the South to be captured."

"I've heard of Mr. Floyd. He was supposed to be involved in the Abstracted Indian Bonds scandal, but the court found him not guilty."

"The charges against him were quashed based on a technicality of the law," said Jed. "I understand he returned to Virginia. Still, the Confederacy gained huge amounts of materiel they should not have. I feared the war will be bloodier for it. How the war will play out depends on how it is conducted west of the Appalachians."

"Out West?" questioned Maura. "Not here in the East?"

"The East is important, but if the Union gains control of the Mississippi River all the way to New Orleans, they will split the Confederacy. That's my assessment. I'm sure President Lincoln and his cabinet have their own plans." Handing his binoculars to Maura, he pointed toward the south. "I believe the steam gun is coming."

A strange wagon being pulled by a pair of horses had a large boiler behind the driver's bench, and something half-conical was covered in canvas on the back side of the bed. Three carriages followed along, and ten militiamen rode alongside as guards.

"Quite the outing," commented Maura as Jed wrote notes on a small pad of paper.

"Pardon?" Then he realized what she meant. "The city paid for the repairs to the steam gun. I'm sure they want to see what they paid for. Militia officers will be here to ascertain the steam gun's capabilities, just like we're doing. They're turning off."

The steam gun wagon and three carriages had turned onto the farm road. Two militia soldiers stopped at the intersection of the turnpike and the farm road to prevent anyone else from following. The remaining soldiers fanned out to search the nearby woods and abandoned buildings.

"Lay down and keep perfectly still," whispered Jed. Maura lay down on her back. "Roll over and keep your face down."

Maura did so. For the longest time, the only sounds were the birds singing, the buzz of winged insects flying by, and the wind rustling through the trees. There was a clop of hoof steps coming closer. Jed's heart beat faster in his chest, but he quieted. Ever so slowly, he moved his hand onto Maura's and squeezed it slightly to give her reassurance.

The hoofbeats came closer and closer, but the foliage blocked any view the searcher might have had. The horse stopped only ten feet away from where they were hidden. The jingle of its tack and the creak of someone shifting in the saddle reached their ears.

Time dragged on, and after what seemed to be an eternity's wait, the rider moved off. Jed let go of Maura's hand and motioned for her to remain still. Noiselessly, he shifted into a squatting position and looked around.

"It's clear," he said very softly. "Keep your voice pitched low."

"Low enough?" asked Maura quietly in a gruff voice ranged as low as she could make it.

Jed snorted in amusement but didn't reply. The steam gun had been pulled onto a field about a quarter of a mile away from the barn. The horses had been unhooked from the wagon and led away. The three carriages were parked beside the farmhouse, and the passengers walked toward the steam gun. Jed didn't need his binoculars to recognize Marshal Kane and Captain Wilcott.

Maura recognized four men as members of the city council, one man as Charles Dickinson who was the inventor of the steam gun, and the last man as a foundry owner Winans. Jed noted down their names and occupations.

From their position on the hill, Jed and Maura watched as a wagon was pushed into position and secured to the ground. A fire was stoked in the firepan under the boiler and soon black smoke billowed from the boiler's smokestack.

"This is taking quite some time, isn't it?" asked Maura.

"Yes, way too long to be of use in the field," replied Jed, making another note. "It would have to be a defensive weapon, probably placed inside a fort." He looked through his binoculars before handing them to Maura. "They're loading it now."

Maura watched a man load five round cannonballs under Dickinson's directions into a hopper at the rear of the steam gun. Dickinson checked the pressure gauges and then motioned to the spectators, who all hunkered down behind a wall as Dickinson pulled a lever.

The steam gun whined and hissed as all five cannonballs shot from it in less than two seconds. The iron balls flew in succession before hitting the ground and bouncing to a stop.

"Great God in Heaven!" exclaimed Maura in utter amazement, forgetting to keep her voice pitched low. "That . . . that thing is pure evil! Did you see how fast it fired?"

Jed's mouth quirked in amusement. "Yes, I did, and it was amazing. However, the rate of fire is only one aspect of a weapon. I have more experience with cannons than you do. Did you see where the cannonballs landed?"

"Out in the field. I really wasn't watching them. I was looking at the steam gun."

"Look at the field. You can see where the cannonballs hit by the gouges in the ground. What can you tell me about where they hit?"

Maura looked through the binoculars for a minute or two. Jed watched the men below. He also kept an eye on the militia soldiers, but none of them came back up the hill.

"I see where the cannonballs hit the ground, but I'm not sure what you want me to notice," said Maura.

"The steam gun was not moved," explained Jed. "It was secured in its position and firing . . . shooting at the same spot for all five rounds."

"But the cannonballs all struck the ground at different spots," said Maura in confusion.

"That means the steam gun is not very accurate. It also doesn't look like it shoots as far as a conventional cannon. Still, untrained troops may experience your reaction and panic when they see cannonball after cannonball fly from this weapon at them. I'll know better after the group leaves, and I can go down to measure the distance."

"What are they doing now?" asked Maura as much to herself as to Jed.

The men had left their meeting and walked to the wagon. Together, they manhandled the steam gun until it pointed at the barn. Maura held her breath as more cannonballs were loaded into the hopper.

She gasped as the steam gun whined again, throwing its ammunition toward the barn. With a loud splintering and cracking of wood, two balls crashed through the upper section of the barn. Two balls hit the lower fieldstone portion; one bounced off but cracked the stone, and the other punched through the wall. The last ball missed completely. The men below were jubilant and applauded its inventor.

"Why didn't they explode?" asked Maura.

"Dickinson must be using solid shot. That's a solid iron ball. The fuses for explosive shells are usually ignited by the gun powder used to propel the shell. There are fuses that use two chemicals in breakable containers that, when combined, explode upon impact. I don't have an understanding of what forces are at work within the steam gun, so I would be very afraid of using that type of fuse."

"As would I," came a voice from behind them.

Jed rolled away from Maura and sprang to his feet. His right hand grasped the butt of his revolver, but the pistol was tied down by the hammer. His left hand pulled out his Bowie knife. Standing with a rifle leveled at them was Lieutenant Frijack.

Chapter 20

Tuesday, May 7, 1861

Lieutenant Frijack's hands tightened on his rifle as he kept it pointed right at Jed. The hammer was pulled back, and Frijack's finger rested on the trigger. The sword by his side rattled in the scabbard as he took a small step away from Jed.

"Drop the knife," he ordered.

Jed sighed and tossed his Bowie next to his saddle bags. Maura was still sitting on the ground with her back to Frijack.

"Now, the belt and the holster."

Jed carefully unbuckled his gun belt and tossed it to the side. The muzzle didn't waiver, but Frijack visibly relaxed.

"I was up on the ridge when I saw movement down here," stated Lieutenant Frijack with smug assurance. "It took me some time to ride down but imagine my surprise when I found two horses. The steam gun demonstration was fantastic. We'll soon chase all you northern scum out of our state. No one can stand up to that type of fire power!"

Jed didn't say anything but let the militia officer rant on. He saw Maura tremble a little, frozen where she sat on the cold ground. Her unmasking would soon be at hand.

"Soon . . . very soon, we'll be sending all of you and that monkey you call a president north of the Mason Dixon line," sneered Lieutenant Frijack. "If I had my way, every northern officer in Maryland would be executed, just like Mrs. Harrison's husband. Imagine having to prostitute yourself to such a man to save her father from ruin!"

"Have you considered the possibility that she loved him?" asked Jed.

Lieutenant Frijack's lip curled in disgust, "And betray her people for someone like him?"

"You never met him."

"I didn't have to," argued Lieutenant Frijack. He prodded Maura with the end of his rife. "C'mon, boy, on your feet."

Maura stood up and turned around to face him. Lieutenant Frijack's face went blank as his mind tried to process exactly who was standing in front of him. His rifle was aimed at Jed, and Jed knew any move on his part would end with a bullet in his gut.

"You whore!" swore Lieutenant Frijack as he swung his rifle up to butt-strike Maura in the face.

The blow never landed because Maura took a step forward and punched Frijack's nose. In an instant, Jed leaped forward and grabbed the rifle with both hands. Frijack's finger tightened on the trigger, and Jed grunted in pain as the hammer came down on his hand instead of on the percussion cap.

Jed wrenched the rifle out of Frijack's hands, but with the pain, he couldn't maintain his grip on it. The rifle flew into the bushes. Frijack shoved Jed away and jumped backward as he fumbled for the grip of his sword. Jed stumbled away from him, ending up on his knees next to his saddlebags. His left hand grasped the Bowie knife, while his right hand fished a tomahawk out of the saddlebags.

"You brought the wrong weapons to a sword fight," snarled Frijack, swishing his sword twice through the air quickly.

Jed didn't say anything but motioned to Maura to move away. Frijack thrust the point of his sword at Jed, which was batted aside by the Bowie. Knowing the reach was too far, Jed didn't make a return swing with his tomahawk, but instead began to circle around. He was hoping the bushes and trees would be more of a detriment to Frijack and his longer reach than to him.

"They said you were a fighting man," said Frijack with scorn in his voice. He made two more lunges which were both parried. "It seems to me you're just scared. If you're an example of northern officers, we'll be whipping your asses in no time."

Maura had moved out of the way of the two men. She glanced down at the men near the steam gun. All except one were still congratulating one another. The one was looking up the hill. The clang of weapon against weapon sounded loud to Maura along with the grunts and snarls of both men. She was sure it could be heard down where the steam gun was.

"I should have known no Yankee would stand up to a fair fight," goaded Lieutenant Frijack as he lunged, only to have his blade knocked away from a killing blow.

"I knew rebels were blowhards and liars," countered Jed. "This isn't a fair fight."

"YEE HAW!" Frijack jumped forward, his blade sweeping down for a vicious cut. Jed would have been cut from shoulder to his abdomen had the blow landed.

At the last second, Jed angled his body away from the trajectory of the sharp steel and swung his tomahawk up to parry. The sword was again knocked aside, but this time Frijack lost his balance and slammed into Jed.

Time froze as the two men stood chest to chest. Frijack began to shake and gasp, then slid to the ground. Maura covered her mouth when she saw the Bowie knife stuck all the way to the hilt into the militia officer's side.

Jed knelt beside him. "I told you it wasn't a fair fight. The Indians have no word for sword, so they call it a long knife. They know all about knife fighting, and they were the ones who taught me."

The lieutenant's hand clutched at Jed's sleeve as his breath came out in one long final exhalation. His eyes stared at nothing until Jed closed them.

Maura averted her gaze as Jed pulled his knife out of the body and wiped it off.

"What are they doing down there?" Jed strapped down his belt and then rummaged through the bushes. "They should have heard his yell."

"There was one who heard the fight," replied Maura, peering over the undergrowth. "He . . . No! It can't be!" She brought Jed's binoculars up to her eyes and stared intently.

"What?" asked Jed worriedly as he found and picked up Frijack's rifle.

He moved to where Maura had crouched. The men below had indeed heard the commotion. All manner of weaponry was appearing out of the carriages, and the Southerners had aligned themselves in front of the steam gun to defend it. What was more troubling was the one man who was directing the mounted militiamen toward the hill.

"He's here!" snarled Maura venomously.

"Who?"

"Duff!"

Jed's head snapped up, and he looked down on the farm. There was no mistaking the whitish blond hair of the Confederate spy standing in the doorway of one of the carriages. Duff was pointing at their location and yelling.

Four horsemen galloped toward Jed and Maura; one was a good hundred feet in front of the other three. They were preparing to move the steam gun.

"Kill him!" urged Maura. "Kill him!"

Jed brought the rifle to his shoulder in one smooth motion. He let out his breath slowly as he aimed. The loud boom of the rifle barely registered before he dropped it. Grasping Maura by the hand, he pulled her along as he drew the revolver from its holster. Leading Maura away, he fired off three spaced shots back down the hill.

"You didn't even try!" hissed Maura, jerking her arm but unable to break Jed free from his grip. "He was right out in the open! You shot that damn horse!"

Jed pulled her to where their horses were and grabbed her shoulders to shake her.

"If I had shot Duff instead of the horse, that rider would have been in our thicket before I dropped the rifle," whispered Jed. Despite his soft words, the intensity of his emotions betrayed an anger so great that Maura quailed before it. "Get on your horse, keep your mouth closed, and follow me exactly. We aren't out of this situation yet. They will kill us if they catch us."

After boosting Maura none too gently onto her saddle, Jed led them away from the hill. He guided them under the trees from one area of concealment to another. Maura almost said something, then she saw four militia soldiers gallop across a field heading south toward the city.

"They're trying to box us in," said Jed, more to himself than to Maura. "I'm guessing two on the road and the four south of us means there are four or more following our trail."

"What if we go east over the ridge?" offered Maura.

"No, too risky. Frijack was up on the ridge. I doubt he was up there alone. He probably had other men spaced out to keep watch. Follow me quietly."

Leading the way at a trot, Jed headed south, turned east and then back north. They remained under the trees, and Maura was impressed by Jed's ability to ride through the forest with minimal sound.

"Jed?" she asked softly.

Jed jerked as he pulled his concentration back from searching for a path and looking out for the men who were after them. He didn't look at her but stopped his horse so she could come alongside of him.

"Yes?" he asked softly, looking around.

"Wouldn't it be easier to get by them without the horses?"

"Undoubtedly," answered Jed. "However, the horses are rented. If Duff and his men find riderless horses, it won't take them long to find the stable and that I was the one who rented them." He gave her a quick smile before turning his attention back to their surroundings. "Besides, I'd rather not pay for the horses and tack. This looks like a good spot."

The area where Jed had stopped was completely exposed, and Maura's face showed her disbelief. There wasn't any underbrush or bushes. He indicated for her to get down, and she reluctantly got off her horse.

Using the bit and bridle, Jed forced her horse down onto its side. It didn't like it and its eyes rolled in confusion and fear. Stroking its neck to calm it, Jed placed a small cloth over its head. He signaled Maura to come over.

"Lay down beside it," he whispered. "Keep its head down and don't let it whinny if it smells their horses. Keep still and quiet. They'll be getting close now."

Maura did as he asked, even though it was clear that she thought they would be easily spotted. Jed got his horse to lay down and put another cloth over its head. He then laid down, patting his horse's neck to keep it still.

Time seemed to drag. The wind rustled the leaves along the ground as birds flitted and chirped in the branches above them. Jed heard Maura's horse try to get up once, but she expertly held it down.

At first he thought it was the wind but then realized the sound was too regular. It was the swishing of hooves through the leaves. Jed breathed out slowly to calm his racing heart and petted his horse to keep it from fidgeting. Cooing very softly, he stroked its neck.

"It couldn't have been a fair fight!" he heard one man say angrily. "They must have snuck up on him from behind!"

"The lieutenant's wound was to the front," argued another, who could only be twenty-five feet away from Maura and Jed. "His sword was out, and the edge was nicked."

"The second one pulled a gun, and they killed him after he was disarmed then," said the first one sullenly. "It doesn't matter. We'll hang 'um, as soon as we catch them."

"We have to find them first!" snarled a third man. "You two jabbering about it isn't helping. Spread out and start looking! Go check those bushes!"

"Yes, Sergeant," came their muttered replies.

The men moved off and were soon out of earshot. As soon as they were gone, Jed rose silently and got his horse up on its feet. He helped Maura and her horse up. Soon, they were headed north away from the city.

"We're not going back to the farm or to the hill," Jed informed her softly. "We'll skirt the farm to the east and head up to Towsontown. We'll stay there for an hour or two and then ride home."

"It's that easy?" scoffed Maura. "I still don't understand how they could have missed us. They were searching everywhere."

Jed chuckled. "We were in a little hollow, and they were downhill and upwind of us. If we had been standing up, they would have seen us. All they saw was the ridgeline of the hollows. Had they been uphill, they would have seen us. We need to hurry. They'll soon realize that we doubled-back on them. Quickly now and no talking."

They rode quickly through the woods, skirting around the hill and bypassing the farm. Once past the farm, Jed led them back to the Baltimore and Yorktown Turnpike, or the York Road as it is sometimes called, and quickly trotted north to Towsontown. The traffic had increased. The farm and drover's wagons kicked up enough dust to choke a regiment.

Unwinding his brown scarf, Jed handed it to Maura. "Wrap it around your neck and pull it up over your nose and mouth."

Maura smiled her thanks, not daring to say anything for fear of getting a mouthful of road dirt.

The large, two-story, gray, stone courthouse dominated the farming town as the ground rose up west of the road.

"There appears to be a lookout up in the cupola," Jed said to Maura.

"I saw him. Where are we going?"

Jed pointed straight ahead past the railroad bridge that crossed over the turnpike. "The Ady's Hotel. I thought we could have a late lunch."

"That sounds good." They rode underneath the tracks. "Uh, that wouldn't be the building ahead on the right with the big Confederate flag hanging out from the second floor?"

Jed's mouth twisted in bitter amusement. "I believe so. Do you want to stop or ride back to the city?"

"Didn't you say we needed to wait?" asked Maura.

Jed nodded.

"Then we'll stop for a meal."

"Keep your hat and the scarf up over your face, even inside," Jed said.

Maura laughed. "That might make eating a little hard."

Chuckling, Jed added, "How about until we sit down?"

They rode to Ady's Hotel. The two-story, white-washed building had a second-floor balcony overlooking the turnpike. Jed looked up at the symbol of a divided nation on the flagpole. Maryland hadn't seceded yet, and it was his job to make sure it didn't. Inside, the ground floor had a bar against one wall with tables and chairs scattered around. A wide set of stairs to the second floor rested against the wall opposite the bar.

Jed led the way to a table in the rear. Going around the table, he sat down facing the front door, Maura's eyes widened, and she straightened her back in indignation. Raising his eyebrows, Jed pointed at the seat opposite him.

Maura blew out her breath and sat down, embarrassed.

"I'm sorry," she said as she pulled down the scarf. "I forgot I'm in disguise."

"Maura, you cannot forget things like that." Jed looked up at the bartender who was approaching them. "Avert your face."

Maura turned her head to the side as the bartender asked, "What can I get you folk?"

"Beer?" asked Jed of Maura. She nodded. "Two beers. Do you have anything ready to eat?"

"My wife's the cook," said the bartender. "There's a pot of stew on the stove and fresh bread that's ready now. We've also got eggs, bacon and biscuits and gravy. I'd have to check on anything else available."

"Stew sounds good," said Maura in a low, gruff voice.

Jed bit his lip to hide his smile. "Two stews with bread and butter."

"Along with two beers, coming right up," said the bartender with a smile.

Jed and Maura were silent as the bartender brought them their pints of beer. His wife placed steaming bowls of stew on the table. The delicious aroma of beef, potatoes, onion, and garlic wafted through the air, followed by the wonderful smell of fresh-baked bread.

The food tasted as good as it smelled. Jed watched Maura pick and stir her stew in quiet contemplation.

"I was surprised when you didn't hold my chair for me," she said.

"I almost did, but I caught myself at the last moment," replied Jed. "How are you feeling? It must not have been easy watching that man get killed today."

"I imagine a lot of young men will be killed before this mess is settled," said Maura morosely. "The lieutenant was doing what he felt was his duty. At least he didn't shoot us in the back."

"No, he didn't. His ego got in the way. He wanted to be the man who captured the northern spy. Does the lieutenant's death bother you like Jonathan's?"

Maura took a deep breath. "No. I do worry about Jonathan's death. He would have gladly died in battle but not cut down from behind like an animal. I . . . I have dreams of his spirit roaming restlessly. I thought killing his murderer would lay his ghost to rest, but now I'm thinking it will take the reunification of this nation to do that."

"So you are giving up on revenge?" asked Jed.

"No," stated Maura calmly. "Duff must pay for his crime." She blew out a long, slow breath to let go of the tension inside her. "Jonathan believed in this nation with his whole heart. He foresaw a time when it would be greater than England . . . or all the countries in Europe combined!"

"Do you actually believe his soul won't rest until . . . this is done?"

"I know I couldn't rest. I fear for Jonathan's spirit. I must do what I can to give him peace."

"Until the end of the war?" asked Jed. "You and I both believe that this war will not be short-lived as most of the people in the North believe."

"You would never quit," scoffed Maura humorously. "You're in this for just as long as I am."

"We'll do what we have to do," said Jed with a smile. "I hadn't taken you for a spiritualist."

"I'm not, but I do believe God gives us tasks to do. I hope Johnathan's soul is in heaven. I've been thinking on this. Jonathan's vision was to help reunite this nation and forge it into a great one. His task is unfulfilled and so it's now mine."

"Pre-ordained destiny?" Jed shook his head. "I believe man has free will—the ability to chase his own destiny."

"Maybe. Either way, I think I must see Jonathan's vision through. There's no doubt Duff must pay for his crime, but I now see a greater purpose. Back to our business at hand, now that you've seen the steam gun in action, what do you think of it?"

"What did *you* think of it? Have you seen a cannon in action?" asked Jed.

Maura shook her head.

"Then you would be like the recruit who just joined the Army. I would like to get your opinion."

"I've heard a cannon before," said Maura. "The town council shoots one every Fourth of July. This one was relatively quiet. I was shocked to see all those cannonballs come shooting out of it. I was very glad not to be in front of it ... but if I was, I wouldn't want to be."

"That's how most of the green soldiers will feel," said Jed. "The troops at Fort McHenry won't discuss it even though I've brought up the subject several times. They're afraid of it. After seeing it in action, I must admit, the rate of fire is astonishing. However, it takes a long time to set up, it's inaccurate, and I'm very sure the range is not as far as gunpowder cannons. That means it could be destroyed without it ever firing a shot; the smoke would give away its location."

"So, it's worthless?"

"Yes and no. I'd hate to be a regimental commander who had to assault one of these in a fortified position without artillery support. Even without exploding shells, the steam gun could decimate closely packed troops and break their morale."

"What do you plan to do about the steam gun?"

"I don't know. I'm hoping they'll take it back to Winans's foundry." Jed sighed. "Something has to be done. It's such a symbol—and bugaboo to the Union soldiers—that it has to be nullified."

"Will we be able to get back to Baltimore?" asked Maura. "I felt very conspicuous riding here to Towsontown."

"I should have brought extra clothes for us."

Maura laughed softly so her voice couldn't be heard beyond their table. "And where would you have put them? You know, it may not be a bad idea to have other places in and around Baltimore with supplies and clothing for both of us."

After a moment or two in thought, Jed said, "And beyond that. If Maryland secedes, I'll have to leave the state. I'm too well known, and my arrest would be immediate. If they find out about you, you can't return to the Confederacy. We should make plans to escape in any eventuality. We'll need places where we'll be safe from detection and pursuit, supplies, clothing, weapons, and hard coin. I'll purchase several properties and hide my ownership the same way I did for the gentlemen's club."

"What do you mean?" asked Maura.

"Mayor Brown and Marshal Kane know you own the club," said Jed. "You have the deed to it. However, as far as public records show, a company—which is fake—at an address that is the same as the club's, owns it. With the deed is a notarized letter stating you own the company."

"I'm afraid I didn't look inside the envelope you gave me," said Maura sheepishly. "You told me it was the deed."

"I apologize. I should have explained it. It's a common practice to hide ownership. A gentlemen's club owned by a woman wouldn't get many members. You 're going to have to give it a name."

"I know," said Maura. "I'll ask Mayor Brown and Marshal Kane for suggestions tomorrow night?"

"Tomorrow night?" queried Jed.

"Ah, you have forgotten. We have a soiree tomorrow night, and I expect you to be my attentive partner."

Chapter 21

Wednesday, May 8, 1861

"He can't do that, can he?"

"I don't know. He certainly seems more than capable of it."

"I wonder if his man really died that way?"

"Well, I'm giving him no excuse to come after us."

"Someone needs to stop him."

"Who? These people in Washington put him here."

The worry and fear in the conversations at the soiree that Jed overheard as he circulated through the crowd was not resentment toward the federal government so much as concern for family and friends. Sighing, he shook his head at General Butler's audacity.

One of General Butler's men had died at Relay House. The general had immediately released a statement that the man had been poisoned by strychnine. General Butler went on to state that if any more of his men were poisoned, he would put soldiers in every household in Baltimore City with orders to use this poison, or *infernal weapon* as General Butler put it, against the people.

The proclamation shocked Baltimoreans. The city officials were quick to protest the accusation. They offered to allow doctors to come down to examine the deceased to determine the cause of death. Letters and telegrams flew like wild birds on the wing between Relay House and Washington.

Jed was appalled when he first read the proclamation in the newspaper. As much as he was disgusted by General

Butler's threat against the citizens, it did have benefits. During his morning ride, Jed saw a change in a lot of people.

It was all well and good to talk about living your life free of government interference, but it was very different when faced with the retaliation that could come by defiance and rebellion to governmental authority. The proclamation did not change those who were firm in their commitments, but it did give pause to those in the city who were on the fence, those undecided about which cause to support.

Another benefit was that the killing of Lieutenant Frijack was completely overshadowed. There had been no problem returning to Baltimore as Jed and Maura rode cross country and avoided the main roads. Frijack's death didn't even make it into the papers. Still, Jed had to watch out for those bent on revenge, and he knew there would be someone.

He looked around at the men and women gathered for the soiree. Soiree, indeed! Instead of the small gathering he had envisioned, it had evolved into a ball with over a hundred people in attendance. The location had been changed to the opulent mansion of a railroad owner. Jewelry and gems glittered on the women in their off-the-shoulder gowns, several of them being a little too off-the-shoulder for Jed's taste. The men were immaculate in their evening wear or dress uniforms.

Captain Boxer stood out in his blue police uniform . He nodded to Jed, who returned the greeting. On his morning ride, Jed had been stopped by Captain Boxer and two other police officers to make inquiries into the death of Lieutenant Frijack. Jed used his cover story that he was in attendance with Mrs. Harrison and Mrs. Petford for a reading of Shakespeare's *The Tempest* for most of the day. Captain Boxer's sigh of resignation and acceptance told Jed that his story had already been verified by the two ladies.

Maura, accompanied by Eunice, arrived just after Jed, evoking quite a stir. Her black gown eschewed the normal high collar, long sleeves and black veil. Instead, Maura's gown was low-cut and off the shoulders. Her blonde hair was done up in a twist that draped casually, but artfully, over one shoulder.

Jed had to agree that the dye work on her gown was superb. Instead of being a black blob in the middle of all the gaily colored dresses, it seemed to shimmer and shine all on its own. The gown's rich shades of ebony enhanced the flounces and patterns of the dress. Life was sucked out of all the pastel dresses near it, and the richer colors just looked garish. Even Eunice's rich, dark-purple dress seemed to be washed out when she was standing next to Maura.

Jed tried several times to talk to Maura or to get a dance with her. She always seemed to be unavailable or had already promised someone else that dance. It was getting frustrating until Eunice passed him by and whispered, "Fourth dance, the waltz."

Jed waited until the waltz was announced before asking Maura to dance. She acquiesced, and he led her onto the ballroom floor.

"I'm sorry, Jed," said Maura softly as she curtsied and he bowed. "With General Butler's threat, I thought it might be best to show my displeasure by snubbing you."

"I, too, was appalled by the man," admitted Jed. "People are being very careful around me."

As they assumed their dance positions, Maura asked, "Would he do it . . . poison all these people?"

"Is he ruthless enough to do it? I don't think so. He's looking out for himself, and I believe he's using the death of one of his soldiers as a ploy to prevent attacks. A very shocking tactic but, as I have seen today, an effective one. I don't know how the solider died, but I would hazard a guess that it was not poisoning. General Butler may not be a good soldier, but he's a very smart lawyer and knows how to manipulate people. I hope you don't count me among his ilk."

"I don't," said Maura with a smile. "I was going to dance with you, but I had to play the incensed Southern lady. I had to make you wait until I got my 'talking to'."

"Talking to?"

"Yes." They glided across the floor in time to the music. "The powers that be had to remind me of my commitments, despite my outrage at General Butler's promise to commit mass murder."

"I sent off a warning to the War Department after I read his proclamation earlier," said Jed. "The reply was short: being handled. In other words, leave it to them."

"That is not encouraging." Maura grimaced. "However, I do have to agree with you about it being a ploy. I noticed fewer people are talking about secession today." She looked aside for a second. "I thought the people here would be angry, like they were during the riot."

"The riot was a mob, rebelling against a visible target," said Jed. "Poison is more insidious. No one I know of would want to be associated with a poisoner. Duff is still a murderer, but the Confederacy can excuse his behavior because he used a pistol."

Maura tightened up in his arms and missed a step. Jed barely avoided stepping on her foot and was rewarded when her heel came down on his toes. He cursed at himself for bringing up such a painful reminder. Even if Maura was now more for seeking justice than vengeance, the killing of her husband was still too recent for her not to be affected by it.

"Oh, I am so sorry," said Maura earnestly, stopping in the middle of the floor.

"It is entirely my fault," stated Jed for the benefit of those around them. "I must practice more often."

"I must say that I am a little worn out," said Maura. "Refreshments and a walk in the garden?"

"I would be honored." Jed offered Maura his arm.

Leading her out of the ballroom, Jed escorted Maura down the hallway to the dining room where a buffet was laid out. The large table held platters of cold ham and chicken, plates of different cheeses and fruit, and bowls of bread. There were also different types of pickle relishes, jams, and honey. At the sideboard, servants poured drinks. Jed handed Maura a glass of champagne before handing one to Eunice, who had followed behind them.

"Did you see that?" asked Jed as he placed slices of chicken on a plate.

"What?" asked Eunice.

"Marshal Kane and his wife looked like they were about to step in here, but he quickly turned back down the hallway." Jed chuckled.

Maura gave a little smirk and Eunice snickered.

"He's the one who gave me a 'talking to'," said Maura as she took a small selection of fruit. "He must not want to interrupt our time together."

"Well, I'm enjoying my time with you." Jed and Maura nibbled on their food and, when they were finished, handed their empty plates to a servant. "When you're done, I would very much like that walk in the garden with you."

"I would be delighted," said Maura. "It's a nice evening for a stroll."

Jed escorted Maura down the hallway and out the back door to the formal gardens. Eunice followed behind them at the proper distance. The sliver of the waning moon did not shed enough light to see by; therefore, torches lined the pathway, giving an eerie, flickering light to the landscape. Topiary, flowers, and hedges created the meandering paths through the garden. Fireflies blinked off and on everywhere as crickets chirped noisily.

"How are you?" asked Jed. "Yesterday must have been a bit of a shock."

"It was . . . was unfortunate that Lieutenant Frijack died, but he chose his path," stated Maura firmly. "I have learned that the steam gun is back at Winans's foundry."

"I have heard the same thing." They reached the end of the formal gardens and turned to walk along the back pathway. "They have it ready for movement by the railhead located inside the foundry. It appears they are afraid of it being seized by the federal government."

"Do you want me to keep a close eye on it?" asked Maura.

"Only superficially," he replied. "I have other people watching it. We need to concentrate on what is being planned for all the weapons, ammunitions, and supplies that have been secreted in this city and elsewhere. It's been alluded to twice that something is going to happen and soon."

Maura shook her head as they reached the other corner of the gardens and started toward the house. "A number of militia soldiers have been transferred out of their units in the city. I saw the rosters on Mayor Brown's desk. A lot more soldiers are being brought in or joining up. There was a notation on the roster, but the mayor was returning. I think it was a date. I'm sorry, but I didn't get a chance to see what the date was."

"Don't be," said Jed. "I'd rather have you safe than caught. The Confederates did the same thing under President Buchanan before they seceded. They put southern officers in charge of vital posts, which were immediately surrendered to the Confederacy without a fight. They are preparing for a rebellion, not simply transferring their stockpiles to the South."

"If Baltimore revolts, what will happen?" asked Maura. "Governor Hicks doesn't want secession that will tear his state apart. The Maryland legislators voted that they could not legally vote for it."

"The eastern half of the state may revolt. Baltimore City will probably be shelled from Fort McHenry. After the riot, Marshal Kane put out a call for assistance, and several thousand men answered that call. They have since disbanded and returned to their homes. I'm not sure how many will or can answer a second call." Jed blew out his breath. "The federal government simply cannot allow Washington to be isolated."

"President Lincoln did tell me that," said Maura.

"I . . . ," Jed suddenly stopped talking and slowed his pace. His head cocked from one side to another, as if he was listening for something. "I . . . I . . . must say how delighted I am that you agreed to take a stroll with me through the gardens, Mrs. Harrison."

"I am the one who is delighted, Mr. Tremblant," cooed Maura, laying a hand on Jed's arm. She whispered, "What is it?"

Jed put a smile on his face and tilted his head down to her ear. "Someone is here . . . nearby. We need to get back inside."

Maura laughed. "Oh, Mr. Tremblant, the things you say. However, I'm feeling a little chilled. I do believe it's time to go back inside."

"Your wish is my command," said Jed with a bow, followed by a huff of disgust from Eunice.

With fake smiles on their faces, Maura took Jed's arm, and they strolled toward the door. The night was dead silent, no insects or birds. The lack of nighttime sounds was what had alerted Jed that someone else was in the garden.

They were only thirty feet away from the rear door when two men stepped out from behind two large bushes to bar their way. One of the men was Captain Wilcott. A rustling noise behind him made Jed turn halfway around to see two more men there. All of them were in militia uniforms.

"Mrs. Harrison, why don't you and your chaperone go inside?" suggested Captain Wilcott. "We need to talk to Mr. Tremblant about the death of Lieutenant Frijack. I don't think he will be bothering you anymore."

Chapter 22

Wednesday, May 8, 1861

Several things occurred all at the same time. Jed's hand reached for the Sharp's derringer he had tucked into his waistband. Maura took a half step forward with an angry look to berate Captain Wilcott. Captain Wilcott reached for his holster, unsure whether it was Jed or Maura that he had to protect himself from. One of the men in the back grabbed Eunice's arm to pull her out of the way.

"EEEEEEK!!!!!!"

At the loud scream, everyone looked at Eunice.

"Help! Help!" she yelled, thrashing the man holding her arm with her purse. "Get away from me! Help! Let go of me!"

The other man in the back moved forward to help his buddy and was rewarded with an inadvertent elbow to his solar plexus. The one holding her arm let go when her purse, which had heavy iron strips sewn into the lining, smashed into his nose. Faces began to appear in the windows, and several men burst out the back door.

"What's going on here?" demanded an older man.

One militiaman, holding onto his chest with one hand, held up his other but could only wheeze in long ragged gasps. The man beside him sat on the ground holding onto his bloody nose. Captain Wilcott and his man held up their hands and took a step backward with total chagrin showing on their faces.

"Everything is fine," said Jed calmly as he walked over to comfort Eunice. She was shaking, but it was more from anger than fright. "It was an unfortunate misunderstanding. These gentlemen came out of the dark, and Mrs. Harrison's companion took fright."

"Yes," agreed Eunice, taking a deep breath to calm herself. "I am so sorry, gentlemen. If I had known who you were, I wouldn't have fought so vigorously."

Several of the observing guests turned away to hide their smiles, and a low chuckling rippled through the gathered crowd. Captain Wilcott compressed his mouth into a tight line, but he shoved aside his embarrassment and stepped forward.

"My dear lady," he said, bowing at the waist. "I must give you my most profound apology. I am entirely at fault. I could not find Mrs. Harrison and feared for her safety. Had I known she was with you and Mr. Tremblant, my fears would have been quelled." Turning toward Jed, he added, "Mr. Tremblant, I am sorry. I did not mean to frighten the ladies."

"No harm done, Captain," said Jed. "Your concern for Mrs. Harrison's well-being commends you. Come inside, and we can have a drink."

"You will have to excuse him, Mr. Tremblant." Mayor Brown approached them. "I need to have a word with Captain Wilcott."

"Mr. Tremblant, would you be so kind as to escort Mrs. Petford inside and see to her needs?" asked Maura. "I'll keep Mayor Brown company."

"As you wish." Jed offered his arm to Eunice.

As they headed inside, Eunice whispered, "Do you think anyone noticed Captain Wilcott had three other militiamen with him?"

Jed chuckled. "Maybe. Everyone was busy laughing in their sleeves that you took down two soldiers with your purse."

"I ripped the lining," grumbled Eunice. "I'll have to get that reinforced."

Once inside the house, Jed whispered, "I must go. I don't like her being out there alone with those men."

"Then what are you standing here for?" she replied.

Eunice intercepted a couple moving toward them. "Oh, my goodness! I had such a fright!"

Jed walked casually through two rooms and out a side door. In the dark, he moved quickly but silently as he circled around to the gardens. Using skills he had learned from the Indians, he stealthily made his way to a shadowy point among the hedges where he could see and hear the group in the garden.

Captain Wilcott had sent his men away. He, Mayor Brown, and Maura had repositioned themselves away from the house, so they could not be overheard. Their path would lead them closer to Jed.

"What in the hell—" Mayor Brown started to say.

"Oh, no, gentlemen," snapped Maura angrily. "I'll start first. I believe everyone in Baltimore City has heard of Lieutenant Frijack's death. As I told Captain Boxer of the police department, Mr. Tremblant was in my company at the time. I was on the verge of finding out what, if any, involvement he might have had in the lieutenant's death. I'll never find out anything now. He'll be on his guard given that you have warned him."

She looked at Mayor Brown. "By your statement, you didn't know about this, which means you have people working for you who are acting on their own volition. Neither of you are inspiring me with confidence! Why don't you just tell Tremblant your plans?!"

"So far, all I've seen you do is have a good time," sneered Captain Wilcott in retaliation. "Maybe you should start *working* on it a little more."

There was no mistaking Captain Wilcott's implication. Maura's face turned white in stark contrast to her black dress, and she brought her hand up to her throat in shock. Jed had to control his urge to soundly thrash the captain.

"Enough! Both of you!" barked Mayor Brown. "That was uncalled for, Captain Wilcott. You will not insult a lady. We cannot be fighting amongst ourselves. We owe it to the people of this city and of the state. We have all made mistakes. I know I have."

Captain Wilcott took a moment before saying, "Mrs. Harrison, I apologize. I have no excuse for what I said. Mayor

Brown is correct that we need to work together. I'm sorry if I have made things more difficult for you."

"We are all under a great deal of stress," commented Maura. "What will happen to the steam gun?"

"How did you know about the steam gun?" asked Captain Wilcott suspiciously.

Maura gave him a look of disgust. "It's been reported in all the newspapers and journals with drawings. Even covered with a tarp, it was easily recognizable when you drove it north from the city."

"Northern forces know it has been repaired and is functional," said Mayor Brown. "They will do their best to capture or destroy it. We must give this some thought. Mrs. Harrison, please find out what Mr. Tremblant knows."

It was clearly a dismissal, and Maura nodded to the two men before heading back into the mansion. Mayor Brown and Captain Wilcott followed a moment or two behind her. Jed crept along behind them to hear what they were saying.

"Do you trust her?" asked Captain Wilcott.

"Yes," replied Mayor Brown. "The information she has provided has been excellent. You should know. That shipment of two hundred pistols would have fallen into General Butler's hands at Relay House had you not intercepted it. Besides, if she were to betray us, she would lose her family, her plantation, and her life."

"So, what will we do with the steam gun? It belongs to the Confederacy."

"I am afraid we cannot keep it here in Baltimore City, as much as I would like to do so," said Mayor Brown. "It's a symbol to the people, but its capture or destruction would be devastating. Getting rid of Mr. Tremblant would not solve the problem."

"No, but I would have felt better," said Captain Wilcott. "After the soothsayer's day?"

Mayor Brown looked up quickly and then glanced around to see if anyone was nearby. "The plans are final, but no one else is informed yet of that day," he warned. "Everyone is prepared, but the notice to put the plan into action will not be sent until the day before."

"It cannot happen soon enough for me. Tremblant?"

"After we have thrown off the yoke of oppression, he will be an enemy spy on our sovereign land," said Mayor Brown with a smile.

"I shall wait for that day with eagerness." Captain Wilcott returned the smile.

The men reached the mansion and walked toward the ballroom.

As Jed tried to decide whether to follow or hold back, a door leading down to the basement cracked open, and a young, black woman quietly stepped out.

"Well, it's a good thing Miss Maura wanted me to work here tonight," said Tabitha Freed.

With an approving nod at Maura's foresight, Jed eased back into the darkness to return to the soiree.

Chapter 23

Friday, May 10, 1861

"Good evening, sir."

"Good evening, Paul." Jed handed his hat and gloves to the butler. "Has anyone else arrived?"

"No, sir. I don't expect anyone else to be here for at least another hour. Miss Maura is in the parlor checking on the arrangements."

"Thank you, Paul. I know the way."

Jed walked to the door on his right and opened it. The piano was still in its usual spot, but all the chairs and sofas had been turned to face it. Extra chairs had also been placed in the room. Maura was arranging music on a stand placed beside the piano.

"Mr. Tremblant, you're early."

"Wild horses couldn't keep me away." He closed the door.

"Are you alone?"

"Yes. I came by to see if you have any more information."

"No, I don't. Do you have any idea what the soothsayer's day is?" Maura asked.

"No more than I had yesterday," admitted Jed. "I even went so far as to interview several of the top spiritualists today."

Maura's breath caught in her throat. "Did . . . did they tell you anything?"

"Nothing apart from the fact I have a strong aura and am facing a time of trial and tribulation," dismissed Jed. He dared not tell her about the one who stated she saw the shadow of a young man hovering behind him. "The Indians I know believe in ghosts and legends of unfinished tasks. I've never seen any—ghosts, that is—but I do know we all have souls. I also believe, given the tales I've heard, a soul may become restless until conditions are met to lay it to rest."

After taking in a ragged breath, Maura let it out slowly. She gave Jed a weak smile and a nod. Her shoulders squared up and resolve filled her being.

"I hope tonight's recital won't be too distressing for you, Jed. Mayor Brown and Marshal Kane won't be here. They have a city council meeting to attend, but the Cary Sisters, Hettie and Jennie, will be here to listen to Miss Natalie LaBlanc perform *Maryland, My Maryland*."

"That song does seem to be gaining popularity," said Jed dryly. "I've been led to understand Jennie Cary wrote the music for the poem."

"She adapted the music," corrected Maura. "She used the tune of *Lauriger Horatius*, more commonly called *O, Tannenbaum*. I told you they are supporters of the Confederacy. They have organized the Monument Street Girls to sew Confederate uniforms. I heard a rumor they are collecting medicines and supplies. They have included me in their sewing circle, but nothing has been revealed, except their distaste for the North. Including this song in tonight's recital ensures their attendance. What do you think of the song?"

"What I think of it is irrelevant. The person who wrote it, a Maryland Man in Louisiana, believes in secession and the division of the United States. What do you think of it?"

"It's a, pardon the expression, damned if you do and damned if you don't situation. I love my home and my state of Virginia. The trouble is that everyone there and in most of the South wants to be left alone to govern their land as they see fit. It's a view of isolation, which cannot work in these modern times. Jonathan showed me that. The Virginia counties west of my home did not agree to secession. I'm afraid it's going to split my state in two."

"It already has," said Jed. "I've received reports that the delegates from those western counties are meeting in Wheeling tomorrow to discuss the issue, and one or two delegates have stated they should make themselves into the state of New Virginia."

"This is what Jonathan warned me about; where we become so divided that it's every man for himself. We will separate ourselves so much that we can expect no help from our neighbors in time of need."

"Events have overtaken us, Maura. The northern abolitionists and southern secessionists won't compromise. Both sides thirst for war. Some want to prove their side is the right one. Some want the glory. There will be those who see opportunity and profit. Very few will understand the cost."

Maura shook her head. "You and I are alike, Jed. We know this war will not be short lived. Before I married Jonathan, we had a party at the plantation. One of the young men there bragged that he wasn't worried about the northern shopkeepers because any one southern could whip ten Northerners. I asked what if there were twenty or thirty. He looked at me in horror as if I had said the most treasonous thing in the world."

"I promise to be on my best behavior with Miss Cary . . . the Misses Carys." Jed chuckled. "Although, how they will react to my presence, I couldn't guess. I'll even sing a verse or two, as long as it doesn't have the words despot or tyrant."

Maura laughed. "I think you just excluded the entire song. They will be on their best behavior. Strange, isn't it? Everyone here thinks you're a northern spy, but no one wants to exclude you from any social gathering."

"It must be my charming personality," quipped Jed.

"More like some very interesting, but mildly repellent, flora or fauna they have never seen or smelled before," said Tabitha, walking into the room. "They want nothing to do with you, yet they can't keep away."

"Tabitha!" chided Maura as Jed roared with laughter.

"No, No. It's actually true from their point of view, and it's working to our favor. They're so busy watching me that they aren't watching the two of you."

"That doesn't help if we can't solve when the soothsayer's day is," complained Tabitha.

"Hopefully, someone will let something slip," said Maura. "Was there something you needed, Tabitha?"

"I'm sorry. The cook needs to see you. There is a problem with the puff pastries."

"Oh, jiminey!" cursed Maura. "I'll be back."

"Is there anything I can help with?" Jed asked Tabitha after Maura had left.

"Not unless you can cook. I've got a few more things to do. Refreshments have been set up, so please help yourself to something to drink. Watch out for Hettie Cary. She's known as the great beauty of Baltimore, but I think she's vain, self-righteous, and enough of a fanatic to do anything to further the southern cause."

"Thank you, Tabitha."

"What for?"

"I've been concentrating on the industrialists and the political leaders and not paying enough attention to the women who support the South," admitted Jed.

With a nod of acknowledgement, Tabitha left the room, and Jed moved to the sideboard where bottles were lined up. Taking a glass off a silver platter, he poured himself one finger of whiskey. It was only a short wait before there was a knock on the front door. Jed looked up when Paul escorted a pretty, young woman in an apricot evening dress and a young man in black tails into the room.

"Miss Natalie LaBlanc and her accompanist," announced the butler.

"Miss LaBlanc, I am Jedidiah Tremblant. Mrs. Harrison is addressing an issue in the kitchen. She should be returning shortly."

"It is my pleasure to meet you, Mr. Tremblant." Her voice was sultry with a resonance that vibrated through a man. Her pitch and diction were perfect.

"The pleasure is all mine," said Jed. "May I assist you?"

"Yes," said the young man quickly as Natalie's eyes seemed to take on a predatory look. "Is this the pianoforte I will be playing?"

"I can only assume so," said Jed.

The young man sat at the piano. After a quick glance at the music, he began running chords to check the tune of each note and the action of the keys. Natalie walked to the stand to check her music.

"*Maryland, My Maryland*," she mused. "You're not a native of Maryland. You're accent and diction give you away."

"I live in Chicago, Illinois," replied Jed.

Natalie frowned. "It's more than that. I have a good ear for such things."

"I served in the Indian Territory for several years with the Army," admitted Jed. "You do have a good ear."

"That's not the only thing about me that is good," purred Natalie to Jed, giving him a direct stare.

Jed swallowed hard as the accompanist coughed and choked. Standing up, the young man headed toward the door. "Excuse me. I need to use the necessary." He left the room.

Natalie's eyes took in the expensive cut of his evening wear. "Well, Mr. Tremblant, have you seen any of my performances?"

Jed almost said, *I'm seeing one now*, but changed his mind. "I'm afraid not," he told her.

"I need a patron. One that is young, virile, and handsome."

"And rich," added Jed.

Natalie smiled and shrugged. "It's the nature of the world, and I'm worth it." She flounced around the piano in exaggerated nonchalance. "Are you staying here with Mrs. Harrison?"

"That would not be proper. She is recently widowed."

"Ah, I have not met her. I see no ring on your finger, so can I say you are not married?"

"Widower," stated Jed flatly. "My wife died three years ago from influenza."

Natalie stopped flitting about and looked at Jed with sympathy. "I am sorry to hear of your wife's passing." She sighed lightly to rid herself of any sad thoughts, then changed the subject. "What are your views on secession?"

"I am against it, as anyone who will be here can attest to."

"To be truthful, I'm ambivalent to the whole thing. I sing the songs I'm paid to sing." Natalie put her hand on Jed's arm and pressed up against him. "I sing even better in private."

"Good evening."

At the sound of Maura's voice, Natalie let go of Jed's arm and casually stepped away from him. Her face showed no alarm or contrition at being caught in such a compromising position. With a knowing smile on her face, Natalie turned to face Maura. As she caught sight of Maura's youth and beauty, her lips tightened, and a bleak look overtook her.

"Miss LaBlanc?" Maura glided forward.

Jed watched Natalie take in and assess Maura's clothes, grace, and poise before Maura took Natalie's hands into her own.

"May I say how honored I am that you are able to perform for us tonight," Maura said.

"The honor is all mine."

"I see you have met Mr. Tremblant. He is of the Tremblants of Illinois, an old and respected family." Natalie's eyes flickered to Jed and back. She knew as well as he did that *old and respected* meant *rich and powerful*. "I sent your pianist to the kitchen for something to eat. May I offer you sustenance or refreshment?"

"Honeyed tea, if you please."

"I will bring you a cup, ma'am," said Paul, coming into the room. "Pardon my intrusion, Miss Maura. Captain Wilcott and Miss Caston just arrived in a carriage. They will be at the door any minute."

Maura's lips twisted into a grimace. "Please excuse me. It appears I have uninvited guests. Paul, have someone set up two more chairs in here. Jed, will you keep Miss LaBlanc entertained?"

Natalie gave Jed a quizzical look as Maura headed toward the front door, and Paul left on his appointed tasks.

"Jed?" asked Natalie rhetorically. "It sounds as if you two are more than friends."

"Her husband was killed in the riot. I was there when it happened and was moved to help her, as I can."

"She didn't seem happy to have Captain Wilcott here. Who is he?"

"He is a captain in the Maryland Militia and a southern sympathizer," answered Jed.

"Ah, she is for the Union then."

The Trail of the Scottish Bluebell

"I'm not sure," equivocated Jed. "Her father's plantation is in Virginia, but her late husband was a Union officer from Connecticut. I think she's upset at having uninvited guests show up. That and the fact that Captain Wilcott would like nothing better than to put several bullets into me."

"No!" Natalie recoiled. "Really?"

Jed nodded. "He objects to my being from Illinois, the state President Lincoln came from, and my being here in Maryland. He also thinks I'm responsible for the death of one of his friends, Lieutenant Frijack."

"I heard about that. Wasn't he the young man who died north of here? You're not in jail, so you're either not responsible for his death, or you're too rich and powerful to be arrested, or are you smart enough not to get caught?"

"Which do you think it is?"

Natalie inclined her head toward Paul, who was coming in with a steaming cup and saucer. "I think I shall take tea."

Maura entered the room. "Mr. Tremblant, are you wearing that very large pistol of yours? Captain Wilcott and Miss Caston will be staying. He is currently divesting himself of saber, firearms, and any other weapon he may have been carrying."

"If one set this to music, it would be like one of my operas," said Natalie. "It's a tragedy when a hostess has to disarm her guests for an evening's entertainment."

"That's why I didn't invite him, Miss LaBlanc," said Maura acidly. "There is bad blood between Captain Wilcott and Mr. Tremblant."

"He told me."

Jed shrugged his shoulders at Maura's glare.

"Well, Captain Wilcott was most apologetic about being here, so of course, I had to invite him and Miss Caston to stay." Maura harumphed. "Now, about your pistol, Mr. Tremblant?"

Jed opened his jacket to show he was not wearing his shoulder holster and Colt. He knew Maura was aware of his derringer.

"No pistol," he said with a smile. "I promise to be on my best behavior, and I'll try to avoid Captain Wilcott as much as possible. Although I do have to wonder how he could have made such a mistake on his calendar."

"You've never made a mistake on your social appointments?" asked Natalie. "I know I have once or twice."

Maura, however, looked thoughtful. Someone employed the knocker on the front door, and Maura, after giving Jed a cautionary look, was forced to leave them to be the gracious hostess.

Couples began filtering into the room. Jennie Cary arrived with her sister, Hettie Cary, who was described as one of the great beauties of Baltimore City. Jed thought she was indeed stunning, though barely a shadow when standing next to Maura.

Captain Wilcott came in with the Cary sisters. He whispered in their ears, and both women shot Jed looks of disgust. If Jed wasn't sure of their sympathies before, he was now. A quick thought flitted through his mind, and he wondered where Miss Caston was. A hand lightly touched his arm.

"You looked lonesome over here all by yourself," cooed Dorothy Caston. "I thought I'd keep you company."

"What of Captain Wilcott?" asked Jed. "You arrived with him."

"We're only good friends. I could have died when I found out we had not been invited! I was mortified! Mrs. Harrison was so gracious to allow us to remain." Dorothy slid her arm through his. "I would be ever so grateful if you would consent to be my escort this evening. I'm too embarrassed to be seen in Captain Wilcott's company."

Jed did not want to escort Dorothy Caston anywhere. Glancing around, he saw Maura engaged in conversation with Captain Wilcott and another gentleman. Jed was well aware of the duels Captain Wilcott initiated supposedly to protect the honor of Miss Caston. This scenario had all the earmarks of a premeditated scandal leading up to a duel at dawn. He searched for some way to turn Dorothy down without insult when a voice spoke up behind them.

"Pardon my intrusion, Mr. Tremblant," said Eunice. "If you would be so kind, Mrs. Harrison has requested you to escort me for the recital."

Dorothy looked mad enough to spit nails, but a request from the hostess could not be ignored. With a fake smile, she removed her hand from Jed's arm and curtsied to him before moving away. Jed let out a sigh of relief.

"Thank you, Eunice," he murmured softly. "I was trying to find some way to get away from her."

Eunice gave a little snort. "You did look like a scared rabbit. Maura warned the rest of the staff and me to be wary of Miss Caston and Captain Wilcott." She gave Jed a knowing smirk. "I guess I don't have to warn you not to be alone with her."

"I'd rather be prisoner to a bunch of Kiowa squaws than be alone with her," said Jed earnestly.

"Mr. Tremblant!" exclaimed Eunice in mortification.

"No, Mrs. Petford. It's not what you think. To put it mildly, I'd rather be a prisoner and tortured by the men of the tribe than by the women."

"Let's move on to another subject. Shall we try the buffet?"

Jed offered his arm, and they headed to the dining room. Cold meats, pickles, relish, fruits, breads, and preserves were laid out for the guests. Paul and another servant served drinks from the sideboard.

"Are they as savage as I have heard?" asked Eunice.

"That depends on what you've heard," replied Jed. "Among the people of their own tribe, they are friendly and generous. Of course, there are exceptions, just like anywhere in the world. Between tribes is a different story. Young men steal or wage war on other tribes to prove their prowess, to make a name for themselves. Life is hard in the West. Even more so, since the white man is encroaching more and more on Indian lands."

"But there's so much land out there," argued Eunice.

Jed shook his head. "No red man owns a single piece of land. The concept is ridiculous and alien to them. To them, the land belongs to all. Imagine if you will, an important spring that has been available to all the Indians for hundreds of years is suddenly claimed by a farmer or rancher. He puts up notices that it's now his property and his property alone. He will not allow anyone else to use it, because he needs it for his farm or ranch. The Indians now believe him to be crazy and dangerous. The white man will defend his property to the death because he believes it's his right."

"Oh," said Eunice meekly. Her face took on a look of consternation.

"It's all right, Eunice," reassured Jed gently. "Let's first see if we survive as a nation."

Paul came over to offer them drinks, and they moved on to lighter topics of conversation. Just as they finished their small repast, Maura asked everyone to take their seats for the night's entertainment.

Jed escorted Eunice into the parlor. When he held the chair out for Eunice to sit, Dorothy barged in to take the seat beside Jed intended for Eunice. Eunice countered the move by sitting in the seat Jed was planning on taking, to the right of the one he was holding. That startled Jed as much as it did Dorothy. Still holding onto the empty chair, Jed inclined his head to Dorothy as an invitation to sit down, placing her between Eunice and another elderly lady.

With no graceful way to refuse, Dorothy had to sit. Jed walked to the other side of Eunice to another unoccupied chair. Dorothy made to rise but was stopped by Eunice's disarming smile and restraining hand.

Maura introduced Natalie LaBlanc and sat in the front row between Jennie and Hettie Cary. As Natalie walked to her stand, Jed saw Captain Wilcott situated across the room. The man had made no move to greet Jed, which was impressive given the smallness of the gathering.

A printed program listing the music for the recital with a short description of each piece was on each seat. The first song was *Maryland, My Maryland*. Natalie began singing and Jed listened carefully. Her tone and inflection were perfect.

A slight movement from Maura caught Jed's attention. She was sitting up very straight, and her knuckles were white as they gripped the arms of her chair. Jed realized the song had a completely different meaning for her. The despot wasn't President Lincoln to Maura but was either Anthony Duff or Jefferson Davis. As to the patriotic gore that flecked the streets of Baltimore, that would be Jonathan's blood, not the blood of the rioters. Jed could see the song rousing and reinforcing Maura's resolve.

When the song ended, everyone, except Jed, stood to applaud, but he did clap to acknowledge Natalie's skill and talent. The song lacked the fire and fervor that he expected from the singer.

Natalie looked him in the eyes and gave him a smile and a wink. Jed inclined his head in thanks, suspecting she had not put her whole heart into the performance.

Maura and the Cary sisters were congratulating each other with a feverish look in their eyes. The sisters were filled with passionate zeal for the southern cause. Maura's fervor, Jed knew, was from reliving the moment when Jonathan was killed and feeling the bitterness and agony all over again. She looked at Jed, and he knew she chafed at the delays he had imposed to keep her safe. They had come close to getting Duff twice, yet he still eluded them. That rankled them to no end.

The Cary sisters gushed over the performance. With the rise of the song's popularity, they were certain that Maryland's secession from the barbaric North was only days away, and they looked forward to joining the nobility of the Confederacy.

Maura smiled, nodded, and moved aside to allow other well-wishers to come forward to congratulate Jennie on her—in their minds—brilliant adaptation. Jed had stood up, so as not to be conspicuous by being the only one seated.

A movement by the doorway caught his attention, and he saw Captain Wilcott ease into the parlor from the hall. Jed caught a glimpse of a silvery gleam hidden by the arm of Wilcott's coat. Before Jed could move, Maura edged up to Wilcott. Jed turned his back but continued listening.

"An extraordinary performance, don't you think so, Captain Wilcott?"

"Truly inspiring," he admitted. "Though, should you say such things with your paramour in the room?"

"He's across the room." Then she hissed, "Put it back!"

"I beg your pardon?"

"Put . . . It . . . Back!" said Maura with a phony smile on her face. "I will not have Mr. Tremblant killed in my home. I will not interfere with whatever plot the two of you have hatched, but Miss Caston's intentions are too blatant. However, attacking him like Representative Brooks attacked Senator Sumner in the senate will generate a great deal of animosity. I will not lose my contacts or my position because of you. So, put it back. My butler will be taking an inventory of the cutlery in two minutes."

Jed expected him to be seething, but Captain Wilcott calmly asked, "You'll not interfere with my plans?"

"No, as long as they do not interfere with mine," replied Maura. "I get instructions. You get instructions. I'm trying to limit the repercussions your independent actions will have upon me. Now, good sir, if you will excuse me. We must finish the recital."

After everyone was seated, Natalie launched into a lively version of *Il Becio, The Kissing Waltz*. Even though the response was more subdued, Jed felt more passion and intensity in Natalie's singing.

The third song was *Ah, Jeris de me Voir, The Jewel Song* from *Faust*, when Marguerite found jewels and a hand mirror left by Mephistopheles to entice her to Faust. Her seduction leads to her downfall and death, but at her death, she returns to the Lord and prays for redemption, which is granted. Jed could see the parallel with the Southern States being led astray.

The next song was *Der Hella Rocle* from Mozart's *Die Zauberflute*. The program's description explained that this was where the Queen of the Night, being denied what she thought was her birthright, plots the destruction of Salastro and the Temple of Light, bringing everything into eternal darkness. Natalie's rendition was flawless, and Jed saw one or two people squirm in discomfort as if they were examining their own motives in the present conflict.

The last piece was *Ave Maria* from Shubert's work on *The Lady of the Lake*. Maura's program description stated it was a prayer for the innocents. Natalie's voice soared and everyone, even the servants, were transfixed in wonder. Though the listeners may not have understood the language of the song, the meaning came through with a clarity that had all the women and several of the men crying. The beautiful aria tugged at Jed's heartstrings, and he was surprised that it evoked both despair and hopefulness about the upcoming civil war.

Utter silence reigned as the last note lingered. A second later, everyone was on their feet, and Natalie curtsied in response to the tumultuous applause. Stepping forward and taking both Natalie's hands, Maura expressed her admiration and gratitude for the exceptional recital. Afterward, Maura invited everyone to help themselves to the food and refreshments.

Eunice turned toward Jed before Dorothy even thought of doing so. Jed couldn't hide his smile at Dorothy's look of startlement and upset as he extended his arm to Eunice. Maura was still talking to Natalie as he escorted Eunice back to the dining room. Captain Wilcott's face was pinched in anger, and he jerked his head at Dorothy to get her to follow them.

Jed placed food on a plate for Eunice and fetched her a small glass of punch. Dorothy tried to approach Jed, and he almost laughed as she and Eunice maneuvered around one another. He was so busy watching them that he was startled when a slim hand slid around his arm.

"Those two look like they're having fun." Natalie chuckled.

"I believe they are," said Jed with a smile. "May I get you some food or drink?"

"As much as I would like to, it might be best if we leave while these two are occupied."

"Us? . . . Leave?" asked Jed.

"Yes, us," replied Natalie. "Mrs. Harrison has offered me your services to escort me home tonight and said I'm not to leave your side. I think she wants you away from Miss Caston and Captain Wilcott before something untoward occurs. Since I am trying to remain neutral between the two sides, Mrs. Harrison believes I'm safe for you to be with." Natalie's mouth quirked up in a knowing little smile. "You are safe with me, aren't you?"

Chapter 24

Saturday, May 11, 1861

Bryce had barely opened the front door before Tanner burst into the foyer.

"Mr. Tremblant! Mr. Tremblant!" he yelled.

"I beg your—" Bryce managed to say as Tanner sprinted upstairs, taking the steps two at a time.

Tanner stopped at the top of the stairs to orient himself. He rushed down the hallway and threw open the master bedroom door before rushing in.

"Mr. Tremblant! They're going to move the steam gun today! They've already loaded it onto a railcar! I rushed . . . OH!"

Tanner choked and turned beet red as his eyes grew as wide as saucers. Natalie's complete lack of clothing and her very, very irritated look made Tanner wish he had a big hole he could just crawl into and die. A door down the hallway banged open, and Jed in his nightshirt rushed into the room. The pistol in his hand didn't look half as deadly as the stormy look he was giving Tanner.

Another clatter of footsteps sounded on the stairs. Before anyone could move, Chrissy ran into the bedroom. She jerked to a stop when she caught sight of everyone.

"Oh!" she gasped out loud. "Oh, my!" She broke out in uncontrollable laughter.

"Enough!" grunted Jed as he put his derringer on top of the dresser. "It's not even first light. Let the lady sleep."

Natalie shot him a sardonic look before sighing deeply and pulling the bed covers up to her neck. Grabbing the giggling Chrissy by the arm, he started toward the door. Tanner gulped loudly and hurried out ahead of Jed and Chrissy. Bryce, standing in the hall and with calm aplomb, pulled the door closed.

"It would have been better if you had checked to see that we were alone first before blurting out your news about the steam gun," admonished Jed in a harsh whisper.

Tanner hung his head in shame. Chrissy snapped, "Don't yous be giving him any grief, Mr. Tremblant! Don't bes getting your tally-wacker all bents out of shape!"

Pointing toward the bedroom, Jed softly said, "That woman in there now knows that the two of you are associated with me. She knows that I'm from the North and that I'm gathering information about the steam gun."

"Oh," gasped a crestfallen Chrissy as everyone took a moment to reflect.

"Nothing can be done to reverse what has happened, Master Jed," said Bryce. "It would be prudent to find out why these two were so intent on disturbing your . . . rest. They just picked the wrong room where you were sleeping. You could have sent her home."

"Appearances, Bryce," said Jed, more to inform the other two than anything else. "After Mrs. Harrison forced Miss LaBlanc on me, I just couldn't send her home."

Tanner blushed and Chrissy snorted. Jed had to just shake his head and smile in amusement.

"I keep forgetting how new we are to this type of business," said Jed. "Mr. Tanner, what is happening with the steam gun?"

"There's been a great deal of argument going on at the foundry between Winans, Dickinson, the mayor, the police marshal, and a couple of the officers from the militia. Winans is worried that troops will break in and seize the steam gun and will take over his foundry. The militia officers said they need it to protect Baltimore when they take over the state."

"Did any of them say when the militia will move the steam gun ?" asked Jed.

"No, but the mayor and marshal told them that the schedule had to be kept and they were worried about how the loss of the steam gun would affect the people of Baltimore. Dickinson said he'd be damned if he'd allow his revo . . . revolutionary weapon to fall into Yankee hands. They were loading it onto a railcar when I left to come here."

"Do you know when and where they plan to rail it?"

"They're sending it south," answered Chrissy. "A couple of customers gots to talking. They're sending it with the mid-morning train to Harpers Ferry because the soldiers at Relay House are searching everything that comes through. Theys also gots people listening in on the telegraph wires."

Jed grimaced as he thought over the problem. If the Confederacy got their hands on the steam gun, it would give them prestige and another victory. The Union soldiers he talked to were afraid to face such as a weapon. The newspapers hyperbole had made it a much more fearsome weapon than it actually was. Jed realized that the value of the steam gun was not the weapon itself, but the made-up myth about it.

"I am going to ride down to Relay House and have General Butler intercept the train," said Jed. "Based on Chrissy's information, I can't send him a telegram."

"Why not send troops from Fort McHenry?" asked Tanner. "They can get it while it's still at the foundry."

"There's more militiamen in the city than there are at Fort McHenry," replied Jed. "Seizing the cannon may make them act. With divided forces, we could end up losing both the steam gun and the fort."

"Ahem, the young lady in your room . . . ?" asked Bryce delicately. "She surely heard Master Tanner's outburst."

"I'll toss out her clothes when I go in to change," said Jed quickly. He had a plan, and he was anxious to be moving, but he stopped when he saw the skeptical look on Bryce's face.

"She's an actress," stated Bryce. "I'm quite sure she would be adept to wearing your clothes out in public."

Jed almost laughed at the thought of Natalie wearing his clothes. Her height and her curves made for an erotic but ludicrous image. However, Bryce was right, and Maura had pulled off posing as a stable boy. Natalie just had to deceive in disguise long enough to get word to the wrong people if she was so inclined.

Pointing at Tanner and Chrissy, Jed said, "You two are staying here to make sure she does not leave. Bryce, I'll need my horse as soon as I come down."

Jed walked back into the bedroom and closed the door behind him. He pulled on an old set of clothes as Natalie watched him.

"Going somewhere?" she asked.

"You no doubt heard what the young man said. I now have a rather pressing matter to attend to. I am sorry, but I must insist you stay here until I return."

Natalie slowly stretched, raising her arms over her head. The bedsheet slid down, and Jed marveled at the sight as she twisted this way and that. Jed felt the stirring in his groin but knew only he had the rank and privilege to get General Butler to go after the steam gun.

"That's fine," cooed Natalie as she snuggled down in the bed. "Do what you have to, but I do have a performance this evening, and I will not let my overly ambitious understudy take my place."

Jed grabbed his clothes and left the room. Chrissy was sitting in a chair outside the door.

"Since I'm usually up at night, I gots . . . got elected to watch her," she said. "You best hurry if you're going to get that steam gun."

Jed nodded and went to the other bedroom to change. The sky was turning gray as he walked out the front door. A groomsman held the reins to Jed's horse as Bryce finished tying a canteen to the saddle horn. Looking at the saddle in weariness, Jed inhaled sharply for strength. Swinging his leg up and over, he took off down the road.

Natalie and Jed had gotten to his house late, and it was even later before they had fallen asleep, but not because of any physical activity. Natalie laughed at him when he told her they would sleep in separate bedrooms, stating that if that got out, it would ruin her reputation. It took not a little discussion and some bribery for her to accept it.

Jed chuckled to himself thinking about the look on Tanner's face when the young man burst into his bedroom—priceless.

As he went south, Jed took an indirect route, in order not to ride too close to any of Winan's operations. It wouldn't do if he was spotted anywhere around where the steam gun was located. It would be assumed he knew about the moving of the gun, and the opposition may change their plans.

As it was, his own plan was dicey. Even if he got General Butler's cooperation immediately, they would still be racing to catch the steam gun train. Jed was sure the train made regular stops, which hopefully would slow it down enough for General Butler to catch up.

Jed's own ride southward was slow after he passed the environs of Baltimore. With everything in such a fluid state, one didn't know whether a fellow traveler was friend , foe or bandit. He rode with his pistol in his hand and didn't put it away until he saw the pickets just north of Relay House.

"I'm sorry, Captain Tremblant." General Butler looked up from his breakfast tray. "You do not have any authority over me or my troops. My orders are to protect the rail line from Washington to Baltimore."

"Sir, I am not issuing orders or trying to undermine your authority," argued Jed. "The steam gun is of great importance. We must keep it out of Confederate hands."

"Must we?" asked General Butler sarcastically.

Jed ground his teeth together. It had been one delay after another. First, he had to wait for the general to wake up. Then he waited while the general shaved and dressed. After that, it was the morning reports. Parker, Butler's aide-de-camp, gave Jed a look of sympathy but did not speak up. He did have the decency during the waiting to have breakfast brought in for Jed.

"Sir, I am out of arguments," stated Jed, trying not to lose his temper. "With your leave, I will return to Baltimore."

General Butler waved him away and returned to his breakfast. Parker escorted Jed toward the door.

"Can we supply you with anything?" asked Parker, trying to soften the blow that Jed had just taken.

"No, thank you. I have sufficient means to . . ." He stopped. "No, Edward. I appreciate the offer. I know the steam gun is on the train, but I must return to find out what the city officials did with the money."

"Money?" General Butler's head jerked up as he asked the question.

"Yes, sir," said Jed. "The five-hundred thousand dollars the city officials raised to finance arms and ammunition to keep federal troops out of Baltimore."

"Five-hundred thousand dollars?" gasped General Butler.

"Yes, sir. They move it around so that it cannot be seized. Of course, with the steam gun being moved so that it would not be taken—"

"Don't try your tricks with me!" barked General Butler. "We couldn't catch it now if we tried."

"Sir, the eleven o'clock train is due here soon," said Parker quickly. "Since troop trains are not going through Baltimore City but around it, it would behoove us to check the tracks, especially in light of Captain Tremblant's report that there are rebels there. The eleven o'clock train is not a troop train, so we can commandeer it."

"An informant's report, not mine," corrected Jed.

"Get two companies of the Sixth Massachusetts ready to board that train," ordered General Butler, standing. "We had better send two cannons with them, in case they use that steam gun against us."

"Yes, sir." Parker hurried out to relay orders. Jed left with him. "What are you going to do if the five-hundred thousand dollars is not on the train . . . assuming we can catch it?"

"Make General Butler the hero of the day for capturing the steam gun for the Union," replied Jed.

Parker shot Jed a look but didn't say anything. There was another period of waiting before Jed found himself on the train platform with a couple hundred blue-uniformed soldiers. Everyone was shuffling around in nervous anticipation as they watched the 4-4-0 engine pulling a set of rail cars chug toward them.

Jed let out his breath to calm his nerves. He was more at home on top of a horse but didn't mind riding on a train.

This time, however, he was doing something new. Parker had asked him to ride in the engine.

"General Butler is riding with the troops," Parker had said to Jed. "I need an experienced officer to ride up front in the engine, especially since we are trying to catch up to another train."

The train pulled up to the platform and stopped with a belch of steam and a cloud of coal smoke.

No sooner had the train stopped when soldiers climbed into the passenger cars to get the civilians off the train. There were protests, but they were not strongly voiced when facing a bayonet. Other soldiers cleared space on a flatbed car for two cannons to be loaded onto it. Jed proceeded to where the engineer and fireman watched the activity.

"You boys taking over the train?" asked the engineer.

"Yes, we need to. We need to catch another train. I'm Jed Tremblant of Illinois."

"Otis Schmidt," said the engineer. He jerked a thumb at the fireman. "This is Jim Laker."

"Do you mind if I ride up front with you?"

Otis looked at Jim before saying, "Nope, no problem, and thanks for asking instead of just telling us. Which train we trying to catch?"

"The mid-morning train from Baltimore to Harpers Ferry. Do you think you can catch her?"

"Only if they made all the stops it's supposed to make, or we cut free from all our cars." answered Otis. "We got enough coal, but we'll need to take on water here."

Jed wasn't happy about another delay, but it was better than having a busted steam engine. "You're in charge. I'm only along for the ride."

Jim said, "You know those fancy clothes you're wearing are going to get a mite bit dirty up here," eliciting a laugh from Otis.

Jed looked at his shirt and pants. They were one of his oldest sets and not even close to what he would consider fancy. "Give me a minute or two."

"We'll pull down to the water tower after they've tied down the cannons," said Otis. "That'll take about ten minutes."

Jed left and soon returned dressed in a Union blue uniform with a canteen and a cartridge box slung over his shoulder. He was carrying a Springfield rifle in one hand and a tied paper-wrapped bundle under the other. "Do you have a place where these will be safe?" asked Jed, holding up the bundle.

"I'll put them in the baggage car," said Jim climbing down and taking the package.

"Uh, that thing isn't going to go off, is it?" asked Otis. "That'd be a bad thing."

Jed looked around at the gauges and pipes inside of the engine cab. "I can see where that could cause a problem."

"Heck! I was talking about me!" Otis laughed. "But a busted pipe would be bad too."

Jim climbed into the engine cab. "Conductor says everybody's on board. Tank is topped off."

"Let's go get that train." Otis released the brake with a clang and pushed forward the throttle.

The four drive wheels spun for half a second before the engine jerked forward. There was a clanking down the line of cars as the couplings hit against one another. Jed had to grab for an iron handhold to keep from falling over. Otis and Jim just swayed with the motion as the train picked up speed.

"We'll be going faster than normal," yelled Otis. "Keep an eye out for critters on the track." He patted the side of the engine. "Ole Duke here don't stop on a dime, you know."

Jed had always wondered why all engineers had a bandana around their mouth until that first fly got caught in his throat. He made himself a bandana out of an old piece of cloth that smelled of oil and coal.

As the train sped along the rails, Jed kept a sharp eye out. He didn't know when or if they could catch up to the other train. He also didn't discount the possibility that the Confederates would tear up track or destroy a bridge to prevent anyone from chasing them, like he was doing now. Jed hoped and prayed, by not using the telegraphs, the Confederates had not been alerted to his actions.

Jed was feeling as nervous as a racehorse. At every curve, he stared intently ahead, hoping for a glimpse of the mid-morning train. After the fourth or fifth disappointment, Jed realized he needed to calm his nerves or risk making mistakes. More than an hour and a half had passed, and on one long stretch of straight track, Jed found himself watching his two companions. Otis, his bandana up over his nose and mouth, was leaning out the side window with his hand resting on the throttle. Jim shoveled coal into the firebox with a smooth, easy motion that spoke of many hours of practice. Jim clanged the firebox door closed with his shovel and tapped the locking bar into place with the edge. He grimaced as he leaned backward to straighten his back.

"Need a break?" asked Jed loudly, holding out his hand for the shovel.

"Appreciate it. This is the longest continuous run we've had in Ole Duke." Jim swapped places with Jed.

"Now, first lesson as a fireman," said Jim, "don't throw the coal in as if it's one big clod of dirt. You want to spread the coal out evenly so that it burns evenly."

At Jed's first attempt, he caught the firebox door with the edge of the shovel, dumping coal all over the floor of the cab and slamming the door closed. It only got slightly better from there, and it wasn't long until Jed's arms felt like lead. Once Jim had rested, he exchanged places with Jed, who was more than happy to relinquish the coal scoop. Mile after mile clickedy-clacked by, and Jed worried if they would catch up to the other train in time. Harpers Ferry was on the border between Virginia and Maryland and had already changed hands a couple of times.

"We're coming up to Ellicott Mills," said Otis a couple of hours later. "I think she's there. I'm seeing coal smoke ahead."

Jed felt a zing of anticipation of danger course through him. It replaced the fear that had been growing inside him about not being able to capture the steam gun. Otis was slowing the train. Ellicott Mills was in a narrow, steep-sided basin. Losing control of the train was one way to end the mission quickly. As they started down the hillside, Jed saw the other train stopped at the station.

"Sound the whistle!" ordered Jed.

Otis grabbed the lanyard, and the engine's steam whistle blasted out two long toots, followed by three short ones.

Jed hoped the troops in the passenger cars were listening because that was their signal to get ready. Jed picked up his Springfield rifle, checked to make sure the percussion cap was in place, and aimed it out the window at the station they were approaching.

There was a small crowd of travelers and families, either saying goodbye or welcome home, on the platform. They watched the approaching train with a good bit of curiosity. Jed didn't wonder why as their train was completely unscheduled.

Otis stopped his train within ten feet of the other one and gave three loud toots on the whistle. Jed searched the crowd but didn't see anyone in a militia or Confederate uniform. The murmur of conversation from the crowd on the platform became gasps of nervousness as two ranks of blue soldiers ran forward to surround the mid-morning train and the station.

"Get everyone off the train!" ordered General Butler, striding forward. "Anyone trying to escape will be shot!"

"Watch my rifle," said Jed as he handed it to Jim. He then pulled out his pistol and jumped to the ground.

"All trunks and packages will be searched for contraband," declared General Butler.

There was a caboose at the end of the mid-morning train, but it was empty when Jed looked inside. The next car was a boxcar, and the side door was padlocked. Looking ahead, Jed saw two soldiers hustling the porter out of the baggage car.

"Hold up!" ordered Jed. The two soldiers gave him a hard look, but the pistol he was holding was not something a common soldier would have. "Does he have keys to the boxcar?"

"Well?" asked one soldier holding the porter's arm.

"Yeah, I got them."

"Open it up," ordered Jed with a wave of his pistol.

The porter did as he was told, and Jed almost gave a shout. Nestled inside the boxcar and strapped down with rope was the big, hulking steam gun. It had been partially disassembled because the boiler had been too tall to fit in the car otherwise.

"General Butler will want to talk to him about the contents of the boxcar," said Jed to the two soldiers. "He'll appreciate it."

The soldiers broke out in smiles, and Jed headed toward the station. Soldiers were going through all the trunks, valises, packages, and carpet bags. Jed hurried into the station to find the stationmaster.

"Are you the telegrapher?" asked Jed.

"Yes, I am."

"Send this to the War Department in Washington. 'Have captured Winan's steam gun at Ellicott Mills with troops from Sixth Massachusetts Volunteers.' Sign it General Butler."

"You sure?"

Jed nodded and placed two dollars on the counter. The stationmaster grinned and started tapping on the keys.

Jed stepped out of the station and almost ran into a couple who were walking away from the stopped trains.

"Where are they going?" he asked the bearded sergeant who was supervising the luggage search.

"Who's asking?" asked the sergeant after taking in Jed's unadorned uniform. "You're out of uniform."

"I'm Captain Jedidiah Tremblant, sergeant!" barked Jed, stepping in close to the man. "Where are those people going?"

The sergeant backed up a step and said, "They didn't have any contraband, so we've been letting them go, sir."

"Was any of them a man in his thirties with whitish-blond hair?"

The sergeant didn't immediately answer, but one of his soldiers said, "Yes, sir. Just a couple of minutes ago. He was with the other man who had those machine parts, sergeant."

"Damn!" cursed Jed as he ran through the station to the other side.

The town rose steeply up the hill in front of Jed. Wagons were coming to and going from the mill on the winding main road that ran through the center of town. Jed stopped just outside the station and closed his eyes in exasperation. Up the hill at the first bend in the road was Anthony Duff. He sat on a horse looking back at the station, and inventor Charles Dickinson waited on another horse beside him. Duff rose in his stirrups and waved.

Only his training and experience on the western plains kept Jed from emptying his pistol at them. The range was just too far. The only thing Jed could do was wave and go back into the station.

Chapter 25

Sunday, May 12, 1861

MAURA AWOKE FEELING REFRESHED, AND the sun was shining. Breakfast—consisting of flaky croissants, a soft-boiled egg, strawberry preserves and coffee—was excellent and made even better by the newspaper reports that the steam gun had been seized by General Butler and his troops in the town of Ellicott Mills. Maura was sure Jed was instrumental in its capture.

Her good mood continued as she dressed for church. She chose to wear a more somber dress with long sleeves and a high collar. Her feathered hat had a thin mesh veil that covered her face. All in all, it was a very stylish dress that would garner attention, despite its black color. Eunice was waiting downstairs for her.

The Basilica of the Assumption was the first cathedral built in the United States and was where the Catholic portion of society worshipped. Maura greeted friends and acquaintances before the service, asking how they and their families were faring. She learned that twelve to fourteen young men had traveled south to pledge their allegiance to the Confederacy, which was about the same number as had joined the Union cause. One family had two sons who had gone to different sides.

Her good mood disappeared, and she felt a little vexed when Natalie LaBlanc sashayed up the center aisle in a hunter green and white, wide-striped gown. Natalie's flat hat was perched on top of her dark auburn hair, as eight ringlets of hair, four on each side, framed her face, drawing people's eyes to it. Her heels clicked loudly on the colorful tile floor. Natalie sat down two pews ahead and on the opposite side of the aisle from Maura. Annoyed and resentful, Maura sat up straight in the pew as the processional hymn started. She glanced over at Natalie, only to see her look inquiringly back at Maura, which irritated her even more.

It wasn't that Natalie was more beautiful than Maura. Maura's father had taught her that her beauty was given by God and not something to be exploited or rubbed into anyone else's face, lest it be taken away. Like her beauty, Maura knew Natalie's superior singing was also a gift from God and from training. Maura knew what was vexing her, even if she didn't want to admit it. She sent Natalie off with Jed the other night.

Sitting in her pew, Maura barely heard the priest drone on with the sermon. The topic was about Jesus chasing the money lenders out of the Temple. However, it was the Northern States and the abolitionists who were the money lenders with President Lincoln being portrayed as a mix between the High Priest Caiaphas and Judas Iscariot. It was just a different variation of last week's mass. Normally Maura paid close attention to the sermon and those members of the congregation around her. She used the oration as a barometer to measure people's responses to the message. It prevented her from committing any faux pas by gauging who was on what side. Secession fever was high in the days following the Baltimore Massacre. However, when the state legislature was unable to vote for or against secession, the rhetoric from the fanatics did not die down, but average men and women started to take a more rational view of the events occurring around them. Trying to get back to her surveillance, Maura turned to look at the people closest to her.

"Stop fidgeting," whispered Eunice. "Compose yourself."

"My apologies," murmured Maura.

Maura had heard that the steam gun was being moved. After not receiving any word from Jed all day Saturday, she concluded that he was chasing after it. Maura knew that any inquiries about the cannon or Jed would bring undue suspicion upon her. She resolved to keep to her appointments and had spent Saturday night at a dinner party at the Cary household.

Facing the front, Maura listened to the end of the sermon. There were no glances or other interactions between the two women through the Rite of the Holy Eucharist. It wasn't until the socialization after the mass that Natalie approached Maura.

"Mrs. Harrison."

"Miss LaBlanc."

"Mrs. Harrison, I was wondering if I could impose upon your time. Since this is my first time here at this cathedral, I hoped that you would be kind enough to show me around."

Maura gave her a little bow of her head. "I have only just arrived in this city myself several weeks ago. I am not very familiar with the cathedral but, if you are willing, may I suggest we explore together?"

"I would like that very much," replied Natalie.

"I would also be honored if you would accompany me afterward for luncheon at my residence," said Maura.

"Thank you. I'd be delighted to attend."

"The two of you take your time," said Eunice. "I'll inform Paul that there will be an additional person for lunch."

"Please, take the carriage," said Maura. "You can send it back, in say, an hour." She looked at Natalie.

Natalie nodded.

"Tell Paul not to wait on serving lunch."

"Oh!" exclaimed Natalie. "I do not mean to take you away from your other guests."

"You are my only guest today, Miss LaBlanc," said Maura. "Unless I have been invited somewhere, Sunday luncheon is a meal that I have with my household staff."

"You do?" asked Natalie in astonishment.

"She does," answered Eunice with a chuckle. "It shocked me the first time, because it was similar to one big family gathering."

"I really shouldn't intrude then," said Natalie.

"Nonsense," admonished Maura. "I'm delighted to spend the day with you."

"I will send the carriage back in one hour," said Eunice.

Maura and Natalie watched Eunice walk away then looked at one another.

"I do have a performance this evening."

"I wish I was attending," said Maura. "You have a beautiful voice. Do you wish to tour the cathedral or just talk in the gardens?"

Natalie's mouth quirked into a half smile. "You're very perceptive."

The two women followed the path around the building until they came upon a bench situated underneath a tall oak tree. The day was warm, with the sun peeking in and out of the clouds blowing up from the south. After arranging their skirts, the women sat on the bench.

The awkward silence that descended between them was punctuated by the whistles of nearby birds and the clop-clop of the occasional passing horses. It was a typical spring day with a slight wind blowing as the women surreptitiously looked around at everything but each other. After several minutes of strained silence, their glances happened to meet, and they both broke out in nervous laughter.

"I'm sorry," they said together, which resulted in dual giggles. "I didn't—"

Maura and Natalie both laughed, breaking the tension that had grown between them.

"This is ridiculous." Natalie chuckled. "I thank you for your patronage, Mrs. Harrison. However, it appears that I have offended you somehow. It cannot be my political views. I have none. In the South, I perform for the South. In the North, I perform for the North. Since our acquaintance so far has been brief, I have to guess that it involves Mr. Tremblant. Mrs. Harrison, it is obvious that you care for him." Natalie held up her hand as Maura opened her mouth. "I am in the theater and trained to notice an audience's reaction. I wanted to tell you that I do not chase after married men or those who have committed themselves to another."

Maura snickered. "What about the married men who chase after you?"

"Ah!" exclaimed Natalie brightly. "A chase is all they get with nothing given at the end, at least on my part. I do not trust those who would so quickly break their vows. However, getting back to Mr. Tremblant, why did you send me with him the other night when you have feelings for him yourself?"

Maura sighed. "Let us assume that what you have said is true. Mr. Tremblant was riding on the same train as my husband and me. We did not know Mr. Tremblant but were all traveling to Washington. Jonathan looked very dashing in his Union uniform. Our train pulled into the station here on April nineteenth, the day of the riots. Jonathan was shot in the back by a Confederate spy who was smuggling weapons into Baltimore."

Natalie gasped in horror.

"We had been married only a few days," continued Maura. "I cannot reconcile myself with his death. I worried myself sick about his soul. Mr. Tremblant helped me through those first chaotic days after Jonathan died. He knew of my rage, my helplessness, my grief . . . even though I never tried to show those emotions to anyone. Though I don't want to, I do care for him, but there is one thing I shall never do."

"What is that?" asked Natalie in a hushed whisper.

"Forgive that spy Anthony Duff for murdering Jonathan," replied Maura in a cold voice. "I want justice so Jonathan's spirit can rest in peace. I will follow Duff to the ends of the earth to do so!"

Maura's color was up, and she was breathing heavily from the pent-up emotions inside her. She looked over at Natalie, who was staring back at her in wide-eyed apprehension. Taking in a deep breath, Maura tried to relax and gain control of herself.

"I am sorry, Miss LaBlanc. I didn't mean to, well, I am sorry for such a public display. The face of the murderer is like a picture in my mind that I cannot get rid of."

"It is much too soon for time to work it's magic on you," said Natalie. "It hasn't even been a month." She gave Maura a little smile. "Would that I could show such emotion during my performances. I would be the toast of New York, London, and Paris!"

Maura had to laugh at that. "It is my Scottish heritage. We hold onto anger and grudges to a fault. I fear I looked like Lady Macbeth just then."

"I know a few Scots. They are also loyal and brave. As for Lady Macbeth, maybe so, but the chill I got was the prediction of Mr. Duff's demise. It put me more in mind of the soothsayer in Julius Caesar."

"The soothsayer?" Maura asked.

"Yes, you know. 'Beware the Ides of March'."

"Oh my goodness!" exclaimed Maura. "The Ides of March is the *fifteenth* of March. The uprising will take place on the fifteenth, Natalie!"

"Yes," replied Natalie, quite unsure of what was going on. "Yes, if you say so."

"I must tell Jed—Mr. Tremblant—about this! He might have gone to St. Paul's Episcopal Church. Natalie, did he tell you where he was going when you left him this morning? It's important!"

"Maura, can I call you Maura? I have not seen Mr. Tremblant since Friday night," said Natalie, taking Maura's hands in her own. "Well, early Saturday morning when a young man came running in yelling that they were moving the steam gun."

"You know about the steam gun?"

"Doesn't everyone?" countered Natalie with a smile. "It was on the front page of every newspaper in the country. He received news about the steam gun and left before the sun was up. My esteem had already taken one serious blow, and that was another. Though, I still have to ask why you sent me to Mr. Tremblant."

Maura looked over to see the street in front of the Basilica empty of any waiting carriages.

"Mr. Tremblant was in a precarious situation. Captain Wilcott of the Maryland Militia wants to kill him. At the recital, he and Miss Dorothy Caston tried to get him to compromise her. It seems to be a scheme the two of them have used before, which results in a lynching or a duel. That could not happen while you were in attendance to Mr. Tremblant."

"Why did you not do it yourself?"

"These black garments grant me certain protections," said Maura as she fluffed her skirt. "There are also restrictions that go with those protections. The other reason is politics. I'm a southern lady who was married to a northern Army officer. That is a very fine tightrope I must walk, because I belong to both sides and to neither."

"I believe we are in the same boat," said Natalie. "As much as I have said I do not wish to choose a side, it is becoming increasingly impossible not to do so. Hetty and Jennie Cary questioned me as to my views on the Confederacy before allowing me to sing *Maryland, My Maryland*.

"I am so sorry." Maura shook her head at the temerity of the sisters' action in her home. "I had no idea they had done so."

"As you said, a fine tightrope we both have to walk. We seem to have gotten off the topic of Mr. Tremblant. I told you that my esteem took a blow. That was because Mr. Tremblant took me to his home and slept in another room. He even locked his bedroom door." She smirked a little. "I tried it quietly. Will you be going to see him as soon as your carriage arrives?"

"You know I am," replied Maura. "You also now know enough to be a real danger to us."

Natalie burst out laughing. "I believe Mr. Tremblant's life is in quite enough danger without my adding to it. May I go with you?"

"Natalie, Anthony Duff is not some villain from a play. He is very real and very dangerous. He shot my husband in the back. He used a knife to kill two men in Frederick simply because they would not follow his orders. He won't brook any interference from you if you thwart his plans in any way."

"And this is the man you're going after? One of those restrictions that you have mentioned is that you cannot see a man alone . . . at least, not in public."

"Do you know what you're getting yourself into?" asked Maura anxiously. "I told you how dangerous this could be."

"Not quite as dangerous as *not* picking a side," explained Natalie. "We shall wait for your carriage and then find the good Mr. Tremblant."

While they sat on the bench waiting for the carriage, they discovered they both spoke the French language, and while Maura was fluent in Gaelic, Natalie could converse in Italian. Maura also discovered that Natalie could not eat seafood.

"I felt like I was going to die when I first tasted a piece of fish," said Natalie. "Now, I avoid all types of seafood. Being Catholic yourself, you can imagine how much I like Fridays."

Maura laughed. Natalie's stomach rumbled, which meant, of course, lunch at Maura's residence. Since it was Sunday and Maura required her servants to attend church, lunch and dinner were usually of the cold variety, unless Maura had a function or party planned for the evening. Today, salted ham, pickled vegetables, various cheeses, biscuits left over from Saturday morning, and assorted fruits were served along with classes of wine.

It took a little bit of convincing on Maura's part to prevent Eunice from coming with them. Natalie was intelligent and already knew or guessed too much of Maura and Jed's activities. However, she was an important source of information and needed to be cultivated. Eunice, unhappily, was forced to agree with her.

After lunch, Maura and Natalie rode in the carriage to Jed's dwelling.

"Good afternoon, Mrs. Harrison, Miss LaBlanc," greeted Bryce as they entered the foyer of the house.

"Good afternoon, Bryce," said Maura. "I'm hoping Mr. Tremblant is in and is available to see us."

"I'm sorry to tell you that he is not in. He left this morning to attend the service at St. Paul's Church and has not returned."

Something in Bryce's tone made Maura apprehensive. Looking closely, she saw the strains of worry reflected in the tightening around his eyes and the hard compression of his mouth. Maura knew that when Jed had not returned home from church, Bryce would have set out servants to find him. They had undoubtedly been unable to locate him, and since Natalie was here with her, Jed could not be having a rendezvous with the singer.

"The club? Fort McHenry?" asked Maura.

"I have sent men to both places," answered Bryce.

"Did you inquire with the police?" asked Natalie.

Maura and Bryce gave her a strange look.

"He could've been in an accident, and they may have taken him to see a doctor."

"More likely a prison cell," murmured Bryce. "The police are not sympathetic to our ... Mr. Tremblant's views, but that isn't to say we should not make inquiries with them."

"I cannot do that, Bryce," said Maura. "I have no scheduled meetings with Jed today and would not be expecting him. Marshal Kane knows this."

"I can go," volunteered Natalie. "If you don't mind his reputation suffering a little. I can say I was meeting him here for late lunch. I, therefore, have cause to be upset that he is missing."

"What of your reputation?" asked Maura.

Natalie laughed. "I'm an actress. If anything, it would enhance my reputation. Enough people know I'm looking at Mr. Tremblant to be my patron."

"Mrs. Harrison, please go home," said Bryce. "Miss LaBlanc and I will roust the police and demand answers."

"Send an urgent telegram to Jed's father," suggested Maura. "My understanding is that he is of a position that cannot be ignored."

"That he is," stated Bryce. "We will send it immediately."

"Bryce, we do have some information that is extremely important," said Maura, while Jed's carriage was being hitched to the horses. "Miss LaBlanc reminded me that the soothsayer's day in *Julius Caesar* is the fifteenth of March. That would mean the day is the fifteenth, but I just do not know which month it is or what is supposed to happen then."

Chapter 26

Sunday, May 12, 1861

AFTER HIS VERY COLD, OUTDOOR bath to remove the train's coal dust and smoke and a quick shave, Jed arrived at St. Paul's Episcopal Church with a few minutes to spare. As he started walking up the front steps to the church, someone yelled, "There he is!"

Looking over his shoulder, he saw three men in rough, dirty clothes hurrying toward him from across the street. They're shaved faces and clean hands gave a lie to the outfits they were wearing. There was no mistaking the pistols they had stuck into their belts. Turning quickly, Jed hurried inside the church.

The sanctuary bustled as people greeted neighbors and talked to friends before the service started. Halfway down the side aisle, Jed stopped to assess his situation. The three men outside had been waiting for him. Despite the low-class clothes they wore, Jed was almost sure they were military men, based on their bearing, mannerisms, and overall cleanliness.

He thought about staying put and leaving with the congregation. That, unfortunately, left too much opportunity for the one of them to get in close and stick a knife between his ribs. If he stayed until after the congregation left, they would send for reinforcements and seize him inside the church. Jed saw his one chance to escape was by getting out now through a side or back door. If the three men split up to guard the doors, it would be a one-on-one situation.

Jed hurried down the aisle to the sacristy door on the right side. Going through it, he found himself in the office portion of the church just as the processional hymn started. Down the hallway, a door led outside. Jed hurried toward the door, only to be tackled by two men who had been lurking in an office.

They all crashed to the floor, and a quick kick to his head disoriented Jed. Punches and kicks followed one after another until he was beaten nearly senseless.

"Whoa, boys, whoa." Captain Wilcott chuckled. "We can't kill him in the church. Tie him up." He knelt to look Jed in the face. "I'm guessing you didn't expect us to be here. My three men up front are beaters to drive you to us. You and I and a certain young lady have an appointment for later this afternoon."

Dragged out of the church, Jed was thrown into the back of a freight wagon. They threw a tarp over him, took him to an unknown location, and tossed him into a basement storeroom. Here he waited for his captors to return.

Flexing his hands to keep the circulation going in his fingers, Jed knew the knots were too tight for him to try to undo. He searched for something to cut the rope, but apart from the broken furniture, nothing was in sight. His one attempt to crawl to another area left him gasping for breath when pain lanced through his knee and side. The pain caused his vision to blur, and darkness crept in on him. Laying still and taking slow breaths kept Jed from passing out.

Jed hurt all over. Groaning from the pain, he rolled over on the dirt floor onto his side. It was difficult with his hands tied behind his back and his ankles bound together. His left eye was swollen shut, and there was the sour, metallic taste of blood in his mouth. Every breath was a struggle because of the pain in his ribs.

Two very dirty windows barely let in enough light to illuminate the murky interior of the storeroom. Jed barely remembered being dragged down here and dumped on the floor. Dusty trunks and broken furniture were placed haphazardly around the basement. Shaking his head to try to clear away some of his dizziness, he felt like a fool. He fell for a trick that would've never deceived him out West, but the environment of Baltimore City had lulled him into a false sense of security.

Jed kept track of time by the progression of what little sunlight came through the basement windows. Conserving his strength, he lay still; he didn't know when, or if, anyone would come for him. Hours passed before the cellar doors were thrown open with the crash. Three soldiers in militia uniforms pounded down the steps with drawn and cocked pistols. Seeing Jed still bound on the ground, they holstered their weapons.

"Wh . . . where am I?" Jed's parched throat made the words come out like a croak.

Without answering, they picked him up by his arms and dragged him across the dirt floor. The mute soldiers pulled him up the steps and dumped him into the back of the wagon, where they covered him once again with a tarp. Every jolt and bump sent little lances of pain through Jed's head, side, and knees. Two of the militiamen sat in the bed with him while the third one drove the wagon. The ride seemed interminable. The road changed from cobblestone to dirt and crossed over two sets of railroad tracks. Jed knew they were well outside the city when the driver pulled the horses to a stop.

The tarp was thrown off, and Jed was hauled off the wagon. Besides the three men who brought Jed in the wagon, Captain Wilcott and Dorothy Caston were there. Looking around, Jed noted the large clearing surrounded by woods. A dirt road led through the middle of the clearing, disappearing into the trees on the far side.

"I'm glad you're here, Mr. Tremblant," said Captain Wilcott. "If a man does not show up for his duel, it would severely damage his reputation."

"Duel?" asked Jed in pain. Two men held him up by his arms with his hands and feet still tied. It felt like his shoulders were being dislocated. "I haven't been challenged."

"Oh, but you were," corrected Captain Wilcott. "You offended Miss Caston the other night by pointedly ignoring her in front of the other people. You made her a laughingstock, and that is an insult that cannot be ignored. Put him over there and cut him loose. Sergeant Ferguson, seeing as how Mr. Tremblant hasn't brought his second, you shall act as his."

Jed was pulled down the road away from the edge of the forest. He gasped in pain and relief as his ankles were cut free and full circulation was restored to his feet. His eyes watered as the ropes on his hands were removed, and the rush of sensation back to his fingers was almost too much to bear.

As he was hauled to his feet, Jed almost collapsed at the anguish shooting through his feet and knee. He remained upright through sheer willpower, though he took a couple of stumbling steps and swayed to keep his balance.

Captain Wilcott pulled out his revolver to check the loads. Sergeant Ferguson produced a handgun from a set of saddlebags and walked to Jed. He fiddled around with the pistol as he was walking and tossed it into the dirt at Jed's feet.

"The captain made me your second," said Sergeant Ferguson. "I wasn't prepared, nor do I want the responsibility of performing such a great position to a Yankee, so I hadn't the chance to get my dueling pistols. I guess you just have to make do with this old pepperbox." He held out his hand with his thumb and forefinger pinched together. Jed extended his hand, and Sergeant Ferguson dropped one percussion cap into his palm. "You might not want to lose that."

Sergeant Ferguson walked away from Jed. He leaned down carefully to pick up the pistol. It was an old Navy Yank ball and cap pepperbox with six .36 caliber revolving barrels. Holding the pistol up to the sunlight, Jed found the one barrel that was loaded. He carefully placed the percussion cap on the nipple and rotated the barrels so that the cap was under the hammer.

"Since it appears you can barely walk, we will dispense with the traditional ten paces." Captain Wilcott walked to a spot about sixty feet away from Jed. "We'll just turn and fire."

He deliberately turned his back on Jed, but Jed saw the other three militiamen point their revolvers at him. Dorothy clapped and giggled in anticipation. Jed felt a deep disgust well up in him. This civil war was going to be bloody enough without those who reveled in death and dying. Dorothy Caston's brand of amusement turned Jed's stomach, but he knew he wouldn't have a fighting chance unless he played along with Wilcott. Slowly, he turned around, and Sergeant Ferguson gave a signal to Wilcott.

"Good," said Captain Wilcott. "I'm glad to see you can at least try to be a gentleman, or as much of a gentleman as any Northerner can be. We'll turn and fire at the count of ten. Sergeant Ferguson, if you would be so kind as to do a slow count to ten."

"Are you sure he can count that high?" gasped out Jed, ignoring the pain in his ribs.

Someone swore out an oath, then Captain Wilcott yelled," Sergeant Ferguson! Get back over there! You can have Mr. Tremblant after my business is completed . . . if he is still alive, that is."

"Yes, sir," growled Sergeant Ferguson. "One!"

Jed took in a steadying breath. His pistol probably only had an effective range of fifteen to twenty feet. After that, who knew where the ball would go.

"Two!"

Jed and Wilcott were three times that distance apart.

"Three!"

Jed knew that Wilcott was using his regular revolver with a rifled barrel. He had the range and the time to line up a shot. Jed's only hope was to fire first and hopefully hit Wilcott in a vital spot.

"Four!"

Jed shifted his weight onto his good leg. He couldn't afford to stumble while turning around.

"Five!"

Taking another calming breath, Jed tried to open his left eye. Without it, he had lost his depth perception. It would also take longer for his right eye to locate Wilcott since he had to turn on his good left leg.

"Six!"

A calm came over Jed. He heard the wind rustling the branches and smelled the wildflowers growing in the clearing. He was ready.

"Seven!"

"Stand fast, gentleman! Drop those weapons!"

Jed froze. He was set and ready to turn and fire on the number ten. These new orders, while reasonable, took a minute or two to process, given his woozy state. He turned slightly to see Captain Boxer and two other police officers approaching them with pistols drawn.

"You and your men need to drop those weapons, Captain Wilcott."

"You have no authority here, Captain Boxer," sneered Captain Wilcott loftily. "We are outside the city limits . . . outside your jurisdiction."

"Drop those weapons!" The militiamen did so, but Jed's mind was still fuzzy trying to adapt to the change in his situation. "Captain Wilcott . . . Daniel, dueling is illegal in the state of Maryland," said Captain Boxer. "Let me arrest him. It will keep your name out of it."

"Leave, Ezekiel," said Captain Wilcott. "It's a matter of honor, and you are outside your jurisdiction."

"He might be, but I am not," said a gruff voice.

Jed turned and stumbled a little. Standing no more than twenty feet away from Captain Wilcott was US Marshal Stockdale. The double-barreled shotgun he was holding looked like the barrels had been sawed off. It was pointed straight at Wilcott and strategically in line with Dorothy Caston.

"Captain Boxer, if you would be so kind as to have your men holster their weapons," said Stockdale. Boxer nodded to his men and carefully holstered his own pistol. "Now, if you four gentlemen and lady would move over to stand beside the police officers."

"Just who the devil are you?" griped Captain Wilcott as he walked over to stand beside Captain Boxer.

"He's United States Deputy Marshal John Stockdale," Captain Boxer informed him. "He's up from Washington, DC, with a murder warrant for one Anthony Duff."

"What!?" shouted Captain Wilcott. His face had lost a lot of its color, but he recovered quickly. "A United States marshal? You have less jurisdiction here than Captain Boxer."

"I don't believe so," answered Stockdale. "I have jurisdiction throughout the entire United States and its territories. Maybe if Maryland had seceded . . ."

Wilcott's face twisted in rage.

"Maybe if the Confederate government was legitimate and recognized by several major foreign powers . . . maybe, but that doesn't apply to our current situation, which is an illegal duel." Stockdale collected the four revolvers lying on the ground. "Of course, this could not be a duel. Only a complete coward would challenge this man in the shape he's in. Good God! He can barely stand or see. Of course, if this wasn't a duel but a planned murder, a lowlife piece of scum would give himself an advantage by using dissimilar weapons, such as a Navy Colt versus a pepperbox. No, Captain Boxer, I would not call this a duel, would you? It must be a sporting event. Maybe Mr. Tremblant heard of Captain Wilcott's pepperbox and wished to shoot it."

"That's it," agreed Jed. Between his beating, being tied up for hours, standing in the sun, and the stress of a mock duel, his mind was reeling. He swayed as if he was drunk. "Just wanted . . . just wanted to see if it would shoot. Didn't think it would."

The shot reverberated loudly in the clearing. A tongue of flame and smoke lanced out of the barrel of the pepperbox, and Captain Wilcott's hat was snatched off his head as if by an invisible hand. Everyone but Jed and Stockdale crouched down amid cries of alarm. Dorothy screamed and collapsed onto the ground. Jed was unable to stand any longer. He dropped the pistol and sank to the ground. Stockdale brought the butt of his shotgun up to his shoulder and pointed it at the other men.

"Easy," he warned them. "Easy. It looks like the gun went off accidentally, but no one was hurt. Captain Wilcott, it is time for you and your men to leave. Go home. Captain Boxer will return your weapons to you. Oh, and don't circle around in the woods. I have several men out there with rifles."

Captain Wilcott, his face pinched tight in anger and fright, stomped to his horse, mounted, and rode off in a gallop. Dorothy stared at his back in horror and incredulity that he had left her there. Sergeant Ferguson assisted her onto the wagon and tied her horse to the wagon before driving off. The other militiamen followed behind them.

Captain Boxer had two men mount up and sent them down the road a quarter of a mile to wait for him. Stockdale lowered the hammers on the shotgun.

"Do you have men in the woods?" Boxer put his pistols into his saddle bags.

"Maybe," answered Stockdale with a smile. "Probably not."

"Don't hold it against me if I don't put much faith in your 'probably not.' How did you manage to find your way here?" asked Boxer sourly.

Stockdale chuckled. "A little bird sang to me. How did you manage to hear about this little fracas?"

"It might've been the same bird," said Captain Boxer. "My songbird is Miss Natalie LaBlanc. It appears that Ms. LaBlanc and Mr. Tremblant arranged to have a meeting this afternoon. A meeting Mr. Tremblant failed to attend. She was a little distraught, alternating between concern for him and being upset that he missed their liaison. I was informed that Captain Wilcott may have had something to do with Mr. Tremblant's disappearance. I simply followed him." He looked over at Jed, who, although he had his head down, was listening intently. "What are you going to do with him?"

"Load him up on a horse and take him to Fort McHenry," said Stockdale. "He can heal up there in relative safety."

"Take him to his house." Captain Boxer gave Stockdale directions to Jed's home. "It is a fortress in and of itself. He's got a loyal . . . Union . . . staff, some of who are fighting men."

"Are you sure you're not just hoping Captain Wilcott will get another chance at him?"

"Captain Wilcott will have his own problems to deal with. I will have to report the suspected duel, and I expect that report will not go favorably with his superiors. Shall we check on Mr. Tremblant? It would not do to have him die on us."

"I know his kind." Stockdale chuckled. "He's a westerner. His eye is swollen shut. He's favoring his right leg, and I'm sure he's got some pain in his ribs, judging by his breathing. Captain Wilcott could've put six bullets into him, and this man would've still killed him if the duel had not been stopped by you. Look at how he shot the hat off Captain Wilcott."

"Missed."

"What?" asked Marshal Stockdale and Captain Boxer together as they looked down at Jed.

Jed groaned and gasped out, "Missed . . . wasn't . . . wasn't . . . aiming for his hat."

"I'll pretend I didn't hear that," said Captain Boxer. "Marshal Stockdale wants to take you to Fort McHenry to heal. I suggested taking you home. Where would you like to go?"

"Home," grunted Jed in pain as they helped him to his feet. "Just get me up on a horse."

"See? Westerner," commented Stockdale. "I brought a spare horse. Hold onto him, and I'll bring the horse around."

After he left to retrieve the horses, Jed looked at Captain Boxer and said, "I can't quite figure out which side you're on, Captain."

"If you mean Union or Confederate—neither."

"Strictly neutral? You know that will be impossible."

"There's a third side. The one I swore an oath to, the people of Baltimore City. They have an affinity for the charm and nobility of the South while, at the same time, have a great liking for the industry and progress brought in from the North. The people of Maryland will join both the Union and the Confederacy in this war. Right now, they're all mixed together. I have enough trouble keeping them apart to be worried about which side I am going to support. I will uphold the law."

"And you were going to arrest me. Is that upholding the law?"

"Would you rather have been in the middle of a gun battle with only one shot in your pistol? I thought it might've been good enough to get you out of here. Once away, I would've dropped the charges and delivered you to your home."

"Wouldn't Marshal Kane have something to say about that?"

Captain Boxer shot Jed a skeptical look. "He will have something to say about this, especially since this location is outside the city limits, but I do not work for the Confederacy."

"Or the Union," added Jed.

"Exactly! The marshal is returning. I would keep a low profile for the next few days if I were you."

Jed quaffed down the better part of a canteen before the other two men assisted him onto a horse. He hurt all over, and his vision threatened to go black, but he managed to hold onto his seat.

"It might be better if we just tie him over the saddle," suggested Captain Boxer to Stockdale as they mounted their own horses.

Stockdale snorted in amusement "I know his type, and so do you. Look at him. Even being beaten to near unconsciousness, he won't fall out of that saddle. He was born to it. Captain Wilcott seriously underestimated him."

"So have some other people." Captain Boxer leaned down and pick something off the ground. He looked at it and then handed it to Stockdale. "I'll have one of my men escort you to Mr. Tremblant's house. You can give this to him as a souvenir."

The object was Captain Wilcott's kepi hat. It was light blue with a black leather border around the bottom and a short, black, leather brim. The shiny brass insignia on the front of the hat was bent from the hole in it. There was a corresponding hole in the back of the cap.

Chapter 27

Monday, May 13, 1861

"Ugh! Ohhhhh! Ow! Ow! Ow!"

Grunting from the stiff knee, bruised ribs, and a splitting headache, Jed rolled over in bed and looked at the clock on the bureau. The face of the clock was still blurry, but at least he was seeing out of his left eye, thanks to the cold compresses Bryson placed over the swelling last night. His right knee was so stiff that he could barely bend it. The doctor didn't believe Jed had any broken ribs, but his chest was bound up tight.

Even though the curtains were pulled back from the windows, the room was gray and full of shadows. Jed focused on the clock and was a little surprised to see that it was a quarter past eight. Gritting his teeth, Jed threw aside his bedsheets and sat up on the edge of the bed. Gasping, he sat there for several seconds until the pain receded to a manageable level. Just before he stood, there was a quick knock at the door, and Bryce walked into the room.

"Good morning, Master Jed. How are you feeling?"

"I hurt all over, but I'm alive."

"I'm not surprised you are in pain, considering what you told me about the incident last night. The doctor told me to remind you that you need to rest and not overexert yourself for at least a week. Let's get you over to the small table. I'm having a tray brought up: roast beef and gravy, sliced herbed potatoes, greens with a vinaigrette dressing, and coffee. It's a heavy meal for this early in the morning, but I thought you would want it to regain your strength."

"Bless you, Bryce." Jed hobbled to the table and sat. "I'm starved."

The tray of food and drink soon arrived, and Jed wolfed it down quickly. Bryce stood nearby, refilling Jed's cup of coffee as needed. Torrents of rain beat against the windows as the shutters rattled in the wind.

"I'm afraid the wind keeps changing direction," commented Bryce. "The storm is going to be stalled over us for a while. Feeling better, Master Jed?"

"Yes, thank you. Also, thank you for getting the doctor yesterday."

"We were all worried about you."

"We? All?" questioned Jed.

"Miss Maura, Miss Natalie, Miss Chrissy, Mr. Tanner," rattled off Bryce. "Miss Natalie put us on to when the soothsayer's day is. She thinks it's in reference to the soothsayer from William Shakespeare's *Julius Caesar*."

"The Ides of March," stated Jed in pleased recognition. "But that date has passed us by."

"Yes," said Bryce. "But if you focus on the *ides*, as Mrs. Harrison put it, it would be the fifteenth of any month."

"That would be the day after tomorrow, unless they were planning on June fifteenth." Jed thought about it for a minute. "No, I perceive that it's a much more immediate time. It must be the fifteenth of May. We cannot have a revolt erupting in Baltimore. It could easily inflame the eastern half of the state."

"Do you think that would happen?"

Jed shook his head. "I think that's what they hope will happen. They've been stockpiling weapons. Anthony Duff was smuggling weapons in on the train. The militia has tried to increase the number of weapons in their armories and has even tried to get a hold of several cannons. What would've happened if the rioters had been better armed on April nineteenth? If that had happened, troops going to Washington would have had to fight their way there all the way from the Mason-Dixon Line. Maryland may have seceded."

"Is it time to notify the War Department?" asked Bryce. "Will they be able to do anything in time?"

"Not in time. There are not enough troops at Fort McHenry to defend the fort and suppress a riot in the city. They could open fire on the city with the cannons as Captain Robinson threatened to do. However, that would be indiscriminate shelling, killing rioters and bystanders—guilty and innocent alike. I'm afraid the closest troops are those that belong to General Butler."

"Could that be why Captain Wilcott tried to kill you yesterday? To prevent you from going to General Butler on the eve of their plan?"

"Undoubtedly, now that I'm aware of the soothsayer's day," agreed Jed. "The War Department will be loath to divert troops away from the defense of Washington. I will have to ride to Fort McHenry immediately to send a telegram to Secretary Cameron."

"You can't!" exclaimed Bryce, his agitation breaking through his normally reserved demeanor. "You're too badly injured! We can send a servant to deliver the message."

"Bryce," admonished Jed gently. "I appreciate your concern, but you know as well as I do that if I send a servant, the commander will send a soldier back here to verify that I sent it. It's only a couple of miles."

A brilliant flash of light from outside lit up the room. It was quickly followed by a loud crack that made both men jump.

"Sir—"

"Bryce," interrupted Jed. "I know what you're going to say. I'm still going." He stood up and grimaced. "We'll need to bind up my knee though."

Standing in the foyer with his knee bound up and wearing his slicker waterproofed with beeswax, Jed was placing the coded message inside a waterproof wallet when there was a loud pounding at the front door. Jed and Bryce shared a quick glance before Bryce stepped forward to open the door.

Gale force winds blew the door open with a bang, despite Bryce's effort to hold onto it. A big ball of windblown, soaking-wet cloth literally flew at Jed, who grunted in pain as he prevented their caller from being whirled down the tiled hallway. A lull in the wind allowed Bryce to slam the heavy door closed.

"I didn't thinks I was going to makes it here without drowning," gasped Chrissy as she fought with the wet, heavy fabric of her dress and cloak, splattering droplets of water everywhere. She finally looked up at Jed, and her expression changed to one of horrified concern. "Good Lord! What's happened to your face? You looks terrible!"

"Good morning to you too, Chrissy," snarked Jed.

Chrissy waved aside his greeting and studied his face. "What happened? Zeke was beside himself when you didn't return home yesterday from church."

"Your diction is improving," commented Jed.

"My dictions be hanged!" yelled Chrissy, which had Jed and Bryce breaking out in grins. "Don'ts . . . Don't you be smiling at me. Tell me what happened!"

Jed described his kidnapping, beating, and the sham duel. Chrissy listened in horrified silence. Bryce left as soon as Jed started explaining to Chrissy what had happened. He returned carrying a large tray as Jed was finishing up his narrative. On the tray was a teapot with steam coming out of its spout, a sugar bowl, a cream pot, and a teacup. After setting the tray down, Bryce poured Chrissy a cup of tea.

"Master Jed, the groom is saddling Sweet Sue."

"Thank you. She's not fast, but she is dependable."

"You're not going out in this, are you?" asked Chrissy in astonishment.

"I have to send a message to the War Department." Jed limped toward the front door but was stopped when Chrissy latched onto his arm.

"You're hurt! Really hurt!" she exclaimed. "Let me go instead."

Bryce cleared his throat. "I've already tried to dissuade him, Miss Chrissy." He gave a critical look at her soaking, bedraggled state. "You can't go back out in this. I'm convinced the only reason you made it here at all was because the wind was blowing in this direction."

"Ha. Ha. Very funny," said Chrissy before she broke out in a smile. "You're not far wrong. I swear there were times when my feet weren't touching the ground."

There was a quick knock at the front door, and the groom's head poked in, admitting the driving wind and rain into the foyer.

"Sir, she's ready," he said quickly. "You sure about this?"

"Head on back to the stables," ordered Jed as he tied an oiled hood around his head. "Keep the horses calm. Bryce, I don't know when I'll return. Chrissy, please stay here until the storm blows over."

"I almost forgot!" cried out Chrissy. "One of the girls overheard a conversation. Ross Winans is coming back to Baltimore City, and there are a lot of people here who blame him for Maryland not seceding from the Union. They're sending three police officers to arrest him. The girl told me she thinks he's not meant to survive."

"When is he supposed to return?" asked Jed.

"Tomorrow."

Jed blew out his breath explosively at this latest revelation. It was just one more thing that needed to be taken care of. Winans was for the states' rights and may have been responsible for trying to ship the steam gun to the South, but he was an important industrialist and inventor. His death could easily be blamed on the North and used to inflame people's passions.

"Let's see if we can find you something dry to wear before you catch your death from cold and get you something hot to eat, Miss Chrissy." Bryce motioned her to follow him.

"I'll take care of it when I get back." Jed pulled open the front door. It took some effort to close up behind him.

SWEET SUE WAS A BARREL-CHESTED Appaloosa that Jed had purchased from an old Arapaho man for two steel hatchets, a skinning knife, and two pounds of beef jerky. Her gallop was barely faster than a trot, but she could go for days on end in all types of weather. The other soldiers at the post made fun of her until she outlasted all the other horses in a series of marches.

The groom had tied her up in the three-sided horse shelter built off to one side of the road.

"Hey, girl," said Jed soothingly as he cut an apple into quarters and fed it to her. "I'm sorry I have to take you out in weather like this, but it can't be helped."

Sweet Sue nickered appreciatively at her treat as Jed untied her reins. Mounting up carefully because of his knee, the they headed out into the tempest.

The rain came down in sheets, and lightning forked across the sky, lighting up the countryside. Thunder cracked like gunshots or fireworks. Sweet Sue plodded forward, not shying away from the storm's fury. Only the occasional flinching of her muscles told Jed of her anxiety at being out in this storm.

With the rain beating down, Jed rode through the deserted streets of Baltimore. His pants were soaked even before he passed the southern outskirts of the city, and he felt the water leaching down his socks into his boots. It was a relief when he saw two soldiers standing on either side of the muddy road that led to Fort McHenry.

"Halt!" yelled one of the men. "Dismount, advance, and be recognized!"

Jed swung a leg over Sweet Sue and lowered himself gingerly to the grass growing alongside the road. He limped forward, leading Sue, until he was three feet away from the two bayonets pointing at him.

"I am Jedidiah Tremblant of Illinois," informed Jed. "I'm here to see the commander."

"Yes, sir," said the dark bearded soldier. "I seen you around. I'll take you up to the fort."

"It might be better if you stay here," advised Jed. "I have had two riders following me. Be on the lookout for them. If you see them, hold them if you can but don't take any unnecessary risks."

Jed mounted up and rode carefully toward the fort. The rain diminished visibility, so he took it slow, not wanting to be shot by a startled sentry. Once inside the walls, he went to the quarters of Major Morris and was soon sitting before the fire.

"I've dispatched a platoon of men up the road to see if they can find those riders," said Major Morris. "Those soldiers are not going to be kindly disposed toward you for taking them out of their nice dry tents."

"I'm sure the two sentries on the road will feel better for the company," said Jed with a chuckle. "What about the message?"

"The telegraph is not working. The wires have either been blown down by the storm or cut. Are you sure there will be a rebellion on the fifteenth?"

"Do I have definitive proof of their plan?" Jed asked. "No, but all indications are pointing toward it. There are also the two men following me, despite this weather. They want to keep a closer eye on me and my activities, which they have not done before."

"There is that," commented Major Morris. "I have enough troops to hold Fort McHenry and Fort Carroll against any threat the rebels throw at me. Unfortunately, I can't quell a rebellion in the city unless I shell it, and I won't do that unless the forts are threatened. We are going to need more troops quickly."

"The only troops I know that are available are General Butler's New England regiments," said Jed. "Any other troops would have to be brought in by the railroad or by boat. Both of which will take more time than I think we have available."

"The storm may break by tomorrow. What happens if you wait until then?"

"Right now, if I were the southern rebels, I would move troops to block access to Baltimore, which would isolate Washington. I would move troops north and south, so Union soldiers will have to fight their way into the city, and I would arm the able-bodied men of the city with the weapons hidden in their warehouses. I'm not aware of what troops the Confederates have south of Washington, but if Baltimore joins the rebellion and if I was Jefferson Davis, I would attack to secure the District of Columbia."

Major Morris looked grim. "Have you forgotten about my fort? I can shell the city from here."

"Would you?" asked Jed. "What if they don't attack you? They could try to blockade you like they did at Fort Sumter."

"I must admit I would be very hesitant to fire upon the city and its inhabitants if the fort is not attacked." He laughed bitterly. "I'm afraid I do not have the troops to hold the city, even if I was willing to give up the fort. No, Mr. Tremblant, if they do not attack the fort, I will not shell the city. I must try to conserve the force I have."

There was a rapping at the door, and Major Morris shouted, "Enter!"

A short, very wet sergeant entered the room and saluted Major Morris.

"Sir, we got one of the buggers," announced the sergeant in an Irish brogue. "The other one was a-horse and skedaddled before we could catch him. The one we caught is in the guard house. He's part of the Fifty-third Maryland."

"Did he say what he was doing around here?" asked Major Morris.

"No, sir. A real tightlipped gent. What should we do with him, sir?"

"I wish you could hang him," muttered Jed to the consternation of Major Morris and the sergeant. "The bruises on my face were given to me by members of the militia, and I'm getting tired of having them under my feet all the time."

Major Morris gave off a nervous laugh. "Lock him up, Sergeant. We'll contact his commanding officer to come and collect him." A crack of thunder crashed throughout the building. "After the storm, of course."

"Sergeant, it was wet work you and your men did just now," stated Jed, placing some coins in the man's hand. "I want all of you to have a round or two on me tonight."

"Yes, sir! A fine gentleman ye are, sir!"

"Sergeant!" said Major Morris authoritatively, which stopped the man from leaving. "Double the guard inside the fort until further notice and cancel all passes. Tell everyone to be especially vigilant. Also, send me the signalman. I want to send a message to Fort Carroll if they can see the flags."

"Trouble, sir?" asked the sergeant.

"You know the sympathies of the militia probably better than I do, Sergeant. We haven't seen any of them this close to the fort in quite a while."

The sergeant looked pensive and then looked at the coins in his hand. With a heavy sigh, he held the money back out to Jed.

"Maybe next time, sir," he said.

Jed moved his hands behind his back. "Hold onto it until you and your men can get to the sutler's shop. I may not be here, and I want to show my appreciation."

The sergeant nodded and put the coins in his pocket. After saluting Major Morris, he turned and left.

"Good man there," stated Jed after the door closed. "He knows something is up, and he wants to keep his men sober."

"He told me that when he was much younger, he got caught being drunk on guard duty. The beating his fellow soldiers gave him made a lasting impression. What are you going to do now? I imagine the wires will not be repaired until tomorrow at the earliest."

Jed grabbed his steaming slicker that had been hung up to dry by the fire.

"One man escaped to tell them I was here." Jed pulled on the cold dank coat. "We need one of General Butler's regiments to be in the city to suppress any rebellious moves made by the militia and to seize the stored arms and ammunition. I will have to ride down to Relay House."

"Does his authority extend this far north? I should have been under his command if it does."

"He thinks it does." Jed put on his hood. He smirked in sour humor. "In a way, I hope that I am and that I am *not* correct about the fifteenth and what may be happening."

"Mr. Tremblant," Major Morris stood and extended his hand, "I would hazard to guess that you are more right than not with your assumptions. Godspeed and good luck. You'll need it in the storm."

It wasn't midmorning yet when Jed rode out for Relay House. Sweet Sue gave him a look of reluctant acceptance as Jed gingerly stepped up onto the saddle. His knee throbbed and his ribs ached, but Jed knew he was the only one who could get in to see General Butler. The big question was if he could make General Butler see reason for occupying Baltimore City. Major Morris sent a runner to Jed's house to inform Bryce of Jed's plan.

The rain lashed him and Sweet Sue. Now more than ever, Jed was glad he had purchased the steady, reliable horse. Gale force winds broke off branches and twigs and whipped them around. A small creek had turned into a rushing stream and washed out a quarter of the road.

Ribbons of lightning raced across the black clouds, looking like a huge, bony hand. The crackle that came from it raised the hairs on the nape of Jed's neck. A ripple of muscles was the only response Sweet Sue made to the storm blowing around them.

Somehow, the storm didn't worry Jed as much as his meeting with General Butler. Could he impart the importance of occupying Baltimore immediately to the man? Would General Butler move decisively, or would he waste time? Would the occupation of Baltimore suppress the rebellious fervor or ignite it? These and many more questions plagued Jed as he rode south through the rain and thunder.

Through all his doubts, Jed was certain of one thing. If Baltimore was not occupied and soon, there would be battles throughout Maryland to keep the railroad lines open to Washington. President Lincoln could not afford to surrender the nation's capital to the Confederacy without serious national and international ramifications. The war would be lost before it even began.

It was almost anticlimactic when Jed rode up to the sentries guarding the road to Relay House. It seemed his name was known as a result of the steam gun chase. The rain had stopped as had the wind, but dark, billowing clouds still rumbled overhead. As Jed rode toward the station, he saw an engine, coal car, and a passenger car lined up on the tracks. The engine was stoked and ready to roll. He was quickly escorted into Relay House and presented to Lieutenant Colonel Edward Parker.

"Good Lord, man!" exclaimed Edward. "You didn't ride down in this, did you?"

"Yes, and it appears I'm not the only one, based upon the two men I saw standing by the telegraph office." Jed peeled off his wet slicker. He was soaked to the bone. "I think they are members of the Maryland Militia. I need to see General Butler immediately."

General Butler, despite his obvious distaste for Jed dripping on his floor, listened to Jed's intelligence report and his theories. At the end, he stood and looked outside.

"Baltimore is undefended as of today," he mused, staring out at the landscape.

"It may not be so tomorrow, sir," stated Jed.

"General Hamilton, who is General Scott's secretary, has sent me a letter to seize all arms and equipment coming from Baltimore destined for the rebels. Today seems like a good day to do that."

"Sir, may I suggest you contact General Scott about this action," advised Edward, clearly agitated.

"Why?" asked General Butler. "The Department of Annapolis is my territory, which includes Baltimore City. I have the right as the commander to move my troops as I see fit. Several weeks ago, my plan to take and hold Manassas Junction was deemed to be too grandiose. As of now, General Scott is planning to occupy Baltimore with twelve thousand troops three months from now."

General Butler's voice had risen, showing Jed his anger and frustration at the old General of the Army.

"Massachusetts soldiers were killed by the Baltimore Pug-Uglies this past April," continued General Butler. "It's only fair that a Massachusetts's unit occupy that city. Colonel Parker, I want one thousand men prepared to leave immediately by train along with two field pieces."

"Sir, if I may interject about Ross Winans—"

"A damn traitor!" General Butler cut Jed off. "He invented that steam gun we captured, and I found out that he's worth fifteen million dollars. You probably saw the train waiting at the station. I am sending a handpicked platoon to Frederick to arrest the man."

"General, the rebel spies will see our troops loading onto a second train," pointed out Edward. "They will be able to warn those in Baltimore before we arrive."

"There's nothing that can be done about that," said General Butler.

"We need a little deception," suggested Jed. "Hook the two trains together with one engine in the front and the other in the rear. Put a guard at the telegraph station. We'll let it be known that we're sending a force to retake Harpers Ferry, and the entire train will initially head in that direction. When we are out of sight of Relay House, you can uncouple the front portion of the train, which will go on to Frederick to arrest Ross Winans. After the trains are uncoupled, the second train can speed right to Baltimore City without making any stops. You can have one thousand men in that city before anyone can react."

"We'll have to go past Relay House," stated General Butler. "Their spies will report the train, even if it doesn't stop."

"Not with guards at the telegraph station, sir," said Edward with a smile.

"Colonel Parker, get the trains hooked up and get a guard on the telegraph station. Get the Sixth Massachusetts ready to board the train. Tell him we are going to Harpers Ferry. Leave all the camp equipment behind with the troops we're leaving here. It can be packed up and shipped to Baltimore City tomorrow. Mr. Tremblant, you will accompany us and guide my troops to that big hill you are talking about."

"Yes, sir," said Jed. "That would be Federal Hill."

Chapter 28

Monday, May 13, 1861

Maura looked out the morning room window at the scuttling clouds in the sky and drenched buildings across the street. The storm had been vicious earlier, and even though the rain had slowed, the boiling clouds showed no sign of abating as the day wore on.

Robbie had stopped by early in the morning to pass on information he had obtained from other cabbies. Justine, the housekeeper, had him come in for a breakfast of biscuits and gravy and coffee. He would normally have reported to Jed, but after Jed's beating and other distractions, it was decided that Robbie could report to Maura. Apart from two suspicious orders—one for 5,000 haversacks and another for 2,000 ammunition pouches—Robbie had no information about any militia movement or gatherings of men.

The storm outside reflected Maura's mood. There was the thunderstorm this morning and now a lull, but pressure was building. At some point, it would let loose. Maura felt the pressure, not only of the storm, but of the waiting violence about to begin in Maryland.

It ratcheted up with Captain Wilcott's failed attempt to kill Jed in that duel. The rumor mill was running full tilt with that story. She had received an accurate version from Captain Boxer last evening. He had stopped by to either warn or threaten her about further shenanigans of this sort.

Despite the storm, several ladies called upon her much earlier than was the norm for the sole purpose of telling her what they had heard. She corrected those whose account was not accurate. It seemed that most of her callers, while not sympathetic to the North, admired Jed's strength and bravery.

The strange thing was that all the callers with southern sympathies seemed to know she was spying on Jed. The ladies talked on about how good it would be once Maryland joined the Confederacy. They would keep the Northerners out and preserve their way of life. Maura smiled pleasantly. While she publicly agreed with them, inside she was shaking her head at their naivety.

Her late husband had shown her the disparity between the northern states and the southern ones. The Union states could get by without the Confederacy, but Maura was sure the Confederacy would fail without the North. It would take years for the South to build up their industry to match the North's. It meant money would be flowing to the North or overseas for goods and services, which was one of the major bones of contention now.

After her guests departed, Tabitha came in to tell her about the message that Bryce had sent.

"He did what!?" exclaimed Maura.

"Jed rode to Fort McHenry to talk to Major Morris and then took off to Relay House in the thunderstorm," repeated Tabitha patiently. "Bryce stated in his message that Mr. Tremblant knew about the fifteenth. He went to talk to General Butler."

Tabitha let Maura think on that for a moment before adding, "Paul wanted me to tell you that Mayor Brown and Marshal Kane are here for lunch and are currently in the parlor."

"I saw them come in. How could Jed ride that far with the injuries he had?" Maura shook her head. "Never mind. I know the answer to that. That man is too much like my Jonathan... ready to do anything to preserve the Union."

"Yes, Miss Maura. Your guests . . .?"

Maura walked into the parlor, and the two men sprang to their feet.

"Gentlemen, I'm sorry to have kept you waiting. Shall we adjourn to the dining room? Mayor Brown, I have just purchased a case of French wine I would like to get your opinion of."

"Of course." Mayor Brown extended an arm to escort Maura into the next room.

"I am delighted you could come for lunch, given the horrendous weather outside."

"It's a shame the good Lord won't create another flood to drown all the Yankees," stated Kane, sitting down after Maura was seated.

"He had better not," said Mayor Brown. "Given the number of them around Washington, all of us in Maryland would find ourselves underwater."

"Not just around Washington," corrected Kane. "Let's not forget about General Butler and his Massachusetts boys at Relay House, stopping and looting every train that goes by them."

"I can't see them doing that to the federal troop trains," said Maura lightly. "Mayor Brown, please do try the biscuits with the Virginia ham pate. At least the Union troops are going on to Washington and not stopping here at Baltimore."

"They shouldn't be in Maryland at all." Kane raised his wine glass in a toast. "Here's to the expulsion of all foreign troops from our sovereign soil in the not too distant future."

"Hear. Hear," cheered Mayor Brown as both he and Maura returned the salute. "A day that is much closer than most people think."

"Really?" asked Maura. "When?"

"Ah, that would be telling," replied Mayor Brown good-naturedly.

"Yes, it would be," added Kane. "It's unfortunate the state legislature chose to cower instead of voting with their convictions. If they had, the throwing off of northern oppression would already be in our past. They are, one and all, traitors to the cause. However, I'd like to make a toast, because they will not be in power much longer."

"I can hardly wait for that day." Maura raised her glass.

"From your mouth to God's ear," said Mayor Brown cheerfully. "My dear Mrs. Harrison, I must say that your choice of wine is excellent."

"Thank you, Mayor Brown. I'm actually forgoing a different selection of wine to drink with our main course, because I think this wine will be excellent with the striped bass."

Mayor Brown took another sip of his wine. "I do believe you are correct."

Lunch continued along this vein with Maura playing the enchanting hostess and the two men making merry. After they had eaten, Maura played the piano while the men smoked cigars and drank brandy.

"Thank you for a wonderful lunch," said Mayor Brown as he and Kane were leaving. The intensity of the storm was starting to increase. "Very soon you will see the culmination of all our work."

"There's one important thing you must do for the next several days," said Kane. "You must keep an eye on Tremblant. We need to know where he is at all times. This is vital and will take precedence over anything else."

"I don't know where he is right now," said Maura, "but he has been invited here this evening for the dinner party that you gentlemen and your wives have been invited to. As for watching him *all* the time, I can't do that, unless you are suggesting something you should not."

"Not at all, Mrs. Harrison," interjected Mayor Brown hastily. "We need to know of his movements and plans to the last detail. This is the information we need you to get. We'll have other people following him around town."

The men took their leave, and Maura went into the morning room to jot down the highlights of the luncheon. After she finished, she glanced down at her black dress. Maura decided what she was wearing would be good enough for tonight's informal get-together. She needed to check with the cook to make sure everything was prepared. As she walked into the foyer, she heard piano music wafting out of the parlor. It was Beethoven's *Fur Elise*.

Tabitha has expanded her repertoire, thought Maura. *I must commend her on this piece.*

Walking into the parlor, she opened her mouth and froze.

"Good evening, Mrs. Harrison," said Anthony Duff as his fingers glided over the keys.

"You!?" gasped Maura. "How did you get in here?"

Duff did not stop playing as he answered. "I must confess that I came in through the cellar door. That ... unfortunate ... wanted poster has put a crimp on my freedom of movement."

"My servants know of that. What will you do when the police come? I can do nothing for you; I did not register that complaint."

"I know. It was our dear Lieutenant Tremblant who did so. I am only the one who made you a widow less than a month ago. I am heartily sorry for any grief I put you through." His fingers paused for a second. "Although, based on the agreement you wrung out of our government and the bits and pieces I gathered about your marriage, it appears that it was more of an obligation and payment than anything else."

"Thank you for that clarifying observation," stated Maura acidly, even though, inside, she was shaking with anger and fear. Had he found her out? Did he know about her sworn revenge upon him? She also cursed herself for leaving the derringer Jed had given her in her room. Never again would she go about unarmed ... even to church.

Duff gave her a sideways glance before resuming the melody he was playing. "You are a smart woman, Mrs. Harrison, ... and clever for one so young. As you may have guessed, I try to leave nothing to chance. There will be no police because your servants are currently performing their duties in the basement under the watchful eye of two of my men." Maura opened her mouth to protest, but Duff preempted her. "They are fine. Think of it as my saving your front door from being broken down."

"What can I do for you, Mr. Duff?" Maura moved into the room and closer to the fireplace.

"Things are coming to a head very soon. You have done well in your assignment and have obtained excellent information concerning the enemy's intent. I must commend you on your skill."

"So, you are my superior," said Maura. "I had thought it was Marshal Kane."

"He passes your information on to me, which I forward to Richmond. I have not revealed myself to you for a variety of reasons. One, I was not sure where your allegiances lay. Two, I could not be sure of what your reaction would be to seeing the killer of your husband, and three, I had other duties to attend to."

"Richmond?" asked Maura in surprise.

"Yes, the Confederate government voted on the eighth to move the capital from Montgomery to Richmond."

"Did one of your duties include Winans's steam gun?"

Duff stopped playing and sighed deeply. "I admit that I failed greatly in that regard. I seriously underestimated Lieutenant Tremblant's capabilities and resources. Who would have thought that another train would be commandeered to chase down the one that had the steam gun loaded on it? I also believe that he was responsible for the death of Lieutenant Frijack but cannot prove it."

Maura's stomach was full of butterflies as she slowly moved obliquely to the fireplace. Facing Duff, her cold stiff fingers fumbled behind her for the iron poker.

"But he was with me that day," advised Maura, a little too loudly in her own estimation. Her fingers found the poker, and she gripped it in her right hand, hiding it in the folds of her dress. "It may have been one of his men, but he never made any comment about the lieutenant's death except to express his condolences."

"It could have been one of his men." Duff concluded the musical piece. He paused for a second before starting a Strauss waltz.

Maura recognized it as the *Irvlichter Waltz, Op. 218*. Its lively tune was seriously inappropriate for the feelings Maura had.

"That person had to be very good to best Lieutenant Frijack in close combat with edged weapons, as I have been told. There is also the possibility that *you* were there that day."

The music stopped, and Maura froze by the fireplace as Duff turned his head to give her a piercing look. "What's the matter, Mrs. Harrison? You appear to be very nervous."

"I have every right to be!" snapped Maura. "A murderer appears in my house unannounced. His . . . his henchmen are holding my servants captive in the basement. I have no idea what your intentions are! You could be here to eliminate a witness to your act. You say you are my superior in this business of getting Maryland into the Confederacy. No one I know of has spoken about you. Not Mayor Brown! Not Marshal Kane! Not Captain Wilcott! Not even anyone from the War Department of the Confederacy! Nervous? You can damn well bet I am nervous!"

Duff turned back to the piano and began playing *Braham's Lullaby*.

"I thought it best to keep you uninformed," he said. "You are extremely young and were married to a northern officer. Despite your protestations that it was a marriage of convenience, I was not prepared to trust you."

"So, do you trust me now?" asked Maura, taking one step closer to Duff.

"Not fully, but maybe a little more than I did. I was surprised you managed to get that concession regarding your father's plantation from President Davis."

"The question now is, why have you come to see me?"

"The future, Mrs. Harrison, the future," answered Duff. "Things will be happening very soon."

"If you mean the fifteenth, I know of it," snipped Maura. "Really? The soothsayer's day? Could you have been anymore melodramatic?"

"It wasn't my choice," growled Duff, striking discordant notes on the piano. "How did you hear of it and who have you told?"

"I have told no one!" Maura took another step closer. She was twelve feet away with small tables and chairs in between them. "Who would I tell? Mayor Brown? Captain Wilcott? I should think that would be redundant. Mr. Tremblant? Oh, I am sure he would be very glad for this piece of information, but he is on the wrong side. As for who I heard it from, your colleagues in the militia need lessons in how *not* to gossip."

Duff sighed heavily and muttered more to himself rather to anyone else. "Too proud . . . too arrogant . . . too full of themselves." He looked at Maura. "Since you are aware of the day, I can be more direct. You are a beautiful and clever woman. With the events that are about to take place here, the decision has been made that your talents will be of better use elsewhere. We are not getting any reports of substance from the territories west of Texas."

"Texas!" exclaimed Maura loudly. "You're asking me to go to Texas?"

"The New Mexico Territory, to be exact," replied Duff as he plinked out *The Yellow Rose of Texas* on the piano. "I want you to establish yourself in Santa Fe. A month and a half ago, the western portion of that territory declared for the Confederacy and is calling itself the Arizona Territory. As I understand it, California is ready to split in half with the southern part of that state also declaring for the Confederacy. That only leaves the New Mexico Territory standing in the way of the Confederacy stretching from the Atlantic Ocean to the Pacific Ocean."

He smiled up at here. "The Confederacy will have a single border with Mexico. The British, French, and Spaniards are not happy with the new government there. Repayment of the loans made to the Mexican government have been . . . sporadic. There will also be a boom to the Confederate economy by opening up trade with the Far East."

Trade with China, Japan, and the rest of the Far East was alien to Maura. She had heard of such places, but they were as foreign to her as the face of the moon. Jed had explained it to her, but her imagination of jeweled cities, yellow-skinned people in silk robes and exotic landscapes kept interfering with her understanding. She did know that an east to west coast Confederacy was a very bad thing.

"You do realize no one knows me there," argued Maura. "I will be just a face among the crowd."

"Just like here." He chuckled. "Your face in a crowd would be like a lighthouse on a dark night. Look at how fast you became a darling of this city."

"Yes, a southern lady with a southern accent in a southern city," countered Maura. Her fear had been replaced by anger. She only had to get a little closer and took a tentative step toward him. "As you have pointed out, I am part of this city now. Would not my talents be best served here?"

"Most likely," agreed Duff, "but I had no say in the matter. I, myself, have been ordered to New Mexico. You are ordered to go for two reasons: one, you report information without modifying it for your own interests, and two, we want you to have Lieutenant Tremblant escort you there."

"You must be joking!" gasped Maura in shock and took a step backward. "It's one thing to invite him to dinners and parties but quite another to travel with him on a long journey."

"My superiors want him out of Maryland and, preferably, west of the Mississippi River. There is another alternative."

"Captain Wilcott tried that one," said Maura flatly.

"Yes, and because of that failure and the death of Lieutenant Frijack, I am loath to attempt that choice."

"When would I have to leave?"

Duff hit a low note on the piano, which sounded like a telling of doom to Maura. "Immediately."

"Impossible! How can I just pack up and leave? What excuse could I possibly give?"

"I do not care," said Duff nonplussed. "You agreed to this. I suggest you pack and leave. The situation in New Mexico is very fluid. Southern officers out there are resigning their Army commissions and joining the Confederate ranks. The Arizona Territory has declared for the Confederacy, but it is unclear if that is a widespread feeling or not. You are needed there as soon as possible. Oh, yes . . . don't forget to take Lieutenant Tremblant with you."

"He's a captain now," hissed Maura, taking a step closer. She was almost within reach.

The front door banged open, causing Maura to spin around in fright. She had not realized how tightly wound her nerves were until she saw the poker shaking in her hand. She looked back at Duff who was regarding her over the barrel of his pistol.

"Hello? Mrs. Harrison?" came a voice from the foyer.

"In here, Miss LaBlanc." Maura walked to the fireplace to replace the poker. Duff returned his pistol to its hiding place.

"I knocked, but no one answered the door," called out Natalie as she swept into the living room. "I know I'm early, but . . . oh! I am sorry. I didn't realize anyone else was here."

"It's quite all right," answered Maura. "I'm the one who should be apologizing. Let me take your cloak. Oh, is it starting to rain again?"

A loud, thundering bang shook the house and everyone jumped. Duff's hand swung down toward his pistol, but he did not draw it.

"It's just staring up again, and it looks bad," commented Natalie with a nervous but relieved laugh. She looked at Duff.

"I swear I don't know where my manners are," said Maura. "Miss Natalie LaBlanc, may I introduce Mr. Anthony Duff. Mr. Duff, Miss LaBlanc."

"It is a pleasure to meet you, Miss LaBlanc. I have attended several of your performances and have thoroughly enjoyed each one."

"Thank you, sir." She jumped a little as a white flash of lightening lit up the room followed by a loud rumble of thunder. "I think this might be worse than this morning's storm."

Before anyone could say anything else, there was a loud pounding on the door. Maura looked at Duff, who just cocked an eyebrow and nonchalantly put his hand on top of his pistol. Maura started toward the door when she heard it open and then slam shut. A rain-splattered Captain Wilcott hurried into the foyer, looked into the morning room, and then into the parlor. Seeing the three people standing there, he hurried to Duff and whispered in his ear. Maura saw Duff's shoulders slump at the news and a resigned look came upon his face.

"Go back to the barracks and gather up your men and equipment," ordered Duff. "Be prepared to head south to Virginia. You know what routes to take."

Captain Wilcott, not acknowledging the two ladies, took off at a run. Silence descended in the room, broken only by the continuous thunder outside and the hard pelting rain against the windows.

"Ladies, I am sorry, but I must take my leave of you." Duff moved away from the piano and picked up his hat off the sofa. "Miss LaBlanc, I am looking forward to listening to more of your extraordinary performances in the future. Mrs. Harrison, will you see me to the front door?"

The Trail of the Scottish Bluebell

Duff didn't walk to the foyer but left by the other door with Maura following. At the stairwell leading into the basement, he called down that it was time to leave. Maura heard a man reply.

"Do you know where Lieutenant . . . ah, Captain Tremblant is?" he asked.

"He is supposed to be here tonight, but with his injuries, I would have to say he is recuperating at his home," replied Maura.

"I thought so as well," said Duff. "We were both mistaken. Go to Santa Fe, New Mexico, as soon as possible. I will see you there. Don't forget to take Captain Tremblant with you."

"You are asking the impossible. It will take time and money."

"You don't have the time." Duff looked around the house pointedly. "It appears you have money."

"My father's wealth, which is tied up in this house," argued Maura. "What has happened?"

"Captain Tremblant has stolen a march on us. He was seen at the Camden Railroad Station, and he brought the entire Sixth Massachusetts Regiment with him!"

Chapter 29

Monday, May 13, 1861

THE PLAN WORKED. THE TWO trains hooked together had pulled away from Relay House heading down the track toward Harpers Ferry. Once it was two miles away, the train stopped and separated. One engine and two cars carrying a platoon of men under the command of Lieutenant Colonel Watson headed toward Frederick to arrest Ross Winans.

Jed could only hope the federal arrest preceded the Confederate one. He hated to think of what would happen if the southern sympathizers in Baltimore City got a hold of Winans.

The second train roared past Relay House without stopping and sped on to Baltimore. General Butler and his staff had taken over the last car. Jed supplied them with the locations of the hidden arms, ammunition, and equipment.

"I want to establish a military presence in two locations," stated General Butler. "I will be declaring martial law and issuing a proclamation. I want to ensure that all manufactories and foundries are working for the Union and not equipping the rebels. It's the militia I am worried about."

"Not all the militia troops are for the South," advised Jed. "There are several units for the Union. I think our concern should be to prevent the citizens from obtaining arms from the warehouses."

Once the train arrived at Camden Station, the plan was to split the soldiers into two columns. Jed, being familiar with the city, would lead the larger column with the artillery to Federal

The Trail of the Scottish Bluebell

Hill. The smaller column would occupy Mount Vernon, based around the Washington Monument.

The train rattled and lurched as it sped down the track, causing a break in their conversation.

"I must first ensure we are entrenched in a defensible position," said General Butler. "Once we are established, I will send companies out to secure the warehouses. Will my proclamation reach the newspapers?"

"Yes, sir," replied Jed. "A squad of your men will deliver a copy of it to each newspaper, to the city hall, and to the courthouse. They will also deliver the proclamation and your message to Major Morris at Fort McHenry."

"Capital!" exclaimed General Butler in glee. "It wouldn't do to have our own troops fire on us as we ascend Federal Hill."

The dark billowing clouds hovered overhead as the train raced on. Despite the earlier thunderstorm, Mother Nature was obviously not ready to call it quits. There was plenty of thunder and lightning, but the rain held off as the train pulled into Camden Station.

Hundreds of men in blue uniforms jumped out of the cars, either to surround the station or to form into ranks. Jed stood beside a boxcar as a ramp was brought over to unload Sweet Sue and the other officers' horses. Loud raucous laughter drew Jed's attention. Four soldiers were crowded around a bench. A frown appeared on Jed's forehead as he caught sight of a maroon skirt showing between the soldier's legs.

"You're a pretty one," leered one soldier, leaning forward.

"She sure is," chuckled another.

"Gentlemen!" barked Jed with more than a touch of authority in his voice.

The four soldiers straightened up and turned to look at him. Their looks of concern turned to one of derision and disregard at the sight of Jed's civilian clothes. Jed saw the soldiers begin to puff up at his interference with their amusement.

"And what might you boyos be up to?" growled a first sergeant walking up to the group. He was obviously a veteran by his age and bearing. The soldiers' expressions abruptly changed to uncertainty. "I don't feel like fighting every Tom,

Dick, and Harry in this city because you want a bit o' fun. Go on! Get back to where you're supposed to be!"

The soldiers quickly shouldered their rifles and moved away. Jed's mouth dropped open in shock when he caught sight of Ruth Goldberg sitting on the bench. Her eyes were concerned.

"You be alright, miss?" asked the first sergeant.

"Quite all right, Sergeant," replied Ruth demurely. "I thank you for your assistance."

The first sergeant nodded to her and left to check on his men. Jed and Ruth stared at each other.

"Are you catching flies, Mr. Tremblant?" asked Ruth coquettishly.

Jed snapped his mouth closed and smiled. "I had not thought to see you again. I am both astonished and delighted. Whatever are you doing here?"

Ruth looked as pretty as ever with her wealth of black hair done up under a bonnet. She seemed poised, but she loosen her grip on her parasol when the soldiers had moved away and she had caught sight of him.

"The legislature is taking a break during this session," explained Ruth. "I think they are letting tempers cool off. They have been arguing over secession, the federal troops that are currently in the state, what should be done about President Lincoln and his request for troops, and a dozen other topics. There's been no agreement on anything, so nothing has been done."

"That is good news for one point; bad news for another," commented Jed. "So, you came home . . . just in time for this."

"And this is, what? I am guessing this is not just a normal troop movement through Baltimore. These soldiers came in by train from the south."

"General Butler is occupying Baltimore." Jed went on to explain what was happening and Maura's deductions about the fifteenth.

"Open revolt?" asked Ruth aghast. "The federal government won't condone that in Maryland. It will mean fighting in the streets. I need to warn my father right away!"

"We do need to get you home where it's safe, and you can tell him about the occupation." He handed her a piece of paper. "This is General Butler's Proclamation that should be printed in tomorrow's papers."

Jed, holding on to Ruth's arm, headed toward the station exit. As they approached, a soldier stationed there held up his hand to stop them.

"I'm sorry, sir, but our orders are to prevent anyone from coming in or leaving. I know you, sir, and those orders don't apply to you . . . just the young lady."

"I see," said Jed. "Miss Goldberg, please wait here under the care of these three soldiers. I'll see if I can find your ride and let him know you can't leave."

Ruth held out the paper. "Please, have him give this to my father immediately."

Jed took the paper, nodded, and headed outside the station. Hundreds of blue-clad men were clogging the street, getting ready to march to Federal Hill. They were waiting for the artillery pieces to be unloaded from the train and hooked up to their limbers and horses. Jed knew he didn't have a great deal of time before he would have to guide these men to the hill.

The sky crackled and lit up the entire city with a stark white light. The glare outlined a man, dressed in black and wearing a Jewish wide-brimmed hat sitting on a wagon. Jed worked his way through the soldiers to the man.

"Mr. Tremblant!" exclaimed Saul, Ruth's older brother. "Have you seen my sister, Ruth? They're not letting anyone in or out."

"She's inside, Saul." Jed looked around and saw only a few small clusters of people watching the soldiers. He handed the paper to Saul. "General Butler is occupying Baltimore City. This is his proclamation of his intent. He's going to declare martial law. Get back to your father and let him know what is happening. I'll take care of Ruth."

Saul gave him a serious look. "Keep Ruth safe."

"On my honor."

"Shalom," said Saul before driving away.

The sound of horse hooves on cobblestone brought Jed's attention back to the station. The horses had been unloaded, saddled, and brought outside. The artillery pieces would soon follow. Jed blew out a breath of exasperation at his limited time and hobbled back into the station.

"Follow me," he said to Ruth, snagging her arm and pulling her after him. He located Corporal Duncan with his squad of soldiers. They would deliver the proclamation after Jed returned from Federal Hill.

"Corporal Duncan, Miss Goldberg. Miss Goldberg, these soldiers will keep you safe until I return from guiding the troops to Federal Hill. Corporal Duncan, do you understand what I am saying?"

"Yes, sir. She'll be safe with us." Duncan rushed on. "I've already sent one man to Fort McHenry."

"Miss Goldberg—" Jed started.

"Go, Mr. Tremblant!" ordered Ruth with a smile. "I'll be here when you get back."

Jed opened his mouth to say something, then realized he didn't have to say anything. He smiled, nodded, and took off for the exit. His knee almost gave way, and Jed grimaced in pain as he slowed his walk.

"So nice of you to show up, Captain Tremblant," griped General Butler as Jed legged up on top of Sweet Sue.

"My apologies, sir. I was checking on my men to make sure they had your notices to post and my instructions. They will wait for my return."

"Ah-hum! Yes, well . . . let's show General Scott how to occupy a city!" announced General Butler gaily. A low, long rumble of thunder answered.

Jed took the lead with General Butler. He was uneasy because no pickets or scouts were to be sent in front of them. Speed and surprise were the cornerstones of General Butler's plan. Even though the air was humid and oppressive, the morning rain had cleared the filth off the cobblestone streets. However, no amount of rain could remove the black coal soot imbedded on the outside of every stone, brick, and wood building.

On top of his horse, General Butler raised his arm, and his subordinate commanders yelled out orders to prepare their men. With a downward movement of his arm, the column of men started southward. They had barely traveled fifteen yards before Jed saw the rain rushing toward them, and the entire column was engulfed in a torrential downpour.

"The rebels will never expect us in this!" shouted General Butler over the crashing thunder and heavy rain.

Jed nodded as lightning streaked across the sky. He looked behind him at the drenched rank and file of marching soldiers. Jed hissed in apprehension as hundreds of bayonets gleamed in the flashes of a brilliant white light. One bolt would incinerate dozens of men. They would be even more exposed on top of Federal Hill.

Faces stared out through water-streaked windows, Jed was all ready for a repeat of the riot of April nineteenth, but it didn't materialize. A few undaunted souls braved the weather to cheer for the Union troops. General Butler acknowledged them with a smile and a wave.

"And here I thought there was no one in this city other than rebels and traitors," said General Butler just before a bolt of lightning lanced downward. The booming thunder was so close that Jed felt the concussive force of it. Sweet Sue shied a little, and it took General Butler several seconds to get his horse under control.

The nature of the neighborhood changed from shops and warehouses clustered around the railroad station to tightly packed residences. The men marched on as the thunderstorm raged above them with an intensity never seen before, Jagged streaks of brilliant, white light streaked across the sky. The thunder was constant, and still, the men marched on.

Federal Hill was at the water's edge overlooking the harbor and the majority of the city. At the base of the hill, General Butler stopped and signaled his men forward. Slipping and sliding on the wet grass and mud, the soldiers surged up the hill. The artillery battery was in the middle of the column. After looking at the narrow, muddy track leading to the top of the hill, it was decided it was too dangerous to have the horses pull the cannons up. Whole companies of soldiers were assigned to get the heavy, cumbersome weapons up the hill. With ropes, pulleys, chocks for the wheels, and quite a few scrapped knuckles, each cannon with its limber was manhandled up the hill and into position.

Jed and General Butler reached the top of the hill. Federal Hill, through some fluke of nature, commanded the entire harbor and all of Baltimore City. It could be easily defended and difficult to attack.

"I believe we are in control here," stated General Butler amidst another terrific crash of thunder.

The rain was still coming down heavily and was whipped around them by the wind. Despite Jed's slicker and hat, he was soaked to the skin.

"Excellent!" declared General Butler, surveying as much of the landscape as he could in the storm. "I have taken Baltimore City with less men than General Scott envisioned and several months earlier! This is glorious!"

General Butler kicked his right leg over his horse's neck and slid off his saddle. No sooner had his feet hit the ground than water squirted out of his cavalry boots to splash into his face.

Jed looked on in shock as General Butler sputtered and gasped from the unexpected watery assault. General Butler wiped his face with his sleeve, looked around, and burst out laughing.

"There's nothing like a dose of humility when one is crowing about his own accomplishments, eh, Captain Tremblant?" he guffawed. "You had best be on your way. We both have a great deal to get done tonight." Turning away, General Butler yelled, "Colonel, send a unit over to that lumberyard to appropriate what we need for breastworks. Assure the owner the government will pay him for his goods if he is loyal to the Union."

The storm continued in all its fury as Jed rode down the hill and back to Camden Station. When lightning lit up the sky, Jed thought he saw a shadowy figure hiding his blond hair underneath the hood of his cloak. Blinking rapidly to clear the spots floating in his eyes, he looked again, but there was no one there and no place for anyone to hide.

Jed found his squad of men laughing and joking with Ruth. The black-haired beauty was smiling and laughing along with the soldiers, so Jed assumed, and hoped, that the men were not expressing any crude humor or inappropriate behavior. He saw that they had all stayed dry under the roof canopies.

"Atten-shun!" yelled Corporal Duncan when he caught sight of Jed dismounting from Sweet Sue.

The men all jumped up and stood straight. Jed, remembering General Butler's dismount, stepped down slowly from his saddle. As his feet touched down on the cobblestones, he felt the water sluicing around inside his boots. Ruth stood with a twinkle in her eyes and raised her hand to her eyebrows in a mock salute.

"At ease," ordered Jed as he sat down on one of the benches to remove his boots. It wasn't until then that Jed realized how tired he really was. He could barely lift his leg to get to one of his boots.

"You two, get his boots off," ordered Ruth, to which Jed gratefully relinquished his efforts to others. As the boots came off, it seemed that almost a quart of water poured out of each one. "And his socks."

"Leave them on," said Jed, a little groggy. Water was dripping from his clothes to create quite a puddle under the bench. "I don't have dry ones, and we need to get a move on."

"Sir, no offense, but you're about all done in," said Corporal Duncan. "My men and I can split into two groups. We have the maps you made for us, and we know who to deliver the proclamations to."

Jed opened his mouth to protest, but Corporal Duncan beat him to the punch. "We can't be dragging a lady like Miss Goldberg around in a storm like this anyway. And it ain't safe to leave Miss Goldberg here neither. We've discouraged a couple of would-be Romeos already. You can take her someplace safe, and we can meet up with you in an hour or two to tell you how we're doing."

"No fighting," said Jed firmly as he stamped his feet back into his wet boots. "That means none, even if it's a single man with a pitchfork. Understand?"

Corporal Duncan and the other ten men all nodded.

"Okay. I'll be at the Washington Monument in one hour, and I'll stay there until all of you show up. Let the man you sent to Fort McHenry know of this. Miss Goldberg, I don't have a carriage, so are you ready for a wet ride?"

"I am certain Saul did not make it home before the rain started up again. I would have gotten drenched if I had gone with him, so I might as well ride with you."

"We found a big square of canvas that should cover you, Miss Goldberg," said one of the soldiers.

Jed had tied Sweet Sue under an alcove to keep her out of the rain. He had already talked to the sergeant in charge of the guards, and Ruth was allowed to leave the station with him.

"Well, Sue, got one more ride in you?" he asked. Sweet Sue nickered and nudged his arm, almost pushing Jed over.

Jed was in a quandary. Taking Ruth to her father's house was a long trip through the city. There was a good chance they would be spotted, and he didn't want to bring that type of scrutiny upon Mr. Goldberg and his family. The club was the closest, and he could easily sneak her up to the third floor. The trouble was he didn't know which clients were being "entertained" up there. It was a meeting place for southern sympathizers and too much of a risk to take Ruth there.

His house was even further away than the Goldberg's and more likely to be under observation. There was only one place Jed thought of where he could take Ruth where she would be safe.

Ruth and the squad of soldiers joined him.

"Up you go," said Jed as he helped Ruth onto the saddle.

"Here's the canvas," said Corporal Duncan as he and another soldier began to pull it up over Ruth.

"Stop! Stop!"

The two men froze at Ruth's command, and she untied the bows to her bonnet. She took it off her head and helped pull the canvas up to her neck, covering the bonnet to protect it.

"Miss, you might want to pull it all the way over you. Like a big ole tent," suggested Corporal Duncan.

"I won't be able to see!" complained Ruth.

"The wind is whipping up out there," said Jed, just a cold blast of air lashed around them. "You'll get soaked otherwise."

"Will it cover both of us?"

"I was going to lead Sweet Sue," argued Jed. "She's traveled quite a distance today in bad weather."

"Jed, you can't! You won't make it ten feet!"

"Uh, we'd better get going," hemmed Corporal Duncan.

"No fighting," reiterated Jed. "I'll meet you at the monument. It's the tall tower with a statue of our first president on top of it."

His men left, and Jed looked out at the storm just as two huge bolts of lightning flashed downward. The resulting double boom of thunder sounded like cannon shells exploding. All of a sudden, he felt a heavy weariness in his bones. He pulled the canvas over Ruth's head.

"Scoot forward," he said as he put his left foot in the stirrup.

"Where are we going?" asked Ruth just before they rode out from under the alcove and the rain pelted at them fiercely. "*Oy Vey!* You rode around in this all day?"

"All day," muttered Jed, holding the canvas cover tightly around her. "There's a house close by the Washington Monument where you'll be safe until I can get you home. I'm hoping to get you there without anyone seeing us. I also don't want to be seen near your father's house."

"I think quite a few soldiers have seen me with you," joked Ruth. "However, I do know what you mean." She stayed silent for several seconds. "It's very strange. I have not seen any police officers or any militia soldiers since I arrived back in the city. There are usually two or three patrolling around the station and the harbor. Have you seen any of them tonight?"

"No, but this thunderstorm may have forced them inside. I'd be more of a mind to say Marshal Kane and Mayor Brown are meeting with everyone to discuss their options regarding General Butler's occupation."

"I understand this is the same regiment that was caught up in the riots," said Ruth from under her shelter. "These soldiers are hoping for a fight. Several of them told me that after the riot, they felt like they had run away. They've sworn not to do that again."

"I'm hoping this occupation will scotch any insurrection today, tomorrow, and in the future," said Jed as Sweet Sue's hooves clacked on the cobblestones and splashed through the rivulets of water running down the streets.

Jed made sure the canvas covered Ruth as the rain came down in sheets. Even under the canvas, she jumped at each brilliant flash of light and the resoundingly loud crack of thunder. He was glad she couldn't see the terrifying spectacle of the jagged streaks of electric bolts slashing across the black sky and lancing down to the ground.

The weather made the trip horrendous, and Jed had Sweet Sue take her time going up the long incline to the top of the ridge where the Washington Monument was located. The troops surrounding the monument recognized Jed and waved him through. A short ride put them in front of Maura's house. Jed dismounted to tie Sweet Sue to a hitching post.

After helping Ruth down, Jed patted Sue on the neck. "I'll get you to a stable right after I get Ruth inside."

The tarp was cumbersome, so Jed and Ruth took care walking up the front steps. Using the large, bronze, lion's head doorknocker, Jed rapped soundly against the door. As the door swung open, there was a white flash of lightning, followed by a loud bang, and then the splitting crack of very close thunder. A small part of the brownstone wall next to the door splintered into dozens of tiny flying fragments, and something whined away off in the distance.

Jed placed his hand in the small of Ruth's back and shoved hard as he ducked and twisted. Another shot rang out, and the bullet whizzed over his head. Doing a side vault over the front stoop railing to move away from the front door, Jed landed on the wet grass as another shot rang out. He lunged and rolled to the cover of a tree, where he undid the leather tie to his pistol and pulled it out of its holster.

Carefully peeking around the trunk earned Jed another bullet shot in his direction. On the opposite side of the street stood Captain Wilcott and Sergeant Ferguson with pistols in their hands.

Cocking his Navy Colt, Jed leaned out, took aim at Captain Wilcott, and pulled the trigger.

Pffft!

The hammer blow set off the percussion cap, but the cap failed to ignite the powder charge. Recocking quickly, Jed took another snap shot at the men.

Pffft!

"His powder is wet!" yelled Ferguson, running toward Jed with his pistol outstretched to deliver a fatal shot.

"Ferguson!" warned Captain Wilcott upon seeing his sergeant rush forward.

Jed came up on one knee and held down the trigger as his left hand fanned the hammer. A highly inaccurate way to shoot, but since Ferguson was only ten to twelve feet away, Jed didn't have much of a choice.

Pffft!
Pffft!
Blam!
Pffft!

The fifth shot went off, and the .36 caliber bullet took Ferguson dead center in his sternum. The impact caused Ferguson's feet to fly out from underneath him, and he landed heavily on the cobblestone street.

Yells and shots of alarm came from the soldiers situated around the Washington Monument. Captain Wilcott looked over and saw movement there. Several soldiers were coming his way with rifles at the ready. With a curse, he turned and ran down the street.

Jed stood up and gave chase. He dropped his pistol back into its holster. As he passed by Sergeant Ferguson, he snatched his gun, guessing there would be only two, possibly three shots left in it. But he couldn't let Captain Wilcott get away. He blatantly ignored the pain in his knee and the stitch in his side.

He had seen Ruth with Jed. If Wilcott escaped, he could and would turn southern resentment toward the Jewish community in Baltimore. Jed wasn't sure the northern military commanders would do much to stop any reprisals.

Captain Wilcott had turned south on Cathedral Street. Jed raced after him in the rain, but his weariness and the pain in his ribs were slowing him down. Wilcott increased the distance between them with each step. Jed wheezed from the exertion. As they neared the Basilica, Jed stopped, aimed, and fired twice.

Wilcott's right leg twisted out and over, spinning the man around. He fell flat onto the wet sidewalk but was up in a second. Limping quickly up the cathedral's front steps, he yanked open a door to get inside.

Jed followed Wilcott as quickly as he could. He pulled open a different front door and rolled inside until he was hidden behind a wall. The shot he was expecting did not happen. Wondering briefly how damned he was for bringing a weapon onto holy ground, he guessed he would just have to add it to his other sins for penance.

"Wilcott!" Jed yelled out. "It's just you and me in here. No fake duel. No two against one. No ambushes. Why don't we take this outside where you can try to take me on an even footing?"

Wilcott's voice came from somewhere within the church. "Only one of us will leave here alive."

Chapter 30

Monday, May 13, 1861

THE BEATING OF THE RAIN against the windows of the Basilica produced a drumming sound that permeated throughout the huge building. The patterning of the rain was broken by the cracks and deep rumbling of thunder. Flashes of lightning coming through the windows created stark contrasts of white and black outlines inside the church.

Jed grimaced. The rain and thunder made hearing small noises impossible. The lightning, no matter how fast he averted his eyes, destroyed his night vision. The good thing was that Captain Wilcott suffered from the same disadvantages.

With Wilcott's sense of southern chivalry, Jed knew the man would not think of leaving once Jed had issued his challenge. Looking around the edge of the wall, Jed couldn't see any sign of his adversary. Row upon row of pews and the columns holding up the vaulted side arches and central domes provided plenty of places for concealment. Crouching down and ignoring the pain in his leg, Jed moved cautiously to his right in a deadly game of hide and seek.

Skirting along the back wall, Jed kept an eye out for any movement. He didn't want to pass a pew and miss seeing Wilcott hiding there. He also kept looking at the pulpit in front of the altar area. It was a raised platform with circular stairs leading up to it. The pulpit was an excellent place to hide and see most of the sanctuary below.

As Jed moved forward, clearing one pew at a time, a flash of lightning revealed how close he was to the confessional booths on his side of the church. There was no lamp lit, so the interior of each booth would be in utter darkness. Just opening the door could get him killed if Wilcott was hiding inside. Bypassing them may turn out to be just as deadly.

Figuring that leaving the confessionals unchecked was too great a risk, Jed sidled up to the first one after checking out the pews nearby. He listened but heard nothing over the pounding rain and rumbling thunder. Taking in a deep breath, he reached for the door handle.

Lightning flashed three times in rapid succession, illuminating the entire interior for a couple of seconds. Wilcott had the same idea as Jed, but he was at the confessional booths located on the opposite side of the cathedral. The men caught sight of one another at the same time.

Jed took a step away from the confessionals, spinning to his left as he brought up Ferguson's pistol. Simultaneously, two tongues of flame boomed out at each other in the darkness. Jed felt a burn along his shoulder blade and knew that, if he had not moved, the bullet would have struck him instead of just scratching him. Ignoring the stinging sensation, Jed quickly moved away from his position to take cover behind a large column.

"Are you alive?" came Wilcott's voice from the far side of the church.

"Yes," answered Jed. "You grazed me along the back."

"Ah, you scored me lightly along the ribs. That's twice you grazed me, but you should be out of shots now."

"Step out and let's see," taunted Jed as he crouched and moved around to get closer. He guessed Wilcott was also on the move.

"I'm not as foolish as the late Sergeant Ferguson," said Wilcott. "You have more than your fair share of the devil's luck and more lives than a cat. However, tonight is when all that luck runs out."

Jed had begun to cut across to the other side, crouching low between the pews. He moved carefully to avoid tripping over the kneelers or knocking into the hymnals. He was halfway across the center aisle when Wilcott appeared about twenty-five feet away.

Wilcott had moved quickly down the side aisle to the back wall of the church and along it to the center aisle. Jed stood as Wilcott turned sideways to him and pointed his pistol toward the ceiling. He then leveled it to take aim at Jed. A shot rang out, ending the duel.

"Too slow," commented Jed as he knelt beside Wilcott who was gasping for breath. A bloodstain spread from underneath his arm. "This was not a duel and totally unnecessary."

"I should—" Wilcott wheezed, breaking into hacking coughs that shook his entire body. "—have guessed you'd . . . you'd have another—" A gasp interrupted his speech, followed by another coughing fit. "—another weapon," he finally managed to finish.

"Four-barrel derringer, .30 caliber." Jed made sure Wilcott's pistol was out of reach.

"I . . . I guess there's . . . no chance for me." His coughing went longer this time as he fought for air.

"I'm sure I hit an artery, and it went through your lungs. You'll be gone before I get half a block away to get help. I'll stay here with you and let your people know."

"You're . . . you're not bad . . . for a Yankee." Wilcott breathed his last breath.

Jed walked slowly out of the Basilica. He was weary deep into his bones. As he walked toward Maura's house in the driving rain he barely felt, Jed could barely put one foot in front of the other. Approaching Monument Street, he heard a sharp whistle ahead of him. It was followed by another whistle farther away. A couple of seconds later, one of his men moved toward him.

"Captain Tremblant, boy, am I glad I found you," the soldier said. "Let's step over to that porch there. The others will be with us soon."

Jed's head was fuzzy, but he tried to keep his thoughts straight. "The proclamation?"

"All delivered, sir. Here come the others."

Eleven soldiers rushed down the street and joined them on the porch.

"Sir, police officers are waiting for you up there because of the shooting by the monument," said Corporal Duncan.

"But you need to know, while we were out and about, we saw a large group of police officers down by a warehouse with several empty wagons. It looks like they're getting ready to move something."

"Which warehouse?"

"The one opposite the Custom House, sir."

Jed grimaced. "That's where the police moved their weapons to hide them from the federal government. We'll have to get some troops down there to stop them."

"Uh, er, sir," hemmed Corporal Duncan. "There are rumors of an attack being bandied about. None of the commanders are letting any of their people go anywhere."

Jed banged his fists on the porch railing in frustration.

"Sweet Jesus!" gasped Corporal Duncan.

"What?" asked Jed, startled by the curse.

"Your back! Your coat's all bloody!"

"How bad is it?" Now that they were talking about it, Jed's back began to throb painfully. He tried to take off his jacket, but it was too wet, and his shoulder hurt too much. "Pull up my shirt and jacket from the back . . . (gasp) . . . carefully!"

Corporal Duncan did the honors. Jed hissed in pain as his shirt pulled free from the wound.

"Looks like you got a three-inch groove along your shoulder, sir," said Corporal Duncan. "It's not deep, but I'm afraid I got it bleeding again. Not too badly though."

"Leave it alone," said Jed. "I'll get it bandaged when I go up the street to talk to talk to the police."

"See the police? Why on earth would you do that?"

"To tell them how Captain Wilcott and Sergeant Ferguson ambushed me. How I shot Sergeant Ferguson there and chased Captain Wilcott to the Basilica. We traded shots in the church and his aim wasn't true." Jed shook his head to clear it. "Something has to be done about that warehouse."

"There's twelve of us," suggested Corporal Duncan. "We can go and stop them."

"You will only get me there if you have a horse you can tie me onto." Jed chuckled, then turned serious and looked pointedly at Corporal Duncan. "Secure it. Try to avoid getting into a fight with them. Retreat if you must. If you can, get inside and barricade the doors. That will be safer than trying to guard the building from the outside. I wouldn't expect anyone to relieve you until tomorrow. Take food and water with you."

Duncan nodded. "We'll get her done, sir."

Jed stepped back into the rain. He heard Corporal Duncan assigning his soldiers tasks to acquire food, water, and ammunition for the night. Jed lost sight of them as he turned onto Monument Street and headed toward Maura's house. There was a police officer standing guard out front, and Sergeant Ferguson's body had been removed. Giving his name to the officer at the front door allowed him access into the house. It was unnaturally quiet inside.

"Mr. Tremblant?"

Jed turned his head to see Captain Boxer standing in the morning room doorway. It took a second for his mind to process.

"Captain Boxer, here to arrest me?"

"That depends." Captain Boxer was dressed in his blue police uniform. "The account I heard from Miss Goldberg indicates that the two of you were fired upon at the front of this house by a man or men unknown. She heard the shots but didn't see anything before you shoved her through the front door. That shove saved her life, but unfortunately, the bullet which missed her killed the butler."

Jed felt a new wave of weariness pervade his body that had nothing to do with his exhaustion.

"I found Sergeant Ferguson shot in the chest outside," continued Boxer. "His holster was empty, and none of the soldiers from the monument admit to taking it."

"You'll find it in the Basilica along with Captain Wilcott's body," Jed told him. "My pistol only fired one shot because the powder was wet." Jed pulled out his pistol and handed it to Captain Boxer. "You'll see that all the percussion caps have been fired, and there are still five balls left in the chambers. I was escorting Miss Goldberg here for safety from Camden Station. We were shot at when we arrived. My one shot killed Sergeant Ferguson. The shooting alerted the soldiers at the monument, and Captain Wilcott . . . retreated."

"Ran away, you mean," corrected Boxer flatly.

"He ran down Cathedral Street. I picked up Ferguson's pistol and gave chase. I winged him outside the Basilica, and he ran inside."

"He took sanctuary inside the church?"

"No, he ran in there to take cover. After I followed him inside, I asked him if we could take this outside. He told me only one of us would be leaving the church alive."

While Boxer thought this over, Jed had to catch himself from falling over in exhaustion.

"You're all done in," Boxer said. "The ladies are in the parlor. We'd better go in and see them."

Jed looked down at his clothes. "I'm not fit to be seen. I'll drip all over the carpet."

"I don't think Mrs. Harrison will mind." Boxer opened the door to the parlor. "He's here."

There were gasps, and a great deal of cloth rustling before Maura, Ruth, and Tabitha burst into the foyer. The chandelier was not lit, but by the light of two whale oil lamps, Jed noted their red-rimmed eyes; all three women had been crying. Both Maura and Ruth kept leaning forward and backward as if they wanted to rush to Jed but were held back by the presence of the other people.

"Are you alright?" asked Maura.

"Tired." His shoulder gave a twinge, and Jed grimaced in pain. "I was hit along the shoulder, but it's not serious."

"What?" gasped both Maura and Ruth. They started speaking at the same time.

"How bad is it?"

"Where's Captain Wilcott?"

"Are you bleeding?"

"Dry clothes He'll catch his death in those wet things!"

"Tabitha, get some bandages!"

"We need to get it cleaned."

"Does it hurt?"

"*Oy Vey*, why didn't you say something?"

"Come! Sit down!"

"Whiskey! We need whiskey."

"Ladies!" said Captain Boxer firmly to silence them. "Captain Wilcott is dead. He and Sergeant Ferguson tried to ambush Mr. Tremblant, who fought back in self-defense. That is the end of the story. You, girl . . . Tabitha? Go get bandages and whiskey. Mrs. Harrison, dry clothes, if you please. Hurry. I can't stay long."

In short order, Captain Boxer had helped Jed out of his jacket and shirt in the foyer. Tabitha returned and gave Jed two shots of whiskey before cleaning the furrow with an alcohol-soaked cloth. Jed's head drooped, and he barely felt the sting in his wound.

The ladies retired to the parlor as Jed stripped and changed into the clothes Maura had brought him. Captain Boxer helped him into the parlor and onto the sofa. Walking over to the door, he asked the ladies to return.

"You're exhausted," said Captain Boxer. "I'm surprised you stayed on your feet as long as you have."

"Is he in trouble with the law?" asked Maura.

"No, although certain members of the police board would not be unhappy to see Mr. Tremblant in prison or just disappear," he replied. "He was seen riding with General Butler this evening. That may give him some immunity, given the present circumstances in the city."

"Which side are you on, Captain Boxer?" asked Ruth.

"The same side I've always been on . . . the law-abiding citizens of Baltimore City. It's a fine line to walk these days. I must leave. It would be best if Captain Wilcott's body was not found in the cathedral. I am sorry about your servant, Mrs. Harrison. I'll bid you good night and see myself out."

After he left, Ruth turned to look at Maura. "I'm sorry to bring misfortune to your door. I don't think Mr. Tremblant would have come here if it hadn't been for my presence."

"You don't know that, Miss Goldberg," corrected Maura. "Captain Boxer saw an opportunity to eliminate an opponent. If Mr. Tremblant had not brought you here, the two men probably would have tried to kill him someplace else . . . with more tragic results."

Ruth opened her mouth to say something more but was interrupted by a knocking on the parlor door.

"Come in," called out Maura. Tabitha entered the room.

"I wanted to see if I should prepare the guest room," said Tabitha.

"Please, not on my account," said Ruth quickly.

"Nor mine," added Jed.

Maura walked over to Tabitha, hugging the young woman compassionately around the shoulders. Maura was only slightly younger than Tabitha but possessed a much greater maturity.

"Tabitha, Miss Goldberg and I will be able to look out after each other tonight."

Jed groaned from the sofa as he tried to sit up.

"We'll get a room ready for Mr. Tremblant as well." Maura said gently, "Miss Petford has already sent word to Mr. Jenkins regarding Paul, but Justine was close to Paul. Go and be with her. I'm canceling all my engagements for the next week. I don't want her having to oversee the housekeeping duties during this time. Go on. I'll come down when Mr. Jenkins arrives."

A single tear rolled down Tabitha's cheek. She gave Maura a weak smile and a nod before heading toward the servants' quarters.

Maura watched her go and her compassionate look changed to one completely devoid of all emotion. "Another loss," she murmured. "Another reason."

"Another reason for what?" asked Ruth.

Maura jerked as if she had suddenly become aware that she was not alone in the room. Jed saw her look over at him, but with his eyes half-shut, she may have assumed he was asleep.

"I beg your pardon, Miss Goldberg, I was wool gathering for a second there. Today has been . . . distressing, for you as well as the rest of us. May I ask why Mr. Tremblant brought you here?"

Ruth smiled. "Don't you mean 'How does he know you?' We met on the train traveling to Frederick for the special session of the legislature. He rescued me from the amorous advances of a state senator." Maura chuckled. "My father sent me to Frederick to report back to him on the secession question."

"He sent you?" asked Maura in astonishment.

Ruth sighed. "Mrs. Harrison, my family is Jewish. I am less conspicuous than my father or brothers, who must comply with our traditions. I understand if this makes me an unwelcome guest in your house."

"I do not know of your religion, but you will always be welcomed here. I have heard preachers portray your people as Christ killers and damned for all eternity. My father told me that the English saw us Scots as slow, stupid work animals. He also said the French were effeminate and prone to mass insanity. What he was trying to teach me was to judge each person on their own merits and not sort them into categories caused by their birth. Why is your father tracking the politics so closely?"

"He's an elder, one of the leaders of our community," answered Ruth. "The slavery question has been an important one to us ever since the Egyptians enslaved us. It is not an issue we can ignore."

"My father owns a plantation, but he doesn't own slaves," said Maura. "He doesn't believe in the institution. That point of view is not popular in the South because of the hue and cry of the abolitionists. However, not having slaves led him to do business with the Harrisons of Connecticut and my late husband, Lieutenant Jonathan Harrison, He was killed during the riot."

Ruth inhaled sharply. "Oh, I . . . I'm . . ." She sighed deeply. "I am sorry, Mrs. Harrison. Mr. Tremblant told me of your husband but did not mention his name. I had not made the connection until now."

"Did he tell you how Jonathan was murdered?" asked Maura coldly. "Did he tell you I feel Jonathan will have no rest until his murderer pays for his crime? Did he tell you how I have sworn revenge on Anthony Duff?"

"Anthony Duff!" exclaimed Ruth. "Jed had him captured in Frederick until I blundered into the middle of it."

"You! That was you?" gasped Maura, standing up quickly. She shook with pent-up emotion, and it took her a minute to regain control. "Jed—as you so informally call him—never told me your name. He only said that he had Duff but for your interference! Jonathan could have been at peace!"

"Ladies," croaked Jed, but he was ignored.

"It's not your husband's spirit who needs revenge," stated Ruth angrily, as she, too, rose to her feet. "It's your own! What happens once you have your revenge? Will you toss Jed aside and return to your idyllic, little world? You are *meshuga*!"

Maura stopped. "*Meshuga*?"

"Crazy . . . insane," informed Ruth with a sneer.

"Maybe so," snarled Maura. Her face took on a smiling, empty-headed look as she added, "At least I'm not the one who just waltzed into a confrontation between two spies!"

"It was Mr. Duff who killed two of his own men to keep me from being compromised. Too bad I don't like his politics, because he was a gentleman and treated me like a lady." She looked fondly at the man on the sofa.

"Oh, and Jed didn't," sniped Maura. "I believe you want Jed for yourself."

Ruth gave out a short, bitter laugh. "For myself? I tried that once before with a Christian. It—" She looked away and waved her hand in the air as if to ward off those memories. "Do I dream of Jed and I being together? Yes, I do, but I know it will never happen. You? You just dream of blood and death."

"I dream of my husband's soul being at peace!" screamed Maura. "It wasn't a battle that he died in! He was murdered . . . shot in the back by a man too cowardly to face him! The man you say is a gentleman!" Tears streamed down her stricken face. "Jonathan opened my eyes to what lay beyond the plantation. He deserves . . . he deserves . . ."

The door to the parlor room flew open with a bang. Maura and Ruth gasped in fright, and Jed jumped to his feet ready to fight. They turned to face the figure in the doorway.

"I heard your voices out in the street." Natalie LaBlanc shook moisture off her skirt. "Be glad the rain is keeping people indoors. This conflict is spreading. There are three more dead tonight, if rumor is true, and you two are arguing over a man exhausted from doing his duty to his country. No one heard my knock, so I let myself in. What if I had been

Anthony Duff? Yes, I do know of him. Who could not with all the wanted posters hung up everywhere?"

Natalie looked shrewdly at the exhausted man as he slumped back down onto the sofa. "I, myself, have been giving information to Jed that has come my way."

"Jed?" asked Maura and Ruth together.

"I'm an actress." Natalie smiled saucily. "No one expects my reputation to be spotless, just discreet. You two should also be more discreet if you want to keep on spying."

Maura and Ruth were stunned into silence at Natalie's comment.

Jed blew out a breath. He had been a hair's breadth away from stopping the argument when Natalie barged in.

Finally, Maura shook her head. "I must be a *meshuga*."

"It's *meshuganer*; a crazy person," corrected Ruth with a smile. "I think I'm there with you. This is unfathomable."

"Is it?" asked Maura. "We all know Jed is a spy."

Ruth and Natalie nodded.

"In fact, I'm sure everyone in Maryland knows he is a spy. I also know he keeps things separate, so that one person cannot give away information on another, like how I did not know of Ruth," said Maura.

Ruth pointed at her. "You must be the wounded woman Jed brought to my father's house. Saul told me she was a blonde woman."

"That was your family?" exclaimed Maura. She looked at the floor as her neck and face flushed bright red. "I am simply mortified by my behavior. I hope you can forgive me."

"I was no better," said Ruth. "Of the three of us, Miss LaBlanc is the only one here with any kind of sense."

"A vengeful widow, a compromised Jewess, and an actress who has enough of her own skeletons in the closet to shame anyone," said Natalie. "Please, call me Natalie. I believe we are going to be very close to one another."

"My name is Ruth, Natalie."

"Maura. I would offer refreshments, but I have given the servants time off to grieve. My butler was killed earlier this evening when two men tried to gun down Jed."

"You told that young woman we could look after ourselves," Ruth reminded her. "Shall we invade the kitchen and see what's available?"

"Let's," said Natalie. "I'm not the helpless darling I portray on the stage. Maura, I'm sorry to hear about your butler."

"Jed, stay put," ordered Maura as Jed leaned forward in an attempt to rise. "We'll bring you back something."

The three of them went out into the foyer, leaving the living room door open. Jed heard Maura lock and bolt the front door. As she was doing so, Natalie stopped to look at the McKenzie family crest.

"What is this flower behind your family crest?" she asked.

"It is the Scottish Bluebell," answered Maura. "It's rumored that the McKenzie family will flourish as long as there are bluebells on our land. Quite a few were brought over from Scotland and planted at the plantation. My father always called me his Bluebell."

Chapter 31

Tuesday, May 14, 1861

Jed woke up to strange smells, unusual noises, an uncomfortable feel to his bed, and bright sunshine. Jerking himself upright, he teetered for a second before falling face-first off the sofa. Raising his head off the floor, he recognized Maura's parlor, and the memories of last night rushed back to him.

He stood up carefully so as to not rip the slightly too small clothes he was wearing. Frowning, Jed flexed his bare toes into the rich woven carpet. Footsteps clicked on the floorboards beyond the far doorway just before Tabitha entered the room. She had tried to enter the room quietly, but after taking one look at the sleeves that were an inch too shirt and pants legs that ended at mid-calf, she burst out laughing.

"I'm glad you're finding this so hilarious," commented Jed dryly before he cracked a smile. He then sobered up. "I am so sorry about Paul. I feel like I am responsible. Is he really gone?"

"Yes, his death won't be the only innocent one taken in this war. Paul's killing has been avenged, and I thank you for it. I know it's wicked to be thankful for the death of two men. I'll be praying for forgiveness in church this Sunday." She was silent for a minute or so, and Jed let her have the time to reflect. "Mr. Tremblant, will this war change things?"

"I really don't know what to tell you, Tabitha. The abolitionists want to end slavery. The Confederacy wishes to set up their own nation. Will these things happen? I don't know. There will be changes because of this rebellion, but who knows what those changes will be."

"Even if the North wins and slavery is outlawed, I don't see my people being treated as equals," said Tabitha. "Even Paul said so. He told me that the end of slavery is just the beginning. Can you give me any assurance that it will end?"

"No, I can't. For slavery to be abolished, it will have to be an Amendment to the United States Constitution, passed by Congress and signed by the president. There are too many variables for me to give you an honest opinion on the subject. Do I wish for it to happen? Yes."

Tabitha nodded her head in acknowledgement. "Your clothes are still soaked. Miss Maura sent word to your house to have them send you a change of clothing. They should be here presently. I have breakfast waiting for you in the dining room."

"Just so long as I don't have to walk up any stairs. I'm not sure these britches will stand the strain."

Tabitha snorted in amusement.

Jed was slathering strawberry preserves on his second piece of toast when Tabitha shooed Bryce and Chrissy into the dining room. In his attempt to rise to his feet, Jed felt a stitch or two give way, and he quickly sat back down, much to Chrissy's bemused delight. Bryce was holding a large, paper-wrapped package.

"Please stay seated, Master Jed," said Bryce. "Those clothes were not designed for strenuous movement." He gave the sleeve length a critical look. "In fact, I would advise from making any type of movement at all. It is well that I have conveyed a complete change of clothes for you. Miss Schaefer arrived at the house just as I was leaving. She has information for you."

"May I get you some refreshment, Mr. Bryce? Miss Schaefer?" asked Tabitha.

Chrissy shook her head, and Bryce said, "Thank you, but no. Where is Paul? I have a question to ask him."

Tabitha stiffened, and her face went gray. Jed grimaced as Bryce's and Chrissy's faces took on looks of concern. Tabitha fought the tears that streamed down her face.

"Paul was killed last night," said Jed wearily. "Captain Wilcott and Sergeant Ferguson tried to kill me last night, and Paul was shot by accident."

"No," gasped Chrissy in horror.

"Oh, my," lamented Bryce. He placed the package on the table. "Master Jed, these are your clothes. If you will excuse me, I would like to give my condolences downstairs and see what help I can offer."

"Of course," said Jed. "If they need anything. Please see to it. I don't know where or when the funeral is to be held."

"I'll keep you informed." Bryce put a comforting arm around Tabitha's shoulders. "Come along, my dear. I am sorrier than you know to hear of this."

Chrissy stood by the table shaking her head. Jed got up carefully and held her chair out for her

"Tea?" He held up the teapot.

Chrissy nodded, and Jed reached for a cup on the tea tray. The fabric of his shirt stretched tight across his chest and his fingers stopped about three inches short of the cup. He could reach no further without either moving or tearing the shirt. Chrissy chuckled and reached for the cup herself.

"I have to get out of these clothes," griped Jed as he poured her tea.

"I'll tell you what I know over our tea, then I'll go so you can get changed." Chrissy added a spoonful of sugar to her cup.

Jed looked quizzically at Chrissy.

"What?' she asked.

"I was wondering who you are. You look like Miss Schaefer and sound like her, but you're not acting like her."

Chrissy took a sip of her tea. "The news abouts Paul seems to have taken something outs of me."

"That dialect . . ." Jed gave her a slight smile. "Forgive me."

"You're forgiven. I'll catches you naked later, but you should know that the soldier boys have taken the gunpowder that was stored at the Baltimore Cemetery and a large number of guns from the warehouse across the street from the Custom

House. There were soldiers insides that warehouse keeping the police from taking the rest of them."

"The rest of them? How many did the police make off with?"

"Just a couple of small wagonloads from what I've been told. General Butler already shut down one manufactory and has cancelled orders that were supposed to go south in other ones."

"Have you heard anything about what the militia is doing?"

"Not much of nothing," replied Chrissy. "A few of the militia commanders who are for the North have approached General Butler concerning their allegiance. The other units seem to be waiting for something. Maybe someone was supposed to give them orders. His superiors are not very happy with Captain Wilcott. At least, that's what a colonel was griping about to one of my girls this morning."

"He's going to be disappointed," muttered Jed grimly. "Captain Wilcott and Sergeant Ferguson are . . . unavailable. I was wondering how a militia captain gained such influence here in Baltimore City. He must have been the liaison between all the rebel factions."

"Soooo, they're all waiting for Captain Wilcott to . . . what? Pass on instructions? By what you have said, that won't happen. So, you ready to get naked?"

Jed spent a little time verbally sparring with Chrissy before he sent her on her way. Chrissy pouted but seemed to enjoy her chase of Jed. For his part, Jed liked their friendship and was certain they were far better off being friends than lovers. Of course, that didn't stop Chrissy from teasing him.

After changing his clothes, Jed went downstairs to express his condolences to Justine and the rest of the staff. Bryce, with Justine's approval, was to send two of his staff over to help her through this time. With Jed's approval, Bryce would be spending the day at Maura's house to help out.

Jed knew Maura's servants had been attending the nearby colored Baptist church. The one thing he did not know was the location of any colored cemetery in Baltimore, but he was sure that Mr. Jenkins knew.

Ruth was not at Maura's house when he awakened. He assumed she had returned to her family. Maura was also not at home and had not returned by the time Jed was ready to leave. Just after midday, he retrieved Sweet Sue from the stables up the street and rode back to his house to clean, oil, and reload his pistol.

After doing so, Jed checked with his informants about how the citizens were feeling about General Butler's occupation of Federal Hill. He also wanted them to be on the lookout for any insurrection or revolt. He saw Robbie with his cab and Timothy at the club. They both told him people were concerned but not angry or antagonistic. Jed wondered if the state legislature's failure to vote for secession had altered the citizen's attitudes. Timothy let him know that a few of the younger members at the club were talking about heading south to join the Confederacy.

The main thing they filled him in on was the Union troops' hands-off approach to the people as long as the people demonstrated a pro-Union attitude. There was no indiscriminate suppression or reprisals. Jed felt this was because Baltimore was more like an industrial northern city than a southern one, but it still tried to hold onto southern values.

After leaving the club, Jed headed south to Fort McHenry. Major Morris gave him a warm welcome, and Jed noted a lot of the anxiety had left the major. Over 2,500 weapons had been brought to the fort from the warehouse by the Custom House, but they had not inventoried them yet. His soldiers were too busy unloading the gunpowder confiscated from the Baltimore Cemetery into Fort McHenry's powder magazine. Major Morris let it slip that he had Ross Winans locked up in the cellblock at the fort.

Jed headed that way.

"Mr. Winans."

"Mr. Tremblant, have you come to gloat?"

The cells in the guardroom had not changed since Jed had seen Tanner inside one of them. Ross looked well-dressed but a little wrinkled with a day-old beard.

"Of course not." Jed pulled over a stool to sit upon. "I learned of your pending arrest yesterday from General Butler. I was visiting Major Morris when I learned of your incarceration here."

"I guess I should feel honored having a whole platoon of soldiers and a squad of Baltimore City police officers come to arrest me."

"General Butler did not send any police officers with his soldiers. They were sent under the orders of Marshal Kane. I received information that certain members around here were not pleased with your stance on secession or with the outcome of the vote."

Ross looked at Jed. "Why should I believe you?"

"Mr. Winans, you are an influential and dynamic person, both in politics and industry. Your stance on secession and state's rights has people worried and is not popular with the federal government. I am telling you this because I find you to be an honest and honorable man. A lesser man would have voted for secession in direct contradiction to the law. As such, I have tried to be honest and honorable with you."

Jed straightened his back and winced from the tug on his wounds. "I had heard there would be repercussions from certain people in the city concerning your vote on secession. I had no hand in your arrest, but when I learned of it, I did nothing to stop it. I thought the soldiers were the most expeditious way to get you out of danger."

Winans sighed deeply. "In truth, I also believe you to be an honest and honorable man. Lieutenant Colonel Watson was clearly surprised by the presence of the police officers who had a warrant to arrest me. The officers were perturbed that Colonel Watson would not turn me over to them, and because his soldiers outnumbered the officers, there wasn't much they could do about it. Not that I like being dragged all over Maryland—Frederick to Annapolis, Annapolis to Relay House, Relay House to this fine establishment." He blew out a long breath. "Please, forgive me. I'm tired, filthy, and arrested without cause. You now inform me that the people with whom I thought I shared a cause, have turned against me, because I would not break the law to meet their agenda."

"Major Morris can't release you," Jed said. "I will speak to him about your comfort and, if you are amicable, to setting some parole conditions."

"Thank you, I would appreciate it."

Jed bid his farewell and spoke to Major Morris before heading toward Federal Hill. The Sixth Massachusetts had appropriated lumber from a nearby lumberyard and were constructing breastworks around the top of the hill. The artillery pieces General Butler had brought along were positioned to fire upon the city.

Jed was informed that General Butler was unavailable. The general was meeting with Mayor Brown and other officials about stopping any arms, supplies, or ammunition from being shipped to the Confederacy. Jed wished him luck, knowing that the southern-leaning officials would do all in their power to circumvent General Butler.

Jed had a pleasant surprise when he saw Zeke Tanner waiting for him at the base of Federal Hill as he was leaving.

"Is there a problem, Zeke?" asked Jed as he led Sweet Sue down the hill.

"Not exactly, sir. Word's come to the factory about Mr. Winans's arrest, and it's made everyone there anxious. A squad of soldiers came by early to see the manager with some paper and to get a list of all the contracts the factory was working on. I left 'cause I heard several of the workers talking about joining the Confederacy. They're planning on boarding a ship called the *Sea Spirit* to sail south. It's supposed to be leaving soon."

Jed frowned. "Do you have a horse?"

Zeke nodded.

"Go to Fort McHenry and see Major Morris. Tell him about the *Sea Spirit*. They may be trying to take as much of the hidden arms as possible on that ship. It needs to be stopped and inspected. I'm going to the docks."

"Yes, sir." Zeke jumped on his horse and galloped off.

Jed headed north to the main piers of the harbor. Because the ship was taking on passengers, it was logical it would be docked there rather than at the shipping piers. As Jed approached the huge, cobblestoned, staging area between the docks and the city proper, it was teaming with people, wagons, crates, and a myriad of supplies.

Being on horseback gave him the height advantage to look over the heads of the crowd. However, it also made him more conspicuous and identifiable. Stopping at a livery stable, Jed left Sweet Sue and proceeded on foot. A few quick answers to his questions let him know that the *Sea Spirit* was berthed at the end of Long Dock.

Dodging around travelers, dockworkers, wagons, stray dogs, and stacks of goods, Jed hurried toward Long Dock. His brow was furrowed by a troubling thought. It was something Zeke had said about factory workers leaving not only the city, but the state to join the Confederacy. Had General Butler's march disrupted the southern plans so much that they were abandoning everything? To Jed, it changed the order of importance away from war materiel to people, especially those with southern sympathies.

Ross Winans was an important industrialist and state senator, but he had been arrested. Mayor Brown and Marshal Kane had shown where their sympathies lay and their abilities to aid or hinder effort to further their cause. Beauregard, Longstreet, Ewell, Stuart, Lee, and other US Army officers had resigned their commissions to join the Confederate Army. Jed had known several of them from his time in the West and counted their worth more than all the hidden caches in Baltimore City.

It made it imperative, in Jed's mind, to find out who was on that ship. He could only hope that Zeke had delivered his message to Major Morris as he ran toward Long Dock. Hurrying around a large, wooden crate, Jed nearly collided with a woman. Dodging around her, he tipped his hat and uttered a quick apology. Turning back, Jed froze, as did Anthony Duff who was standing ten feet away.

Both men reached for their pistols at the same time but didn't draw them from their holsters. A young boy, about eight years old, stood in between them calling for his mother, who was the woman Jed had almost collided with.

"This is not a place to get into a gun battle." Jed took his hand off his revolver.

"Agreed." Duff removed his hand from his weapon.

"Are you leaving?"

"It would seem to be the prudent thing to do," answered Duff with a smile. "The barbarians are no longer at the gate but inside the city. I have no desire to be arrested and tried by a northern court. I am just the tiniest bit pleased that you survived your encounter with Captain Wilcott last night."

"I'm immensely pleased," said Jed grimly. "I'm sure if the outcome had been different, you wouldn't have lost any sleep over it." Jed balled his hands into fists. "Shall we get on with this?"

"Not calling for help?" Duff also balled his hands into fists.

"No, for the same reason you are not doing so." Jed crouched into a fighter's stance. "Who knows who will come to one's aid?"

"Indeed. I—" Duff's eyes widened in shock.

Jed wasn't paying attention. He was stunned by what he saw behind Duff.

The men reached out to the other.

Blam!

The gunshot rang loud in Jed's ears as the bullet whizzed by his shoulder. Men yelled and women screamed. Everyone nearby began running this way and that. One dockhand banged into Jed, staggering him into the crate. Jed pulled out his pistol and turned to face Duff, but the man was gone. So was the person who had been behind Duff with a pistol.

Spinning around, Jed was astonished to see Dorothy Caston sitting on the cobblestones, crying, and cradling her right hand. Jed picked up a stiletto on the ground next to her. Along the handle of the knife was a groove.

"My hand! My hand!" cried Dorothy.

"Let me see it." Jed pulled a handkerchief out of his coat pocket.

Dorothy sniffled and held out her bloody hand. She hissed in pain as Jed gently dabbed her palm. From the angle of the slice in her palm. Jed guessed that the bullet hit the handle of her knife and travelled up between it and her palm. Jed wrapped his handkerchief around her hand and tied it in place.

"It . . . it should have been you," whimpered Dorothy.

Jed hid her stiletto in his coat pocket. "He tried," said Jed as a police officer ran up to them. "This lady has been hurt and needs to see a doctor right away. I'll stop by the police station later to give an account to Captain Boxer."

"Yes, sir," replied the officer.

Jed turned away before the officer could stop him.

The delay nearly cost him. The *Sea Spirit* was just starting to pull away from the dock as Jed sprinted toward it. Jumping the five-foot gap between the dock and the ship wasn't hard. He grabbed the railing as his feet landed on the gunwale. With a slight spring, he vaulted over the rail onto the lower deck. As he landed, pain shot up through his knee. Only his iron grip on the railing kept Jed from falling over. The only person there was a black boatman who, at the sight of Jed's pistol, decided to stay still right where he was.

Jed, holding his pistol down by his side, hurried up the stairs to the wheelhouse. Looking to the right and left as he headed up to the top deck, he tried to spot Duff among the passengers but to no avail. The captain and another hand were inside the wheelhouse.

"Sir, you aren't allowed in here," said the captain firmly when Jed opened the door.

"Sir, I believe you have a Confederate spy on board who is wanted for murder." Jed lifted his pistol to point it at them. "There will be a boat from Fort McHenry with soldiers who will board this vessel. Please stop near the fort."

"As you wish," said the captain. He turned to the hand. "Tommy, tell Bart to be ready to drop anchor and have the passengers assemble at the bow. Tell them we must stop for an inspection."

After the captain notified the engineer via his speaking tube, Jed asked him, "Are you transporting any arms or equipment to the Confederacy?"

"The Confederacy?" exclaimed the captain in surprise. "We're bound for New York City with several stops along the way. This ship is carrying nothing for the rebels."

"New York City!" Jed couldn't believe his ears, but as the ship was fast approaching Fort McHenry, he couldn't follow up on the inconsistency.

The Trail of the Scottish Bluebell

A boat with ten soldiers and four oarsmen had put out from the fort's dock. Two signalmen were sending a message to the ship from the top of the lower, water gun, battery escarpment. Jed saw Major Morris and Zeke standing there, just as six cannons were run out to point at the *Sea Spirit*.

The captain steered closer to the fort, then let out two blasts on his steam whistle. There was a loud metallic clanking as the anchor dropped into the murky water. Jed heard a rise in the volume of conversation coming from the passengers one deck below him.

A series of thunks told Jed that the boat of soldiers had come alongside the ship. Men cursed as they climbed from one vessel to the other.

"You had better head below," suggested the captain. "Trust me. I have no desire to see my ship sunk."

Jed nodded and hurried down to the cargo deck. A lieutenant was directing his men to search through the cargo.

"Lieutenant, I am Captain Jedidiah Tremblant. We need to look through the cabins and passengers for a spy."

"Yes, sir. Major Morris told me you may be on board." The lieutenant pulled out a folded paper and opened it. It was a wanted poster for Anthony Duff. "This man, sir?"

"Yes," replied Jed. "He's dangerous. Make sure your men search in teams of three."

Jed and the soldiers searched through every cabin, every nook, and every cranny. They had each passenger walk past them. Duff was nowhere to be found on the ship. A search of the cargo revealed nothing that was going to the Confederacy.

At the end, Jed had to sigh." Lieutenant, get your men back on the boat. I'll be going with you. I'll be down as soon as I have talked to the captain."

Jed had reached the top deck and was heading toward the wheelhouse when he glanced over at another side-wheeler passing alongside. The large signboard on the starboard railing announced the ship's name as *Roanoke*. Standing by that railing was Anthony Duff. He lifted his hat to Jed as the ship steamed on by.

Chapter 32

Tuesday, May 14, 1861

It was well after dark when Jed rode up the path to his house. He handed Sweet Sue's reins over to the groom and started toward the front door. Sighing deeply, he contemplated the day's events.

General Butler was firmly entrenched on Federal Hill, effectively securing southern-leaning Baltimore City with all its industrial capacity for the Union. Ross Winans had been arrested as an agent for the Confederacy. The funny thing was that Winans had voted against secession because he felt the Maryland Charter didn't give him the authority to do so. The death of Captain Wilcott seems to have cut all communication between the various rebel factions, and to top it all off, Anthony Duff had escaped again.

That last thought rankled Jed more than anything else. He had been duped and had fallen for it hook, line, and sinker. Somehow, Zeke had been identified as being one of Jed's informants and had been given false information. It had taken Jed an hour to convince Zeke that he was not at fault for not recognizing the ruse.

However, as perturbed as Jed was about Duff's escape, it was not the most disturbing thing on his mind. He was profoundly upset by the incident concerning Dorothy Caston.

Jed had been prepared to fight Duff barehanded on the docks when they had both seen something to distract them. Shaking his head, Jed couldn't believe he jumped forward to protect the Confederate spy. A spy the Union could do without.

Of course, he was certain that Duff was trying to stop Dorothy from stabbing him in the back. Duff's movements at the time were more protective than confrontational. The gunshot from behind Duff that had disarmed and wounded Dorothy had frozen both men and caused a panic. Duff then escaped into the crowd as did the shooter.

Jed blew out a long breath. Yesterday had been grueling and the culmination of today's events were depressing and painful. As he opened the front door, he decided to just shelve everything and wait until tomorrow to sort things out.

"Good evening, Master Jed," greeted Bryce as he took Jed's hat and gloves. He frowned as Jed took off his shoulder holster and laid it with his Navy Colt on the foyer table.

"Good evening, Bryce." Jed retrieved his pistol before he was reprimanded. "I'm sorry. I'm just tired."

"I'll take that." Bryce relieved Jed of his weapon. "Your day is not over yet. You have guests in the dining room."

"The dining room?" Jed raised his eyebrows.

"Sir, you need food and rest," said Bryce. "Your guests have been here since late afternoon, so go in and have dinner with them. Everything is still hot."

"I'll need you in there if my guests are who I think they are," said Jed with a smile.

"Someone must serve the wine, sir. I'll be right in."

Jed entered the dining room. As he had guessed, Maura was seated at the table. What he did not expect was that Ruth and Chrissy were there also. Bryce came in and held out the chair at the head of the table.

"I take it Miss LaBlanc could not attend." Jed walked around to sit down.

"She has a performance tonight," said Maura. "Jed, I—"

"Thank you, Maura," interrupted Jed earnestly. "I had no idea that Miss Caston was behind me. I can only imagine what it cost you to take that shot instead of the other one. Although, how you managed to shoot that knife out of her hand, I'll forever be in amazement."

"I didn't intend to," admitted Maura, "shoot the knife out of her hand, that is. Did you capture Duff?"

"No," sighed Jed. "After the shot, everyone panicked. He disappeared into the crowd before I could even lay a hand on him. He escaped on the steamer going south."

Maura looked stricken. Ruth reached over and took her hand in sympathy. Even Chrissy looked a little grim.

"Maura, I made a promise to you," Jed assured her. "I will keep it, no matter how long it takes."

Maura stood quickly and moved to look out the window. "I'm having trouble believing that. He's escaped so many times. I . . . I had him, but . . ."

"Yes, he did escape. I should have paid more attention to my surroundings," stated Jed.

"Maura, you and Jedidiah have thwarted Mr. Duff at every turn," said Ruth. "His effectiveness in this state is at an end. The world has become a smaller place for him. We will get him."

Maura didn't answer or move away from the window.

Chrissy finally gave out a long sigh. "I need to return home. I'm sure Mr. Tremblant will be so kind as to grant us the use of his coach. It can drop me and Ruth . . . take Ruth and I to our homes. Mr. Bryce, would you be so kind as to get the coach ready? I would like to show Miss Goldberg Mr. Tremblant's collection of Indian . . . thingamajigs in the other room."

"Of course, Miss Schaefer," said Bryce, who escorted her and Ruth out of the dining room.

"She's younger than I am, but more aware of the world than I'll ever be," mused Maura, still looking out the window but with a little smile on her face.

"Our experiences shape us all. I'm more at home in the West than I am here in these big cities. No doubt you are more at home in the mountains of Virginia, even though you have traveled more than most of the citizens of this country."

Jed moved to stand behind Maura.

"Maura, I care for you deeply. I know it's only been a month since we met. When my wife died, I wanted to shut myself off from everyone and everything. I did that for far too long."

"You had nothing to distract you or occupy your time, from what you have told me. What could you do? Avenge yourself against an illness? I had a purpose but not the experience to fulfill it. I would have been—and have been—rash and impetuous. It nearly got me killed." She turned around to face Jed. "You have given me the benefit of your experience for which I am grateful."

Jed couldn't help but twist his mouth into a slightly forlorn smile. He opened his mouth, but Maura stopped him from saying anything by placing a hand upon his chest.

"Wait, Jed. Please, give me some time."

Jed gave a soft laugh and said gently, "I'm not trying to rush you or force you into anything. I know how much time it took me to get over a loved one's death. While I did try to dissuade you from this perilous course, events overtook us. Time, however, is not a quantity we have in abundance."

"What do you mean?" asked Maura.

"I received a telegram from the War Department. The two of us have been ordered to take the first train tomorrow to Washington, DC to speak to Secretary Cameron. By the tone of the message, I gather that other people will be there."

"President Lincoln?"

"Possibly. I am loath to have you come. It's one thing for me to be seen walking into the War Department or to have a meeting with Secretary Cameron. It is entirely another thing for you to be seen there. It would be reckless and foolhardy. It's a risk that is not only dangerous to you but also to your family. I have worked with southern officers who were ignorant, but not one of them was stupid."

"I've been seen with you here." She sighed. "I was so hoping to meet President Lincoln again."

"He would not want you to place yourself in a position of danger," said Jed. "Neither do I. We both know this war is not going to be short-lived. With what happened last night, I realized I should not waste another moment without telling you of my feelings." Jed held up his hand when Maura opened her mouth. "I'm not expecting any kind of reciprocity. You are newly bereaved and both of us were thrown together in this . . . I guess I would call it a shadow war, since most of it will never see the light of day."

"If the truth be told, I think I jumped into this and dragged you along with me," said Maura with a rueful smile. "Are you sorry?"

"No, I would gladly do so again," said Jed, "for you."

"Thank you," murmured Maura, gently touching Jed's cheek. She took in a deep breath. "You will go to Washington tomorrow alone to meet whoever you need to see. You are right about the risk, and I have a couple of things that need to be done here."

"Be careful," said Jed seriously. "Mayor Brown and Marshal Kane have not been removed from their positions. There are also Union soldiers strutting about. Ruth was accosted by some of them."

"Strange, isn't it? If it hadn't been for Jonathan, I probably would have favored Virginia and the Confederacy. He was the one who showed me what the United States could be," mused Maura. "What time does your train leave in the morning?"

"Six o'clock. Robbie is taking me to the station. I should be in Washington by nine o'clock. Faster than the boat trip we took. Of course, it's a further distance to travel by water than by rail. As Ruth said, the world is shrinking."

"I promise to be careful, Jed. We had better join the others."

Jed and Maura found the two women and Bryce in the morning room.

"Bryce, my apologies to your coachman, but I can take Miss Goldberg and Miss Schaefer home," said Maura.

"It's no trouble, Mrs. Harrison," said Bryce. "Let me inform him."

After Bryce left, Jed looked at the three women: Maura, breathtakingly beautiful in her black, high-necked gown; Ruth, dark-eyed and exotic in her brown skirt and white blouse; and Chrissy, impish and playful in her pink, long-sleeved dress. All three looked very young, even Ruth who was only a couple of years younger than Jed. Too young in Jed's eyes to be mixed up in this kind of business. Jed shook his head, knowing there was nothing to be done about it.

Jed sensed that a change was coming, but he couldn't put his finger on what that change might be. They all stood around in awkward silence until Chrissy broke out in a fit of giggles.

"Here's we are, acting like it's the end of the world, just because one little spy escaped." She laughed. "Of course, the fact that he would have got rid of the lot of us, if he could, has nothing to do with it. Right?"

Maura snorted in macabre amusement, much to her embarrassment. Ruth tried but couldn't hold in her laughter at Chrissy's audacious, but accurate, statement. Jed just shook his head as he felt a great weight lift off him. Altogether, they had defeated Duff's plans, and he had been forced to flee.

"We had better leave, ladies," said Maura. "Jed has a long trip tomorrow."

"Oh?" asked Ruth. "Where are you going?"

"To Washington. When I return, I'll let everyone know what the War Department wanted with me."

"Goodnight, Jed," said Chrissy, pulling his head down to kiss him on the cheek. "For good luck."

Ruth kissed him on the other cheek with a soft lingering kiss. "For good luck. Although you do tend to make your own luck."

Ruth and Chrissy walked out to the foyer. Jed felt a fluttering in his stomach as Maura approached him. It was a feeling he had not had in a long time. Her blue eyes looked inviting as she unconsciously licked her lips. A soft hand came up to caress his cheek, sending an intense shock of pleasure through him. Her head tilted a little to the right and upward as her eyes half closed. Jed bent down toward her soft lips.

A knocking at the door broke them apart before their lips even got near one another. Maura, blushing furiously, turned around toward the side window. Jed closed his eyes and sighed in exasperation before bidding the person to come into the room.

"Oh! Good evening, Mrs. Harrison. Good evening, sir," said Zeke, looking in and then walking into the room. "A message came for you at Fort McHenry, sir. Major Morris gave it to me to bring out here."

"Are the others still in the foyer?" asked Jed with just a little irritation in his voice as he took the paper from Zeke.

"No one is in the foyer," replied Zeke in surprise. He went over to the front windows and looked out. "Here they are. They're out on the front porch. I came in through the back entrance."

There was a period of awkward silence as Maura continued to look out the side window, and Jed tapped the folded piece of paper against his leg. Zeke shuffled from one foot to another as he twisted his head from side to side to look at each of them in turn.

Zeke, Maura, and Jed spoke at the same time.

"I'll wait outside."

"I should get the other ladies home."

"Can you give us a few minutes?"

Zeke clamped his lips together, and he turned bright red in embarrassment. Maura's mouth twisted this way and that as she fought to keep from laughing. Jed chuckled good naturedly as Zeke rushed out the door.

"I really do need to leave," said Maura. "Jed, please be careful on your trip. I . . . I will . . . your words mean a great deal to me."

"I understand that you have feelings and emotions for Jonathan, Duff, me . . . feelings and emotions that you need time to sort out. Let me walk you out."

"Thank you, Jed."

On the front porch, Ruth and Chrissy were sitting on a swing bench suspended from the porch roof. Bryce and Zeke stood at the bottom of the steps beside Maura's coach.

"Oh, pooh!" complained Chrissy. "It's time for us to leave."

"Sir, Master Zeke has informed me that he has stopped working at the manufactory," said Bryce. "May I suggest he move in here and accompany you tomorrow? I would feel better if someone was with you."

"What do you say, Zeke?" asked Jed. "Are you ready for a train ride? Do you need anything from your rented room?"

"Yes, sir. No, sir. I mean, I'm ready to go, and there's nothing I need to get from the room."

"It might be best if Master Zeke doesn't return there," said Bryce. "I'll send someone tomorrow to retrieve whatever is there and notify the landlord. Come along, Master Zeke, we have packing to do."

"Ladies, we need to leave ourselves," said Maura.

"Aw, all of us don't have to leave," whined Chrissy. "Why don't I stay and keep Jed company?"

"Why don't we all stay?" Ruth laughed. "Go on and get in the coach!"

Chrissy made an exaggerated pout but followed after Maura and Ruth. Jed helped the ladies into Maura's coach and closed its door.

"Ruth, Chrissy, we need to talk," he heard Maura say seriously as the coach started off into the dark.

JED'S COACH DELIVERED HIM AND Zeke early the next morning to the Camden Railroad Station. Jed carried his old carpet bag, while Zeke touted a worn, battered valise.

They were surprised at the station. "Chrissy! What are you doing here?" asked Jed.

"I have something to give you, but you has to promise to gets on the train," said Chrissy nervously, clutching an envelope.

"I promise." Jed held out his hand, knowing how nervous she was by the way her diction had lapsed.

"Youse nots going to kills the messenger?"

"Spank her, maybe?" joked Jed with a smile. He could see a thrill go through Chrissy as she, too, broke out in a wide smile. "Go tell Maura her letter was delivered."

"How'd's ya know it's from Miss Maura?" asked Chrissy in astonishment.

"It's her handwriting on the envelope," replied Jed. "I, hopefully, will be back tomorrow." Chrissy's face fell, and he added, "It's all right, Chrissy."

"Any messages you wants delivered?" she asked.

"None until I have read this." Jed held up the envelope.

"You sure?"

"Chrissy, I told Maura my feelings last night. Both of us have issues that need to be addressed and that will take time. I want you to watch out for yourself. Even with Union troops in the city, there are still enough southern sympathizers to cause a great deal of trouble and damage."

Bursting into tears, Chrissy threw her arms around Jed's waist and hung on as she sobbed. A couple of early morning passengers looked over at them and smiled at what they thought was a farewell moment. After a few moments, Chrissy regained control of her emotions and kissed Jed on the cheek before stepping away from him.

"I'll see you when you return," she said to Jed. She hugged Zeke tightly, much to his consternation. "You take care of yourself, too." She leaned against him to kiss him on the cheek. "You both had better . . . Oh! Oh, my! I'm . . . ah . . . extremely flattered, Zeke. Want to walk me home?"

"The two of us have a train to board," interjected Jed before Chrissy killed the boy from embarrassment. "Quit rubbing against him and let him go!"

"You're no fun!" pouted Chrissy as she stepped back and flounced out of the railway station.

"Sir, I—"

"Train," ordered Jed. They quickly boarded their passenger car.

"Sir, are you and Miss Schaefer . . .?"

"No." Jed chuckled. "I think she likes the chase. I think if we ever culminated our pursuit, it would ruin our friendship, and I believe I would be tarnished and debased in her eyes." Jed looked down at the envelope in his hands.

"Do you think it contains bad news, sir?"

"I won't know that until I've read it," answered Jed with a shrug. "Let me read it first before we borrow trouble about what we think may be written."

"Yes, sir." Zeke stowed their luggage in the overhead racks. "I'll sit over here to give you some privacy."

"Thank you." Jed used his knife to slit open the envelope. A single piece of paper was inside.

My Dearest Jedidiah,

By now, you should be on the train enroute to Washington. I apologize for doing this in a letter instead of in person, but I am afraid you will not approve of what I plan to do. If I saw you face to face, I know, with your Yankee ingenuity, you would be able to talk me out of it.

I am honored and flattered by what you told me last night. It took courage and integrity, but I already knew you had those sterling qualities. I must say that I have feelings for you too, but I cannot tell you exactly what those feelings are. There are times when thoughts of Jonathan evoke such emotion that I get overwhelmed. I feel such rage at his murder and such despair about whether his soul will able to rest if Anthony Duff escapes divine judgement.

I cannot seem to put these emotions aside and I have tried. This is the part that you will not approve of. I have decided that, while I could stay in Baltimore, I would be of more use in Richmond. Ruth and I have talked to Mr. Goldberg, and Ruth will be accompanying me.

Since Eunice is a vocal abolitionist, I dare not take her into the Confederacy. Eunice will stay behind at my house to act as the central collection point for information. Natalie LaBlanc will also be staying in Baltimore in my house. She will be hosting dinners and parties there.

I have spoken to Mayor Brown and Marshal Kane about the Union troops occupying Federal Hill. I expressed my fears of being arrested. Marshal Kane assured me there was no danger, but Mayor Brown agreed that it would not do for me to be detained since I was to travel to Santa Fe in the New Mexico Territories. Interesting that he should know that, isn't it?

I will send you reports as soon as I have established myself in Richmond. I will also try to clarify what the trip to Santa Fe entails and keep you informed.

I end this hoping for your understanding. I also decided to use an affection I had as a child. My correspondence to you will have this drawing of Scottish bluebells on it. The flowers mean gratitude and I am grateful to you . . . and maybe more than that. There is a tale that witches changed into hares and hid among the flowers. I plan to change and hide well in Richmond.

With Great Affection

"Sir, is Mrs. Harrison well?" asked Zeke.

"She is well, Zeke. We won't see her for quite a while, and from now on, we'll refer to her as the Scottish Bluebell."

####

Excerpt from

The Travels of the Black-eyed Susan

May 18, 1861

RUTH LOOKED UP FROM HER diary when she heard a knock at her door. Before she could say anything, Maura peeked her head in.

"Are you ready to leave?" asked Maura.

"Let me just finish writing down this last thought."

Maura walked into the room and sat down primly on an upholstered stool, arranging her hoop skirts over it, so they would not wrinkle. Although Maura was eight years her junior, Ruth felt that she possessed the maturity and common sense of someone much older. Ruth concluded that it was probably due to her husband, Jonathan, being killed in April during the Pratt Street Riot in the City of Baltimore. Ruth snuck a glance at Maura, who saw it and winked back at her.

Maura fanned her hands from her throat downward and outward before saying, "What do you think of my dress?"

"It's beautiful, but not exactly the type of mourning clothes they will be expecting," stated Ruth.

The only things that was sober about Maura's dress were the shades of black in the material. The billowing skirt was flamboyant, while the off-the-shoulder style was daring. The decolletage was half and inch above being totally scandalous for any woman, but for a widow... Ruth had to admit that the dress was spectacular and, combined with Maura's ethereal beauty, made the entirety of it stunning.

"I had it designed to attract attention," said Maura, preening delightedly. "Wearing the high-neck collar, the concealing veil, the black gloves, and everything else would make people avoid me. Duff disappeared from the City of Baltimore when General Butler seized control and placed all of our other contacts under constant scrutiny. They are all now inaccessible. We need to reestablish our connection to the Confederate government."

"As you have said before." Ruth shut her diary.

Indeed, during their five-day trip from Baltimore to Richmond, Ruth and Maura had discussed their objectives and options. Although they had not spoken it aloud, Ruth knew that Maura's primary goal was to exact revenge on Anthony Duff for killing her husband. Ruth didn't believe in spiritualism, but Maura did. The idea that Jonathan would never find eternal rest until justice was served was firmly entrenched in the young girl's mind.

That still didn't keep Maura from thinking clearly. With all the confusion, tension, and chaos caused by General Butler's occupation of Baltimore City, Maura decided that she and Ruth should not go to Richmond through the City of Washington, DC. General Butler commanded his troops to stop all trains going out of or through Baltimore, except for troop trains. Anyone traveling southward would be detained.

The ladies' best bet was to travel overland to Front Royal where they would be able to take a train to Richmond.

Ruth's father, Samuel, had secured for them a heavy, two-horse freight wagon upon Maura's assurance that she could handle the team. Not only was it able to carry their personal trunks, but Samuel had the rest of the wagon filled with cases of French brandy and other spirits, bolts of canvas, boxes of tea, and a large number of medical supplies, including a quantity of morphine. Maura added non-perishable foodstuff, like canned and salted meat.

The food turned out to be fortuitous because, when the two women were half a day out of Baltimore, they were stopped by a band of men. The leader was well dressed, according to

Ruth's eye. The other five wore clothes that ranged from fair to poor. The men carried a variety of weapons from shotguns to old flintlock rifles. One man even carried an old blunderbuss. The leader had his rifle slung over his shoulder as he stood in the middle of the road with his left hand raised to stop the wagon. His right hand rested on the butt of his pistol.

"What can we do for you, gentlemen?" asked Maura sweetly.

"Ma'am," said the leader, nodding in acknowledgement to Maura's black dress. "It's sure an unexpected pleasure to hear the dialect on one's own home. I'm Lieutenant William Burkegrave of the Third of Virginia. My men and I answered the rally cry from the elected officials of the fair City of Baltimore. However, as you may surmise, the bluebellies stole a march on us. I am endeavoring to return myself and my men back to our fair state. To that end, unfortunately, I must commandeer your wagon."

"Lieutenant!" gasped Maura in horror. "You would strand two women out here in the middle of nowhere?"

"I apologize for the inconvenience, but the two of you can return to the city with little risk, whereas my men and I face incarceration or worse."

"Here, now, Lieutenant," drawled one heavy set man dressed in homespun. "My feet are killin' me!"

Burkegrave turned to face the man but froze when Ruth clicked the hammers back on her shotgun. It was followed by a third click. Glancing over his shoulder, he stared at the small pistol in Maura's hand and the double-barrel shotgun pointed at him from under Ruth's blanket.

"Lieutenant?" whined the man impatiently.

"Be quiet, Purdey," said Burkegrave quietly. "We're both looking at the wrong end of a shotgun, unless I miss my guess. Jack, take the men down the road to that fallen tree."

"Yes, sir," said Jack, a young man in good quality clothes, but not up to cut of Burkegrave's outfit, who had a mischievous smile. "Let's go, boys. Down the road with you lot."

"But—" Purdey started to say but was cut off when Jack flicked his wrist to point down the road. Purdey, with a dour look on his face, headed in that direction, followed by the others.

"Now that my men are safe, shall we continue our discussion?" A hint of a smile played on Burkegrave's lips.

"You can talk all you want, Lieutenant Burkegrave," stated Maura. "When General Butler occupied Baltimore, we gathered up what merchandise we could for the Confederacy. I will not cast these needed supplies aside so your men do not have to walk."

"Miss…uh…I do beg your pardon, but I did not catch your name."

Maura pushed her black veil aside. "I am Maura Harrison of Virginia. This is my good friend and companion, Ruth Goldberg."

Burkegrave inhaled sharply and bowed. "My sincerest apologies, Mrs. Harrison. I do recognize you. I was fortunate enough to attend one of Mayor Brown's balls where you were present." He smiled. "My understanding is that the Cary sisters were most put out when you decided to live in Baltimore City. Am I to assume you are returning to the state of your birth?"

"You may indeed, and what the Cary sisters think is of no concern to me."

"The Confederacy may have had a setback in Baltimore City, but we will soon teach those Northerners about sticking their noses into our business." Burkegrave grimaced. "If we can get up-to-date weapons. Are you sure you…?"

"If I could have retrieved the weapons Marshall Kane had stored in and around Baltimore City, I would have." Maura sighed. She wrapped the reins around the brake handle and got down. "Come and take a look at what we have."

Burkegrave held up his hands. "No, no. I believe you have no weapons in the wagon."

"I know," said Maura, "but we may have some items that may be of use to you and your men. You can also see how limited our space is inside the wagon."

"As long as Mrs. Goldberg doesn't object." Burkegrave smiled and held out a helping hand to Ruth.

"I am unmarried." Ruth climbed down off the wagon on the far side away from Burkegrave. She retained her hold on the shotgun and stood several feet away from him.

"Miss Goldberg, you've hurt my feelings." Burkegrave smiled again, but his eyes had a glint of hardness in them.

"My apologies, sir," said Ruth. "However, I think it is better to have a little hurt feelings than to be hurt by making an error in judgement."

"I'm not afraid of you," said Burkegrave.

"I'm just giving you a friendly warning," replied Ruth. "I'm not the one to be afraid of if you cross us."

Burkegrave snorted and glanced at Maura.

She gave him a smile that didn't quite reach her ice-blue eyes.

Burkegrave took a half-step back and licked his lips at the coldness in her stare. His eyes swept over Maura's black dress and the pistol she was still holding before he nodded an acknowledgement to both women. "I am afraid I have not placed myself or my men in the best light. Let me make it up to you by escorting you and your wagon to wherever you are going."

Acknowledgments

THIS NOVEL WOULDN'T BE POSSIBLE but for the help I'd received along the way. First, I have to thank my wife, Irene. She patiently proofread my drafts, made me correct confusing passages that made perfect sense to me, and kept my nose to the grindstone to finish it. Without her love and understanding, this would have been a pile of papers gathering dust in my filing cabinet.

Second, I'd like to thank my editor, Dawn Brotherton. She helped me refine this work from something I liked to something I'm proud of.

www.ingramcontent.com/pod-product-compliance
Ingram Content Group UK Ltd.
Pitfield, Milton Keynes, MK11 3LW, UK
UKHW042005230426
12048UKWH00009B/561